MOTHER

ALSO BY S.E. Lynes

Valentina

MOTHER

S. E. LYNES

bookouture

Published by Bookouture
An imprint of StoryFire Ltd.
23 Sussex Road, Ickenham, UB10 8PN
United Kingdom
www.bookouture.com

ISBN: 978-1-78681-221-6
eBook ISBN: 978-1-78681-220-9

For Mum

The past is not a package one can lay away.

Emily Dickinson

Good Friday, 17 April 1981

Still the man thrashes against him, wild as a trapped animal. His arms flail; his shoes scuff against the damp gravel of the canalside. His feet gain purchase. His legs lock. His rigid torso thrusts into Billy's chest. It's a powerful blow and Billy staggers backwards at its force. They'll both end up in the water at this rate, he thinks. But he must keep tight hold of the rope. This is his very life he's holding onto; he's come this far and nothing will make him let go now.

The man writhes, cries out – choked, desperate. He clutches at the rope to try to prise it from his failing throat. The twine chafes against Billy's knuckles, sends blood slick across his aching white fists. The man gives a guttural cough, an internal retching that seems to come from Billy's own chest. Together they lurch, wrestling twins, a two-headed beast, until the man's scrabbling boots blanch under the street light. Billy freezes. They have left the cover of the bridge. Someone might see.

With a roar, he drags his raging victim back to the dark, heels scoring twin trails in the loose stone chippings until, to his relief, the shadow of the bridge slides over them once again. Billy's nostrils flare; his mouth gapes. Not enough air; he must suck in all he can. Overhead comes the rubbery rhythm of cheap shoe soles on stone. One person only – the brisk, offended strut of a good-time girl who has heard one joke too many tonight. Soon there will be more people along this way. He must hurry.

The man bucks, his belly rounding like a bedsheet on the breeze. With all his strength, Billy pulls the rope. He has begun to cry, to sob with a kind of grief. It is all so wretched, but he has not been able to grasp the exact nature of the wretchedness until now. This is how it is to kill a man. This is how it feels.

His body is numbing with cold and pain. His nose is running; no hands free, he has to lick away the gritty trail of mucus from his upper lip. His wet hair falls into his left eye. He flicks his head to clear it, but it falls back. He blows it up, this stubborn lock, but it drops again as soon as his breath fails. It is so bloody awful, this business of death. It wasn't meant to be this hard. It wasn't meant to be this messy.

He yanks at the rope again, and this time, at last, the writhing stops. Billy could let go of the rope now, but no, it is not worth the risk. He will finish this, and after it is over, then will be the time for putting things right. Then will be the time for atonement.

'I will do only good.' His voice is little more than a croak; his biceps sear for lack of oxygen. 'Only good from now on. I swear by Almighty God.'

He gives one last pull. The rope is in spasm, his hands in spasm with it. His teeth hurt; he fears he might press them into his gums. He cannot hold on.

The tang of urine fills his nostrils. The man collapses. His feet splay, his body heavy as a gravestone. Silence rushes under the bridge and stops there, filling the space with its terrible sound. Billy clutches the rope, but already the tension is gone.

'Only good now,' he says, and falls to his knees. 'Only good from now on. Oh God.'

Footsteps overhead: clack, clack, clack – the whinny of tipsy female; the bass notes of the male who thinks his luck is in. Billy's chest is a pump. The jagged path digs into his knees. If those above could see him here below: filthy and crying, snot-smeared and pitiful. What foul troll is that? they would ask themselves. What monster?

He sucks at the cold damp air, air that smells of moss and dirt. Monster. With his bloody hands he wipes his face but feels only mud and grit. Monster. He is still weeping: for this death, for his own saved life. If they could see him, if anyone could, oh God.

The pain of the evening's exertions claws at his bones. He must rally. He hauls himself to his feet, tries to lift the body, but it is too heavy. He has to kneel again and push with all his remaining strength to roll it towards the water. *It* now. At the edge, he stops. He can feel the ugly set of his own disgusted mouth. His skin itches and cracks. He closes his eyes for a moment. He is already kneeling, as if the decision to pray has been made for him.

'Lord God,' he whispers, closing his hands together, hoping he can remember at least some of the words. 'As we commit the earthly remains of our brother to the earth… that is, to the water, grant him peace until he is raised to the glory of new life promised in the waters of baptism. We ask this through Christ our Lord. Amen.'

A strong shove is all it takes to roll the body over the side. Barely half a second passes before the dull splash of oblivion breaks the quiet. Billy groans, lies full length on his stomach and stretches his hands into the water. Scooping up handfuls, he splashes his face clean. Baptism, he thinks. I baptise myself. I am born again.

CHAPTER ONE

12 June 1981

What I want to say before we start is that I loved him. I loved him. And he loved me.

There. I can begin.

Write it all down, they tell us in here. *Writing is therapy*. They had to say that. I haven't spoken since I got here. I suppose writing's a bit like confession, isn't it? Head bent to the desk as behind the grate – *bless me, Father, for I have sinned*. But today, sitting here covered in shame and regret, I know that nothing I can write will change what happened. All I can hope for is that it will change how I feel about it. I'm not looking for forgiveness. I am beyond forgiveness. I'm looking for understanding. Peace, maybe, maybe not. I'm certainly not holding my breath for a full night's sleep, a meal I can finish, a packet of pills I can toss into the bin. But I no longer have the heart to pray, so I suppose writing it all down is better than doing nothing. What I don't know for certain, I will imagine, but what I imagine will be within reason, given everything he told me at the time – everything I believed at the time.

'I'd always known,' he used to say. He would say this often. 'Even before they told me. Even before I could put it into words, I'd always known.'

I would take his hand in mine. His hands were pale, with soft tufts of dark hair on the backs of his long fingers. Pianist's fingers, I'd call them, though he didn't play.

'It's nothing to be ashamed of,' I told him. 'It wasn't your fault.'

I used to think listening was a privilege – to have another person entrust to you their darkest secrets, their vulnerabilities, the private insanities we all have. There's an intimacy that comes with that. Love comes with that. It could be that love is not possible without it. I don't see listening that way any more obviously. But what choice did I have? He came to *me*; he trusted *me* – what else could I do? Once he'd started, I saw the momentum gather within him like a blackening cloud. And then, my God, the words fell like rain. Slowly, then faster: a million beaded droplets in the longest, heaviest downpour.

And I took that sodden weight from him with love.

'It's OK,' I told him.

But it was not. It was not OK.

I remember once he told me about how, as a boy, he used to run the hot water into the sink in the bathroom, let the steam cloud the mirror and watch himself disappear.

'I used to stand back,' he said, his brow furrowing at the memory. 'I'd screw my eyes up to see if I could get myself to come into focus.'

Anxious then – though of course he'd sought his own anxiety – he would wipe the wet fog from the mirror with his pyjama sleeve, sigh with relief at the sight: him, himself, Christopher Harris.

'A normal boy in a normal bathroom,' he'd say. 'In a normal semi-detached house in a normal street in a normal seaside town. And Christopher, well, that's about as normal a name as any, isn't it? Did I tell you I was named after St Christopher?'

He was so particular about his name. *Christopher, not Chris, please*, he would correct, in that quiet voice of his, anyone who attempted to abbreviate him. Not that he was the type to make a fuss, but as he always said, *Names are important, aren't they? They tell you who you are.*

His hesitant smile, his brown eyes meeting mine. He was looking for himself there, I realise now. He was always looking for himself.

*

And then there was the rope.

That was how he described the knot he'd carried in his chest ever since he could remember – a knot that, no matter how often he picked at it, would never loosen. The knot persisted throughout his childhood, into his teens: a tight confusion of endless loops, without beginning without middle without end. Ironic, then, that as a young lad he loved to skip. He never made it into the football team, you see, and his parents weren't ones for physical exercise for its own sake.

And so, alone on the back patio in the evenings, he would jump over the skipping rope his father had made for him, the wooden handles worn smooth by the long hours' gripping. At night, he would unscrew those wooden handles, untie the knots within and slide the handles from the cord. In the dull yellow glow of his bedside lamp, he would make the figure of eight, the midshipman's hitch, the fishermen's bend – tongue out, eyes flicking every now and then to the pages of his *Knots You Need to Know* book, a tenth birthday present from his parents. I wonder if he thought about all this as he crossed and slid the braid through his fingers, as he pulled the cord tight. Could he almost hear the step, whip, step, whip, the whoosh of revolutions in the close air of the yard, the refrain he would repeat in breathless, half-swallowed words: *salt, mustard, vinegar, pepper, salt, mustard, vinegar…*?

I have so many questions and this is one: if it weren't for the maintenance grant, would Christopher ever have untangled the rope? If it weren't for the grant, he would never have gone to university in the first place; his parents could never have afforded it. Were it not for the grant, he would not have found the suitcase in the dark loft space at the back of his attic room.

But he did. Hidden behind the smarter cases his family used for holidays, Christopher, being Christopher, took this dilapidated, dusty old thing, not wanting to use the more decent luggage for himself. When he pulled the case towards him, the catch popped. The lid sprang open. Inside, a greyish blanket no more than a yard square and knitted in a cross-hatch design. It smelled strongly of mothballs, of dust. As he gathered it up from the case, a piece of paper flew out. He picked it up and opened it.

St Matthew's Convent
Church Road
Railton
Liverpool L25
13 March 1959
Dear Mr and Mrs Harris,
    We write to inform you of a baby boy, born only yesterday…

He dropped the torch and fell back, fingers sinking into the itchy pink insulation strips that ran between the ceiling joists. The thirteenth of March. The day after his birthday.

In the dark, cramped space, the fallen torch shone a spotlight on the brick wall: cobwebbed, damp, crumbling.

He was born on 12 March 1959 – in Morecambe, Lancashire, so he had believed. His parents had never told him otherwise. Not that Jack and Margaret Harris were bad people. They were what you'd call traditional, but like all parents, they did their best. Don't we all? Christopher's treatment hardly marked him out as in any way special, not at that time. *I want doesn't get. Because I say so. Don't come back till teatime.* Phrases you would hear ten times a day. And like most kids, his backside was no stranger to the palm of his father's hand, his ears more than accustomed to irritated quips from his harried mother. *Stop fidgeting, for goodness' sake, hold your fork properly, you can't go to Mass dressed like that.*

He was an only child until the new baby came in the winter of 1967. Perry Como on the Dansette, ice on the inside of his bedroom window. Hooked over the Kodak Brownie in the lounge, his father snapped his mother's belly, huge and round under its patchwork cheesecloth smock.

'Don't take any more, Jack,' she said, shooing him away with her hand. 'You'll waste the film.'

Christopher thought she meant to save some for him, perhaps for the Scalextric track he'd built by himself in his room. But she didn't come to see it, and his dad didn't bring the camera out again until the baby was born – which happened a week or two later. That night, midnight-ish, he shivered on the bottom stair while from the front bedroom there came a cavernous lowing he could not equate with his mother. He dared not go up to see if she was all right – could not imagine what he would see if he did.

After what seemed like hours, his father came clattering down the stairs in his pyjamas. 'I have to phone for an ambulance, son.'

From the blue Wedgwood dish on the hall table he dug pennies and ha'pennies, closed his fingers around them before grabbing his overcoat and throwing open the front door. He turned back, raised his forefinger as if in afterthought and said, 'Wait there and don't bloody move.'

The door slammed shut. Long minutes passed. Christopher did not bloody move. Then the key, crunching into the Yale. The front door swung open, a blast of cold air, his father's eyes bloodshot and wild.

'Right, lad.' His sandy hair flew in one piece from his balding head like the top of a boiled eggshell. 'Ambulance'll be here in a bit.'

The ambulancemen carried his mother downstairs, one at each side of her, as if she were a chair and they were trying to keep the wallpaper from scuffing. They puffed with the effort. She was still mooing, and he thought of the Friesian cows in the field next to last year's holiday cottage in Ffos-y-ffin. Her face was pink as raspberry jelly, her matted hair darkened to the colour of brown paper, stuck in pointed fronds to her glistening forehead.

'Mum,' he called out to her as they carried her into the street. 'Mummy.'

But she was panting and moaning, and she did not look at him.

The next morning, his mother was not at home. There were no fresh socks, so he put on yesterday's, and at breakfast his father did not put butter or jam on Christopher's toast.

'You're eight, aren't you?' he said, eyeing Christopher's knife stilled in mid-air. 'Should know how to put butter on toast by now.'

That afternoon, Mrs Whiteside, the lady from next door, picked him up from school along with her own little boy, whose name he had forgotten by the time he came to tell me all this. She gave them both a jam sandwich and a glass of milk in her back kitchen.

'Do you know where my mum is?' he asked her.

'Your dad's with her,' she said, taking his plate before he'd finished his sandwich. 'Now off you go, the two of you – get out from under my feet while I peel these spuds. I suppose I'll have to do extra.'

He was playing marbles with the neighbour's son after tea when the long shadow of his father darkened the rungs of their filthy doormat pitch.

'A boy.' His father's silhouette, so much stockier than the shadow, eclipsed the light. His face was invisible. 'Do you hear me, Christopher? You've a brother now. He's called Jack.'

'OK.' Christopher returned to his game, pressing his knuckle to a cat's eye the size of a gobstopper, a silver and blue ripple frozen inside its heavy glass. An important shot this. They were playing keepsies.

It would be years before he thought about the fact that his brother's Christian name was the same as his father's.

*

Louise came a year later. She and Jack Junior were their own unit: Irish twins, his dad called them. Their fair hair and bright, freckled faces did not match Christopher's own black locks, his pale skin.

'I was the blank canvas,' he said to me once. 'They were the works of art.'

'No, no,' I remember replying. 'Don't say that. You're my work of art. We're all a work of art for someone who loves us.'

But his siblings' easy way with their mother – the way they climbed onto her lap if she ever sat down, hid under her skirt while she gossiped with the neighbours on the street, laughed when she scolded them – served only to remind him of his own stiff stance, his inability simply to hold, or be held by, another human being.

'No one is born unable to hug,' I told him. 'It can be learnt, and I'll teach you.'

I thought I could teach him everything. Confidence, that was all he needed, I thought. A sense of his place in the world. But I could not give him that.

At ten years old, Christopher was moved into the loft, into a room made by his father.

'Your brother needs his own space,' his mother said, by way of explanation. 'He's gone two.'

Fine by Christopher. Jack Junior was a pain in the neck, a whinger. The sooner they stopped sharing, the better.

The box room became a nursery for Louise, who was getting on for fourteen months by then. Christopher, already taller than his mother by this point, wasn't far off being taller than his father. He could not straighten up to full height in his new bedroom without banging his head on the eaves, but the floor space was bigger than the one downstairs.

His father built the windows for the loft room, put the electrics in and lined the walls with fresh woodchip, which he painted cream. His mother ran up curtains from fabric she'd found at Lancaster market, made him a valance sheet with what was spare. His parents bought him a new pine wardrobe from MFI on hire purchase.

The trapdoor was left as it was – with a U-shaped handle. Whenever Christopher went up to his room, he would take the long hook from its holder on the landing wall, loop it through the handle on the trapdoor and pull. With a heavy metallic clatter, the stepladder would come shuddering down like a magic staircase summoned from tin clouds. At ten, this made the room feel like a den; later, like a temporary guest room.

And later, when he did start to look at it in that way – that is, with the seed of bitterness he wished were no part of him – he would think about how nothing had ever truly belonged to him. Nothing had really been his. To and from school, he would tread as lightly as he could so as not to wear out the soles of the shoes that would be Jack's – try not to suck thin the grey cuffs of his school blazer.

'Try and keep it nice for your brother, can't you?' His mother, Margaret, shaking out his father's work shirts over the kitchen table. 'We can't be buying new blazers every five minutes.'

It seemed to Christopher sometimes that his life was spent trying not to ruin anything, trying not to bite his nails, not to put his elbows on the table, not to pull out clumps of his own dark hair. By the time he was twelve, his eyebrows were no more than black tufts where he had plucked out patches along the length. They never grew back, not completely.

And always the knot, always the rope.

I will say this: things were different then. People had different ideas. People went to church every week, went most places on foot, often came home from work to eat at midday. No exception, Christopher walked the half-mile from St Luke's Primary home for his dinner at 12.15 p.m. sharp: something like boiled potatoes, mince or battered fish, peas, carrots followed by steamed pudding with custard or white sauce. His mother, flushed from battle with the twin tub, muttered: 'I feel like I've been through the ruddy wringer…' unwrapping her pinny from her thin waist – 'Don't have time to be running a restaurant…' pulling the turban from her forehead – 'Call that hand washed? Go and get some soap on it now before I give you a thick ear…' fixing her hair in time for the stomp of his father's boots on the path.

Five around the table, heads bowed, the smell of carbolic on his praying hands. *For what we are about to receive…* After dinner, or lunch as they call it now, his father grabbed his tool bag and returned to work. Christopher wandered back to school, while his mother pushed the pram from the butcher's to the grocer's and on to the baker's. There was no rest for the wicked.

In 1972, the black-and-white television was replaced by a colour set. By then he was at Morecambe Grammar. Lemon-curd crust and a glass of milk in hand, he sat cross-legged on the floor after school and watched the *Clangers* or *Blue Peter* or *Bewitched*. Then he would go up to his loft and study to the soundtrack of the week's Top 40, which he taped without fail every Sunday night on his radio cassette player. Homework complete, he would climb back through the hatch – the clank, clank of those metal steps – and watch the news with his parents.

'You'll get square eyes, you will,' his mother would say, his father muttering behind his paper about the brain-rotting capacities of the idiot box. But then, his father didn't like books much either.

Christopher never understood what square eyes were, though by the age of fourteen myopia had furred his world like the inside of an old kettle. His mother took him to the optician, and two weeks later, spectacles were pushed onto his face, adjusted around his ears. And there they would stay, in various sizes and subtle variations, for the rest of his life: his world clear now but gated off in dark tortoiseshell.

He worked hard, always. He made no apology for that. Caught the bus to school, stayed for dinner, played British Bulldog sometimes on the tarmac. 'Rubbish' at woodwork and art, 'all right' at English and history (he excelled, though he would never say it). Loved to read, loved music. The seventies brought decimalisation, all mod cons, though Morecambe still seemed a decade behind, judging by the clips on *News from the North*. The seventies were happening elsewhere, just as the sixties had, but news of them still came through the television. A tide of change: IRA bombs in London, Margaret Thatcher knocks Edward Heath off the Conservatives' top spot, a prostitute murdered in Leeds.

Like any sixteen-year-old, Christopher was more concerned with youth club on Friday nights in the church hall, watching but not speaking to girls whose pastel dresses had been replaced by flared trousers and low-cut T-shirts stretched tight, girls who threw back their heads when they laughed, who smoked in dangerous blue clouds; boys with long hair who, unlike Christopher, knew what to say. Sundays at Mass, an altar boy, a chorister, his alto broke, turned baritone. Having no distractions at home above the distant whoop of his siblings downstairs, his schoolwork progressed apace. Three A grades at A level – a place at Leeds University to read history.

'What do you want to go there for?' his father asked, sipping tea from his mug in the kitchen. He meant university, not Leeds. He set aside his newspaper, peered down at the results sheet as if it were a secret code, up at Christopher, then back down at the sheet. 'That a trade, is it, history?'

So, you see, his father might not have let him go to university at all, might have steered him into a steady job doing real work for real money, money he could chip in for rent. *University of Life!* Christopher might have ended up with an apprenticeship like most of his peers, were it not for the maintenance grant.

He might never have opened that suitcase.

*

Christopher picked up the fallen torch, pulled the case from the eaves and into his room. There he dusted it down with an old inside-out vest and into it placed the clean clothes his mother had left folded on his bed along with his books and the new brushed-silver fountain pen she had given him for university. After that, he unscrewed the handles of his skipping rope and tied it around the case to be sure it wouldn't pop open again. He carried the case downstairs and left it in the hall.

In the kitchen, his mother and father and Jack and Louise sat together around the table. Christopher handed his father the piece of paper. His father took it from him, his expression no more than that of mild enquiry. He pushed his reading glasses onto his nose and studied the letter for no more than a second, his expression changing instantly – nothing anyone would have noticed if they were not watching closely; no more than a clench of his jaw, a flare of his nostrils. He placed his forefinger and thumb to his brow and, handing the letter in silence to his wife, dispatched Jack Junior and Louise upstairs to their rooms.

To Christopher he said, 'Go and wait in the front parlour.'

Christopher sat on one of the armchairs, firm, almost hard, the raised pattern of the fabric running like Braille beneath his fingertips. His teeth chattered. The front room was cold. He had only ever seen one other person's front room – his school friend Roger's, when they'd laid out his grandfather's body. And here, now, with no corpse to speak of, he felt death in the room just the same. In his chest, the rope tightened.

Long minutes later, his father came in, followed by his mother, who brought a tray with three cups and the teapot, a jug of milk, the sugar bowl, and set it down on the low table, as if the ritual of tea could protect them from the chaos Christopher felt coming.

'Christopher.' It was his mother who began, skinny knees pressed together, hands bunched on her fraught lap; his father, beside her on the settee, smoked his pipe in silence.

'Me and your dad,' his mother said. 'That's to say, we're your parents, of course we are.'

'Yes,' Christopher said, falling towards what she had to say, helpless as a stone pitched down a well.

His mother looked towards his father, who sucked on his pipe and nodded for her to continue. Trusted her with so little usually but now appeared content for her to take charge. Seeing no shift from her husband, no move to help her out, Margaret returned to Christopher, her glance flashing like guilt itself.

Don't say it, he willed silently. *Don't say what it is you are about to say. Let us drink our tea and say well here we are and shouldn't we be going and don't want to miss that train.* But they did not drink their tea, and they did not say those things. Instead, his mother said the words that were already travelling up her windpipe, forming themselves on her tongue, which now pressed itself to the floor of her mouth to let in the gulp of air she took to ready herself and say:

'Christopher, you had another mother and father.'

And like that the rope uncoiled, snaked wildly in the sudden vacuum.

A girl in trouble. This was all they knew. This, and more, he heard through the electric buzz in his ears, a white heat searing the cave of his chest. His parents – familiar strangers who sat in front of him now and looked anywhere but at him – these people had picked up his infant self from a convent on the outskirts of Liverpool. They had brought him home and called him Christopher. Here in their semi-detached house with its back patio and its converted roof space, that baby had grown, had learnt to skip, to read, to not spoil things, to not claim things for his own. And somewhere along the line, the natural child that had been denied them had come after all. He had come, and they had called him Jack.

'Why didn't you tell me?' he asked.

'You had opportunities here,' said his mother, pressing on, deaf to him. 'Dread to think what would've happened if we hadn't taken you. We left a note for her, told her we'd look after you. Yes, truth be told, you were much better off here with us.'

Here, where his black hair had never been mentioned as anything unusual – or indeed as anything at all. He thought now it must have been a subject everyone avoided. His height? No more than a handy attribute when a jar was needed from the top shelf of the pantry.

'Happen that's where the brains came from,' his mother added with a merry laugh that choked on itself and died. 'Goodness knows they're not from me. And your being so tall, like, what with us being short and that. We were going to tell you on your birthday, but we didn't want to upset you, did we, Jack?' She cast a glance towards his father, but it landed short. 'We wanted to wait until you were old enough. We thought that were best. But then…' She brought the lumpen handkerchief from her sleeve and dabbed her eyes. 'I don't know. It's not an easy thing to say, love, and it just seemed to get bigger, and then it was too big. You're our son, Christopher, and that's all there is to it.'

How quiet his mother's voice was, as if the silence in the house were yet one more thing that must not be ruined. Christopher. Even his name had not been his own. Jack Junior had been given his name, the best family crystal; Christopher the lesser glassware: serviceable and of reasonable quality – nothing you could complain about.

'We've told you now, at any rate.' His father's pipe had left his mouth but hovered near, just in case. 'Doesn't change anything as far as I'm concerned.'

He coughed into the thick roll of his plumber's fingers, his other hand cupping the bowl of his pipe. He did not take his wife's hand, though she looked like she might shatter for lack of touch. Deep creases ran across her forehead, her mouth set in a soft rectangle of angst. On the mantelpiece, the carriage clock chimed quarter past the hour. The shiny palm leaves that grew in patterns up the wallpaper seemed to sprout from his father's head.

Father? The word stopped Christopher's thoughts dead. But his mother was already standing, brushing at her skirt.

'Yes, well,' she said. 'Happen it's better to know than not, eh.'

But as he said to me, he'd always known. And this is really what this story is all about.

CHAPTER TWO

Nurse just came. She stands over me while I take my meds.

'There you go, my darling,' she says. She is Irish, middle-aged, a no-nonsense type. That's what you become, I suppose, if you're dealing with broken people all day long. Can't waste your time getting sentimental – where's the use in that?

'What's that you're writing there?' she asks. 'A book, is it?'

I shrug.

'Well now.' She eases the little plastic dish from my hand. 'I'll leave you to your book.'

Part of me is sorry when she goes, sorry that I didn't extend the basic courtesy of talking to her. Writing, not talking, is preferable. I don't want to hear the words coming out of my mouth. And if I write it, I can burn it without ever having uttered a syllable.

I'd always known. That's where I'll start today. I asked him once what he meant by that. He'd taken me to the pub – he had a thing about pubs. It was the Traveller's Rest on the hill, as I recall, and we sat in the little side room with the log fire. It was late afternoon and we were the only ones in.

'What I mean is…' I added when he didn't respond. I was worried I'd pressed on a nerve, that I'd upset him. 'Do you think that feeling came from actual concrete events, or was it something… I don't know… more of a sixth sense?'

He picked up his glass and, without taking a drink, placed it back on its coaster. He picked up another coaster and tore off the corner.

'I think it started with my brother,' he said, tearing off a second corner. 'When my mum was in hospital having him. She was away for ten days. That's an eternity to a child, and I began to feel distressed.' Christopher talks like that – quite formal in his way of expressing himself. 'Towards the end of that period, I actually began to believe that she'd died and no one was telling me.' He sipped his bitter and licked the froth off his lip. 'She wasn't dead, of course, but the feeling never went away. Was it concrete? No, but I could breathe it in the air. It was a secret, but it wasn't a secret because a secret is something one person knows or maybe two or three. It was the opposite of a secret. It was something everyone knew but no one said anything about.' All four corners of the coaster torn away, he began to worry it between his thumbs and forefingers.

'But surely that's paranoia?' I said.

'Paranoia, yes.' He shrugged. 'I came and went on that for years. But later, I knew it wasn't, and it wasn't one single event either. It was a multitude of little things – chance remarks, sudden silences if I came into a room, glances exchanged between my relatives. And I don't know exactly when I knew it absolutely – maybe only when they told me – but I'd felt it long before.' He stared at me, his eyes shiny and dark as treacle.

'I can remember Margaret coming home with my brother,' he said. 'She told me to go and say hello to him. He was in a basket on the living-room floor by the fire.

'I crossed the carpet in pin-steps. I could feel her eyes on the back of my neck. I looked at our Jack, little Jack Junior. He was all red, snarling even though he was asleep, with tight fists raised above his head like an angry little boxer. I didn't know how I was supposed to say hello to a baby, so I reached over and prodded his forehead with my finger. He started crying.

' "Careful, Christopher!" Margaret shouted.'

He had mimicked her and now stopped to laugh, though not happily. 'Margaret could never keep the irritation out of her voice,' he went on. 'But she always spoke to me that way, so I was used to it. "You have to be gentle with babies, Christopher," she said.'

'What did you do?' I asked him.

'I ran out into the yard. There was a spider's web I'd been watching for days and it was still intact, stretching across from the roof overhang down to the drainpipe. The spider was a big one; it had a body the size of a raisin – you know, one of those spiders that have knees. I'd shown it to my friend Roger the day before and he'd said it was a whopper. So then I ran my finger down the edge of the web and pulled the whole thing away.'

'And the spider?'

'Went scuttling – but not fast enough. I caught it. I could feel its little body frantic in my hand.' Seeing the horror cross my face, he laughed. 'It was only a spider! Anyway, I crouched down and let it out onto the patio stones and… and I crushed it with my foot.'

He picked up his glass and drank. I said nothing.

'A week or two later,' he continued, 'Margaret told me off for nearly suffocating Jack. I told her I'd been trying to tuck him into his blankets, but I hadn't. I'd pushed the blankets over his face and held them there.'

'Why?' I asked him.

He shrugged. 'I don't know. I can't say I wanted him dead. It wasn't as clear as that. I just wanted to hold the covers over his face and…'

'But you were just a kid.'

He shook his head – no. 'There were other things too, when I was older. When I was fourteen, they gave him my Scalextric set. They didn't ask me, they just gave it to him. I wasn't playing with it by then, but that's not the point. It was mine.' His voice had hardened; he had become agitated. He bit down on his bottom lip then drank. On the tabletop, the coaster lay in frayed pieces. 'So later, when no one was looking, I took his teddy bear from his room and put it in the compost heap. I dug down and put it in with all the smelly rotten vegetable peelings, and I covered it over and thought: there, take that.'

He raised his eyebrows and smiled, as if to say: *See? I'm not as nice as you think.* But it didn't change my opinion of him. As I said, I loved him.

But I digress. Christopher was on his way to Leeds, wasn't he, after his parents had told him the truth of his origins. He recalled nothing of that journey, could not remember how he got from the train station to Devonshire halls of residence. That was the shock, I think, erasing his thoughts, or refusing even to form them in that moment of pure suspended animation. His world had stopped on its axis. And now that very world was waiting for presence of mind to return so it could go on spinning. The next memory he had was sitting on his bed in the room he shared with Adam, although of course he didn't know Adam yet.

He was sitting on his bed staring at his open hands, he said. He was studying the way the creases arched across his palms, tracing, some believed, his destiny. He had seen a palm reader once, he told me, on Morecambe pier. He'd have been around sixteen, had gone in for a dare. An old gypsy woman, with a headscarf with thin silver coins sewn into the hem, had held his hand and studied it.

'Here, that's a shock,' she'd said after a few moments, pushing her forefinger to the middle of his hand. The thick black kohl under her eyes had smudged, crumbed in the corners of her bloodshot eyes. 'It's coming soon. It will change your destiny.'

He'd dismissed her words within seconds of leaving the booth, but they came back to him now, dissolving, re-forming as another damn sense, yet more invisible particles floating in the air. He was not, no longer at least, the simple, shy eighteen-year-old history student he had anticipated being. That much was certain. Rather, he was a trembling boy scout, no older than twelve, who had been given a penny and a candle and told to get from Land's End to John O'Groats. He could almost feel the chill wind on some distant hilltop blowing into his face. He was not equal to the task. He was but a child.

It was a daydream from which he knew he had to wake up, and that this waking up had something to do with being or becoming the man he had now to be. *Man.* For a couple of years now, people had been referring to him that way. He had left home, which was what men did, but the rite of passage had been marked by a revelation too big to hold in his aching head. And the rope? The rope was still there. Only now he had a diagnosis, and the diagnosis cast a shadow as astonishing as a superpower. Footsteps rang louder on the pavements, strangers' clothes separated into threads before his eyes, and on the station platform, on the train, on the university campus, people everywhere seemed to stare only at him, as if to ask: *Are you family? Are you blood?*

Somehow, in that terrible trance, he had made his way to this twin room, sat down on this worn bed and stared at his open hands.

'Well, well, well!'

Christopher looked up to see a smiling ginger-haired man bounding into the room. He swung his suitcase onto the other bed, put his hands on his hips and, seeing Christopher, threw back his head. 'I say, shall we go in search of a hostelry, my good man?' Northern vowels infiltrated his attempt at a Home Counties accent. He laughed and gave in to them. 'Just kidding, man. I'm Adam. First man on earth. Never touch apples.' With two long strides, he was in front of Christopher, one arm out, apparently intent on shaking hands. 'Pleased to meet you. Hey, do you like T. Rex, man?'

He wore tight blue flared jeans, a black polo-neck sweater and a black leather jacket with square pockets. He was studying electronic engineering. He was from Newcastle. Outskirts. (That explained his accent.) His mother was Irish. He had family in Liverpool – his auntie on his mother's side. He liked women. He loved women! He liked T. Rex – did he already say that? Fleetwood Mac, ELO and Queen. Hated ABBA. They were crap, but his sister liked them. His sister was eight – a mistake; his mother had thought it was the menopause. She got on his nerves – his sister, not his mother. His second name was Wells. He couldn't wait to get stuck in. To what Christopher didn't ask.

'Thought we could take a wander,' Adam continued, 'see if there's a pub sells beer? See if we can find ourselves a couple of birds? We should stick together, I reckon. Us grammar lads. What do you think, man?'

Christopher saw his belongings through Adam's eyes. His peeling case tied with rope, his donkey jacket. No gold-monogrammed luggage where he came from, no woollen coat, no tweed.

'I need to unpack,' he said.

'You can unpack tomorrow.' Adam pushed out his bottom lip. 'You've just got out of jail free. Live a little, man.' He leant in closer and patted the pocket at his hip. 'Besides, I've got some fine weed.'

A flare of panic. Weed? That meant marijuana, Christopher was pretty sure.

'Don't freak, man,' said Adam. 'It's not purple hearts, only a bit of grass.'

Christopher feigned the best laugh he could manage. 'N-No, really,' he stammered. 'You go on. I'm fine. Next time.'

'Suit yourself.' Adam shrugged, turned away and loped towards the door, leaving his bed with his luggage still closed upon it. 'See you later then.' He left, whistling his way along the corridor. A door hinge squeaked and squeaked again, the whistling faded; his carrot-topped room-mate was no more.

Before Christopher had time to think about anything else, more chatter echoed in the corridor – two or three boys, he thought, maybe four – arriving to other rooms. One of them could be his brother. His twin, why not? The one his birth mother had kept, perhaps, or given to another family. Was that it? Was that his story? A twin, a brother, who would look like him and like the same things and have his mannerisms even though they'd never met. What a thought.

Back in Morecambe, on the way to the station, he had stayed silent in the back seat of his parents' car and all the while they'd waited for the train. Now they were gone, he was full of questions. He had not asked his birth mother's name. He had not asked his birth father's name. He had not, come to think of it, asked his own name.

But he could not. Not now, not ever. The subject had been opened like a library vault, only long enough to retrieve this lone and dusty book before being closed and locked forever. Jack and Margaret would never, could never, speak of it again.

Out in the corridor, more doors whined open, slammed shut. The smell of floor cleaner, of damp, of sheets washed in different detergent. He lay back on his knitted hands and stared at the ceiling.

'Karen,' he whispered, to try it. He liked the feel of that name, the shape his mouth made when he said it. 'Where can I find you?' he asked of the ceiling. 'Or are you Denise? Julie? Barbara? Valerie?'

He did not imagine names for his father. But there, where there had been only air thick with doubt, was now the shadowy shape of a woman. The shadow needed detail, features he could recognise: a broad nose like his, perhaps, or his brown eyes or black hair. If he could only see her, clear the fog – meet her eyes with his. He should register with the adoption agency, or bureau, or whatever it was called. Perhaps the local council was his best bet. Lancashire. No, Liverpool. The letter had said Railton, so it would most likely be Liverpool City Council, wouldn't it? There was only one way to find out.

The way he told it, that was the moment he leapt up from his bed, scooped the loose change from his overcoat pocket and headed out. The university rep who had given him his key changed a pound note and pointed him in the direction of the phone, and after several false starts and a few wasted two-pence pieces, Christopher reached the Adoption Records Office in Liverpool.

After going round the houses, he said, he spoke to a woman called Mrs Jackson, who took his name. After a few more questions, she asked, 'How does two o'clock a week this Friday sound?'

'Two o'clock next Friday,' he said. 'I'll be there.'

He took the stairs two at a time, his heart thudding against his ribs. Mrs Jackson had spoken to him kindly, yet as he entered his room, it occurred to him that she had given him no hope. Her only assurance, thinking about it properly now, was that they would meet soon and get the process under way. What the process would deliver had been left unsaid. She had promised nothing.

He threw himself once more onto his bed. No matter what Mrs Jackson had said, he, Christopher Harris, had started upon a journey that would lead him to his mother, and no amount of polite obfuscation could prevent this… this *knowledge*. He would find her. The certainty quickened the blood in his veins. Blood she shared! Through her he would locate himself in the world. She would tell him his name. She might already have left her details with the relevant officials. She might be waiting for him to get in touch *right at this moment*. She wouldn't know him as Christopher, of course, but by the name she herself had given him. His jaw tightened at the thought.

But then he shouldn't get his hopes up. His birth mother might not have made any attempt to find him. She might not be expecting him to search for her, might not want him to. Oh, but if he could meet her, he could tell her that everything was all right. He could go to her like Jesus, and say, *I forgive you*. No, that was too grand. Who was he to forgive anyone? But he could at least make sure she was well, happy, settled. He wouldn't even have to tell her who he was. He could just… watch her.

CHAPTER THREE

I suppose at some point I need to think about Benjamin, whom I found out about too late. Perhaps that's the real disaster. If I'd known about him sooner, we could have worked something out. I could have prevented all of this – and if that isn't enough to drive a person out of their mind, I don't know what is. When I think of Ben, I'll admit the idea I have of him is romantic. If you never get to know a person well, you can keep them in your mind as a kind of idealised dream, and that's what Ben is to me. When I picture him, it's morning, sometime in early 1981, and he's throwing an espresso down his throat and grabbing his keys from some artsy kitchen table in a boho apartment in San Francisco. He has floppy brown hair and a lopsided, boyish grin and moves with a kind of easy charm that people don't notice straightaway. It's only later that they realise they find him attractive, find that they want to be around him, though they can't pinpoint why.

I see his apartment somewhere near the bay, on the fourth floor maybe, somewhere with a view. Or maybe he and his girlfriend Martha rent a room in one of those painted-lady houses on Alamo Square with a pot-smoking landlady like Mrs Madrigal from *Tales of the City*. Whatever, I see him soft-footed and cartoon-creeping into the bedroom where Martha is still sleeping. He bends over her and kisses her soft, warm cheek. It is still dark out. He has brought coffee for her, which he sets down on the bedside table. The steam seems not to snake upwards but to trail down, fanning out into the cup from some invisible point in the air.

'See you later, honey,' he whispers.

She stirs and, even in stirring, eyes still shut, rewards him with a lazy smile.

'Are we going out for dinner later?' Her voice is slurred and hoarse with sleep. He could just crawl back into the bed and press his face against her belly.

'Sure. We're meeting the others downtown at eight.'

She opens her eyes. They are green, like his. Oh, how lovely she is.

'Are you going to do what we talked about?' she asks him.

'Sure,' he says. 'I'll do it today.'

He reaches the office at 7.30 a.m. Outside, the Golden Gate Bridge throws its arcs against the still-black sky. Plenty of time to run through his presentation one last time before the 9 a.m. meeting. Barring any major reversals, he's just about to win the biggest client in the history of United Graphics: Oakland, a range of olde-worlde kitchen and picnic ware that evokes *Little House on the Prairie* and capitalises on the current craving for all things Americana. Not bad for someone who's been in the company less than a year. But if you were to count up the man hours he has put into this project and change them into dollars, that kind of professional victory has not come cheap. Ben has worked so hard these last months that even when he does get some precious leisure time, he barely knows what to do with it any more, can barely recall the long, glorious, smoke-hazed hours he frittered away at college. Seriously, he thinks, as this private moment of pride pushes a grin across his face, what has happened to him?

He reaches for his cue cards and the acetate slides from his desk drawer, and takes them into the conference suite. He switches on the overhead projector, fusses with the neck angle until he's centred the white square of light on the white back wall. Outside, lights still twinkle in the bay. But the late-September sky is bleaching now, a nascent pink glow rising from the horizon. Martha will be in the shower. After that, she will get dressed, have her breakfast and go to work, then come home and wait, eager to tell him about her day spent at the mercy of thirty eight-year-old children. He never hears about her days lately. When they first met, he wanted to know every detail, her every move and thought. He still feels the same. He lives with her and yet he misses her. But these last months he hasn't had or hasn't made the time to listen. And now the habit has been lost. This afternoon he will make sure he gets home before she gives up and goes to bed. They will walk together to the restaurant, hand in hand. He wonders if they'll have sex before they go out, a thought that sends a bolt through him. He should take some time off – spend it with her.

Will you do that thing we talked about? she asked him again this morning.

I'll do it today is what he said.

He will do it. If Oakland goes well, he will do what he's promised. He'll do it this afternoon.

He lays the acetates one by one on the projector, whispering his way through the cue cards, throwing out his hands, pausing for the laughter he knows he'll get. He's always a little keyed up round about now, an hour or two before, but the nerves or adrenalin or whatever the hell you want to call it are what make him good at this stuff. They give his performance the edge that has made him stand out, get him so far so fast. The cue cards? No more than a pre-show comforter, a talisman to ward off the heebie-jeebies. Once he's started, he won't look at those cards, not even once. He's a talker – could talk his way into and out of just about anything.

By the time he's finished his rehearsal, a flash of Titian hair through the glass office wall tells him that Donna, the office secretary, has arrived. After a brief but flirtatious conversation in which he gives her instructions for the set-up, he leaves her to furnish the conference suite with the white Conran cups and saucers he ordered from London. There are croissants too, from

Schubert's. No expense spared. Important not to skimp on the details. Petty short-term savings most often mean losing out in the long term.

Over in the kitchen booth he fixes himself another espresso. Returning to his desk, he dials into his answerphone and finds a call from 6 p.m. on Friday – he was here finishing the storyboard but didn't hear it come in.

'Benjamin, hello darling, it's your mother calling.' Her voice slips but is not so slurred as to be incoherent. 'Could you call me back? I won't try you at home since I'm sure you're not there.'

He checks his watch: 8.33 a.m. If he calls now, he can say he's heading into a meeting and it won't be a lie. Plus he won't have the call hanging over him, and that will leave his mind clearer for the presentation. He punches in his parents' number, and in the precise moment of realising what a mistake this is, she picks up.

'Benjamin, there's a surprise.'

Four words and already she's breaking his balls.

'Dorothy. Listen, I'm heading into a meeting but I saw you'd called Friday. I only picked it up now. Nothing urgent, I hope?'

'You're very busy, I know,' she says.

He waits. Things being what they are, she will have been up since 5 a.m. Vodka knocks her out by early evening, but the trouble is, it wakes her up early too. Double-entry bookkeeping, Martha calls it, the pluses and minuses of every goddam decision you ever make.

'It was nothing urgent,' she goes on. 'You go to your meeting.'

'George OK?'

The suck of his mother's lips on the gold tip of her Sobranie cigarette. 'You know your father.'

Ben checks his watch. The guys from Oakland could be here as early as quarter to. He should never have made the call.

'I was wondering if you and Martha would be coming for Thanksgiving,' she says finally.

Nuts in the crusher: check. September and she's talking about Thanksgiving, for Chrissakes. It's *Put your good shoes on; we'll be late for Mass* all over again. On a loop. With different words.

'Listen,' he says. 'If it's nothing urgent, maybe I can call you back later?'

'I don't know where I'll be later, but sure, if you're too busy, I guess.'

Through the glass wall he sees two suits, Donna's red hair weaving between them. She is pouring them coffee, her lips moving nineteen to the dozen.

'Dorothy,' he says, 'I'll call you back.'

He rings off but decides to wait before hitting the conference suite. The rationale behind calling his mother was flawed, and he needs a few minutes to settle himself. She always does this – gets under his skin, makes him feel like he's doing something wrong. The worst of it is, she thinks she's easy. Genuinely. If he were to say to her, *Dorothy, quit busting my balls*, she would fall down with the shock. She would cry and wail. She's given him everything; all she wants is a conversation once in a while, is that too much to ask? Is it? No, it isn't worth blowing oxygen into that particular fire – better to pretend he can't see its embers glowing in the hearth. People don't change. People never go through those epiphanies you see in the movies. Scrooge would have finished up the same old tight-ass eventually, once he'd gotten over the shock of his crazy Christmas Eve acid trip, and his mother is no different.

He straightens his tie, pulls in a lungful of air and heads into the conference suite.

CHAPTER FOUR

Understandably, I think, Christopher's first week at university passed in a blur. Not that he skipped lectures, no. Christopher would never have done that. He attended all his classes with the diligence that was so much a part of him. *Consensus and Contention: Investigations in International History; The Crusades and Medieval Christendom; Empire and Aftermath: The Mediterranean World from the Second to the Eighth Centuries*... whatever the module, the message was the same: 'It is history that tells us who we are... it is only history that can put us and everything we know into context...'

Grey-haired academics lectured from dog-eared stacks of paper at the front of vast halls, radiating a bored air of wanting to be elsewhere. In another century, perhaps, he thought.

Christopher took rigorous notes, borrowed books from the Brotherton Library – a reading list as long as a phone directory – and bought more hardback tomes second-hand in the union shop. His best distraction from the terrible anticipation of his meeting with Mrs Jackson from the Adoption Records Office, he told me, was to begin research for his first assignments. Adam scarcely to be seen in the evenings and over that first weekend, Christopher found himself alone with his books. On the Sunday, he found a church – Our Lady of Lourdes in Cardigan Road. There he attended Mass and lit candles for the mother he longed to bring from the shadows of his imaginings. He prayed for her to be delivered to him as he had prayed as a child on Christmas Eve, guiltily requesting toys for himself when he knew he should be thinking about the poor and the sick. Though Friday's appointment with Mrs Jackson never left his mind entirely, once back in his room in halls, he took up his books. As he had for much of his life, he took his refuge there.

Friday came around at a speed, I remember Christopher saying, that made Edwin Moses look like a sloth with a bad leg. It later transpired that this was one of Adam's catchphrases; Christopher did like to try them out for himself sometimes, and if anyone laughed, his face would break open in surprise.

That morning, the cold air met him at the exit to Liverpool Lime Street station. Not that this bothered him. He was above all delighted to have made it through the week, and besides, it had been colder and windier back in Leeds. He walked in what he hoped was the direction of the council offices, he said, head bowed, map pressed to his chest, heat building in his belly. All the way to Liverpool, he had thought – had not been able to stop thinking – of the infant taken in by his parents eighteen years earlier. He had tried to picture that baby in the shawl he had found in the case – washing it in his mind from grey to white. His mother had wrapped Jack Junior and Louise in soft white wool she herself had crocheted, but when he tried to put himself in such a blanket, Christopher could only conjure the image of Jesus in the manger. Not even Jesus, but the time-yellowed plastic doll they used in St Stephen's for Christmas Mass.

Of course the baby his birth mother had wrapped in swaddling bands and laid in a manger was not Christopher at all.

'That child was but a *baby*,' he said to me once, 'a being yet to form.'

His birth mother had not left *him* at the convent, no, not at all. She had left an unformed being, no one she knew. In fact, that baby had nothing to do with the person he was now. Nothing whatsoever! His birth mother didn't *know* him. Not the boy, not the man, not the name. If she could see him now, that would be different; she would know him as soon as her eyes met his. He hoped he would know her in return, felt sure he would. He might love her – why not? And she might love him. Was that so impossible? It would be in a different way perhaps than had she raised him, but all the same… there would be a lifeline connecting them, linking one to the other. What else was this coil in his chest if not that very lifeline, his silken rope to throw out to her and say: 'Here. Grasp this. Rescue me.'

I'll admit that when he told me, my heart tightened for him, poor boy. I find it's often the way that the hopes of someone you love are heavier to bear than your own.

He reached the council buildings in Henry Street, gave his name at reception and a few minutes later, a woman came to collect him. She was very small. She wore a burgundy skirt suit and high spike heels. Her hair was short and grey.

'Mr Harris?'

He nodded and stood, dwarfing her.

She shook his hand. Her pale blue eyes looked up into his. 'Samantha Jackson,' she said. 'We spoke on the phone. Pleased to meet you.'

'Yes. Thank you.'

'Great stuff. Now, if you'd like to follow me. Can't abide the lift, so we'll take the stairs, all right?'

'Yes. Yes, of course.'

She went ahead and he followed, kept his head down for fear of finding himself staring directly at her small but round rear as it swung from left to right in its tight pencil skirt.

'How was your journey?' she said over her shoulder. 'It's Christopher, isn't it? Are you all right with Christopher, or do you prefer Chris?'

'Christopher please. Thank you.'

'You came from Leeds.' This she added as a statement before turning and heading up the next flight. Her steps echoed against the hard institutional flooring. 'So do you like football? Do you have a team?'

'Ah, yes. Yes I do. Liverpool in fact.'

'Good man. And what do you think about Dalglish, eh?'

'I…'

'Four hundred and odd thousand they paid for him. Obscene, isn't it?'

'Yes,' he said. 'It's a lot of money.'

'It is for kicking a leather bladder round a field with twenty-one other blokes.' She stopped and placed her hand to her chest, rolled her eyes and puffed. After this brief performance of tiredness, she pushed open her office door. 'Now. Come in and have a seat.'

Inside was a desk, a bookshelf, two easy chairs facing each other and a G-plan-style coffee table on top of which lay a faded red cardboard folder.

'Go on in, take a seat, Christopher, you're all right.'

When he told me this, I could just imagine him standing there, not knowing whether to go in, whether to sit down. He'd been uprooted – of course he felt that way. The confidence he eventually found came much, much later.

Seeing Christopher hesitate, Samantha gestured to the chairs. Without saying anything more, Christopher sat on the smaller, apparently less comfortable of the two. It was hot in the office and the air smelled of heating, of cigarettes. Samantha Jackson sat in the other chair. Behind her, a low winter sun shone through the dusty window – through the gap where the blinds did not reach. She picked up the file and held it, closed, against her chest.

'So, Christopher,' she began, and smiled as if in afterthought. 'I'm what's called an adoption counsellor. I'm basically a social worker specialising in adoption, if you like. In cases like this, the council provides someone to help you through the process should you decide to go ahead. Is that clear?'

He nodded.

She plucked some half-moon glasses Christopher had not noticed until that moment from a chain on her chest and slid them onto her nose. She peered at him over the top of them. 'So as a starting point, Christopher, it might be best if you tell me what you're hoping for today.'

'Hoping for,' he repeated, suddenly with no idea why he had come or how to put what he wanted into words.

'I mean, in terms of making contact. What is it you're hoping will come out of it?'

'I suppose,' he began again, just to say something in the hope that more words would follow, 'I was wondering whether my mother had left her details at all. Or if she'd been in touch. Or tried. I mean, I don't know if that's even possible. I… I don't really know how it works. I only found out I was… I only found out the other week.'

'That's all right.' She nodded, her blue eyes fixed on his. 'You must be feeling quite up in the air with it all.'

Up in the air. That was it exactly. A red helium-filled balloon floating in a vast blue sky. He nodded his agreement, tried to smile. At the maddening prickle in his eyes, he blinked, coughed, pushed himself back in his chair. He crossed his legs, uncrossed them – crossed his arms instead. He wished she would not look at him and stared down at his knees.

'What I'm trying to ascertain, Christopher' – her voice was gentle, so gentle, but still he could not look up – 'is whether you feel ready, potentially, to start a search. Actually, you won't know this, but none of this was possible up until this year really. The law didn't change till 1975, and these things take a while to filter through. So you're lucky in that sense. Before now, you'd have been on your own.'

'On my own,' he repeated. Again, she had said exactly what he felt, as if she were him and he her. On his own – he had felt this since his mother, Margaret, had told him the truth of his life. Before that. Perhaps always.

'That's right,' she said. 'In terms of any investigation you might have wanted.'

When she didn't say any more, he made himself look at her. Her eyes were such a vivid blue, like the celestial paintings in church. They made him want to tell her everything about himself, to start talking and never stop. He looked away.

'I suppose I'd like to find out who I am,' he said, to the window. 'My real name, that sort of thing. Where I belong.'

'You don't feel like you belong at home?'

'No. Yes. Of course. I mean, of course. It's just that, when they… my parents… my adoptive parents told me, I… I can't really explain it. Except to say I already knew. I didn't know. It's not that. What I mean is, is that common? Is that normal? To know something like that before you're told?'

'People feel all sorts of things, Christopher. Everything's normal in that sense.'

The sound of traffic from outside. She had paused, was looking at him. He spoke – to fill the silence. 'I knew my brother and sister were natural, or biological, or whatever it's called, and that I was… different, is maybe the word. I knew they were biological because I saw my mother with… with… you know, pregnant. And I don't remember being born, obviously – I wouldn't expect to. I don't remember any *before*, in terms of the feeling. What I mean is, I suppose I always felt…'

In another office, a phone trilled twice and stopped. He heard a man's voice, though nothing of what he said.

'No one else in my family has dark hair,' he went on – couldn't help himself. 'Not even aunties and uncles. I'm the only one.' He stopped, attempted another smile, feeling his face grow hot.

'Anyway, sorry, I was hoping, I *am* hoping, that maybe if I could see my actual biological mother I would see where... where I fit, I suppose. Where I make sense. In the world, I mean. That probably sounds ridiculous.'

'Not at all.' The counsellor still had the file held to her chest. 'OK,' she said. 'All right. Now, of course, there's the possibility that you won't feel that. These things are never perfect.' She spoke with such gravity, Christopher felt, as though she were a surgeon come to deliver the worst possible news to the next of kin. Except here there was no next of kin. At least, not yet.

'Never perfect,' he said. 'Of course. I understand.'

'You have to take that on. And what I also have to tell you is there is the possibility that your birth parents are no longer with us.'

'Of course.' He had not considered this eventuality, and the thought hit him flat in the chest. 'That... that stands to reason.'

'There's also the possibility, and I'm not saying this will happen or it won't, that she or they won't want contact. It happens. But in the eventuality that they do want contact, we advise getting in touch by letter first and then perhaps by phone before an actual physical meeting.'

In his mind's eye, a faceless woman fought to emerge. She was holding a red balloon, holding it out to him: *Here*, she said. She let go. The balloon floated away before he had a chance to grasp it. The woman was gone.

'I understand,' he said.

Samantha Jackson laid the file on the coffee table, opened it and drew out a document. 'This is a form for you to apply for your birth records.' She held it out and he took it from her. 'You'll have to fill that in and send it to the Registrar General.' She pulled out another paper and laid it over the first. 'This is another form you can send to the court overseeing the adoption, which in this case is Liverpool. There's some more information for you here.' More documents landed, until a small pile of papers lay on his lap.

'I've photocopied the relevant information on adoption contact registers. You can register a veto, you see, if you don't want to be contacted. And that's obviously a possibility.'

'I have no expectations,' he said, taking hold of the papers and stacking them on his knee. 'I just want to know.'

'I'll put a call in to NORCAP. Sometimes birth parents register their details there. I've got a colleague there – Robert. He'll have a look and see if your mother's been in touch. All right? In the meantime, you have my number if anything's troubling you or if you need to ask me something or talk to me, OK?'

'Yes. Thank you. Thank you so much.'

And that was it. I remember thinking how photographic his memory must be. And along with the visual details, he was able to relay the conversation too, verbatim, as if it had happened the day before. What I've written here is an approximation, of course, but everything he said stayed with me long after he'd said it. That's the way, I think, with the people who become important to you, who impact your life. And Christopher did more than impact mine.

He destroyed it.

On the return journey from Liverpool, he took out his book, but the words swam, dissolved, blackened like a swarm. He felt as if he were floating, looking down on himself there in the train carriage trying to read. But at the same time he was in his own body, sitting down with the book in his hands, the words fidgeting on the page.

After a few minutes he closed his eyes, pushed his head back into the headrest and saw at once the documents that would lead him to his birth mother. Forms he would have to sign: Christopher Harris. Funny, he'd always been so particular about his name, and here he was on the brink of claiming another. *Christopher please, not Chris.* How pernickety that seemed to him now, watching the northern towns shuffle by: Huyton, Eccles, Rochdale, Halifax. *Christopher please, not Chris, thank you.* As if the shortening of his name diminished him in some important way. Had that all been down to the rope, to *that* feeling? Yes, he thought now, it probably had. A self always so precarious it could stand no further alteration. Perhaps if he had been less of a stickler, he would have found himself picked for lunchtime football games instead of consigned to the bench, summoned only when they were short-handed or needed someone in goal. And later, perhaps he would have known better what to say to the girls at youth club instead of standing at the edge of the room, mouthing the words to the hits, flat R White's cream soda warming in his sweating hands. He had kept too tight a hold on himself – he saw that now. Perhaps that was normal, under the circumstances. Perhaps it had been the only way to prevent himself from unravelling.

And so a new name would soon be his, if all went well. If he could choose from all the names he'd ever heard, he would not know which he would prefer, only that he no longer wanted Jack, as he once had. Jack belonged to his brother, to the Harris bloodline, not to him. He, Christopher, or whatever his real name was, had his own line now, flowing from a past he had yet to discover all the way to this moment, to this train carriage, to this young chap called Whatisname. The line ran through his present and on to the man he was to become. All would become clear. His history would tell him who he was, who he could be. His history would give him his future.

'Who am I?' he asked the vacant railway carriage. 'What is my name?'

A change of air. He opened his eyes. The carriage door had opened and opposite him a woman with white hair was arranging her small case on the overhead rack. As she sat down, she stared at him through grey haloed eyes.

'I'm sorry, did you say something?' she asked.

'No. Sorry.'

'No, I'm sorry,' she said, without taking her eyes from his. 'I thought I heard you say something as I came in just now.'

'Nothing.' Christopher looked out of the window and saw trees, pines, all bent the same way. 'It was probably the wind,' he said with a polite smile.

He closed his eyes once more and returned, this time in silence, to his imaginings.

Hello. Yes, hello. I'm David. I'm Thomas. I'm Matthew. I'm John. I'm Matthew Mark Luke and John, next-door neighbour carry on… A rose by any other name. A name, a name, what's in a name? I am your son. My name is Harry, JimBob, William… He could almost see her, his mother. She was tall, like him. Yes, tall. And she had black hair, like his, a lock that fell over her eye when she was reading or cooking or whatever it was she liked to do. He could not see her face but could feel its kindness on his skin like sunlight. *Hello… Doris, Daphne, Julie, Jean, I'm… I'm Peter I'm Michael I'm Zachary, your son. You can shorten it, customise it, call me what the heck you like. I am your son. I am your son. I am your son.*

CHAPTER FIVE

Christopher arrived at the halls a little after six to find Adam lying on his bed in his Y-fronts, reading *Tyke*, the Leeds rag magazine. On the front was a cartoon. Of what, Christopher could not make out, apart from a speech bubble: *Only 20p!*

'Chris, man,' Adam said, jumping up as Christopher walked in. 'Dark horse, where've you been all day?'

'Christopher please. I prefer Christopher.' Did he? Was that true any more? Force of habit had made him say it, nothing more. 'I've been… out.'

'Out, eh? Why aye, man. What's her name?' Adam laughed.

Christopher envied it, this laugh that seemed to live permanently on his room-mate's rather pink, generous lips.

'Oh, nothing that exciting, I'm afraid.' Christopher sat on the bed, crossed his legs and recrossed them, before giving up and standing once again. He thrust his hands in his pockets, wondered what he could find to ask his room-mate about.

'Lectures go all right?' was what came to him, after a moment.

'Skived the five o'clock,' said Adam. 'You bloody art students don't know you're born. We're slaves compared to you.' He lengthened the word *slaves*, rolled his head like a wolf howling at the moon when he said it.

'I'm not exactly an art…' The words fell away. An entire day off campus and he had missed but one lecture, it was true.

'Valuable drinking time is being missed, Chris, man. Christopher, sorry. Speaking of which, you don't fancy a pint, do you, by any chance? It is almost Friday.'

'It is Friday.'

'That's what I said. Friday. Holy crap, is it? Jesus, where did the week go? Come on, you didn't come out last weekend, and I'm not letting you get away with it this time. The books can have a night off, eh, what do you say?'

Adam's face was set in an expectant expression Christopher thought might be mischief. Going for a pint would be a normal thing to do, he thought. It was what men who knew who they were did, men who were not sticklers for the minor alteration of names, men who even had nicknames like Jonesy or Budgie or Bones. Now was no time to admit he had never seen the inside of a pub. Now was the time to come off the substitutes' bench and claim his place in the team.

'All right,' he said. 'As it's Friday.'

'Great.' Adam looked him up and down. 'I'll lend you some decent jeans.'

Adam was already striding ahead. His hair pushed thick against his coat collar, orange as the vitamin C tablets Christopher's mother had made him chew on winter mornings when he was a child. Shoulders high, head down, hands deep in his donkey-jacket pockets, he hugged himself against the cold. Christopher had not worn Adam's trousers – they were too short and too small, a fact obvious just from holding them against himself. Adam had volunteered to ask around but, mortified, Christopher had said no.

'It'll be dark anyway,' Adam had said. 'But tomorrow we're going into town and sorting you out with something decent. You will never get laid like that, man. Not unless she's blind.'

Now, Adam jabbering all the way, they headed out of the grounds and up Cumberland Road. Christopher made himself look up, notice, see. On the corner with Headingley Lane, the looming tower of City Church, its gothic arches, its blackened sandstone. He thought of Morecambe, with its semi-dilapidated funfair, its smooth pink promenade where he had roller-skated as a child, the grey sea, the pale miles of sand. Here in Leeds, sturdy sandstone walls ran along the pavements, giving the place a pleasing sense of a past solid and near enough to touch, to fall against. One that would not crumble.

'We could take a bus, but it's not that far to walk,' Adam said, guiding Christopher to the right with a light touch to his elbow. 'The Oak's just down here, on the Otley Road. Work up a thirst. Put the pennies we save in the beer jar, eh?'

'Yes,' said Christopher. 'I don't mind walking.'

On the way, Adam filled him in on his week. He had lectures pretty much all day, he said. Went straight to the library afterwards, knocked off *the old homework*, then hit the pub around nine. This was why Christopher hadn't seen him – at least not in the evenings. He wondered where he ate, if not in the halls canteen, and how he afforded it. He didn't appear to take his breakfast at the halls either. Mornings, the two of them had settled into a routine of grunted greetings, Christopher making his way down to breakfast, Adam – a shambles in a rather incongruous paisley silk robe – to the showers.

The Original Oak was crowded – *Christ, it's heaving*, Adam said – and so hot, Christopher's glasses steamed up the moment they stepped inside. The thick air made his eyes sting and he blinked over and over, almost glad of his momentarily opaque lenses. Slowly his glasses cleared. The place was full of students – distinguishable by their scruffy clothes, the bold burgundy and white of Leeds University scarves on some of them, and their age too. He wondered how they had the money to drink, to smoke, on the maintenance grant before remembering that of course not all of them would have such a thing – that it was their parents who were paying. There was no one Christopher recognised from his course or from the halls, but then since his arrival, he had been mostly lost in daydreams.

Adam, the ends of his fingers dipped into the tight pockets of his faded denim jeans, was looking around intently as if to take some sort of inventory, and rocking back and forth on his heels.

'So I guess we just go to the bar?' said Christopher.

'That is where they sell the beer, mate. You have been in a pub before, haven't you?'

'Of course. Lots of times.'

Adam made no move.

'What would you like to drink?' Christopher said, after a moment.

'Very kind of you to offer, sir. A gin fizz… no, a dry martini, shaken not stirred.'

'Dry martini. Right.' Christopher took a step towards the bar.

'Hold it!' Adam caught him by the arm. 'I'm kidding. Jesus! Who do you think I am, James Bond? I'll have a pint of Tetley's, if you please, and a packet of pork scratchings if you can stretch to it.' He turned and strode towards the window, reaching into his jacket pocket and pulling out his packet of cigarettes.

Christopher stood a moment, fighting off nascent panic. At the thought of going to the bar, his chest constricted. He had hoped to watch Adam, see how it was done, and was overcome now by something else, something darker, like anger but not anger – not exactly. His father came into his mind, coming home late one night, soundlessly placing his tool bag on the kitchen table like a burglar, creeping across the linoleum in his stockinged feet. Christopher, no older than ten, up for a glass of water, had watched the pantomime of him from the kitchen door.

'Hello, Dad,' he had whispered, only to see his father leap into the air, clapping himself on the chest.

'Sweet Mary and Joseph, Christopher, what the dickens are you doing there, son?'

His father's pub was the Time and Tide, near the bay. He went every Friday after work – payday. He had done this ever since Christopher could remember. Why had his father not taken him, once he came of age? All right, so Christopher did not know how to fix a broken flush or fit a tap, had little time for *The Sun* newspaper and the shouting headlines his father favoured, but would it have been so terrible to spend an hour drinking beer, as men, as father and son? He, Christopher, would have been so much more comfortable now, had his father done this small thing. Perhaps, he thought then, this ritual had failed to happen due to the lack of rope tethering one flesh generation to the next, the lack of blood. That his brother Jack would be taken to the Time and Tide the moment the icing on his eighteenth birthday cake had set, Christopher had no doubt.

Steeling himself, he approached the bar. There was a cigarette machine on the right, near the Gents. He considered buying some, had noticed that Adam smoked Players No. 6, but had no idea of brand or strength; the passed-round fags behind the school lavvies another ritual in which he had not been included. The barman was dropping change into the hand of another man, young enough to be a fellow student. Christopher raised his eyebrows, then, on seeing the barman engage with a bearded chap at the far end, coughed and studied his feet.

'Yes, sir, what can I get you?' The barman appeared before him.

Christopher felt himself blush to the roots of his hair, but, eyes fixed to the dark wood of the bar, pressed on. 'Yes. Thank you. May I please have two pints of Tetley's beer and two packets of pork scratchings, please, if you have them?'

'Right you are, sir.'

'Thank you. Thank you kindly.'

And like that, it was done. The tightness in his chest eased. It was with some small shock that he witnessed the exchange of a pound note from his own hand for two cool pints of ale, snacks and a little change. He pocketed the change, hung the two packets of scratchings from his mouth and, fighting the urge to grin at his small and private victory, carried the drinks over to Adam.

He found his room-mate sitting between two women on a sofa near the window at the front of the pub. Both women had long straight brown hair; one wore flared jeans and what his mother called *one of them pouffy blouses*, the other had glasses – hexagons rimmed in thin gold – and was dressed in denim dungarees and a tight brown T-shirt. Her eyebrows were no more than thin lines, the lenses in her glasses looked to be tinted, but only a little, and behind them her eyes were dark – and looking directly at Christopher. His face grew hot, and for one horrifying moment he imagined upending the glasses and pouring beer all over the table.

'Christopher, so glad you could finally join us,' said Adam.

Christopher set down the drinks. Join them? Wasn't he already part of the arrangement? Whatever, Adam lunged forward and grabbed one of the beers, pushing the glass against his open mouth. He drank deeply. So deeply that when he set down his glass, half the pint had gone, industrially suctioned into the tank of his belly. He wiped the back of his mouth with his hand and said, 'Cheers, man.'

All this happened in seconds.

Christopher was about to speak but could not think of anything to say. He realised he was still standing and so slid into the armchair opposite. He picked up his own glass and sniffed it, smelled malt but in the same moment realised to his shame that this drink sniffing would not be considered normal behaviour. He sniffed again, more loudly this time and not near the glass, as if his nose were running a little after the outdoors. After a second or two, when the interval felt right, he took a sip. The foam tickled his top lip and he licked it away. The cool beer washed down his throat. The taste was neither sweet nor savoury, he thought, taking another short gulp. Not bitter either, as the name suggested. Creamy, perhaps, a taste of yeast or bread, yet sharper, and liquid obviously.

Adam had taken off his coat and his Aran sweater, and the tight black T-shirt he wore underneath revealed him to be thin and taut. He lit a cigarette for both the women, then lit his own and shook the match.

'Shouldn't light three fags with one match.' He winked at the women. 'Bad luck. Comes from the trenches, get your head blown off. Anyway, Christopher, let me introduce you to these two lovely ladies.'

'Women,' said the one in the glasses, once she'd taken the cigarette from her mouth and blown the smoke towards the ceiling.

Adam raised his hands. 'Sorry. Women.' He slapped the back of his own hand. 'No more condescending patriarchy bullshit from you, boy.'

'I'm Alison Jones,' said the one without the glasses, ignoring Adam. 'And this is Angela Greaves. Angie. We're both reading English. Pleased to meet you…'

The women seemed educated – they had that sound to their vowels. Christopher was about to introduce himself, say what he was 'reading', when Adam spoke again.

'And this luscious god of a man is Christopher Harris. He's tall, as you can see, he's reading history so he must love the past, but don't call him Chris because he doesn't like it.'

'Hello,' Christopher said. 'Delighted to meet you both.' He held out his hand, as his mother had taught him to do. The first woman, Alison, shook it, then exchanged glances with her friend and smiled. He wondered what that meant, that smile, if anything.

'Christopher,' said Adam, picking up his already empty pint glass and wiggling it. 'Are you going to offer these women a drink or what?'

'Oh golly. Of course, so sorry.'

'Actually, I'll have another while you're there. This one seems to have gone down without touching the sides.'

Adam did eventually, as Alison put it, break the seal on his wallet, adding that he should be careful he didn't kill a family of spiders just by opening it. Perhaps feeling slighted and wishing to prove himself generous, he added food to his turn: two packets of KP peanuts, which he threw on the low table, announcing, 'Dinner,' with a stifled belch. He did keep the conversation going, however, asking everyone how they'd celebrated the Queen's Jubilee during the summer. To much appreciative giggling from the women, he told the story of the *disaster of a street party* in his road in which two of his neighbours had come to blows over an egg-and-spoon race, and a kid had hit himself in the face with a Swingball bat and had had to be taken to hospital.

'Wrong choice of uni though,' said Alison, once the laughter had died down. The statement appeared designed to elicit a question, perhaps from Adam, who was by now apparently glued to her side.

'How can you say that?' he obliged. 'You've met me now, what's wrong about that?' He grinned.

'Meeting you's one thing,' said Alison. 'It's *him* I don't want to meet.'

'The Ripper,' Angie qualified. 'Two women killed since we finished sixth form. One of them last month – that Jean Jordan. It's terrifying.'

'They're prozzies though, aren't they?' said Adam. 'Don't think he goes for ladies like you two – sorry, women.'

'Prostitutes are women.' Angie shot Adam a narrow look thick with disdain. 'And anyway, the one in June wasn't a prostitute. You know, this is the reason why the police aren't getting on top of it. This *they're only working girls* bullshit. You watch, he'll kill

someone you'd refer to as a normal woman and there'll be all hell
to pay. It's sexist bullshit, the whole thing.'

Bullshit was the word of the evening, it seemed. Having
never heard the term before outside American television dramas,
Christopher enjoyed hearing the women say it. *Bullshit.* The word
made him want to cheer and laugh. Fly, even. But the topic of the
murderer seemed to have made them all rather serious.

'We're like prisoners,' said Alison after a moment. 'We're having to
organise ourselves into groups just so we can go to the pub. It's ridiculous.
We need a comprehensive minibus service. I daren't even take a taxi.'
She looked at all of them in turn. 'I mean, what if he's a cabbie?'

Talk slowly returned to the safer ground of music. Alison
became more and more engrossed in Adam's apparently encyclopae-
dic knowledge of bands. In wonder, Christopher watched his new
friend's arm manoeuvre its way around her shoulder, watched him
break the flow only to laugh as her head flew back in amusement
at something he whispered into her ear. Christopher's own head
felt strange: as if all the internal parts of it had come loose – his
teeth, his tubes, his tongue – and were sliding about inside every
time he moved. He worried he had become silent.

'Are you all right?' Angie was looking at him, still with the
expression of ironic amusement she had worn at the beginning of
the evening. Her eyes were brown, he thought. Like his. 'You've
gone quite white, you know. Green actually.'

The urge to vomit came then, as if in response.

'Excuse me.' He stood, but stumbled. His head spun, the loose
components no longer rattling but suctioned fast to the walls of his
head, like teenagers on the wheel of death back home. A pressure
at his elbow. Angie, two-handed, was steering him through the
thick smog towards the doors.

'Just keep putting one foot in front of the other,' she said, and
it seemed to Christopher that her low voice was kind. 'That's it.
You're doing really well. Soon be there.'

Outside, the fresh air hit him like cold water. He felt it splash on his forehead and down the collar of his shirt.

'My coat,' he said.

'I've got it here,' said Angie, urging him to sit on the pavement.

'I'm going to meet my mother.' He felt the pavement, cold under his buttocks.

'Oh yes, what, tomorrow?'

'No, not tomorrow. One day. Never mind.' He sighed, pushed his head into his hands. Possibly his imagination, but it seemed that Angie had her arm around him. Then not. She lifted his arm and he felt his jacket being coaxed onto his body, the warmth as it lay across his back. The need to be sick abated.

'Thank you.'

'Not used to this, are you?' he heard her say.

'Yes,' he protested. 'Just haven't eaten today, thassall.'

'Do you think you could eat something? There's a chippy not far away.'

'Thank you, that's kind, but no. Not chips. Where are you from, by the way? I missed it earlier.'

'Blackpool.'

'You don't sound like you're from there.'

'Ah, no, well I went to school… elsewhere. But my family home is there.'

'I'm from Morecambe,' he said. His own voice struck him as sad. 'We have illuminums… illuminames… you know, lights. Like Blackpool. Down along the prom.' Watching from the back of the car as a child, thighs stuck with sweat to the black vinyl seat, his siblings, in their separate world, scrapping over something or other. The cold of the window pressed against his nose, rainbow colours haloed against the dark Atlantic sky.

'Oh yes, Blackpool Illuminations,' said Angie.

'Angie,' he said. Angie. She was lovely, he thought. But she might be mocking him.

Angie helped him up. Her hands were soft, her fingernails pink as potted shrimps on the ends of her long thin fingers.

'Thank you, Angie. Angel Angie.'

'Oopla, that's it. Watch your step.'

He stopped. 'Angie, this is all wrong. I should be walking you home.'

'And here was I thinking you were different from your friend.'

'I am.' That was wrong too, made him sound like he thought he was better, which he did not. 'I mean, what about, you know, the way things are? Like you said, there was a victim only last month. You can't walk home by yourself – it isn't safe. Besides, if you do, I won't sleep. So you'd be doing me a favour, you see. You'd be helping me sleep.'

She laughed, and despite the booze, his heart fizzed at the sound. She was lovelier than any girl he had ever met – not that he had exchanged more than a greeting with the girls back home.

'All right then,' she said. 'Since you put it like that. To be honest, I would never have gone by myself; the girls would kill me, and like you say, the way things are.'

'Do you think we should tell Adam?'

She shook her head, gave a brief laugh. 'I think Adam's in good hands, don't you? It's Alison I need to check on.'

She disappeared, returning a few seconds later.

'Looks like Adam's seeing Alison home safe. No surprise there.' Angie threaded her arm through his. 'Come on, let's go.'

They walked. He focused on keeping step with her in case she should take her arm away. It seemed to him they were going further up the Otley Road, away from his halls, then off right somewhere. He let her talk, soothed by her idle chatter. She liked Blackpool, she said, but it was too full of tourists in the summer. She liked to walk along the beach in the autumn and the winter.

'Do you have the rockets?' she asked. 'How about a big dipper?'

'Big dipper yes,' he said. 'But no rockets, though it's years since I've been. I only went when I was little. There's a death slide, I think, in the House of Fun.'

'Death slide, not sure I fancy that. Do you like candyfloss?'

'No.'

'Me neither! Disgusting, isn't it? Like eating sugary hairsprayed hair.'

They seemed to have been walking for a long time – about half an hour or so – when she turned right down an alleyway, which led to a gate; beyond, to the left, were playing fields, what looked like flats at the far end.

'This is Oxley,' she said. 'It's a bit of a way, I should have warned you.'

They walked down to the flats and came to a sandstone building that was almost entirely black, neoclassical arches on a kind of porch. She stepped up into it and he followed her. It was very dark there. He leant back against the wall, felt it shore him up.

'Oxley halls for women,' she said, something scoffing in her tone. 'Can't wait to get out, get my own flat. Listen, it was kind of you to walk me home. Germaine Greer is marvellous and everything, but she'd be precious little use if I met *him*, wouldn't she? Unless she had a knife.' She mimed a slashing motion with her hand. 'Here, cop hold of this, Mr Ripper…' She was doing an Australian accent – quite well, he thought. 'I'll turn you into a bloody eunuch myself, you bloody pervert.' She laughed at herself then sighed. He stared at her in awe. She was pretty, he thought.

'He could be out there right now.' She shook her head, serious again. 'I wish they'd catch him.'

'It's a terrible thing.' He smiled an apology, on behalf of whom he had no idea: himself, perhaps, for being of the same sex. He looked at the floor, and when he plucked up the courage to look at her again, she was taking off her glasses. Her eyes were large, so large they seemed to see right through him, to all that he did not know. She slid her specs into the breast pocket of her jacket and smirked at him as she had when they were introduced.

'Well,' she said, and looked towards the upper windows. One of them was open – the faint strains of Pussycat's 'Mississippi' trailing out into the night. He wondered which window was Angie's, what her room looked like, what it would be like to go there with her.

'Your coat is thin,' he said. 'You must be cold.'

She placed her hand on his cheek and smiled. 'Warm hands, see?'

His heart beat faster, in fear. 'You should go in.'

'We could sneak up to my room. I'd like to find out what's going on in *there*.' She tapped him gently on the side of his head: once, twice. She was still smiling, her fingers light on his neck, bare where he had neglected to bring his scarf. 'Might get expelled though. Making cocoa in the presence of a male. Honestly, you'd think it was the fifties.'

'I don't have much to say.' He closed his eyes briefly at the sensation of her long fingers reaching into the back of his hair, the soft scratch of her nails making his scalp tingle. 'I'm afraid the illuminations were the highlight of my repertoire. Ill-um-in-ations, ah, see, must be sobering up.' She had his head in her hands now and had begun to caress his scalp with such tenderness he wanted to rest his head on her shoulder and say nothing more except *Don't stop.* 'I mean,' he continued, struggling now to concentrate on anything other than her, her hand in his hair, 'you were right, I've never even been to a pub before. Before tonight. Don't tell anyone, will you?'

'Won't tell a soul.' She leant in close, her breath warm as freshly baked bread against his ear, her teeth no more than a gentle, blissful bite on his earlobe. He felt himself stir, stiffen; the thought of her discovering him this way filled him with terror. But she did, had discovered him, her other hand now on his crotch, her mouth closing over his. 'Open your mouth a little,' she whispered. 'It's OK. I've looked after you this far, haven't I?'

'I haven't…'

'I know. It's OK.'

He opened his mouth, matching hers as best he could. He wished he knew the things that others knew, that Adam certainly knew. He wished he could show her instead of her showing him, but she was too far ahead. Her tongue touched his, their lips pressed together; he felt himself harden further against her touch. She ran her hand down the length of him, up again, as if trying to build a picture by touch alone. Up and down, her mouth never leaving his. He wanted to tell her to stop but could not, did not want to. And then—

'Oh God,' he whimpered. 'Oh God, no.' His head fell into her shoulder just as her hand sprang back. 'I'm sorry. I'm so sorry.'

'It's OK,' she whispered, and stroked the back of his head. 'That's normal for a first time.'

He could not raise his forehead from her shoulder. He did not want her to see his face, knew she would see even in the low light that he was burning.

'You won't tell anyone, will you?' he whispered.

'There's no shame in it, Christopher.' She hugged him, though their bodies only made a clumsy A-frame in the darkness. He wanted so much for her to leave him, but could not stand the thought of her seeing the dark patch he knew must be there on the front of his trousers. 'You look after yourself, all right?'

Thankfully, she turned as he released her. She waved, though without a backwards glance. He wrapped his coat around himself and watched her walk away, through the door of her halls, into safety. She did not turn back or wave again, and he wondered if this was out of discretion or disgust. He should have initiated their kiss. He should have slowed her hand. He should have known things like she did, like others did. She had said it was normal. But it was not. He was not.

CHAPTER SIX

You have the devil in you, Ben's mother used to say when he was naughty. And growing up, he was inclined to agree. The insinuation was that the devil came from his real family, though she never said this out loud. He had always understood he was adopted, at first in the amorphous form of feeling, a form to which words gave shape much later on. But his parents had always been honest with him about that, at least, explaining to him in simple terms that he was a gift to them from another mommy and daddy but that he was theirs now and always would be and they loved him. They loved him all right. And you can't choose how you're loved – he knows that because they told him that too. You just have to give thanks to the Lord that someone somewhere is looking after you, and suck up the rest. And whatever devil there was inside him had got him this far.

To ward off the devil, there was church. Ben remembers how, on Sundays, his mother would lead him to Mass through the streets of Virginia, walking too quickly so that he had to half-run to keep up with her. He never asked why she couldn't walk more slowly, why his father got to stay home. Come to that, he never asked why she was one way in church – holy, smiling and soft-voiced as an angel; another way at home – hard-voiced and not smiling, never smiling, and not like any angel he ever saw. Passing the Negroes coming out of Little River Southern Baptist Church, he often wondered why they looked so much happier with their

God than his congregation did with theirs. Those joyous hymns, they sang them so hard he could hear them coming through the swinging double doors as his mother dragged him on by.

Once, long ago, he had fantasised that his real parents were those very Negroes who sang so gaily in the church down the road. He used to wonder whether one day his skin would darken to the colour of coffee beans and he would discover, finally, that he did not belong with white folks at all. It would all make sense then. He would walk into Little River and take his place on the pew and sing those joyous hymns at the top of his lungs. But as he got older, he realised with a feeling of intense sadness that he would never be darker skinned than a glass of cream, would never sing with the people who smiled even outside the church. He would instead stay the same: Benjamin Bradbury, white, straight-haired, origin unknown. No one else was like him. At school, none of his friends had been adopted. The only other adopted children he had heard about were something to do with the war. Although they were called orphans, which was a different thing. As far as he knew, his birth parents were still alive. How could that be? Who would give away a child? And why?

Of course, he is an adult now; life has already taught him that such questions are not math – they cannot be answered like that. And yet the questions persist, in a more sophisticated form, even as his world, once black and white, fuses into a spectrum of greys. Doubt. Even now, so young, his certainties are dropping like leaves in fall. Martha wants children. He wanted children, but now… Somewhere in his own childhood, though he cannot recall exactly when, his parents stopped being Mom and Pop and became Dorothy and George. Not overnight – it was a much slower thing, as if the words *Mom* and *Pop* had been written on his mind with magic ink, designed to fade over time. And as the years passed, he became aware that *Mom and Pop*, as well as being the people who'd taken him in or however the hell you said it, were what they called well-to-do. That his father's Harvard education and career as an attorney in DC were big bugaboo, at least in their neighbourhood.

They had met at Harvard, though Dorothy had never worked so far as Ben could remember. *Enough to do with you scooting around my feet all day.* What came between his parents' meeting and the cocktail parties they hosted in their large suburban house was a mystery, like an episode of *The Rockford Files* he never got to see. That Dorothy was not happy he had concluded by the time he reached his teens from a series of clues: her thirst for vodka tonics from around three in the afternoon, her clumsiness when she fixed dinner and the way her knuckles paled when she held onto the kitchen counter.

He wondered if this had to do with him.

As a teenager, like many teenagers, Ben spent most of his time in his room. He drew, in secret, constantly. His parents could not see the point.

'It's right here on the end of the pencil,' he once sassed.

Evenings, pretending he needed to finish an assignment, he would lock his bedroom door, put on a record or a cassette tape and lose himself in Aretha Franklin, Ray Charles, Stevie Wonder, and in the endless lines that followed his pencil around the white pages of his sketch pad. First he copied, relentlessly. Cartoons, photographs, lettering from magazines – anything. Copied until the lines went their own way and made new forms of their own. Oh, how he loved that: the first mark, like the first footprint in snow. The mystery of what would take shape.

Knock knock. 'Benjamin, can you hear me?' Dorothy at the door. He could tell by the way her voice projected sideways that her ear was pressed to the wood. 'I don't know how you can concentrate on history with that noise going on the whole time.'

'It's OK, Dorothy – I got it. Don't worry about it.' He turned the music up, just a little, whispering, 'History of soul, sister, history of soul.' Blowing smoke out of his bedroom window by this time, spraying his room with Blue Stratos, feeling the groove of the pencil across the page. 'Rock Steady', 'Hit the Road Jack', 'Superstition'... until evening stole the sun from outside his window and he felt his stomach hollow as a cave. After supper, more drawing, collage, paint – until it was time to shin down the outside wall and meet his friends and smoke fat joints in the park. His bedroom was a wardrobe that led to Narnia, he often thought. You opened the door, made your way through the coats and behind lay a whole secret world.

The years passed. Dorothy and George tried to stop him from *drawing and so forth* and make him concentrate on *something worthwhile*. These attempts failed: when he was four, he drew with the soap bar on the bathroom tiles the time they took his coloured pencils away. At fourteen, pocket money withdrawn for the quintillionth time, he jumped the barriers so he could take the train into DC – to the National Gallery, the Smithsonian, the Renwick. When his folks said no to art school, he stood on George's stepladder and poured three different colours of emulsion paint onto the concrete garage floor. By then, he was seventeen. The bud of his early sass had bloomed into the full flower of frank and open rebellion.

'Damn,' he said, admiring the results in front of a horrified Dorothy. 'It's like Pollock or some shit.'

Speechless on the steps that led into the garage from the main house, his mother returned to the kitchen and pressed her lips directly to the bottle neck of the Smirnoff.

At last, his parents conceded that, if he wasn't going to follow his father into law, then a career in graphic design would be the least shameful option.

'Graphics,' said his father at his farewell dinner, served by the help, Constance. 'At least that's one up from art, for Chrissakes. What do I know anyway? I can't even draw a goddam stick man!

And you can't draw either, can you, Dotty?' He shook his head, seemed about to say more but was silenced by a look from his wife. While they had been open about Ben's origins, it was not a matter to be discussed, least of all at the table.

'I guess I'm just a genetic blip,' Ben said, smiling through his meatloaf and thinking about how awesome it would be at California School of the Arts – how much weed he would smoke, how many times he would get laid (already a respectable number). How much distance he would put between himself and these people, and how fucking relieved all of them would be.

CHAPTER SEVEN

They were trying to persuade me to take a shower just now. What a laugh. What a farce. What's the point? I'll never feel clean again. I don't even care about them seeing me naked. My body is a separate thing. I observe it from the outside with a detachment that is almost interesting. It is thinner. My shoulder bones protrude at the top like knots, my eyes look bigger, darker – all iris and no whites. Meds, exercise in the courtyard, food. What's the point? What's the point of any of it?

They helped me into my jogging bottoms and a loose white T-shirt.

'OK, my darling,' Nurse said as she left. 'You'll get on with that book of yours now. There'll be someone right outside.'

And here I sit. Not quite alone, because that is not allowed. Shower, meds, food. And this: as pointless as all the rest, I'm sure, this merry exercise I've got going for myself. But with no sharp objects to hand and a nurse outside the door, there's nothing else to do.

I'm glad Christopher had Adam. It was Adam who sorted out his appearance, who took him into Leeds town centre to buy clothes – *Those trousers are a bloody disgrace, man, who bought them, your mum?* (She had.) Under Adam's benign duress, Christopher bought flared jeans, an Afghan coat, T-shirts and two shirts with long collars.

'That's better,' said Adam. 'You'll be fighting off the birds with a shitty stick in that get-up.'

Adam persuaded him to do the Otley Run with a bunch of lads from electronic engineering. Christopher vomited into the gutter outside the Three Horse Shoes, a fact that, rather than singling him out as a weakling, appeared to bestow hero status upon him for days after. With Adam, he went to see The Damned at Leeds Union, to a club called Le Phonographique in the Merrion Centre. Whenever Adam proposed a night out, he never seemed to mind Christopher's initial reticence, seemed to understand that he needed a harder push than most but that, once cajoled, he would come along and he would be glad. Christopher worried he was a charity case, that Adam would tire of him sooner rather than later. Having no one to share these worries with, he kept them to himself.

'I tell you what,' Adam said one night. They were in their room at the halls, about to go down to the Union for a drink. Having dressed in one of his new shirts, a tie and his flared jeans, Christopher was sitting on his bed, waiting while Adam tried on different shirts, turning this way and that in the full-length mirror he had brought from home. 'All's you need is a bit of chutzpah and you'll be flying.'

'Chutzpah?'

Adam turned from his reflection, apparently satisfied with this, his fifth choice of shirt: a brown and beige stripe, tight around the body, the collars long, the neck open lower than Christopher would have dared. 'I mean, look at you. You've got the looks, the height; you've got the smarts. You've even got the big brown peepers the chicks love, you bastard. If I had half what you had, I tell you what, there'd be no stone left unturned.'

'You want to unturn *more* stones?'

Adam laughed. 'Good point. I can't complain, and Sophie is a peach.'

A peach, not a stone, although peaches contained stones, Christopher supposed. 'Sophie? I thought you were with Alison?'

'I am. She's a peach too. But I've sort of got a casual thing going with Sophie. Nothing major, but that's not the point I'm making. It's you, my bashful, bespectacled friend. How short-sighted are you?'

'Quite.' What *was* Adam's point?

Adam had sat down on his own bed and was pulling on his ankle boots. 'I mean, on a scale of one to ten, where one is you can't read the lecture notes on the board and ten is you can't get out of bed because you can't see the floor, how short-sighted are you?'

'I'd say about a five,' said Christopher. 'I wouldn't be able to find my way across the pub, if that's what you mean. But I could probably get out of bed and get my feet into my slippers.'

'Right.' Adam frowned. 'So the glasses we make a virtue of – don't want you falling over a table, that's not smooth, is it? Unless you're going for the *Some Mothers Do 'Ave 'Em* school of charm, which you're not.' He narrowed his eyes, scrutinising Christopher. Christopher shifted on the mattress, coughed into his hand. 'Your hair's better than it was,' Adam continued. 'You've got two decent pairs of britches, a few shirts and that coat we picked up, so all we need now is… the chutzpah. A bit of bravado. What you've got to understand, mate, is that sometimes when women say no or stop they mean yes, carry on, and a bit of cheek is what tells you when to listen and when to take no bloody notice.' He stood, his boots all but covered by the wide sweep of his jeans. Christopher stayed sitting on his bed, aware that Adam was about to deliver one of his talks.

Sure enough, Adam spread his hands. 'You've got to look at it like this. You chat up some bird – she knocks you back. So what? You move on, no big deal. Unless there's that tiny hesitation, in which case keep going. And basically you keep going until one of them takes the bait.'

'The bait?' What were they – fish?

'That moment when they bite. But the thing is, the more you get knocked back, the less you care. So you've got to almost want to get knocked back, if you know what I mean. And this is the sheer beauty of it, my friend. The more you get knocked back, the less you care, and the less you care, the better you get. Do you see? And then eventually you find a woman, she likes what you're saying, or she gives in to what you're saying, or she just can't be bothered to fight you off, it doesn't matter. Then it's just a question of keeping going till they relax. They're uptight, most of them. They want a bit of action as much as we do; they just need to relax and see that none of it matters. Because it doesn't! We're all here to have a good time; it doesn't need to be *War and Peace*. It's just a drink, a laugh, a fuck if you're lucky, and the sooner you can get them to relax and realise that, the sooner you're on.' He stepped closer. 'Stand up.'

Christopher stood, found himself almost nose to nose with Adam, now two inches taller in his boots. To his surprise, Adam took both his hands in his and Christopher had to fight the urge to pull them away.

'Don't worry, I'm not going to jump you.' Adam let go, took a step back and placed his hands on Christopher's shoulders. He pushed down. 'Get these from round your ears for a start. You'll develop a hunch if you carry on like that.'

Christopher lowered his shoulders. His back made a low cracking sound.

'Well that's a hundred per cent better for a kick-off.' Adam moved closer and grinned. 'Now, pretend I'm a gorgeous bird. Gorgeous as you like.'

Christopher felt himself blush. *Forget it, let's just go to the pub,* he wanted to say but couldn't.

'You want me to pretend you're a woman?' he asked instead. 'Are you serious?'

'Deadly. Don't worry, I'm not trying to make a pass, not that way inclined; just want to get you to feel the force, like Luke Skywalker. You need to get some use out of your lightsaber, Lukey baby.' He was mucking about, pretending to be solemn, had put his hands together in prayer. 'Pretend. Use the Force.'

Christopher opened his mouth to protest. Adam grabbed his hands and placed them on his own waist.

'Adam, I…' The heat in his face spread down his neck. He looked at the floor – the orange scratchy carpet that Adam said was made from Brillo pads.

'Trust me, flower. I'm Obi Wan. You're Luke Skywalker. Now. Pull me towards you.'

'I can't.' Horrified, Christopher stared at the tips of Adam's silly boots, his own brown brogues polished to a high shine. This was utterly ridiculous. 'We… in my family… we don't really…'

'We don't in mine either. Just relax, will you? Look, your shoulders are right back up again; what are they on, string? You're not a puppet. Get 'em down.'

Christopher obeyed, rolled his head to loosen his neck, but still could not look at his room-mate.

'Now, pretend I'm a bird and pull me towards you. Stop groaning, Christopher. It's called a hug. Women love it. It's tender without being predatory – before you get predatory, although we don't say that and that bit I'll be leaving to you, mate. Go on, pull me in.'

'I…'

'Do it.'

'I don't…'

'Do. It.'

Christopher sighed. Impatient, it was Adam who pulled Christopher towards him until their bodies almost touched. There was no room to keep his head at a downward angle, so he found himself obliged to tilt it back a little and direct his gaze over Adam's left shoulder.

'That's it,' said Adam. 'Steady as you like.' Without warning, he wrapped his arms around Christopher's shoulders and pulled him into an embrace. Now their bodies touched, all right. Christopher could feel the strength in Adam's arms, his hard, thin torso against his own. His neck had almost locked itself over Adam's collarbone, the tip of his chin against Adam's back. It was all so different from the way it had been with Angie, or slow-dancing at the youth club with the girl with greasy hair. He kept his eyes on Adam's T. Rex poster on the far wall

'You see, mate,' said Adam. 'It's not that bad. But you are as tense as a tightrope. Try and relax, will you, for crying out loud. At least try. *I'm not here to jump you* – this is what this position says. *I'm your friend*, it says, *you can trust me*, all that.'

Adam leant to the right, then the left, keeping tight hold of Christopher all the while. He repeated this once, twice more. Every muscle in Christopher's body clenched, but he concentrated on keeping his shoulders down, as if relaxed, in the hope that Adam would stop.

'Hug me back,' Adam said.

Christopher lifted his arms a little and closed them tighter around his friend. Their chests connected; he could feel the side of Adam's head against his own, could smell the Brut cologne he kept on his bedside table.

'That's it. Now. I'm a girl. I'm a girl and I'm thinking,' Adam switched to a high-pitched parody of a woman's voice, 'here's a strong fellow who can hold me tight. He'll look after me, he'll protect me from that nasty Ripper man.'

Christopher closed his eyes, but it was useless – he felt his knees lock.

'This guy is strong and I can trust him,' Adam continued, still in the silly girlish voice. 'This guy will look after me – he will protect me against perverts and nasty men in raincoats, and murderers. I think... I think I'll let him feel my tits.' He jumped back and laughed.

Christopher shook his head, unable to stop himself from smiling. 'You're a lunatic, Adam,' he said. 'An absolute lunatic.'

Adam clapped him on the shoulder. 'Come on, you stiff bastard, let's go and get pissed.'

In moments like this, Christopher said, he wondered whether it was Adam he liked so enormously, or Adam's view of him. In Adam's eyes, he, Christopher, was no more than shy, perhaps a little square but still, essentially, one of the boys. In Adam's view, he, Christopher, was normal.

Despite Adam's mischievous influence, Christopher studied hard. He still found refuge in solitude, books, his Top-40 tapes. 'Denis', 'Sheena Is a Punk Rocker', 'How Deep Is Your Love'. He found St Urban's in Headingley, resumed his weekly visits to church. He prayed for patience, lit candles for his mother, whoever and wherever she was.

Oh Lord, protect and care for my real mother, whose son was taken from her. Keep her in your light and let her know that I'm looking for her. Tell her I will find her, if not in words then in a feeling of peace. Amen.

The Sex Pistols went to number one, the students protested outside the Parkinson Building to show their support for the firefighters. He called Samantha Jackson, who asked him to call her weekly, for a chat, which he did. She was easy to talk to, easier over the phone. When he expressed frustration, she counselled him against rushing, against taking matters into his own hands. And still no word came from the Registrar.

December. A Christmas tree went up in the Union building, another outside the Queens Hotel in City Square. Another strike by the Ripper: Marilyn Moore, who survived. Christopher bought *The Telegraph*, *The Guardian* and the *Daily Mail* and cut out the articles relating to the attack. He bought a scrapbook and glued the cuttings in there, along with photocopies from newspapers he had found at Leeds City Library down in Calverley Street, covering the Ripper's victims to date: Emily Jackson, Marcella Claxton, Irene Richardson, Tina Atkinson, Jayne MacDonald, Maureen Long and Jean Jordan, the woman Alison – or Angie, was it? – had mentioned in the pub.

Now that this last victim had survived, a nation pinned its hopes on her description of the man they were calling a monster, a coward, a psychopath. But her account, plus some matching tyre tracks amounted to nothing much. Not enough, certainly, to stem the fear that had infiltrated the mind of every female student on campus. At the Union, a minibus was organised to take women to their places of residence. Those who refused to be prisoners in their rooms collected in parties to walk to and from the pub. Stories abounded of women reporting their husbands, their brothers. *Do you know this man?*

Christopher fell into the habit of cutting out any newspaper clipping he saw – *Mob Jeer Lorry Driver*; *Why Can't They Catch Him?*; *Prostitutes Go in Fear* – and into his cheap scrapbook he stuck them all. Sometimes, when he'd finished his reading, he would flick through the scrapbook, poring over the headlines and the words, the photographs and the photofits, imagining what dark details lay invisibly there where the grey newsprint smudged the thin white page. What secrets, what horrors.

Towards the end of term, he was walking back to Devonshire Hall when he was filled with that familiar feeling of knowledge. And sure enough, there in the pigeonhole marked H was a letter addressed to him. At the sight of it, his insides flamed, because he knew in that moment, he said, that the rag end of an old year was about to be brought to life with the promise of something new.

The envelope was large – three times the size of the standard rectangular official letter. There was another envelope too, white, squarer, upon which he recognised Margaret's handwriting. He took both letters up to his room, placed Margaret's letter to one side of his desk and held the brown envelope to his chest. On the bookshelf, Adam had rigged up a plastic Christmas tree, no bigger than a Tiny Tears doll. He had bought it from Leeds market for thirty pence. A lone strand of ratty silver tinsel snaked around its body like a helter-skelter, and disappeared down the back of the shelving. Christopher opened the large envelope and pulled out the pinkish document.

CERTIFIED COPY OF AN ENTRY OF BIRTH
Pursuant to the Births and Deaths Registration Act, 1953
Registration District: Liverpool
Birth in the Sub-district of: *Liverpool*

'Liverpool' was handwritten, in fountain pen. Below, columns – all filled with the same handwriting.

When and where Born	Name, if any	Sex	Name, and surname of father
Twelfth March 1959, Liverpool Maternity Unit	Martin Anthony Curtiss	Boy	Mikael Dabrowski

I often think of him holding this handwritten document in his hands, of how he described that moment to me. His arm dropped to his side, he said, as if deadened by a hard thump. He had to steady his breathing, hand against his mouth. He could smell the ink in the sweat of his palms.

'Martin,' he whispered. 'I am Martin.'

A memory surfaced, until now suppressed. A woman he used to see sometimes on Hestham Avenue when he was a boy. She wore a headscarf made of blue patterned silk or satin, tied under her chin, but that was all he could recall except that he did not recognise her as one of his neighbours. But now, seeing his name on the birth certificate, he remembered this woman, how she had talked to him once and made him afraid. He had been no more than ten or eleven and out on his bike – a second-hand Raleigh Chopper, the best thing he had ever owned. He had been cycling up and down the road, hungry and a little bored, trying to do wheelies like the other boys, when the chain had come off. He'd turned the bike upside down and rested it on its handlebars while he teased the oily links back onto the cog's teeth. Someone had grabbed his arm, and when he turned, he saw it was the woman – he recognised her scarf.

She had called him a name, her grey eyes searching his.

'No, sorry,' he had replied, politely as he had been told. 'I'm Christopher.'

'Christopher? Are you sure? You're not…'

Oh, what had she called him?

She had been younger than her coat and headscarf suggested, that much he could remember – no older than his schoolteacher, Miss Briggs, who was getting married. But she had a wild look to her. Nothing he could have explained – she wasn't raging insane like the madwoman from the town centre who kept dogs and sang in the street, but there was something in her face, in the way she insisted on pushing a name onto him like the gypsies on the pier pushed their lucky heather, a name he hadn't asked for and didn't want. I must look like someone she knows, he had thought at the time, but now, staring at his birth certificate, he realised with a burning feeling in his abdomen that she might not have been mistaken. Perhaps she did know him after all? Was it possible? No, no of course not. But he had seen this woman more than once, always on the street, never going into anyone's house or talking to anyone or moving with any sense of purpose. She had been there the day he left for university, he remembered. He had seen her at the corner when his parents pulled out onto the main road. As they passed, she had turned her face away. He had seen only the sky blue of her headscarf.

After a moment, he brought the certificate to his eyes once more.

Name, surname, and maiden surname of mother	Occupation of father	Signature, description, and residence of informant	When registered
Phyllis Anne Curtiss	Merchant sailor	Phyllis Curtiss, mother, 22 Greenway Road, Runcorn, Cheshire	Sixteenth March 1959

He tossed the certificate onto his desk and dashed out of the room to the lavatories, where he relieved himself with a sigh. The hot stream coursed from him, splashing into the porcelain with the force of an open tap.

'Martin,' he said to his reflection in the rust-corroded mirror. 'Martin Anthony Curtiss.'

Martin. House martin. Martin Luther King. St Martin of Tours, who gave his cloak to the beggar at the gates. Was he, Christopher, kind enough to do something like that? Could he be a Martin? He studied his eyes, his broad nose, his chin, which struck him now as almost square. A square jaw, that was a good thing, wasn't it? Martins had square jaws in a way that perhaps Christophers did not. Adam always teased him about his height – *you lanky bastard, fucking leggy bugger* – had once shaken his head and told him his appearance was wasted on him. Angie had kissed him, she had…

He hoped never to see her again. If he did, he would pretend he hadn't.

Back in his room, he pored over the birth certificate until he could see it even when he closed his eyes. His mother was from Cheshire. He could go to the address listed on this document – he could go now. His mother, Phyllis Curtiss, wouldn't live there any more, of course, but perhaps her parents did. His grandparents! The thought hit him in the solar plexus. His mother was probably young; that would mean his grandparents would not be too old – early sixties, maybe, or younger if they too had had children early. Children! He might have an auntie or an uncle. They might all get together at Christmas – sing carols around the piano like the pictures on the front of Christmas cards. He wondered whether they drank alcohol, like Adam and the other students, or were sober like Jack and Margaret – whether they went to Mass together on Christmas Eve, or not at all. He wondered if his birth father was still around – Mikael, a sailor; it was unlikely. He sounded foreign – Polish, perhaps, or Russian. The thought mattered less than the rest.

But, he said, Samantha Jackson had told him to wait, to proceed through the proper channels. He would make another appointment with her – that was the correct course of action.

The light fell. His window greyed, blackened. In his mind's eye, his family posed before him: a faceless group shot of his ancestry, imagined smiles in a darkroom developing tray. Uncoiled, the rope cast itself towards them. He would tie himself there and, finally, moor.

CHAPTER EIGHT

He called Samantha Jackson the next morning. She told him to photocopy the certificate and send it to her, which he did, skipping a lecture so as to catch the post.

A week later, there was an official-looking letter in his pigeonhole. He had known it would be there. He plucked it out and tore it open, unable to wait until he got to his room. His eyes cast about, fishing for and catching the sense without any logical reading. *Liverpool City Council* read the letter heading, a coat of arms underneath: two mermen, two birds – herons or cormorants possibly. His eyes flicked to the bottom: Mrs S. Jackson, Adoption Counsellor and Liaison Officer. Beneath, her signature scrawled in blue ink. He could not train his eyes to read in any kind of linear way.

… NORCAP… colleague… pleased to inform you a Mrs Phyllis Griffiths, née Curtiss…

Dear God! He read the letter again, made himself do it properly this time, one hand clapped over his mouth. His mother had registered her details on his birthday, 12 March. One Phyllis Griffiths, aged thirty-three. Samantha looked forward to hearing from him. He folded the letter and headed up to his room. He sat on his bed, the letter still in his hand.

She, Phyllis, had searched for him.

A strange and lovely warmth filled him. It spread to his bones, his stomach, his heart. His skin felt ticklish, his hair lifted on its follicles. His mother. His mother, Phyllis, was waiting for news. She was waiting for *him*. If all went well, if he could keep his cool, next year, 1978, would be the year he would finally meet her. In his chest, the rope untangled, tied up anew in what he imagined as a bow. A bow around a gift. He laughed. Had he not imagined the rope tied to the harbour, ready to pull him in? Ah yes, he had envisaged it in all sorts of ways, but a mooring was the better image. A mooring post and a rope – yes, perfect. He could feel the water beneath him, guiding him towards her.

Only days later did he remember the letter from Margaret. He was studying at his desk (no sign of Adam as usual) when he saw the corner of the white envelope protruding from his books.

With a feeling of tiredness laced with guilt, he drew it out and opened it, but at the sight of his own address in the top right-hand corner, he smiled despite himself. Margaret had worked in a typing pool for years before leaving to get married – such an old-fashioned idea, now he thought about it. And so sad, actually, holding beneath it as it did the assumption that she would soon be in the family way, which of course she was not. And here, writing to the boy she had taken in when her body failed her, she had not forgotten the rigours of official correspondence. The address present and correct even when writing to her own son, who, after all, lived there. Underneath she had written:

Dear Christopher,

I hope you're well. Me and your father are muddling along. Your father had sciatica last week but it's easing up now.

Louise and Jack are both in the juniors' nativity play. Jack is the narrator and Louise is a horse in the stable. Me and your father are looking forward to seeing it.

Your father is looking forward to some days off at Christmas, provided no pipes burst in this cold weather. I hope you're wrapping up warm.

Can you ring sometime and tell us when you're coming home
for the holidays?
From,
Mum

Still with this persistent feeling of tiredness, Christopher urged himself from his desk and went to the payphone to call Margaret. He had *mountains of work* to catch up on, he told her. Ignoring her silent disappointment, he added that he planned to be with them on 23 December.

'But that's almost Christmas Day,' she said, and tutted before brightening as best she could. 'You'll be with us for Christmas Eve Mass, I suppose. That's something.'

He did not tell her about his birth certificate, his birth mother, or about the appointment with Samantha Jackson. He told me this was not out of a need for secrecy, nor because he was dishonest. It was because he could not find the words to say it. And it strikes me now, years later, that not finding the words to say what we need to say is one of life's biggest tragedies.

The day of his second appointment with Samantha Jackson came. A late-December snow flurry threatened the Liverpool train with cancellation, but no, it went ahead, thank goodness. And so, instead of taking the coach to his home in Morecambe on the last day of term, he slid instead through the sleet-slashed Liverpool pavements, to the council offices in Henry Street.

This time in a navy suit with matching navy shoes, Samantha Jackson led him up the stairs to her office.

'Done your Christmas shopping?' she asked him.

'Not yet.'

'Me neither. Probably do it on Christmas Eve like I always do. Have you many to buy for?'

'Just my family. My adoptive family, I mean. Just four.'

'Never know what to get, do you? I don't anyway. Whole thing is a consumerist farce, really.'

She gestured towards the same chair as the time before. He sat, pressed his back to the chair, then leant forward, flattened his foot to the floor to stop his leg from jiggling.

'Now,' Samantha said, pulling out his file and slipping her half-moon spectacles onto her narrow ski-jump nose. She looked up, over the top of her specs. 'You all right, love? Do you want some water?'

He nodded, coughed. 'No thank you, I'm fine. A little nervous.'

'Of course, that's normal. You will be.' She pulled out a sheet and scanned it, making little clicking noises with her tongue. 'So, as I said in the letter, your birth mother did approach NORCAP. March the twelfth... ah, I see, that's your birthday, so in principle that's a good sign. She couldn't have done it any sooner, to be honest, not legally; she'd have had to wait until you were eighteen. It means she desires contact. Sometimes they don't, and we have to respect that.' She laid the paper on her lap and fixed Christopher with her clear blue eyes. 'What we recommend, Christopher, is that you write a letter first of all. In our experience, it's best to go slowly, try and build a relationship through some correspondence before you arrange to meet, if that's the way it pans out. Tell her about yourself – ask her about herself. How does that sound?' She drew the glasses from her nose and held them by the arm. 'It really is better not to rush these things.'

She had sought him out the moment the law had allowed it! On his very birthday! He wanted to go to her now, now this minute, and take her in his arms and cover her face with kisses and say, *Mum, Mummy, it's me, your son, Martin.*

He coughed into his fist. 'Yes,' he said. 'A letter. It sounds like the right thing to do.'

'Good. In that case, the next thing is to talk about your expectations. How do you feel about that?'

'Whatever you think.'

Samantha Jackson spoke for a long time, kindly, looking at him all the while as if checking he were still there. These things could and did sometimes go badly, she told him. Sometimes the child or the parent was not happy – sometimes they could not connect. Was that something he was ready for, should it be the case?

'Rejection's a tough thing to deal with,' she said, 'in anyone's book, especially in these circumstances.'

She had said this in their first meeting. Little did she know that he had experienced rejection every day from the moment Jack Junior was born. Nor could she possibly realise that he, Christopher, had an ability to know things before they happened. He almost said, *Don't worry – I already know the meeting will go well. I can feel it the way others can feel a change in the weather. I can feel my mother, her light, inside my chest.* But he did not, since that would not have been a normal thing to say.

'I expect nothing,' he said once Samantha had finished. 'She doesn't know me, after all.'

But she would know him the moment she saw him, and she would take him in her arms and cry sweet tears into his hair. *Martin*, she would say, *my darling Martin, at last I have found you.* He knew this.

Samantha was smiling at him. 'She's an English teacher, I believe, in a secondary school. She's got two kids, twin boys, I think.' She handed him a document, in which details about his mother had been typed. He imagined someone taking notes from her during a phone call. Or perhaps she had presented herself in person. He envied whoever had met her that day – envied the proximity they had enjoyed while she answered their questions, shy, abashed, but determined.

He scanned the document. 'Her address is in Runcorn. That's on my birth certificate.'

Samantha took the document from him and held it up against his birth certificate. She frowned and said, 'Yes, that's right. Not the same address though. Looks like she settled near her parents. That's good too, potentially, means they managed to work it out. When it comes to having babies adopted, often these girls don't have much choice in the matter.' She frowned at the page. 'It's the outskirts of Liverpool, bit further than outskirts actually. Mersey estuary. There's a big chemical works, ICI – I know someone who works there.' She gave a little laugh. 'Not making it sound very glamorous, am I? Anyway, when you write, do make sure and put your contact address on your letter; that way she can reply if she wishes to. I know I sound like I'm stating the obvious, but you'd be amazed how many don't. Is that clear enough?'

'Yes,' he said. 'Very clear. Extremely clear. Clear as day! Sorry, yes, thank you. Thank you so much.'

He walked from the offices in wonder, he said. He had the impression that he, his very self, was coming into focus, his outline defining like a figure stepping out towards him from the fog. So it had been when he had wiped the steam from the bathroom mirror as a boy: himself, quite simply there, except this time he was wiping away the fog of his life and claiming his place not in a house but in the world.

'Phyllis.' He said her name over and over as he walked, laughing like a child at his own footprints in the snow, his jacket flying open. He paid no heed to the cold. He jumped over a puddle where the snow had melted to slush. 'Phyllis Curtiss.'

She taught English, which meant she liked to read, as he did. They could talk about books! They would have so much in common! How clear it all was. How right he was. Hadn't he known he was adopted before Margaret had told him, before he had found the note in the case? And now… now he knew his mother and he would be friends, more than friends – family, once again. Phyllis Griffiths, who was still so young – only thirty-three. She must have been younger than him when she… why, yes, she would have been no more than fifteen. A child. A poor child in a terrible predicament.

Samantha had told him that Phyllis had two sons now with her husband, whose name was David Griffiths. But things had been different for her when she had given birth to these other sons, his half-brothers. She had been settled, older. Happy. But she had not forgotten him. She had not forgotten him.

Back in Leeds, the halls were deserted already for the Christmas break. Although from the state of Adam's half of the room, it looked as though he was still here. Perhaps he, like Christopher, was delaying his return home. This seemed unlikely, for such a happy-go-lucky chap. Adam seemed the very embodiment of Christmas cheer, of family gatherings and merriment. He hadn't mentioned his family, Christopher realised, but he imagined them, Adam and his father, their hair flame red, their cheeks bright pink, drinking pints of bitter and singing carols down at their local on Christmas Eve. He imagined Adam surrounded by friends and relatives, the life and soul, his homecoming something everyone looked forward to.

Whatever, Adam wasn't there right at this moment, so Christopher threw off his coat, took his writing paper and his fountain pen from his desk drawer. He would write the kind of letter that someone at the council, someone like Samantha Jackson, might advise him to write. After a moment, he bent to his task:

Dear Mrs Griffiths,
I have been advised by my adoption counsellor at Liverpool Council, Samantha Jackson, to contact you by letter first of all. I would have

contacted you long ago, but my adoptive parents only told me the truth of my situation in October of this year, the day I left for Leeds University, which is where I am now. My name is Martin Curtiss. I am your son. I was born on 12 March 1959 in at Liverpool General Hospital.

I will be for a brief time at my adoptive parents' home in Morecambe for the Christmas holidays, but you can contact me here at the halls of residence, as I will return in early January. I will include my halls address in this letter.

I must confess I am nervous at the thought of contacting you.

He stopped – bit the end of his pen. He sounded formal, too formal. Stiff. But that was better, wasn't it? Familiarity at this point would be too much – she might become suspicious, doubt his intentions. He should keep his feelings in check. Goodness, if he were to write what he felt! *My adoptive parents only told me the truth of my situation in October of this year,* he had written, when what he wanted to say was: *I have always known about you, all my life! I feel you in my heart as I feel the very pulse of life!* But he did not. He had to keep close rein on himself. He could not possibly say even half the words that ran around his head, nor admit to the myriad scenarios that had begun to infiltrate his thoughts: he and his birth mother sitting beside one another in some pink-hued room, sometimes laughing, sometimes heads bent together, deep in conversation, sometimes even lying side by side on a large apricot-coloured bed, addressing their deepest desires, fears, insecurities to the ceiling. Their hands would clasp, the light would fall on these conversations without end. She would stroke his hair.

Martin, she would whisper. *My darling boy.*

But such images were not for this letter. Not yet, perhaps not ever. Better to tread with cautious steps. He continued:

I almost took English for my degree, but plumped for history in the end. I read in my spare time though – I love reading. I have just finished The Shining, by Stephen King. I like thrillers especially. Honestly, if you were to ask me if I prefer a night out on the town or a quiet night in with a novel, it would be the second choice all the way!

He stopped, looked at the exclamation mark with disapproval. Keep a tight rein, Christopher. Hold yourself back. Don't frighten her away.

He squeezed a full stop after the y and made the exclamation mark into an I.

I have a room-mate here in Leeds. His name is Adam. I enclose a picture of us taken last week in Leeds town centre. It isn't very sensible but I hope you find something familiar in it. It was taken last Saturday so it is recent. You can't see in black and white but I am the one with the darker hair because mine is black. The other idiot is Adam.

Out of his wallet he dug two photo-booth snaps. In his desk drawer he found the Swiss army knife his father had given him as a boy (when he still hoped for a Swiss-army-knife kind of son) and used the scissor gadget to cut free a single snap. It had been Adam, of course, who had persuaded him to have his photo taken in the booth in WHSmith.

'Come on, man,' he had said, already feeding coins into the machine. 'It'll be a right laugh. We can have two each. I'll give one to Alison – help her survive Christmas without me. You can keep yours in your wallet or… or give them to your ma or something.'

Christopher had acquiesced, as he always did. And here he was, staring at himself staring into the camera while Adam appeared to be growling into his right ear. Adam's hair was beyond shoulder length now. The faintest trace of a smile on Christopher's own lips gave away that he was in fact trying not to laugh, and he thought

Phyllis would like that. She would see that he knew how to muck about, that he had a friend, but that he wasn't an out-and-out Jack the Lad.

Jack: that name again, how peculiar.

He read the letter back, but worried he'd come across as harsh, calling Adam an idiot. What if she didn't know he was joking? *Adam isn't really an idiot*, he added. *He is tremendous fun actually. You would like him.* She might like him more than she liked Christopher. He pushed the thought aside.

> *I am Adam's 'project'. He is teaching me how to dress more fashionably and how to talk to women. He has the gift of the gab but I don't, not in that way. Although I'm sure I would enjoy talking to the right person. Adam says I should let my hair grow, which I have done, a little. It does save on barber's fees, I suppose, which is an advantage on the maintenance grant. Not that I'm complaining. I like it very much here.*

He regretted mentioning money. He copied the letter out again, missing out the reference to his grant but keeping Adam. He did not mention that Adam had taught him to smoke, made him try marijuana, which he had hated, nor did he write about his adoptive family other than to say he had been well looked after and that he was grateful for the opportunities they had given him.

When he had finished, he signed off:

> *I look forward to hearing from you, if you wish to have further correspondence with me. I very much hope you do.*
> *Your son, Christopher, né Martin Curtiss*

The risk he took, sending that letter. It took courage, I'll say that even now. But it's always a risk, isn't it, reaching out to someone? Simply telling a person you love them, in whatever context, is to expose yourself to any damage they might wish to do to you, should they so choose. I guess all we can ever do is reach out anyway and hope to God they do us no harm. That's what I did. That's all I did: reach out, little knowing that I, that both of us, would come to such terrible, terrible harm.

CHAPTER NINE

Morecambe, Friday, 23 December. Margaret and Jack met him from the station, their faces set in anxiety. Christopher could see no reason for this beyond a certain nervousness around trains, travel, change of any kind. But seeing them, so diminished, on the platform, their eyes darting so that they might catch the earliest possible glance of him as the train ran past, he felt a pain in his gut. He had acted in secret, behind their backs. There was no getting around it. He should have told them he had initiated contact with his birth mother, but he hadn't. The wrongness of that struck him with full force only now, seeing them in all their bewilderment on the cold railway platform. They deserved better. And here they were to welcome him home from his first life's adventure. Just like normal parents.

The train whined and shuddered to a halt. He jumped down and ran to them, writing silent apology into the energy of his actions: *See how I run! See how pleased I am to see you again!*

'Well, lad, that's a pair of trousers all right.' Jack's first words and he, Christopher, had barely said hello. His father was shaking his head. 'Loon pants, is that what they're called?'

'They're just jeans, Dad.' He braced for his father's opinion on his Afghan coat, which was surely imminent.

'Your hair's grown,' said his mother. 'It's down over your collar. What's that coat? What is it, sheepskin? It reeks. Jack, smell his coat. It smells like a dog.' For once, Margaret had beaten her husband to it.

'You both look well,' Christopher said, smiling, while to his relief his father ignored his wife's request and instead wrenched the tattered, rope-bound case from Christopher's grip. 'Give us that, son, go on.'

Son.

Christopher let go without a fight. 'It's good to see you both anyway. Jack and Louise?'

'At home wrapping presents, I should think,' said his mother. 'Last-minute Annies, the pair of them.'

'Ah yes, well I must go and buy mine tomorrow.'

'Haven't you done it yet? What, none?' The tone of his mother's voice was more suited to having just heard he'd lost all his belongings in a fire. Now that he looked at them closely, it seemed that their lifetime of angst had been drawn on their faces with wrinkles. Their foreheads particularly were scored with deep lines.

'There are only four to buy, Mum.'

'Aye well, happen so, but tomorrow's Christmas Eve! There's practically nothing left in Woolworths.'

Her accent sounded strong – both their accents did, his ears accustomed to different voices these last months. Outside the station, rain fell in diagonal rods; a queue of taxis rattled as if shivering in the cold. His mother took out a small square of clear plastic from her pocket and unfolded it to make a rain hood. This she tied under her chin before dashing tiptoe out to the car park, giving small shrieks of disgust at the weather. His father followed, case flat over his head. Christopher walked behind, wondered when he would get his next cigarette.

'We'll drive past the pier, show you the wreckage,' said his father.

'Wreckage?'

'The pier! Washed away, last month. Didn't your mother say?'

'I put it in the letter,' his mother said. 'A storm. Terrible, it were.'

'Of course,' Christopher said, feeling himself blush, glad of his place in the back of the car. Which letter was that? One he had not even opened possibly. 'Sorry, I wasn't thinking.'

'Well.' His father's mouth clamped shut in the rear-view mirror, opened again but only just. 'Don't suppose it's of any great interest to you now.'

'Too busy out on the randan, I expect.' His mother, her words artificially light as ever, faltered as they always did under the persistent weight of her husband's. 'Chasing girls.'

Girls.

Through the streaked windows, his hometown rose before him: the beach and the promenade, the blackened skeleton of the pier. *Girls.* He had not seen Angie since that night in the Oak. He had not returned to that pub with Adam, who had moved on to the Bricklayers, nearer the campus, the Union bar sometimes, where the beer was cheap, and sometimes a string of pubs in town: the Cobourg, the Pig and Whistle, the Albion.

They had reached Hestham Avenue. The sight of the house made him catch his breath. For one suspended moment, familiarity and strangeness stood side by side. Time had done this. Knowledge had done this. And he could share none of that knowledge with Jack and Margaret.

His father swung the car onto the drive. Rain pooled in the pockets where frost had popped the tarmac. Christopher had to be careful to step over puddles when he got out of the car. He loved his new trousers but they sucked up water from a mile away. Determined not to lift his trousers like a long skirt, especially in front of his father, he tiptoed to the front door. He stepped inside, into the smell of the bathroom drifting down the stairs: damp towels, Imperial Leather soap, lily-of-the-valley talcum powder.

'I'll put my bag up,' he said, and climbed the stairs.

His brother and sister were in their rooms. Jack Junior said hello when Christopher showed his face at the crack in the door but

Jack was too engrossed in Christopher's old Scalextric to bother looking up. Louise did look up and gave him a thumbs-up. She was kneeling on her pink bedroom carpet, brushing the blonde nylon hair of what looked like the disembodied life-sized head of a girl. There were lipsticks scattered on the floor, bright plastic hair clips, a vivid blue square of eyeshadow.

'What're you doing?' he asked her.

She set the brush aside and divided a lock of the plastic head's hair into three strands. 'Girl's World.' She folded one strand over another, her brow knitted, her chin jutting forward in concentration. The expression was so exactly like Margaret's when she darned socks or sewed buttons back onto his father's shirts, it took Christopher aback.

'I'll leave you to it.' He reached the pole from its neat mount on the landing wall, pulled down the trapdoor and banged his way up the metal steps. His room was as he had left it, though it smelled of polish and there were stripes in the burgundy carpet where his mother had obviously passed the Ewbank. He took off his wet coat and hung it over the back of his desk chair. He took off his shoes and socks as they too were wet and put all of them on the oil heater, which was ice cold. He turned the dial and heard the click-click as it began to warm. His own breath clouded before him.

He sat at his desk. What he was about to do felt wrong, but he had not had time until this moment and would not delay it further. It was why he had come up to his room after all. He grabbed his writing set from the drawer where it had lain undisturbed all term, placed the bold lined sheet beneath the top sheet and wrote:

Dear Phyllis,

I realised on the train that I had quite forgotten to wish you a Merry Christmas! So I will send this second letter right away in the hope that it reaches you between Christmas and New Year.

He sat back and stared at the words on the page.

Love is where the idle mind wanders, he had once heard someone say – or perhaps he had heard it on the television, or read it somewhere. If that was true, then he loved her, Phyllis, even though he had not met her. Yes, he must do, since his mind went to her whenever it was unoccupied, sometimes even when he was trying to focus it on his books.

'Christopher.' From the bottom of the stepladder Margaret was calling up to him. 'Cup of tea, love.'

'Coming now,' he answered, scribbling frantically:

I must dash!

   Merry Christmas, Phyllis, although you won't get this until after. I hope it is all the merrier for me contacting you. I know it is for me. Yours,
Christopher

He wrote her name and address on the envelope and sealed it. His heart raced, battered in his chest. A second letter without hearing back from the first – he had not reined himself in, not really. Too late now! He grabbed his coat, his wet socks and shoes. He put on the shoes without the socks, which he stuffed into his coat pocket, the letter in the other. He would run out to the postbox as soon as he'd drunk his tea. Perhaps leave it half an hour for form's sake. He had no intention of hurting anyone's feelings, after all. And I believe that, even after all that has happened, Christopher would never hurt anyone, not intentionally.

On Christmas Eve, Christopher did his gift shopping in haste. That evening, he told me, he made himself eat three extra-strong mints to disguise any whiff of No. 6, then sprayed his room with Denim deodorant before heading down his metal staircase at quarter to eleven in time to go to Midnight Mass with the people he had called his family: Margaret, Jack, Jack Junior and Louise. Margaret was waiting for him on the landing, coat on, bag clutched at her waist as if someone were threatening to snatch it. He had not yet reached the bottom step when he turned to see her pained expression.

'Christopher, are you wearing those trousers?'

He stepped onto the landing and looked down at his dark navy flared jeans (an absolute bugger on the stepladder, not that he would have admitted it) and his new black ankle boots with the snazzy block heel. 'I was going to, why?'

'Do you have any that aren't… loons?' She looked like she might cry, and he thought of Adam, of what he would say when Christopher told him about this. *Loons?* he would say, in a silly shocked old-woman voice. *For the house of God, Christopher?* It was all Christopher could do not to laugh out loud – it was only a lack of cruelty that prevented him.

'I'm wearing a shirt,' he said. 'I don't think God will mind.'

'Don't blaspheme.'

Know God's taste in fashion, do you? was what he did not say, seeing the futility of argument just in time.

'I can change,' was what he did say. 'I've some old ones in the wardrobe.'

'Aye,' she said, her nose wrinkling at the bridge. 'Happen.'

He returned to the loft, the clank of shoe on metal serving only to amuse him further. Adam again, there in his mind's eye: *Flares, Christopher? In a church, Christopher? What are you, a murdering, drinking fornicator?* How ridiculous. And it did not escape him that this ridiculousness was something he would not have seen back when he lived here, but three short months ago. And yet he could not pinpoint when or where he had learnt to view the world this other way. When had this happened to him?

At least in his loft room, he thought, his mother could not see the smirk on his face.

He searched out his old grey school trousers and changed in haste. They were too short and a little tight on the waist after a term of steamed puddings and beer, but not, at least, flaring out like the very devil incarnate. *Stop it, Christopher. That's enough.* He put on his old black brogues, thought about wearing his school tie as a protest but instead grabbed an old purple tie and knotted it under the wide collars of his brown shirt. Over this new outfit, his Afghan coat must, he thought, look a little odd, though there was no mirror to check, and besides, he could hardly argue it mattered – not now. He returned to the main part of the house, repeating the dreadful and comic clonk-clank-clonk on the stepladder, his old woollen trousers airy around his knees after the skin-tight wrap of his jeans and the straight leg of course a cinch on the metal steps.

'That's better,' came his mother's voice from behind him, and when he turned to look, he saw that she was holding out a woollen coat. 'Maybe pop this on,' she said. 'It's only your father's.'

'Of course.' He shrugged off the Afghan and let it fall to the floor. His mother was already at his back, spreading out his father's coat, which smelled strongly of mothballs.

'This was your dad's going-away coat,' she said. 'Don't think it's been worn since 1952.'

She slid it onto his shoulders then bent to retrieve the rejected Afghan from the floor. He studied his father's coat a moment: the body fitted well enough, but the sleeves were too short, the cuffs of his shirt protruding by a couple of inches.

'Do you need this?' Margaret asked him.

He looked up to find her holding out the letter.

'Ah yes.' Chest tightening, he snatched it from her hands and shoved it into his father's coat pocket. 'I need to post that, thanks.'

'Who's it to?' She was smiling at him. 'Your sweetheart?'

He managed to return her smile, went so far as to wink. 'Perhaps,' he said.

Margaret had not moved. She was still looking at him. 'What's her name?'

'Ah. She's… she's called Phil.' He felt his cheeks flush.

'Phil? Isn't that a man's name?'

'It's short for… for Philippa.'

He transferred the letter into his trouser pocket – it would not do to leave it in his father's coat – and followed her down the stairs, wondering if she had seen the address. If she had, would she recognise it? No, it was a different address, and besides, there was no reason to think she would know or remember the original one. And he had written Mrs P. Griffiths. That could be anyone.

In the hall, his father, Jack Junior and Louise were waiting like strangers in a pungent cloud of Old Spice. Louise had on a pale blue wool coat Christopher had not seen before, a darker blue velvet Alice band in her hair. Jack Junior's hair, a short-back-and-sides, was slicked to the side with Brylcreem, his parting a thick white stripe. He looked like a prat.

'All set, finally?' There was an indigestive strain to his father's face and voice. His hair, Christopher noticed, was styled in the exact same way as his son's.

'Oh yes, all set,' said his mother. 'All ready for offski, and don't we all look smart?'

His father opened the door and held it, his mouth set in a flat line, while they filed out into the road. 'Off we go then.'

'You look weird,' Jack Junior said as they walked towards the church.

Christopher bent to whisper into his ear. 'Well you look ugly. But at least I can change my trousers.'

'Dork.'

'Mummy's boy.'

'Poof.'

'Wet the bed recently?'

'I'm telling Mum.'

'Go on then.'

Christopher walked on ahead, buttoning up his borrowed coat against the bite of the wind, tying his scarf tighter and thrusting his cold hands into his pockets. St Mary's Church would at least be a break, he thought, from this, this constant and pervading feeling of orbiting like Sputnik that grew with every passing hour. At this very moment he was floating in space, looking down upon the surreal scene of himself in his father's coat, too short in the sleeve, his school trousers, too short in the leg, a change of clothes deemed better, no, deemed *necessary* to go and worship a God who supposedly saw all men as equal, presumably regardless of their sartorial choices. What had happened to him? He had not felt changed until he had come back here. But he had changed. He had become Bowie's space oddity.

In the comforting dimness of the church, he lit a candle for Phyllis, wherever she was, and another for his father, Mikael. Crossing himself, he offered a silent prayer for them both, for their safety and happiness, for their lives. The priest, Father Donald, followed by the two altar servers, one with the cross, the other with the thurible, marched in sombre procession to the front, diffuse grey coils rising. The air filled with a thick sweetness and with the sweet, striving harmonies of the choir.

Alleluia, Alleluia.

Father Donald arrived at his chair, and the choir and congregation fell silent. Closing his eyes, he crossed himself. 'In the name of the Father, the Son and the Holy Spirit ...'

'Amen.'

The service began. At the mention of Christ's birth, Christopher thought of his own, of Phyllis, swathed in blue, the sweat on her brow, her cries of pain, the moment she first held him in her arms, knowing she could not keep him. His eyes prickled but he fought and recovered himself. When he sang, he sang the words to the statue of Our Lady at the front of the church and thought only of her – Phyllis, a vague notion, a shadow in the smoke.

By 11 a.m. on Christmas morning, he was itching to go into the garden for a smoke. But he had not the courage to light a cigarette in front of his parents. A drink too would be welcome, come to think of it – the small sweet sherry his father would pour at midday would hardly take the edge off. A physical urge to leave made it difficult for him to sit still. He wondered how long he could stay.

'I'll probably head back to Leeds on the second,' he said once they had sat at the table for Christmas lunch, once they had said grace and pulled their crackers, once they had argued against Margaret's annual voicing of her disappointment: *The turkey's dry again. No, no it's delicious, Mum, not dry at all.*

'That's a flying visit,' Margaret said. Her glasses had a lean to them and the sherry had turned her nose red. 'Can you not stay longer?'

'I have to study,' he said, loading his fork with a greedy mouthful but avoiding Margaret's gaze. 'Essays and so on. There's a lot of work at university, you know – they don't just give you a degree.' He was, he knew, using their ignorance against them and it pained him.

'What do cannibals play at parties?' Jack Junior read from the cracker joke slip.

'Is your room warm enough?' his mum persisted.

'Swallow my leader,' said Jack Junior, and laughed.

'It's fine,' Christopher assured her. 'Everything's fine. There's nothing wrong; I just have to study. I want to get at least a two-one.'

'Is that the same as a degree?'

Helpless, Christopher glanced towards his father, who hadn't said a word. Perhaps he had not heard, too busy helping Louise put on her paper hat. Perhaps he had drunk some of the sherry in secret, lucky bugger.

Christopher shook his head. 'I can concentrate better at the halls, that's all.'

'Why do French people eat only one egg at a time?' Louise read. 'Because one egg is un oeuf. What?' She frowned. 'I don't get that.'

Christopher laughed, though no one else did. 'It's because *un oeuf* is French for an egg,' he said, smiling at his little sister. 'And *un oeuf* sounds like *enough*.'

Louise threw the joke aside. 'That's rubbish. It's not even funny.'

'They eat frogs' legs over there,' came his father's contribution to the cultural discussion. 'What d'you expect?'

After dinner, they opened their presents. Jack Junior and Louise emptied their pillowslips onto the lounge carpet and tore through their gifts: books, a chemistry set, a Galt science kit, a game called Buckaroo. His mother handed him an envelope.

'We didn't know what you'd need,' she said. 'There's ten pound in there.'

'Thank you. That's too much.' He thought of the travel fares ahead, once he was allowed to go and see Phyllis, and put the money in his pocket. 'But thank you.'

Christopher gave Jack Junior two new cars for the Scalextric, to Louise he gave a jumpsuit for her Sindy doll and to his parents a bottle of Warninks Advocaat. A mistake. His father peered at the bottle as if he were reading the instructions on a tin of paint to check which solvent he needed.

'Warninks,' he said, pronouncing it 'warnings'. 'Isn't an advocate some sort of lawyer?'

'You mix it with lemonade,' Christopher said, kneeling up to point at the label on the back. 'It's called a snowball. It's a popular cocktail at Christmas apparently. Thought it might make a change.'

His father's eyes creased in disdain.

'It's a pretty colour anyway,' trilled his mother. 'Lovely warm yellow, isn't it, Jack?'

'Not sure I'm too keen on cocktails,' said his father.

'No,' said Christopher, hearing his own voice quieten. 'Me neither really. It was just supposed to be a bit of fun…'

CHAPTER TEN

They made me walk around the yard earlier. Nurse linked my arm, said I was doing grand.

'This'll give you an appetite,' she said. I wonder at her indefatigable hope. It is like a plant that blooms again no matter how many times you cut off its flower. And I am a weed, I suppose, killing it by stealthier means.

She stands over me while I eat, urging me on as if I'm running a marathon. Chicken broth. God only knows what's supposed to be floating in it – they look like fridge magnets. I manage half and push my bowl away.

'Another mouthful, come on, my darling.' She picks up the spoon and scoops up the thin soup. 'Come on, for me.'

I watch myself from above: opening my mouth, being fed like a baby. I know that if I let her feed me, she will leave me alone. Then I can get back to Christopher. Ironically, it is Christopher who is keeping me alive.

Christopher returned to Leeds on Friday, 6 January, as a compromise. His parents took him to the station, and as he waved them off, he found himself wondering when he would return, then if he would return. It wasn't that he no longer wanted to see them; only that, since the only meaningful conversation possible between them was the one they could never have, he wasn't sure what there was left to say.

At Devonshire Hall, he found the longed-for letter from Phyllis in his pigeonhole. He told me he'd known it would be there before he saw it; it was why he had come back early. He rushed up to his room, threw down his case and tore open the envelope.

Morecambe, 26 December 1977
Dear Christopher,

Well stop calling me Mrs Griffiths for a start! I'm Phyllis – please call me Phyllis from now on. Promise?

I prayed this day would come! You have no idea. I've waited for it for so long, and since I gave my details to NORCAP, not a day has gone by that I haven't checked the post in case there was something from you. So you can imagine how excited I was to receive and read your marvellous letter. I have read it many times since then, I can tell you. So many I think I must know it off by heart! I'm guessing the adoption counsellor told you I'd registered with NORCAP – did you know I did it the very day of your eighteenth birthday? I prayed you would look for me – I lit candles for you at St Edward's at the end of our road, and lo and behold, you did look for me! I should pray more often because now here you are and here's me, sitting in my bedroom, where I can be in peace away from the rabble, so that I can write back to you. Only now I've started, I hardly know where to begin!

I never wanted to give you away, that is the first thing I must say to you, something I have wanted to say to you all your life. You were my flesh and blood. You are my flesh and blood. I have felt the loss of you all these years as if I had lost my own foot. But, you see, I still felt the itch in my toes all that time, and that's because you were out there, alive, and I could feel it. If I tell you nothing else besides, if you know at least that, then I will have at least a small comfort. The thought of you thinking I'd abandoned you has just about killed me these last eighteen years. I was fifteen when I fell pregnant, you see, and I had no choice but to give you up. My parents would not have supported me and your father was long gone. He was a sailor, he was Polish and his name was Mikael Dabrowski, but you know all that by now, I think. You didn't ask about him so I've assumed that is so. I'm afraid I have no idea where he is. I don't even have a photograph of him. I wish I could tell you he was the love of my life, but he was not. He was very handsome and I was very sheltered. Parents think they should protect their children, and of course they should. I would have protected you had you been allowed into my care. But too much protection results in greater danger sometimes. At least it did for me, and I paid a terrible price.

But all that is in the past. Here you are and here I am and it strikes me that forward might be a good way to go. What do you say, Christopher? After eighteen years, we're maybe a few letters, maybe a couple of months away from one another! And it's funny, because now we are so close to finally meeting, the months we have to wait seem almost longer than all those years. Do you feel like that? Although I suppose you have only known about me for such a short time, whereas I've known about you your whole life.

I have been told we should go slowly too, but now that I have found you, I am so impatient to see you. I wish to get to know you, Christopher. I wish to meet you, if not immediately, then at some point. Please write and tell me we can. I have to hope, please let me. I want to know every little thing about you – how you take your tea, what television programmes you like, all about your childhood. I hope that doesn't scare you. I would not want to frighten you, but the truth is, Christopher, I'm frightened too.

I am married to a good man called David. He is happy I have found you and is really supportive of my wish to be reconciled. We have two boys, twins. Their names are Darren and Craig, and they are eight years old. I have not told them about you yet, but I will, should you decide you wish to take things further. My mum and dad don't know about all this yet, but when they find out, I'm *sure they'll be delighted, and that means you'll have grandparents to meet too. When you were taken from me, I did not speak to them for a long time, but that is all in the past now. I also have a sister, Miriam, so she would be your auntie! I'm sorry, I'm saying too much. Don't worry if you're not ready for any of that – we can take our time. I could write to you all day, all week, and never stop. I feel like I could burst with all I want to tell you.*

It is, of course, up to you. I cannot lay claim to anything at all – I know that. I will take my lead from you. I'm sorry if I've said too much already. I can't help myself!

I'm asking for you to give me a chance. What do you say? I used to kiss your baby photo each night. Now I have the one you sent. You are so handsome! I carry the picture in my purse. One day I hope to be able to take it out and show people and say, there, that's my boy, that's my son.

To be reunited has been my dream for more than half my life. None of what I have written in this letter can convey the strength of my feelings. My feelings are stronger than words.
Yours,
Phyllis

He pressed the letter to his chest. The radiator gave a loud bang, which made him jump. The wind blew outside, rattled the loose sash windows in their frames.

He had worried about the power of his feelings, so much so he had not dared to reveal them. But she, Phyllis, had dared to write her feelings – all of them. She had not been able to, perhaps not even wanted to, rein herself in. It had not occurred to her to try. She loved him as he loved her. It was as he had thought. As he had known! They were connected, in tune, as one, before they'd even met. This, this was his gift and his curse – his knowledge of how things would be before they had come to pass. She wanted to see him every bit as much as he wanted to see her. He had not doubted it. He had *known* it.

With his coat still on, he took up his fountain pen and wrote:

6 January 1978
Dear Phyllis,
    I have just this moment returned to Leeds and to your wonderful letter.

The page swam. He touched his cheek and found it to be wet. He sat back from his desk, unable to continue. This was preposterous. He did not cry. He had not cried since he was a child, and only then it would have been after scuffing his knees on the paving stones in the back garden. But he wasn't in pain. It wasn't that. Yet here were tears just the same – hot and streaming down his face, girlish, shameful.

There was no one there to see him, so he pressed his fists to his eyes and let it happen, let himself sob and shake, slump and slacken. The surprise of it gave way to something he could not name but which was not unpleasant. Relief, something like that, a draining down of his very blood – like when his father, Jack, bled the heating and as a boy he would watch and hear the hiss of the air as it blew out of the radiators, the softening of the hiss as the pressure fell, until, with a gurgle, the brown water came and his father would wind the T-shaped key and stop it. She had said her feelings were stronger than words – how right she was. How could anyone contain such feelings? It was not possible. They were too big. Only now, in the release of this strange weeping fit, did it occur to him what a strain it had been within the walls of his family home to feel his every word scrutinised and censored, to be watched for signs of change as one watches for a malevolent outsider. He was the outsider. Had been even before he had left.

University had changed him, but it was knowledge – knowledge that had pushed him out of his home, possibly forever.

Was it wrong to have changed? Was it wrong not to belong? The wrong here, perhaps, was neither of those things themselves but the secrecy of them. Why had he kept hidden his search for his birth mother? That did not mean he was seeking to replace the mother and father, the brother and sister he already had, did it?

Not necessarily.

But by saying nothing to his parents, he had lied to them. And no matter how you looked at it, that was a sin. But the sin had been committed, the air had been bled out, and it could not be forced back in now.

He wrote,

You have been braver than I in expressing your true feelings. Your bravery has given me the courage to share my feelings, although in these matters I am by no means an expert. My adoptive family are good people, but when I look at them I do not see myself – no browline, no jaw, no eye or hair colour. That is no one's fault.

Mrs Samantha Jackson at Liverpool Council did indeed give me your details, and yes, I knew you had registered with NORCAP. I knew you'd had me when you were very young and that my father was called Mikael and a sailor. I knew that you taught English and that you were married with twin boys. Samantha urged caution but I think she meant where there was hesitation on the part of the parent or child. There is no hesitation here. Far from it! I would be agreeable to a meeting as soon as February if that is all right with you. Oh my, I am aware of sounding formal! I keep making mistakes. Forgive me – I can't help it. I am rather quiet, you see. I am studious by my room-mate's standards and I hope that is OK. I was not brought up in a family that laughed very often. I don't mean that critically, it is just the way we were. But I have laughed a lot with my friends here at the university and find that I understand more easily now when people are pulling my leg. Adam pulls my leg all the time.

Adam came into his mind, standing at the door of their room one evening before Christmas on his way out to meet Alison, or Sophie, or some other woman.

'You need to get laid, man,' he'd said. 'That's your trouble.'

Christopher dismissed the thought and returned to his letter.

Do you have a photograph you could send? I would love to have a picture of you, if that is not too forward. Did you feel like you recognised me at all from my picture? What I mean is, did you recognise yourself or perhaps my father? I suppose the picture was too small to tell.

I await your reply. Please write soon. It doesn't need to be a long letter. We can tell each other everything if and when you decide you would like to meet, if you still do. For my part, I would like to. I vote we write not one or two long letters but many short letters and aim to meet next month but not if you have changed your mind. I don't want to rush you.

With love,

Your son,

Christopher

8 January 1978

Dear Christopher,

My darling boy. Your letter came this morning. Of course I recognised you in the picture! I'm sorry, I should have said. You have your father's nose, I think. And he had dark hair too. My hair is brown – nothing special, I'm afraid, what you'd call mousy. Typical English rose, I suppose you'd say. I don't tan and I go red in the heat. I can't see much of me in your photo, but then I can't see much of me in the twins. Everyone says they are the spitting image of David. My genes are obviously weak.

And don't you be apologising for yourself – I won't allow it! You sound perfect just as you are. You mustn't feel like you need to be any other thing than yourself, do you hear me? No more apologies. I can't be doing with fake people anyway. I get enough of airs and graces from David's colleagues' wives at the estate agent's. They drive me bonkers with their holidays to Spain and their Mateus Rosé. Stuck-up lot. As if putting wine in a basket makes it a big deal, honestly. Listen to me. Now it's me who is writing nonsense!

I think writing short and sweet letters is ideal. But let's write lots! And yes, a meeting in February would be fabulous. The sooner the better, I say. I don't see what's to be gained by waiting. I've waited long enough! How does Saturday the 11th sound? If that's too soon, don't worry. We can make it later – it's just a starting point. Let me know anyway. I will write again.

The thought of seeing you at last is too much to think about. Your photo is in a frame on my bedside table. I kiss it every night, but then I can't get to sleep for thinking about you. I have imaginary conversations with you all the time – I can't tell David for fear he'll think I'm barmy. I lit another candle for you at the weekend. Our church is at the end of our road, St Edward's – I think I told you that already. I try to go most Sundays if I can. Do you still practise?

I've enclosed a picture of me. It's not very clear, but it'll give you a rough idea. It was taken last year in Conway. As I said, I'm nothing special, just an ordinary human being – or human bean, as the twins say sometimes when they're mucking about. And yes, we laugh in this house. I am glad to say that David brought laughter to my life a long time ago and that's exactly why I married him. Don't tell him I said that – it'll go right to his head!

All my love, until we meet,

Phyllis xxx

Christopher wrote back by return of post, agreeing to the date. He kept his letter light, avoided the subjects that troubled him – his adoptive parents, his love life, sex. He could not tell her about Angie, nor about the only other girl he had ever touched – from the girls' school one time at the youth club. He couldn't even remember her name, only that he had spent a long slow dance to Chicago's 'If You Leave Me Now' staring up at the cornicing in the church hall to avoid the smell of her greasy hair. He worried these things would make him sound weird, and with that monster on the loose – and in Yorkshire – she might think it was him. The idea filled him with a cold, sick feeling. The Ripper's victims: bodies mutilated and abandoned in wasteland, behind cemeteries or left to rot in parks. When he thought of these women, these murders, these bodies, something dark niggled away at any peace, however short-lived, he might feel. He thought he knew what they meant by 'bodies', the fathomless dark the term concealed. All around him, he could sense the terror that still permeated the female student population, judging by the frenzied conversations he had overheard in the shuffle of the lecture halls, the squash of the corridors and the clatter of the university canteen. Normal women had been murdered. Normal women, just like them.

And if the victims included normal women, he wondered, was the Ripper a normal man, a man as normal or as troubled as any other – a man like him?

Sometimes, when Christopher thought of the killer referred to increasingly simply as *him*, he found himself unable to stop imagining how the circumstances had progressed from transaction, in the case of the prostitutes at least, to terror. The mere word – *prostitute* – provoked in him a strange mix of excitement and revulsion. He thought of dark streets, of the smell of rain and rotting rubbish, the whirr of refuse trucks in the small hours of the night. When he thought of the five-pound note the police had found in that handbag, he thought of other banknotes, grubby, crumpled, dug out from pockets and handed over, stuffed into cheap purses in haste. He thought, could not help but think, of a faceless woman in a damp alleyway, underwear yanked down and away, the monster's trousers dropped, hairy white legs bent, knuckles bleached by the weight of buttocks, paler legs wrapped around the thrusting hips of a shadow man, the glint of teeth and eye all that was visible of his murderous grimace.

And then, what then? The climax, the aftermath – sensations he had (if he didn't count Angie) only ever experienced alone, by his own hand. He knew at least the rush, what the French called *the little death*, and the melancholy that followed. But at what point did it turn for *him*, the Ripper? Or was there no such preamble? Did he attack them from behind, send them falling before they even knew he was there? Did he confront them and bare his yellow teeth? Or did he talk to them, flatter them, walk with them a while before turning, horribly, the knife raised in his sweating hand? Did he kiss them? Did they touch him? Did they caress him, the Ripper, as Angie had caressed him, Christopher?

At the thought of that business with Angie, he felt a fresh sting of humiliation. Her kindness had been worse than cruelty. Women had that power. They made you lose control. Maybe that was why the Ripper killed them – revenge for reducing him to his basest, animal self. Women were the authors and the witnesses of his shame and as such had to be terminated.

Something along those lines, perhaps, though Christopher was no expert in these matters. Adam was an expert. He appeared to have no problem with issues of the body, talked openly, proudly even, of his bowel movements and his sexual conquests as if they were no more embarrassing than eating a sandwich. He had finished with Alison now and had taken up with a language student called Rosemary, a very tall woman who made him look like some sort of garden gnome. These disparities didn't faze him. He wore his charm as if it were the most comfortable old cardigan and took what came to him as his right. He was lucky. Like the first man on earth he often joked about, he had claimed his place in the world. His name fitted him perfectly.

Christopher sighed, locked in his private, interior world where such thoughts looped, dived and dissolved – looped again infinitely. There were things he would never tell anyone, not even Phyllis. For her, he would be everything she was hoping for in a son. He would be a boy she could not refuse. For Phyllis, he would be normal.

CHAPTER ELEVEN

Between 12 January and 11 February 1978, Christopher and Phyllis wrote a total of ten letters each. During this time, the Ripper killed again: Helen Rytka, an eighteen-year-old prostitute from Huddersfield. Christopher cut out the relevant newspaper articles, stuck them in his scrapbook and returned to his letters to Phyllis. Writing to his birth mother, he told me, became his favourite way to wind down after an evening lost in medieval studies or the horrors of the Holocaust. With each letter came the momentary appeasement of his all-pervading desire to be in constant communication with her. But barely a day, sometimes barely minutes after he had written, the need to reach for her renewed itself, stronger still. It moved me to hear him say this. *Love is where the idle mind travels.*

And so, when the InterCity pulled into Warrington station at 2.25 p.m. on Saturday, 11 February 1978, Christopher found himself, rigid with tension, at the window of the train door. He had stood there since Manchester Piccadilly, unable to sit a moment longer, staring out of the window as if she, Phyllis, might appear skirting along the hedgerows like a phantom.

The photograph she had sent was indeed blurry. In one of her letters she'd mentioned that she hated having her photo taken and always looked a fright. She was, he thought, saying that out of modesty, but I know she didn't have a high opinion of the way she looked. Despite the poor focus, Christopher thought the photograph showed a pretty young woman not too much older than him. She was holding an ice cream, though the sky at her back was grey, and her light brown hair blew up and across her cheeks in the wind. She was smiling, and when he looked into the photo, as he had done every day since, he imagined her smile was for him.

He had tied all her letters together using the scraggy tinsel from Adam's miniature Christmas tree and stored them in a shoebox under his bed. A nightly routine had become to unwind the glittering thread, pick one at random and read it before he went to sleep, a routine that almost always finished in him taking out every one of the letters and reading them from first to last. He would close his eyes and think of her and him together, always sitting or lying close, hands clasped, heads bent in a soft apricot light. He wondered sometimes where this light came from, and what it meant.

He stepped down off the train and waited for the crowd to thin. One by one the horde dispersed until only one remained: a young woman in a burgundy wool beret, a woman once blurry brought suddenly and shockingly into focus. She was standing in front of a blow-up image of Jimmy Savile – *InterCity. This is the age of the train* – her face the very picture of anticipation.

'Phyllis? Phyllis Curtiss?'

But she was already walking towards him. She wore bell-bottomed jeans like his and a long black woollen coat. She could have been another student, maybe a PhD student. Her arms flew out like wings, but almost immediately she clapped them to her sides as if she did not know whether or not to fly.

'Christopher?' Her hair was fair rather than brown as she had said, but her eyes were dark – brown, like his. Margaret's eyes were blue – he shook the thought away. 'Christopher, is it you?'

'Yes,' he said, almost too choked to speak. 'Yes. It's me.'

Her eyes shone, a rim of tears at their edge; her mouth pressed itself into a tight smile. She took a deep breath, her nostrils flaring, her shoulders rising, her chest seeming to inflate. When she exhaled, she gave a short gasping laugh – of surprise, of joy, of something neither of them could identify but which filled the air, the sky, and on.

After a moment's hesitation, she came forward. Her hands flew up and dropped and flew up again, and when she was close enough, she reached and touched him lightly on the arm, as if to check he was really there. He found himself unable to move, filled with a kind of burning. She stood back, straightened, gave another half-gasp, half-laugh. Her hair was not black like his but her nose was not thin at least, perhaps a little like his own, and her eyes were definitely brown and carried a smudge of grey beneath. He reached for where she had touched his arm and held himself there, as if injured. But he was not injured.

'Here you are,' she said.

He nodded, all ability to speak quite gone.

She reached up and placed a forefinger under the inner corner of his eye, then traced her finger down a little, the way a tear might run. As if suddenly aware of what she was doing, the intimacy of it, she withdrew her hand and placed it flat against her own flushed cheek.

'Sorry,' she said. 'Just … my dad used to say that my eyes had been pushed in with sooty fingers. And yours have that too…' She covered her mouth with her hand. Her eyes brimmed, overflowed at last. 'I can't believe it.' She laughed that small gasping laugh again and took a step back. Her eyes did not leave his.

'I…' he began but could not continue.

'Let's get you home,' she said gently, reaching into her coat pocket for a tissue and dabbing at her eyes. 'To my house, I mean – if I can manage to drive. I don't know if I can, mind you, I'm shaking like a leaf here.'

With her arm at his back, she ushered him out to the car park and then walked a little ahead. Every other step, she turned and gave a laugh, as if embarrassed or as if to apologise for something.

'This is our chariot,' she said, and stopped.

They had reached a bronze-coloured Austin Princess. The bodywork had rusted in patches and the black vinyl roof had started to peel. 'Bit of a banger, but she goes.' She unlocked the passenger door first, touched his arm again, the lightest tap, before making her way around to the driver's side. In her wake, he smelled flowers, though he could not have said whether it was perfume or soap.

'Get in,' she called over the top of the car. 'Excuse the mess.'

Inside, in the footwell, were six or seven green toy soldiers of the type he himself had played with as a child: no bigger than a thumb, their feet moulded to small flat rectangles so they could stand and fight. He guessed they belonged to the twins, whose names he had learned off by heart from her letters: Darren and Craig. Despite being messy, the car was comfortable, with soft rust-coloured velour upholstery. It smelled of sports kit, of trainers. There was a box of Kleenex tissues on the dashboard, four or five tapes in the square recess next to the gearstick, what looked like a woman's handbag of tan leather on the back seat.

Phyllis started the engine. A blast of music came from the cassette player – French: Blondie, 'Denis'.

'Sorry,' she said, turning down the music. 'David tapes the charts every week for the car.'

'I used to do that,' he said, filled with inexplicable joy. 'Every week.'

'So you like music, then?'

'Yes, very much. Do you?'

'Love it. I like Fleetwood Mac, do you like Fleetwood Mac?'

'I love Fleetwood Mac. I like the song… what is it… the one from the new album… "Dreams"? I like that one best.'

'That's my favourite too!' Her voice had risen both in pitch and volume. She flapped her hand in excitement, her engagement ring flashing next to her wedding band. She turned to him for a second and smiled. One of her front teeth crossed the other – he had not noticed that until now – and it was all he could do to stop himself from reaching over and drawing his thumb down the squint line made by the overlap.

She grasped the steering wheel, laid her arms around its rim and rested her head against her hands.

'I'm not sure I can drive,' she said, and laughed. 'Just give me a minute.'

'I understand,' he said. 'I don't think I could drive now either.'

'Thanks.' After a moment, she pulled herself upright and rubbed her forehead. When she spoke again, her voice shook. 'Dig around in the glove compartment,' she said. 'I think the Fleetwood Mac's in there. I need Stevie Nicks to calm me down, I think.'

Christopher opened the glove compartment. Three cassettes fell from the jumble onto his lap. They were mostly BASF, all copies, all with labels scribbled in black felt-tip pen: the Best of Motown, the Bee Gees, Billy Joel. Phyllis had let down the handbrake and was now edging out of the car park, into the traffic. All the while, she drew in short breaths, making a soft whistling sound, blowing out those breaths again as if after a shock. Though all he wanted was to drink her with his eyes, he made himself look away, wanting to leave her some privacy in the height of emotion seemingly too raw, too powerful to conceal. He understood – more than she could know. He'd had to flatten his feet to the floor to stop his legs from trembling.

He busied himself with the tapes and found a grey TDK with *Rumours* scribbled on the label.

'This is only just out, isn't it?' he asked. 'You've got hold of a copy very quickly.'

'That's David does those,' she said. 'A right old pirate, he is. Terrible.' She was negotiating a roundabout, glanced at him as she turned left and onto a dual carriageway. She had taken off her hat, and against the sun her hair spun a wispy halo.

'I can't believe you're in my car.' She seemed to have recovered her voice and her tone had levelled. 'I just… I can't believe you're here. My baby. My baby, Martin.'

'I can't either,' he said. 'But I am.'

'You are.'

They had been together less than fifteen minutes and already happiness had flooded into him, warmed his insides like wine. He wondered if he had ever felt so happy. He doubted it.

'I think we have the same nose,' he said.

'Do you? You know what they say about noses. Run in the family, don't they?' She laughed, and he laughed too, conscious still of keeping himself in check, aware that if he didn't, he might howl for the near pain of such joy.

Minutes later, they came to a bridge: pale green, industrial looking – steels, rivets, arches. It held the road that they drove over now, another bridge to their right, its sandstone blackened with soot. To their left, what looked like a town; beneath, a river shone brown.

'That's the railway,' she said, gesturing at the blackened stone bridge. 'The Leeds train doesn't stop there. The road we're on now is called the Runcorn–Widnes Bridge,' she said. 'David's grandfather had a hand in it. Literally. Lost his hand when one of those beams hit him. T'other side is the estuary, and that's the old town further on. We were in Widnes just now, and when we reach the other side we'll be in Runcorn.'

'Is that Runcorn?' he asked, nodding towards the town.

'That's what I meant when I said the old town, sorry. But yes it is, love.'

Love.

They drove off the bridge and onto another dual carriageway.

'The Mersey,' she said, anticipating his question with, he thought, a kind of telepathy. 'The Runcorn–Widnes Bridge is like the Golden Gate Bridge except with twice the fog and half the sunshine. Just kidding. The canal's down there, did you see it? One of the teachers where I work lives on a barge somewhere along here. I've never been on it though. The barge, I mean.'

'Do you live near?'

'Not too far now.'

In the wing mirror, the pale structure of the bridge shrank behind them. They left the dual carriageway, turned right and right again – Christopher lost track until Phyllis turned left into a road of semi-detached houses, about the same size as his parents' but with leaded bay windows and larger front gardens, dwarf walls, hedges. She pulled into a driveway, at the end of which was a garage, set back from the house.

'Home sweet home.' She turned off the engine and opened her door.

He got out and followed her back up the drive and around to the front of the house. Phyllis chattered as she let them both in. Inside, it was warm, almost hot after the cold of the outdoors.

'I left the heating on,' she said. 'Take your coat off and hang it with the others.'

He did as he was told, putting his jacket over a child's anorak since there was no free hook. His hat and gloves he stuffed into the pockets. She was already in the kitchen; he could hear her clanking about, the flush of water.

'Tea?' she called to him.

'Thank you, yes.'

She was singing to herself: 'Dreams'. The song had stuck in her mind, no doubt after they'd listened to it together in the car. He sang it too, softly, while he took off his ankle boots. On the floor underneath the coats were a pair of men's walking shoes, two pairs of boys' football boots and a pair of women's tan leather boots with a heel. His own boots he placed neatly on the end, in the row.

Minutes later, he and Phyllis were sitting at the small Formica kitchen table, hot tea in ivy-patterned china mugs before them.

He had imagined this moment so many times but had not been able to envisage the sight of her until now, smiling at him as she was through the lazy steam, her hair a little fuzzy from the damp air. There were fine lines at the edges of her eyes. Her skin had pinked a little, making her look like a schoolgirl. She put her hand over the mug to warm it. The house smelled sugary, as if she had been baking. He could feel his toes throbbing as they warmed up.

'David's taken the boys to the football. It's Liverpool at home, not sure who they're playing. I thought it'd be better if it was just the two of us today.'

Phyllis sighed. For a moment neither of them said anything. As if synchronised, both placed their lips to the rims of their cups, despite the obvious fact that the tea was too hot yet to drink.

'Can you tell me?' The question came out before he had a chance to stop it. 'I mean, do you think you can talk about it – about me, that is?'

She put her tea down and smiled at him sadly. 'I can.'

'I shouldn't have asked,' he said quickly, feeling himself blush. 'I shouldn't have asked like that. I'm sorry.' He stood, took off his sweater, sat down again. 'Sorry, I'm overheating.' He reached for his drink, but she caught and held his hand.

'What did I say about apologising? You should save it for when you've done something wrong. And you've done nothing wrong.'

'Sorry. For apologising.'

She laughed, cocked her head as if to study him. 'You're shyer than your letters.'

It was his turn to laugh, out of embarrassment. 'I was hoping you wouldn't notice.'

He turned his hand in hers, flattening the back against the cool tabletop. Their hands lay palm to palm, the tips of her fingers at his wrist, his fingertips at hers. Her hand was much smaller than his, her skin pinker, her nails longer. Her watch was a blue Timex.

It looked like a boy's watch and he wondered if it belonged to one of the twins. Beyond the strap, her pale arm vanished into the burgundy wool sleeve of her sweater.

'What do you want to know?' she asked him.

He made himself meet her eye. 'Everything you can tell me, but only if you can. I don't want to upset you.'

She took his hand in both of hers and lifted it as she stood. She led him through to the living room and told him to sit down.

He sat on the sofa, felt it sink beneath his weight. The fabric of the cushions was velvet – green, the colour of wine bottles. The carpet was paisley – greens and yellows, thick under his stockinged feet. Although the room was warm enough, she crossed to the opposite wall and lit the gas fire all the same, as if the merest chill could not be allowed, as if she were in fact trying to keep him warm forever now she had brought him in from the cold. Above the fire were photographs in frames. He wanted to go over and look at them but did not.

Phyllis returned to him, took his hand once more in hers and laid their knotted fingers on her leg. Normally such a gesture would have filled him with angst, but it didn't, not with her.

'When I got your letter…' She stopped and inhaled deeply. She was dressed much like the girls at university – a casual sweater and jeans. Not like Margaret – not like a mother at all.

'You don't have to tell me right away,' he said. 'It's enough just to be here for now. It's a miracle to be here with you.'

'It is.' It was barely a whisper. Her fingers tightened around his. 'It's an absolute miracle.'

He could feel the warmth radiating from her. Human warmth. A *human bean*. The line where their thighs ran down to the sofa's edge was dark. He could not see the cushion beneath. He wondered if he had ever sat this close to his mother, Margaret.

'You don't have to explain yourself to me,' he said. 'That's not why I came.'

'I want to.' She looked up into his face and smiled. Her eyes were wet – they had not dried in all the time they had been together – and she reached up and tucked his hair behind his ear. The tenderness of the gesture was almost unbearable. He closed his eyes a moment and opened them again.

'You're Christopher now,' she said.

'Yes. But I was Martin. Your baby.'

On the mantelpiece, a carriage clock ticked. The gas fire hissed. A car passed by, though he wasn't sure if the noise came from the road in front of the house or the one behind.

'Every morning,' she began, taking his hand again, 'when the post drops through, I get a moment where I feel this little pulse of excitement. And then when I see there's nothing but bills, bank statements and the like, the feeling drops like a stone and all I feel is disappointment. Most people get that probably, but I think it's more so for me because of what I'm always hoping for. Maybe I'm no different to anyone else. Maybe we're all longing for something special to happen. Maybe life is just a constant process of readjusting our expectations.'

'But that day you got my letter,' he interrupted – couldn't help himself.

'Yes,' she said, and squeezed his hand so tight it hurt. 'That day I didn't have to readjust anything because something special did happen. There was your letter in its little white envelope, all neat and precise.' Her left eyelid lowered halfway in a comic expression, as if she were joking or being ironic, or perhaps she had something in her eye. He did it too, felt his eyelid tremble. 'And the address was written in this painstaking handwriting. Black ink. So neat. It was addressed to me, of course. And I knew. I just knew. I was shivering before I even opened it. Standing in the hallway shivering.'

He said nothing, stayed utterly still, held his breath in case the sound of it stopped her from continuing.

'Of course it was five o'clock by the time I got to read it. The house was like Clapham Junction. I had to do the packed lunches, get the kids sorted, go to work. God knows how I did. Then after work I had to pick up the twins, get their dinner, get them settled. I fed them early then put them in front of the television, took the letter upstairs and into the bathroom. It's the only room with a lock in this house. Not very picturesque, I know, but I sat on the loo and read your words, and I felt as if my bones were melting. Literally, Christopher. You should've seen me. I was crying so much my jeans were covered in wet spots. You'll think I'm romanticising, but I'm telling you it was like that. It was like forgiveness and redemption all at once, except I only realised in that moment that I'd been waiting to be forgiven, if that makes sense. I'd waited for your letter for over half my life and there it was in my hands, and all I had to do was hold on, not mess up, and I had a chance of seeing you again. Even as I was reading your words, I thought: this will be my first story for him, this right now, sitting in this bathroom on this loo seat, crying over his letter. I'll lighten it up for him, I thought. Joke about having the loo paper right there, how handy that was to dry my tears.' She sniffed, smiled, rolled her eyes, as if to suggest she was silly.

He wanted to tell her there was nothing silly in anything she had said, but could not speak. He had imagined her reading his letter in her room, perhaps, or in the kitchen. But it didn't matter. None of it mattered.

'I hadn't forgotten your birthday,' she said. 'How could I? So on the twelfth of March last year I knew you'd turned eighteen, just as I knew you'd turned one and two and every year in-between. I had nothing of you except for the smallest picture, no bigger than a credit card, black and white. You were barely a week old when…' She stopped again, threw her eyes to the ceiling, blinking fast. He placed the flat of his hand between her shoulder blades and told her it was OK, that there was no rush.

She nodded, closed and opened her eyes, passed her hand over her brow. 'I'd registered with NORCAP on your birthday, and since then I'd been running for the morning post much like I used to run for my *Bunty* comic when I was eight. Except *Bunty* used to come regularly, on a Thursday I think it was. Whereas your letter never came.'

'I'm sorry. I didn't know.'

'Don't be sorry, love. Nothing for you to be sorry about. It's me that's sorry.'

'No. Don't say that.'

'Well I won't if you won't, eh? How about that?' Her left eye closed again but only a little way – her tic or mannerism or whatever it was – and she laughed the small gasping laugh he now recognised as hers.

He laughed too, in a similar way, and again closed his left eyelid a little. 'And then?'

'Then? Then nothing. The months passed. Spring, summer, autumn, and before I knew it, it was Christmas. David said I should forget about it, but I couldn't. I thought you must have decided to live your life without me, and that was fair enough.'

'No!' Christopher raised their tangled fingers to his lips and kissed the knot they had made. Odd, that he felt no strangeness in doing this. Just the opposite, in fact.

'It's all right,' she said. 'You'd every right to make your choice, love. I couldn't say I'd made mine back then, but that was my fate.'

'What do you remember about me?'

'Your smell,' she said quickly, and smiled. 'The way your head smelled, especially in the morning, the day after you were born. I inhaled it like it was Vicks, and I remember thinking, I could live off that smell. I wouldn't need food or water or anything, just that. And your head was so soft and your eyes were so round and wise, as if you'd been here before and you were looking at me as if to say, *What are you doing here?* And then I suppose my most vivid memory after that is handing you over. Sister Lawrence. She had this placid smile and I wanted to punch her, punch that smile right off her face. Not that that would have solved anything. She was all right, one of the nice ones. And I was fifteen. I had no real idea of what I was doing – I couldn't grasp the enormity of it. I put my baby into a stranger's arms because that's what I was told to do. But my hands had become hot and sticky with holding you and they got stuck under your head. Sister Lawrence had to slide her own hand between your head and my hand and kind of prise you away.'

'Where was this?'

'At the convent. We were in the mother superior's office. Some girls had their whole pregnancy there, but I was allowed to stay at home. I wasn't allowed out of the house once I started to show, but at least I wasn't at the convent. Bloody miserable place.'

'Were you alone?'

'No. If my memory serves, my parents took me there with you in my arms and drove me back alone. And that's when I left you. There was no conversation before, and when they drove me home, no conversation then either. The subject was never mentioned again. You were never mentioned again. Nothing, not a word, as if removing a whole human being from our lives was little more than the end of a chapter. It was all at best inconvenient, at worst unfortunate. Any attempt to speak of it beyond that day was to pay too much attention to something best forgotten.' She stopped, rubbed her forehead, ran her hand over her eyes. 'Different times.'

'You don't have to say any more.' It cost him all his will to say it. He wanted more. He wanted all of it. Every detail played out, second by second.

'It's OK,' she said. 'They know about you, Mum and Dad. Now, I mean. They're looking forward to meeting you. Thing is, we're not going to get anywhere looking backwards and blaming people, are we? It was a long time ago.'

How wise she was – how good, how kind.

'Are you all right?' he asked her.

'Of course, love,' she said, patting his hand. And then, after a moment, 'Gerard, that was the mother superior's name. This was at St Matthew's. I missed my O levels. I took them a year later at college. I'm grateful to my parents for that. They were very particular about that, and I would never have become a teacher without them. I was bitter at them for years, of course, but now I think they were trying to do right by me, that's all. I'd always been bright at school and they didn't want to see me waste it.' She breathed deeply, shook her head as if to clear it before continuing. 'The mother superior's office was a drab old place though. You should have seen it. Brown, everything brown, although that could just be how I remember it – maybe I've got it in sepia tones in my mind or something like those old photos. When I think of it, I can smell dust even though there wasn't a speck. Incense, too, and something else, which I think now must have been carbolic soap or some such. None of your Shield there, I can tell you – none of your Impulse body spray or what have you. No smell, no colour. Even the books were brown – it's a wonder I didn't develop a hatred of them right there and then, a wonder that they, not God, became my salvation.'

'Salvation?'

'Yes, love. Education. Look at you, at university. It's fabulous. You'll get your degree and you'll be able to get a decent job rather than stacking shelves or emptying bins like some of these poor souls. You're going to have a good life, Christopher. There's nothing stopping you.'

'No,' he said, feeling his chest loosen and swell. 'Not now.'

'I'm already proud of you and I've only known you five minutes.' This time when she laughed, he laughed with her. He had known she was going to laugh, had seen her eyelid begin to quiver, so was able to meet her laugh with his own. As he laughed, he felt his left eyelid lower and wondered if he'd always done this and was only noticing it now.

'And that was it really,' she said. 'I had to sign some papers, I remember, though I can't remember any of the words. I just signed. Insidious duress, I'd call it now. I was fifteen, did I mention that? It outrages me even now. Signature! I didn't have a signature! What fifteen-year-old has a signature? I didn't even have a chequebook! I just wrote my name in my best handwriting, that was all. I consigned my Martin, you, to the arms of a nun not much older than me, and that was it.' She began to cry. 'Sorry, ignore me. I haven't talked about it for a long time.'

He pushed his arm all the way around her shoulders. Her shoulders were narrow; in the cup of his hand he could feel the small square of bone at the top. It was only after he had put his arm around her that he realised he had done it. But even then, on realising, he had no desire to pull it away.

'I didn't cry,' she said, composing herself, reaching into her sleeve for a handkerchief. 'Not then. I signed, and then I gestured to Sister Lawrence to let me take my baby one last time. I wanted to press my nose into the soft folds of his... of your neck. I wanted to breathe my last breath of you. Your own baby's neck, the softness, the sweet smell... I can't even put that into words, Christopher. I only hope you get to experience it one day and you'll know what I mean. I thought if I could inhale you, I could breathe you into my marrow or bottle you and stopper you inside me or something, but they wouldn't let me take you. I can remember my mother turning me by the shoulders and walking me to the door. It was all so bloody gentle, so bloody quiet. But inside I was a volcano. And I've played that moment over too many times to count and each time I wonder how I didn't scream, why I didn't throw my mother's hands from my shoulders, snatch my baby and run out of there and never come back. I could have taken my chances. You and me against the world. But I didn't. And that's what I'm sorry about. No amount of confessions can remove the weight of that.'

She pressed her hands flat over her face and wept. He pulled her small body towards him. She let her head rest against his chest and sobbed into her hands, and he kissed her hair and told her it was all right. It was all right. It was all right.

'I'm here now,' he said. 'No one can take you away from me.'

CHAPTER TWELVE

Ben reaches the apartment a little before six. When he steps inside, Martha gives a sweet cry of delight. He has kept his promise. That it's enough to make her squeal in surprise opens a chasm of guilt in his chest.

He holds up the bottle of Moët & Chandon he has picked up on the way home. 'You, my beautiful one, are looking at Benjamin Bradbury, future senior designer and winner of the Oakland branding contract.'

She whoops, claps her hands and laughs.

He takes her in his arms. 'Wait a second.' He puts the sweating bottle on the table and takes hold of her once again. He buries his mouth and nose in her soft neck. She smells of the coconut soap she favours, and the downy softness and sweet smell of her skin make him want to tear off her clothes and forget about everything but her. He runs his hand down her neck, onto her breast.

'Come on,' she says, taking hold of his hands. 'Not so fast. Let's do a toast.'

'A kiss.' He pulls her back into him and kisses her deeply. She responds, sliding her hands to his buttocks before pulling away again.

She pushes her thumb against his lips. 'Don't look at me like that. Pour your woman a drink, at least. I'm not some cheap floozy, you know.'

She fetches two glasses. He opens the champagne with a pop. He pours it, raises his glass but changes his mind. He puts his glass aside and drops to one knee.

'What are you doing?' She's still holding her glass, waiting to drink.

'I don't have a ring or anything, Martha,' he says. 'I wasn't planning on doing this right now, but I just realised I can't wait another second to ask you if you'll marry me. So, Martha, will you? Will you marry me? Please?'

The room has stilled, the air turned thick. For a moment, fear clenches his jaw. She kneels down on the kitchen floor, pulls his glass from the tabletop and hands it to him. She meets his gaze with her steadfast green eyes.

'Idiot,' she says. 'Of course I will.'

Later, when they have made love and drunk the rest of the champagne and shared a light joint in bed, he lies with Martha dozing in the crook of his arm. Only now, in the warm peace, does his phone call with his mother come back to him. He should call his parents now, he thinks. Call and tell them the news. It is in moments such as this that he is filled with regret.

Physical distance had been his only intention going to college so far away from them. He didn't hate his parents or anything. But once the first semester in California was through, the thought of returning to Washington brought with it only dread. So he didn't go, pleading a flu virus that had swept through the university. A particularly virulent strain, for such a complete fabrication.

'But you didn't come home for Thanksgiving,' Dorothy had said. 'Will you even be here for Christmas?'

He'd listened for the chink of ice in the glass but had given no answer.

By the end of his final year, Dorothy called but once a month, and only to ask if he was eating enough, whether he needed any money. He had not spoken to George, his father, since they'd fought over Nixon. Carter was in the White House now, of course, but the damage had been done.

'Well I guess I should let you get on now,' Dorothy always said when she herself could no longer bear the strain. 'Your father says hello.'

'OK, Dorothy. Thanks. And thanks for the money. Tell George I said hi, OK?'

Ben had stopped saying he'd go visit real soon. Martha had pulled him up so many times for lying. It was only through her that he'd realised he did lie – out of habit. She taught him that there was rarely any real need to lie, that actually the truth was almost always easier. By then she was his world, his refuge, his home.

He'd met her in his final year. She was in the university bar with a bunch of girlfriends and had stood up to use the bathroom. The alcohol hit her – at least that was what they decided when they discussed it afterwards – and she fainted against his back. When she came round, he was sitting on the floor of the bar, her head in his lap.

'Hi,' she said and smiled that sweet and sleepy smile. 'I was playing quarters.'

'You should really give that up,' he said. 'You suck.'

'You're right. I need to find another game.'

They said nothing else for maybe five or ten minutes.

'Listen,' he said eventually. 'I feel bad, but my thighs have gone numb and I really need to move my legs…'

'Oh, sure.'

He helped her raise her head, pressed the glass of water to her mouth. She drank, eyeing him like a child taking the host from the priest.

'Thanks,' she said, getting herself upright now. 'I'm reading anthropology. I'm not usually this wasted, but I was doing it for research.'

'Is that right?'

'Uh-huh. Effects of tequila shots on the contemporary human.' She held out her hand. 'My name's Martha Edwards.'

'Ben Bradbury.' He shook her hand. His left, her right: awkward, more like a step at a barn dance than a greeting. But he held on anyway.

After graduation, he asked her to move in with him and felt his life start. She felt it too, he thought – there was a new seriousness about her, a desire to put the madness of college behind them and find something more substantial. She applied to train as an elementary-school teacher, and he resolved to find work in design: something good, something *impressive*. Martha was proud of his commitment. She said it came from love. But he wondered later, looking back, whether it came from nothing more noble than a desire to prove George and Dorothy wrong – about art, about politics, about everything. And when George pulled in a contact and found Ben a job at a reputable design company back in DC, a fact communicated to Ben via Dorothy, he said thank you, he was real grateful, but he preferred to stay with Martha in California.

The gamble paid off. An impressive portfolio and a certain relaxed charm that can only be acquired by misspending at least some of your youth on marijuana, girls and good times soon found Ben a job at United Graphics, a company specialising in corporate-identity branding. The open-plan office in downtown San Francisco came complete with fashionable red chairs and desks of black-stained wood. His job title was Junior Illustrator, apprentice to a creative manager called Darko, whose glasses were pieces of electric-blue plastic with lenses dropping onto each cheek and whose designer sneakers Ben was determined to fill once Darko became senior creative director. By '82 – that's his aim.

He feels Martha stir beside him.

'My shoulders are cold,' she says. She sits up, her long back lean and strong, the hint of a tan line at the bottom. 'I'm thirsty, do you want some water?'

'Sure.'

She reaches to the end of the bed and rifles through the clothes they threw there. Pulls out his black T-shirt and puts it on. He watches her walk out into the light from the hallway. His T-shirt reaches the top of her thighs, and at the sight of her he feels himself stir.

She comes back with two glasses and hands one to him, climbs back into bed and pushes her feet under the quilt.

'So did you do that thing?'

'Not yet.'

She drinks her water. 'What've you got to lose? Maybe they could put you in touch. I know they like to go slowly with these things. You have to write them.'

'I'm not doing it that way. I've decided. These people are bureaucrats. Doing things the proper way takes way too long, man. Trust me.'

In his mother's purse all those years ago had been a small black-and-white photo of a baby in the arms of a nun. On the back was the date, and the name of the convent. He had pocketed the photo and, with the passion of an eight-year-old child, resolved to set off that very evening. He packed a bag with some clothes, some sandwiches and the card for his Child Saver bank account. Figured he'd hitch a ride across America then stow away on a boat. After that, it could not be far to the convent. He had looked on a map and Liverpool was right there on the coast – on the near side of England! He would simply show up and ask to look at their records. But that evening Dorothy made chicken casserole with dough balls and it smelled good, so he put the photo in his tin safe and locked the padlock and kept it safe for the following day.

Week.

Month.

Year.

'I know where the convent is,' he says now, to the love of his life, a woman so unlike Dorothy, who cares no more for cocktail parties than for a trip to the moon, a woman who is happy if you so much as smile and lay your hand against her cheek. 'I have a photo. All I need to do is rock up there and ask. They'll have records, they must do. I just need to find the time is all.'

Looking at Martha now, her strawberry-blonde hair mussed up from the activities of the last hour, he thinks that if he leaves it much longer to find out who he really is, he might be halfway to being a father himself.

He lays his head on her lap. She takes his head in her hands and brings her face down to his to kiss.

'I love you,' he says.

'However you want to do this thing, you should do it now,' she says.

'I should. Then we can get married.'

'Then we can get married.'

The day after the Oakland deal is finalised, he books the flight: an open return to London. From there he'll hire a car. He's going to need the flexibility. He'll need his own steam.

CHAPTER THIRTEEN

It was the first Saturday in March. Phyllis had asked Christopher to come and stay for the weekend. I can picture him, standing outside the front door, palms sweating around the cellophane wrap of carnations he told me he'd picked up from the garage. For each of the twins he had bought a Marathon bar, a packet of Chewits and one of Spangles. He was generous, was Christopher. That's something you should know about him. He only ever wanted to please.

Since his first visit, a few weeks ago now, he and Phyllis had agreed that he would phone her every Sunday evening. No such arrangement with Jack and Margaret; Christopher saved all his coppers for Phyllis, for the moment he would head down to the payphone and queue behind the other students waiting to call their families.

The sound of her voice down the line was a drug, the days between calls cold turkey, the shakes coming in the form of vivid dreams in which nothing more happened than the two of them talking in the soft pink light he always imagined, her head on his chest. He could still feel the small square bone of her shoulder in the cup of his hand, could still watch her laugh in his mind's eye whenever he wanted, replay and replay the way her left eye half-closed when she heard or said something funny or peculiar or embarrassing or suspicious. When she spoke on the telephone, he pictured her in this way, her face, the way she smiled. He thought of her hair against his lips, the soap fragrance, the silence in the warm living room.

The two of them sitting together on the sofa while she told him the story of his birth had been exactly as he had imagined.

In-between calls he wrote to her with the kind of news he could never share with Jack and Margaret:

Another night out with Adam and the electronic-engineering boys last night. Siouxsie and the Banshees were playing at the Union. I lost count of how many pints I drank – those boys are a bad influence all right! Back to the library with a sore head for me today… I shall do well not to fall asleep at my desk.

He said to me once that it was as if he had found in Phyllis a personality for himself that had been his all along, as if she had been its custodian these past eighteen years, and now that they had finally met, she had handed it over to him. Her lightness took away his weight, he said. Her love untangled the rope.

Newsflash! I have grown a beard. All Adam's idea, of course, part of his Christopher project, but he says it suits me. You shall have to tell me what you think when you see me. I'm not at all sure.

She replied:

A beard, eh? Heavens! I can't wait to see you with it. I bet you look swish… Our Darren's been in another fight at school. Takes after his dad, obviously. Bellicose little bugger… I'm doing Tess of the d'Urbervilles with my fifth years this term, have you read it? Do you like Thomas Hardy? We're doing Antony and Cleopatra too, and Keats. I love Keats, do you? 'Beauty is truth, truth beauty!' … David and I are off out to see Star Wars with the twins at the weekend. I wish you were coming with us.

Phyllis's letters were informal, chatty, but in them were flashes of the English teacher she was too. He read them over and over. On the page as in life, she flitted from subject to subject with a restlessness he'd noticed when they'd met. He had this same restlessness, he thought. He must have got it from her. He borrowed a book from the library: *Poems of John Keats*. He copied quotes from it into his letters, to please her.

He did not tell her he had kept their reunion secret from Margaret and Jack.

She did not ask.

The weeks passed. Every moment not spent talking to her, writing to her or reading her letters he endeavoured to fill with studies or trips to the pub. Drink helped. And though he told Phyllis all about his drunken antics with Adam and the boys up and down the Otley Road, he made no mention of her to them. But on such high-jinks nights in Woodies, the Three Horseshoes or the New Inn, Phyllis would be with him, there in his head and heart, laughing along in that way she had. In these moments a strange and secret happiness brought to his reticent lips a smile over which he had no control, and he felt himself unfold, thought he might one day wrap himself around life the way Adam did. One day.

Love is where the idle mind wanders.

And now he was here, at her door, bracing himself to meet his other family, the 'mad family' as she called them. He saw the coddled shape of her through the bevelled glass and felt his stomach lurch. She opened the door and smiled with such apparent delight that he found himself catching his breath. This delight was for *him*. It was because of *him*.

'Christopher!' She had already reached out for him, was already pulling him towards her. The cellophane rustled against his chest. He feared she might crush the flowers but she stood back and took them from him. 'Love the beard! You look older – not sure I want that, eh? Just kidding. And you brought flowers! Aren't you lovely?'

Lovely. 'I…'

'Come in, come in, we're all here.'

Inside, he could hear the television, and then the door to the living room opened and a boy's face appeared around the jamb. He grinned and disappeared. Christopher heard the television die, then came whispering, then a man stepped out, smiled and came towards him.

'Christopher – pleased to meet you, lad. I'm David. Come in, come in, come and meet the troublemakers.' He shook Christopher's hand, his grip firm, his brown eyes not leaving his. He was clean-shaven, his dark brown hair long at the back, the front spiky as a sea urchin at the top of his wide forehead. Christopher estimated his age to be around thirty-five. 'So glad you made it over. We've heard a lot about you. Honestly, I'm glad you're here because I thought Phyl was going to explode, and I'd hate to have to clean that lot off the walls.'

Phyl. 'Hello, David, pleased to—'

'Give over.' Phyllis had closed the front door and now ushered him further into the house. 'Take no notice of him, Christopher. He's a big bloody tease.'

Guided by Phyllis – Phyl – he followed David to where the twins were wrestling on the living-room floor.

'Oi, you two, pack it in.' David separated the boys and held their wriggling forms by the hand. He lifted the hand of one, like a referee announcing the winner of a boxing match. 'This is Darren,' he said. 'He arrived first so is technically the oldest.' He let Darren's hand drop and lifted the other's. 'And this is Craig.'

Both were dark like their father, dressed identically in navy blue polo shirts and jeans that hovered around their ankles. At the waists, they both wore red-and-blue-striped elasticated belts with

S-clip fasteners. David shook them by the arms so that they danced like puppets, making them both giggle. 'Say hello then, you two.'

'Hello then, you two,' Darren said.

'Cheeky bugger,' said David.

'Hello,' said Craig and buried his head in his father's belly.

Phyllis had been right. The boys didn't look like her at all and the realisation made Christopher sigh with relief. He could see David in them though – in the line of their brow and eyes, the set of their mouths, especially now as they grinned and threw sideways glances at each other. Behind them, on the television, the Incredible Hulk smashed up an office in silence.

'Pleased to meet you both.' Christopher stepped forward for a handshake, hoping that was the right thing to do. One after the other and both still giggling, the boys took his hand and shook it rather limply. 'Oh! I almost forgot, these are for you.' He dug in his canvas army-surplus bag and took out the sweets.

'Yes!'

In a flash, the goodies were swiped from his open palm.

'Oi, you two,' said David. 'Don't snatch! And say thank you to Christopher.'

'Thank you to Christopher,' said Darren, which earned him a cuff around the ear. 'Ow!'

'Thank you!'

'Come into the kitchen, Christopher.' Phyllis's hand was on his shoulder. While David admonished the twins for their bad manners, she led him into the kitchen and gestured for him to sit at the table. 'Let me get you a drink. Tea? Something stronger?'

'Tea's fine, thank you.' He watched her walk over to the kettle by the window. She was wearing a dress this time; the soft plum-coloured fabric swung around her calves as she moved. She was so much younger than Margaret. Not like a mother at all. He wanted to talk to her all day, exhaust himself discovering all her mysteries until he knew her back to front and inside out. He should not, he felt, voice this thought aloud.

'What's this about tea?' David had come into the kitchen. 'We can't be drinking bloody tea on a day like today, mate.' He walked past Christopher to the fridge, opened it and pulled out a bottle of wine. 'This is a big celebration. You don't get to meet your grown-up stepson every day of the week, do you? Lambrusco. Can't run to champers, I'm afraid, but at least this has bubbles. Do you like frizzy, Christopher? I've got some tins of Greenall's or I've got larger. You name it.'

Christopher wondered which was the right answer, and whether David had said frizzy and larger on purpose. It was the kind of joke Adam might make, so he decided not to question it.

'I like anything,' he said. 'Lager?'

'Larger it is. Good man!'

To Christopher's relief, David gave him a thumbs-up before retrieving two cans of Carling Black Label from the fridge and bringing them over together with the wine. 'You'll have vino, won't you, Phyl?' He winked, inexplicably, at Christopher. 'She is très sophisticated, your mother.'

Mother.

Christopher felt his heart in his throat. Instinctively he looked over to where she stood at the sink. Beyond her, he glimpsed the garden and the shed through the back window. The curtains were made from pink gingham – bright and fresh – and on the windowsill was a pot of shiny green chives. This house, the way it felt to be here, was lovely. David had opened the cans and was pouring Christopher's lager into a glass with bottle-top windows and a handle, a pint glass like they had in pubs. He held it out to him, its froth an inch thick at the top.

'Ice-cream-cone job, I'm afraid, but it'll calm down.'

'Ice cream?' Christopher took hold of the glass.

'The head. Too much froth. I poured it too fast, sorry.'

Still Christopher had no idea what his stepfather was talking about, but again he decided to leave it.

'This'll knock her out, you'll see.' David opened the wine and poured a glass for Phyllis. 'She's not had a wink of sleep, it'll go straight to her head.' He held up his beer glass. 'Here's to you, Christopher. I for one am very glad to meet you, and I want to say thank you right from the word go for making my missus a very happy woman.' He coughed, as if embarrassed, and touched his glass against Christopher's. 'If I could make her half that happy, I'd be doing very well indeed.'

For a moment Christopher couldn't move. He wanted to pick up his own glass but there was no strength in his hands. And she, lovely Phyllis, had come over to the table and sat across from him, and now the three of them were sharing a drink at home on a Saturday afternoon like it was the most natural thing in the world. Phyllis was smiling at him, her eyes soft, as if he were her little boy and had done something that had made her proud. But he had done nothing, only walked into the house and sat down.

Later, while David went to the parade of shops further up the road, Christopher helped Phyllis with the dinner.

'This is so nice, isn't it?' Phyllis said, reading his mind. 'I mean, it's nothing special, is it, peeling carrots at the kitchen table with your eldest son, but at the same time, it is, so very special, do you know what I mean?'

'I do.'

'I mean, not that I'm glad I've been without you, but if you hadn't gone away and come back, I might never have appreciated a moment like this.'

Moments like this were all they had, he thought. And it was enough. He passed her a carrot and picked up the next one.

'I think perhaps I'll learn to cook,' he said. 'I can't even boil an egg.'

'Boiled eggs are the hardest. You can't tell what's going on inside, can you?'

'No,' he said. 'No, you can't.'

She nudged his elbow with hers. 'I'll teach you. If you come back, that is.'

'I'll come back,' he said, too quickly, his voice louder than he had meant. 'I'll come back as often as you'll have me.'

'Every weekend then.'

He knew she was joking, but at the same time she was not. And nor was he, not entirely, when he replied, 'Every weekend it is.'

Phyllis got up, brought a second bottle of wine from the cupboard and held it up.

'We don't usually drink red wine,' she said, a little abashed. 'David said we should buy it because you were coming and he said to buy red because we're having lamb chops. Do you like red wine, Chris?'

He shook his head. 'I don't know. We have sherry on Christmas Day, but that's it.'

'Heavens, you must think we're alcoholics!'

'I don't. No. I would never—'

'Relax, Chris, love,' she said. 'I'm only pulling your leg.' She laughed, but tenderly, and stroked his hair. 'Let's get this open anyway.'

The rattle of the key in the lock, the muffled chaos of the twins coming in. Christopher's chest sank.

'We're back!' David came through first, bringing the cold from outside with him into the kitchen. 'Good man, you're opening the red, what's it like?'

'We were waiting for you, weren't we, Christopher?' Phyllis said, glancing at Christopher, meeting his eye. From this look, he understood that he should agree, even though they had been about to drink it without David.

'Yes,' he said. 'We were waiting for you to taste it.'

The evening passed like none Christopher could remember. They ate hungrily, talked easily, as if they'd known each other for a long time. The light fell, and when the plates were clean, Christopher jumped up to clear them away.

'Stay where you are, you,' said David, pushing him with some force back into his seat. 'You're our guest.'

A little drunk by now, Christopher became aware of fussing behind the open fridge door.

'Close your eyes, Christopher,' Phyllis called.

'All right.' He closed his eyes, though not tight.

'Watch it,' came Phyllis's voice, though she was not talking to him. 'Careful.'

'Let me do some.' Craig – almost definitely.

A glow, dim against the brush of his eyelashes. He opened his eyes. Phyllis was walking towards him, flanked by the twins and holding a cake covered in candles.

'Darren,' she said. 'Go and turn off the big light.'

Darren ran and flicked the switch. The room darkened.

'It's someone's birthday next Sunday,' said Phyllis. 'March the twelfth. Ring any bells?'

Christopher's cheeks burned. He was about to protest, but David was already counting one, two, three, and then he, the twins and Phyllis were singing 'Happy Birthday' at the top of their voices.

Christopher pressed his hands to his face, a sob catching in his throat. They finished singing and cheered.

'Come on, Christopher,' said Phyllis. He heard her nearness in her voice – she was right there at his knee. 'Blow out the candles then.'

He breathed in as deeply as he could, his breath snagging with emotion. He could not take his hands from his face.

'Come on, my love,' said Phyllis again. 'Don't hide.'

Composing himself as best he could, he lowered his hands and blew out all the candles in one go.

'Great pair of lungs,' said David.

Phyllis passed the cake to her husband, muttered something Christopher didn't catch. He wiped his face, unable to speak.

'Come here, you big daft thing.' Phyllis took his head in her hands and hugged it to her stomach.

'I'm sorry,' he said, the warm, soft flesh of her belly against his cheek.

'Is he crying?' said Darren.

'He's a bit overcome, that's all,' said Phyllis. 'It's a big day, is this. A big day for all of us.'

'Can we eat the cake now?' said Craig.

'Shut up, Craig, before I brain you,' came David's voice, and Christopher wished they would leave him and Phyllis alone, to have this moment together.

Phyllis squeezed his head once more before pushing him back gently and kissing him on the forehead.

'My darling, darling boy,' she said, thumbing away his tears. 'It's all too much, isn't it? Of course it is.' She pressed her forehead to his. 'My precious lad. You've no idea how happy you've made me.'

And Christopher did make people happy – I believe that even now. He made me happy. We made each other happy. But sometimes, when we lay our hopes for happiness in another person, we become blind. To others, to ourselves. That kind of happiness cannot last. It did not. It could not.

CHAPTER FOURTEEN

Ben picks up his hire car from Heathrow Airport. A red Ford Fiesta, an upgrade he got by charming the woman on the desk. It is a trip, driving on the left-hand side of the road, but he gets used to it quickly enough. He is still tired from the flight but determined to push on. He only has a week, after all.

When he's made it clear of Heathrow, he pulls into a service station so he can check the map. He's bought an Ordnance Survey book of Great Britain from a shop in the airport called John Menzies and flips it open now on his lap. He takes notes – the road names, the junctions he will need.

The drive goes smoothly enough. Outside Birmingham he stops and buys a cup of coffee and a bacon sandwich, which he eats in the car. The sandwich is damp, the bread flaccid and the coffee bitter. Still, this isn't a gourmet tour he's on. Nor is it business. He should probably stop soon, maybe find a motel, if they even have those here – his flight was so early – 6 a.m. And here it's only 2 p.m., which feels weird because that's still 6 a.m., as if time has stood still. He figures if he pushes himself he can reach Railton by 5 p.m. English time. By then for him it'll be 9 a.m. He should still be OK – won't be the first time he's put in crazy hours. Besides, once he's found the place, he can book a hotel somewhere near. He wonders if they'll see him today. He hopes so. He is very persuasive, so Martha says, and anyway, how hard can it be to persuade a nun?

He pats his chest and feels the documents in his pocket. His birth certificate, his passport. They're enough, he hopes. They'd better be.

CHAPTER FIFTEEN

Thursday 9th March
Dear Christopher,

Happy birthday! I hope this card arrives in time! We loved having you here. Me especially, but David and the boys too. The boys are asking after you, asking if you'll come again the weekend after this one. They want you to play football with them – they go to the town hall grounds, which aren't too far away. So will you come? I'll be in on Thursday night and David's out at football training (all football mad in this house), so if you give me a ring, we can arrange it. If not, the following weekend or whenever you're free.

He held the card to his chest. He had promised Adam he would go out that weekend but knew already, had known as soon as he'd read her invitation, that he would head back to her, to Phyllis, instead.

The following Friday morning, he took the train once more to Warrington.

'I've invited my parents for dinner tomorrow,' Phyllis said as soon as they were in the car. 'I hope you don't mind.'

He remembered their pictures above the gas fire, and later how he and Phyllis had flicked slowly through the family album together. He had been right: his grandparents were young – fifty-six, only six years older than Jack and Margaret. In the photos, they wore jeans. Christopher had never seen either of his parents wear jeans.

'Do you have a photo of my father?' He had found the words to ask her.

She had shaken her head, no. 'I'm so sorry. I have nothing. But he was tall, like you, with lovely green eyes. And he was kind, like you, I think. He had a kind way about him.'

He could not meet Mikael, could not study him for a likeness. It was not the end of the world, he thought. In fact, he said, it was better that way.

'In that case…' Phyllis was saying now as she pulled onto the roundabout. Christopher wondered what she'd said before that – he had been miles away. 'I can tell you I've invited our Miriam, her Brian and their teenage kids, Sophie and Ian. Oh, and David's mum – his dad passed away last year. She's lovely, is Helen – you'll like her.'

A wave of nerves passed through him but he hid it.

'I'm sure I'll like all of them,' he said. 'I only hope they like me.'

'Of course they'll like you. They'll love you. What's not to love? You're my son, aren't you? Listen, we've never been allowed to speak about you all this time, so any opinion they have of you will be from now on, fresh-slate type thing. Even with our Miriam I've only talked about you a handful of times. It's funny – we've always called you Martin. It's the only name we had obviously. But don't worry, I've told them to call you Christopher. I've told them you're not Martin any more.'

At the house, Phyllis told him more about his father: how he had spoken with a Polish accent – she imitated him – how he had taken her to the Scala in the old town and to the Cavern once in his friend's car, and how she, no more than a girl, had been impressed by this.

'I'm sorry I can't tell you more,' she said, holding his hand as she always did. 'Only that the last time I saw him, he took my cigarette lighter and he never gave it back.'

'I know plenty,' he said. 'He was kind. He was tall. He was a Polish sailor. Maybe I'll meet him one day.'

'Well, if you do, tell him I said can I have my lighter back.'

Theirs was a conversation begun late, yes, but without end. He made no move to withdraw his hand from hers until, at 4 p.m., the boys arrived from school – all limbs, satchels and coats. Christopher sat quietly in the corner of the kitchen while Phyllis fussed them, gave them jam butties and glasses of milk. After saying cursory hellos to him, his presence apparently nothing special, they disappeared off with their football. Phyllis followed them to the front door and called after them, 'Zip your coats up, boys. You'll catch your deaths. And be careful crossing the big road.'

And like that, once again he and Phyllis were alone and he felt the thrill of it in his body. She opened the bottle of Lambrusco he had bought from Morrisons on the way down to Leeds station. 'You shouldn't bring stuff like a guest,' she said, pouring the wine. 'You're family now.'

'It's nothing.'

He had walked everywhere all week – from the halls into the faculty and back again – and put each bus fare towards the bottle.

She smiled and held up her glass. 'Here's to you, kid.'

'No. To you.'

They were two thirds down the bottle when the front door banged.

Phyllis pulled her hand from Christopher's. Christopher's chair scraped across the linoleum, but before he could stand or move further from her, David was at the kitchen door, looking from him to Phyllis and back again. Something flashed in his eyes, no more than a glance, before he grinned in his usual way.

'Christopher brought wine,' Phyllis said quickly. 'I know you don't like this one so I thought there was no harm opening it.'

'I don't know,' said David, shaking his head and pulling a can of Carling from the fridge. 'Boozing in the afternoon. I'll have to watch you two.'

*

The next day, Saturday, while David took the twins to the swimming baths in Ellesmere Port, Christopher helped Phyllis prepare the buffet for the family. She giggled when he turned to her from the oven, floral oven gloves up his forearms, his glasses fogged up from the heat.

'What?' he said, which made her laugh more.

At last she stood back from the table, her brow furrowed. Together they took an inventory: mushroom vol-au-vents, prawn cocktail vol-au-vents, chicken vol-au-vents, a quiche Lorraine, an army of sausage rolls – *that's the collective noun for sausage rolls*, said Phyllis – sandwiches of egg mayonnaise, ham and mustard, cheese and pickle; chicken drumsticks that Phyllis had cooked the previous afternoon, Quavers, Skips and crisps, Twiglets, cheese straws with cream cheese inside, skinned peanuts and raisins…

'Do you think we've got enough?' She turned to look at him, her eyes pleading.

'I can't remember what the tablecloth looks like,' he said. 'Yes, yes, there's enough. More than enough.'

'Are you sure?' She rubbed her hands and bit her bottom lip. 'There's two Sara Lee cakes, so we should be all right, and I've got a tub of Wall's Neapolitan in the freezer.'

'Phyllis.' He laid his hands on her little shoulders. It wasn't the food she was nervous about. Of course, why hadn't he seen that before? 'Relax,' he said, to himself as well as her. 'It will be fine.'

'Only it's… that this is all so wonderful, what's happened.' Her eyes brimmed. 'But it's so wonderful it's making me panic.' She pressed her head to his chest and threw her arms around his waist. He found himself with no choice but to put his arms around her. She was warm against him, and he felt the pulse of her life beating against his belly. He closed his eyes, wanting to savour the feeling, but was conscious that David would be back at any moment. Taking hold of her hands and pushing her back gently he said, 'I'll go and have a wash, I think.' He smelled his hands, as if to reinforce his point. 'Yes. I smell of egg mayonnaise.'

He was upstairs, bent over the bathroom sink, when he heard the doorbell. He came down, expecting to see David and the boys, but when he went into the living room he was met instead by an older couple. His grandparents then. Here they were.

'Christopher.' Phyllis rushed to the door to meet him and took his hand. 'This is Norman, my dad, and Pat, my mum.'

They smiled at him and said hello. The moment was so very strange, he told me. He was studying them so hard for a likeness to himself, for acceptance too, that when they smiled and said only hello, a sigh escaped him.

Phyllis squeezed then let go of his hand. 'It's OK,' she whispered.

He stepped towards his grandparents.

'Pleased to meet you.' The words caught in his throat. He coughed into his fist before trying again. 'Pleased to meet you. Sorry. Yes, I'm Christopher Harris, your... I'm – I was – Martin.'

'Pleased to meet you, young sir,' his grandfather interrupted, saving him. He was tall, Christopher noted with relief, and though his cuff of hair was grey now, in the photos it had been black.

'Pleased to meet you,' came his grandmother's echo. Christopher scrutinised her face but found no evidence he could seize and make his. 'You're a fine lad. Isn't he a fine lad, Norman?'

'He is that.'

They shook hands. A silence followed. But of course these were the first few seconds of something so new, so unrecognisable, that it was all any of them could do, Christopher felt, not to scatter over the floor like so many spilled cocktail sticks.

The others arrived soon after: his aunt and uncle, his cousins, David's mother, who would be his step-grandmother, he supposed. Christopher examined them all for clues, for features he could point to and say, *Look!* Sophie and Miriam both had dark hair; Miriam also had a broadish nose, broader than Phyllis's. Norman did not have that nose but Pat did, perhaps, or similar, and smiley eyes that gave her a myopic, laughing expression. Ian was tall, almost as tall as Christopher. And then there was his real father to think about, who Phyllis had said was also tall. None of them shared Phyllis's way of closing one eye a little whenever she joked or found something peculiar. This was something of her that Christopher alone shared. The thought warmed him, like an illicit secret.

'Tuck in,' Phyllis said – almost cried out. 'Don't stand on ceremony. We're all family here.'

Was it all too much too soon? I find myself wondering that, here, now, thinking about everything he told me. For the rest of that term, Christopher spent every other weekend with Phyllis, and it strikes me now that he went from stranger to son quicker than acquaintance to friend, quicker than most people agree to a second date. But that's the way it happened. Only fools rush in, but love makes fools of us all. And foolishly perhaps, Phyllis helped him with his train fares when she could, money he refused but which she pressed upon him, too insistent and generous for him to fight. She encouraged him to bring his washing, which he did. They spent Saturday mornings watching the twins play football; afternoons, Phyllis taught him to cook in the cosy back kitchen. On Sunday mornings, he went with the family to Mass at St Edward's Church at the end of the road – was introduced to the priest, Father Jacob, as Phyllis's son. After Mass, he helped Phyllis prepare the roast dinner while David took the twins to the swimming baths or to the park for a kick-about.

Happiness altered Christopher's physical appearance. I saw it in the swell of his chest, the way he pulled his shoulders back and how his mouth became an almost permanent smile. During this time, Margaret wrote once a fortnight with news of family life back in Morecambe. Her letters always included his own address in the top-right hand corner, as if to remind him of where he lived. *When are you coming home?* she asked. *Will you be here for Easter Sunday Mass?*

But Phyllis had invited him to come with her, David and the twins to Anglesey for a week at Easter.

Dear Mum and Dad,

   I won't be able to come home at Easter unfortunately. I have been invited to stay with some friends in Anglesey, so if it's all right, I think I will do that.

   I am still working hard. There is a lot of work, more than I thought there would be. But I am keeping my head above water. Thank you for the cheque.

Love,

Christopher

The letter was clearly dishonest, but there was a lie of omission here too. Nowhere in it did he admit that he would be away only for the last week of the Easter break, which left plenty of time free for him to visit, time he had chosen not to spend with them.

Easter came, and with it the news that the police had uncovered another victim: the woman, Yvonne Pearson, another prostitute, had been found under a discarded sofa. She had been there for months.

'God, that's terrible,' said David, closing the *Mirror* in disgust and throwing it on the coffee table of the rental cottage in Aberffraw. It was mid-morning and he had just returned from the paper shop. 'That man is pure evil. Who could do that to a woman? Why would *anybody* do that?'

But it was the thought of the sofa that plagued Christopher. He found himself wondering what kind of fabric covered it, floral or plain, whether it was traditional in style or modern, whether the Ripper had had sexual intercourse with his victim on it prior to putting her body under it. He did not share these thoughts, but once David had finished with the paper, Christopher put it in his bag to take back to Leeds for his scrapbook.

'Let's get out,' said David. 'How about a walk along the beach at Llanfaelog?'

'You go, love,' said Phyllis. 'I fancy a read.'

'Well I need to clean that monster out of my head,' David replied. 'Come on, Christopher, finish your coffee and let's give your mother a break, shall we? Boys! Get your coats!'

Christopher would rather have stayed and talked to Phyllis, but something in David's manner told him he had to go along. David took the cricket bat and ball, and once on the beach, they stopped to play French cricket. The clear air, the crashing of the waves and the game itself raised their spirits. Soon Christopher found himself laughing at almost nothing – the tennis ball falling through his hands, David and the twins crying out *butterfingers*, the way David managed to block every ball, with a cry of *Did you see that? Boycott's got nothing on me!* performing a silly victory dance in full view of the other holidaymakers. The cold, damp shaggy tennis ball in his hand, Christopher pitched it towards David's legs but missed.

'Suffer,' Darren shouted. 'You're rubbish!'

'He's too tall to throw all the way down there,' said David, laughing. 'And his flares get in the way!'

'And his hair,' Darren countered, overexcited as ever, winding his arm like a professional bowler. 'And his beard. He looks like the Ripper!'

Darren pitched the ball. It hit David on the back of the leg. But only because David had already thrown the cricket bat to the ground.

'Don't you ever say that again.' He was striding towards his son, shouting as he went. His face had darkened, the veins on his neck like cables. Darren shrank away from him, a blush deepening. 'I don't want to hear anyone in this family mention that sick bastard, not to me, not to anyone, have I made myself clear?' David's chest subsided, giving him a crestfallen look in the aftermath of his rage. 'Let's head back,' he said quietly. 'It's getting cold.'

'I think Christopher looks like Jesus,' Craig said, his voice full of apology and hope.

When they got back to the cottage, Christopher went straight to the bathroom and studied his face in the mirror. He had seen the artists' sketches of the Ripper on the news, sketches that his mind now overlaid onto his reflection. Darren had a point. With his black beard and hair, he did look a little like those pictures – that is, like *him*. He leaned into the mirror and met his own dark eyes. The hint of blood in the whites, the flecked and deepening brown of the irises, the pupils, dilating now a little, black and unending as an abyss. Were they the eyes of a man? Or a monster?

Later, Christopher helped Phyllis to prepare a cottage pie while David and the twins watched the football. She told him about her work, about the other teachers at the comprehensive school; he spoke mainly about Adam, who was now onto his third girlfriend.

'This one's called Lorraine,' he said, peeling the last strip of skin from a potato and plunging it into cold water. 'But she's not the only one he has on the go. There's Alison, who finished with him but I think he still sees her from time to time. And Sophie, who...' He stopped. Sophie, Adam had said, was just a sex thing, whatever that meant. 'I don't know how... well actually I do. He's not bad looking but he's not a film star or anything. It's more that he always seems to know what to say.' He picked up another potato and began to peel it. 'He calls it chutzpah. It seems to mean not taking no for an answer – at least he doesn't. He simply goes up and talks to them, and then if he gets no response or the wrong response he has this ability to brush it off and move on. It doesn't bother him. Rejection doesn't bother him.' His voice carried an edge. He fell silent.

When after a moment his mother didn't reply, he looked up, worried for a moment that he'd said the wrong thing. She was looking at him very directly, her expression sad.

He set down the potato and the peeler. 'I didn't mean to upset you. What have I said?'

She shook her head and smiled, but even her smile was sad. 'You sound jealous, my love. I know you're not, not really, and you mustn't be. You're worth ten of Adam. Honestly, I wish you could see how handsome you are, Chris. Look at you. You're perfect.'

Christopher felt himself blush but said nothing.

'Now you listen to me,' she went on, quite, quite serious. 'Any girl would be lucky to have you, don't you forget that.'

'Oh, I don't know.'

'Well I do. And I'm a girl, aren't I? And I can tell you with some authority that lots of women like quiet men. God knows there are enough gasbags in this world. There'll be someone out there, someone who really, really, truly gets who you are and who loves you for it. I wonder if Adam will ever have that. You maybe need to realise that it's better to have one person you truly connect with than a thousand girlfriends.'

He thought of Angie. He didn't think what had happened between them could be called connection exactly. More like a short circuit.

'I did have a girlfriend,' he said. 'But it didn't work out. What I mean is, I didn't know what to do.'

'It's like anything else, love. Takes practice. And that person, that girl I'm telling you about, she will understand that because she will understand *you*.'

'You understand me.' It felt like he needed all his courage to look at her.

'I do.' She took his hands in hers. 'I love you, and so will she.' He nodded, unable to speak.

David's shadow fell across the mess of vegetable peelings. Christopher withdrew his hands from Phyllis's, picked up a potato, which slid out of his hand and fell onto the table, then onto the floor. He jumped from his seat and retrieved it, stood to see Phyllis, also out of her chair, giving her husband a kiss on the cheek.

'What's this, a palm-reading?' said David.

'It's called a heart-to-heart,' she replied. 'It's what people who are in touch with their feelings do. I'm trying to give our Christopher some confidence in himself.'

'What's not to be confident about?' David pulled two cans of lager out of the fridge and three glasses from the cupboard. 'Good-looking lad, plenty of smarts. They must be like flies round—'

'Don't you dare, David Griffiths,' Phyllis said, hitting him playfully on the shoulder. 'I've told him he's handsome and clever, but he's more worried about how to chat them up, that kind of thing. You talk to him. You're a right old gobshite, aren't you?' She turned to Christopher and winked.

'Cheeky sod.' David shared the beer between the three glasses. He appeared to be devoting his full attention to this simple task. Perhaps to avoid an ice-cream job. 'You don't need to chat up anything,' he said, handing a glass to Phyllis and one to Christopher, though he was still looking down at the table. Christopher followed his gaze, but saw only potato peelings. 'Questions,' David continued. 'That's what women like. Questions. You need to get out there, find yourself a nice girl your own age and ask her a load of questions.'

There was a pause. When Christopher looked up, he saw that David had raised his glass.

'Cheers,' he said, something expectant in his face, as if he had been waiting for Christopher to look at him, to meet his eye. He turned to Phyllis, pulled her towards him and kissed her slowly on the mouth. Christopher watched, helpless, his hands clenching into fists.

After dinner, David suggested that he and Christopher go for a pint at the local pub. Christopher would have preferred to stay in the warm, next to Phyllis on the sofa, but David had already stood and was pulling his coat from the back of the chair, and for the second time that day, Christopher's gut instinct told him he had to say yes. Once they were outside, however, David appeared to change his mind.

'Actually, let's just go for a walk,' he said. 'I've had enough beer for one night.'

'All right.'

The air had turned chilly now that the sun had set, and Christopher pulled his coat tight around him. Together they walked in the dusk towards the beach, which was at the end of the short road, its sand spreading up onto the tarmac. An anxious feeling had overtaken him. He wondered if David was cross with him, though he could think of no reason for this. Perhaps it was because of the boys this afternoon, Darren's clumsy mention of the Ripper, though why that would make David cross with him, he couldn't fathom.

He followed David to the shoreline, the soft rush of the sea like car tyres over gravel, an orange sun all but melted into the horizon. David picked up a stone and skimmed it across the water.

'She's a very special woman, your mother,' he said.

'Phyllis? I know.'

'She's kind. She's too kind actually.'

Christopher said nothing, but the anxiety he had felt surged inside him.

'It's great that you've found her,' David went on after a moment, bending to pick up more stones to throw into the sea. 'And I can see that you've become close.'

'Close,' Christopher said. 'Yes.'

David stopped skimming stones and threw his arm around Christopher's shoulders. With the other hand he grasped Christopher's waterproof where the hood met the body. There was nowhere to look but into David's eyes, which were strange and blackish in the fallen light.

'She loves, does Phyllis,' he said, his voice thick. 'She's a very loving person. She makes people feel special.'

'Yes.'

'When I met her, I knew from the word go I was going to ask her to marry me, did I ever tell you that?'

'No.'

'Well I did. I knew I'd never find anyone else like her. She's my absolute world.' He looked out towards the sea but kept hold of Christopher's jacket. 'She is my world,' he repeated, turning back to him, those eyes again like nails. 'You understand that, don't you?'

Christopher nodded, fear in his chest and throat like fire.

'I understand,' he said.

David held on for a few more seconds before patting Christopher on the chest as if to flatten it.

'Good,' he said. 'Good man.'

CHAPTER SIXTEEN

Seeing no sign of Adam, Christopher made his way along to the Skyrack for a pint. David had given him a lift back after the holiday and he needed to stretch his legs after the stultifying hours in the car listening to Queen and to David, who had sung along pretty much the whole way.

The Skyrack was packed. He hadn't expected it to be so full on a Sunday, but, he supposed, everyone would be back from their Easter holidays and keen to get back into student life. Seeing no space to stand without feeling self-conscious, he stayed at the bar and lit a cigarette. When Adam had first given him a Players No. 6, Christopher had coughed so much he was almost sick. Now he loved to smoke. It solved all the problems of what to do with his hands.

'Hello, stranger.'

With a pang, he recognised Angie's voice, and when he turned, sure enough, she was standing behind him. Unsure whether to shake her hand or kiss her cheek, he did neither.

'Angie,' he said. 'I… Hello.'

She didn't have her glasses on. Her eyelids looked heavy, with booze perhaps, but her eyes had not lost their mischievous, mocking stare. Her plucked brows were raised, adding to her overall ironic expression. To his annoyance, he felt the heat of a blush creep up his neck.

'Haven't seen you all year,' she said, cocking her head and smiling in the way he had not forgotten. 'October, wasn't it? And here we are about to go into the last term.'

'I've been busy.'

She looked him up and down. 'So I see. Buying clothes. The beard. You look different.'

He took a drag on his cigarette, a slug of Tetley's. 'Different in a good way?'

'Yeah. You don't look quite so much like your mum dressed you.'

He stared at her a moment, unsure, but then she smiled and he smiled too. She was only pulling his leg.

'Adam dresses me now,' he said.

She threw back her head and laughed. He had meant it as a joke, yes, but he hadn't thought it was quite so funny.

'Oh, Christopher,' she said, and sighed before fixing him again with her mocking eyes. She leant towards him and looked up through her eyelashes. 'Between you and me, I think Adam likes telling people what to do. Dangerous charm, that one. Still, Alison's over it now.' She motioned to a group of people – women, actually, about eight or so. Christopher recognised Alison and also Sophie Hampton-Something-or-other, Adam's so-called sex squeeze. He had a date with her the following evening; Christopher remembered him talking about it just before the holidays. He wondered if Alison knew about Sophie and vice versa; wondered just how many women Adam had slept with already, how many he was sleeping with at the present time. It hardly seemed fair.

'That's our collective,' Angie was saying. 'Safety in numbers and all that. Anyone who fancies a drink just has to wait in the foyer at eight.'

'So you all walk together?' He winced. State the obvious, why don't you, Christopher.

'That's the idea, although Sophie's a bit of a one for going off on her own, silly cow. It's really going home alone after dark you have to watch. It's not great coming in a big group, but it's better than being a prisoner.'

'Of course.' He nodded. 'Listen, can I buy you a drink? I mean, is that allowed?'

'You're so funny.' She did not mean amusing, that much was clear, though she spoke, he thought, with affection. She met his eye and raised her eyebrows, and again he had the impression she was drawing him into a conspiracy of sorts, or a trap. She was pretty, very pretty actually, not unlike Phyllis in her colouring and in the indescribable lightness she had about her. 'Go on then,' she said, 'as it's you.'

He bought two pints of Tetley's and brought them back to where Angie waited for him. She had lit a cigarette and offered him one, which he took, to be polite. They talked about how their first years were going so far, about their Easter holidays. Christopher remembered David's advice and asked as many questions as he could, sometimes thinking so hard of the next question that he forgot to listen to the answer. Angie had been home in Blackpool for the whole of Easter but had come back that morning. She made no mention of the disaster that had occurred between them, and he remembered the way she had pocketed her glasses and pressed her warm hand to his face.

'So the streets are no safer but you women have found a way,' he said, but the words sounded clumsy even as he said them, maybe because he knew where he was leading to – trying to lead to, at least.

She shook her head. 'I wish they'd hurry up and catch him. We're terrified, all of us. Alison's not sleeping. That one in January…'

'It's a terrible business all right. And the police don't seem to be any nearer.'

She met his gaze and shook her head. 'They seem to be chasing leads, but they're all dead ends.'

'Angie,' he said, his heart thudding in his chest. 'I know you have your group, but I wondered if you'd let me walk you home?'

He pulled out his jacket and showed her the lining. 'I'm unarmed, as you can see. But I suppose you're organised with the others… forget I asked.'

'I'd love you to,' she said. 'You're all right, you see. I know you – you're safe. Hold on there while I let the girls know. God knows, there's enough of them.'

He watched her wander over to the group. From a distance, it looked as though they were angry with her. Alison glanced over and appeared to scrutinise him for a moment before her face relaxed. She had recognised him, apparently, and gave him a wave. Unsure of how to respond, he crossed the bar to say hello. He thought that might be the normal thing to do under the circumstances but was not sure.

'This is Christopher,' said Angie. 'He's trustworthy. He's walked me home before.'

'You're Adam's room-mate, aren't you?' It was Sophie who had spoken, through a cloud of smoke. She sounded like an actress or a princess or something. She was blonde, which he had not expected, with pale blue eyes. He had imagined her with black hair for some reason, and red-painted lips.

'I am, yes.' He tried to smile, felt like he should apologise or something, but she was still staring at him, her eyelids low, her head tilted back a little.

'He didn't say you were so good-looking,' she said.

'I… ah…'

She threw her gaze to Angie. 'Lucky, lucky lady, Angie.'

'Come on,' said Angie, taking Christopher's arm and rolling her eyes at Sophie. 'Don't let her intimidate you. She eats men for breakfast, lunch and dinner, that one.'

Sophie laughed. 'Don't forget supper, darling. Especially supper. Goodbye.' She waved with only the tips of her fingers. 'Goodbye, Christopher, darling.'

It was a relief to turn away and follow Angie out of the pub. He would walk her right up to the door of her halls, he decided, and give her a friendly hug. It would be an investment.

'They were not happy,' Angie said as they stepped outside. 'But I told them you could be trusted.'

'I'm harmless,' he said, and smiled. 'No victims so far, at least.'

As they walked up the Otley Road, their fingers brushed against one another's once, twice, and on the third time, he took her hand. She did not refuse him. Now that they were walking, he found it easier to talk to her, and he told her about his holiday, about going cockling with the twins on the sands at Newborough Beach.

'You have to wiggle your toes about in the soft muddy part by the sea,' he said, delighting in her groans of disgust. 'And when you feel something sharp or hard, you reach in, and if you're lucky, that's a cockle.'

'Sounds like fun,' she said. 'So these are your brothers?'

'My dad and my twin brothers. They're terrors, those boys. They're good kids though. We're a very close family. They're my world.'

'Aw,' she said. 'You are sweet.'

Angie suggested they go the back way this time, turning right at the Three Horseshoes and heading up Weetwood Lane.

'It's quicker this way,' she said. 'But a lot quieter. It leads all the way to the back of Oxley. I wouldn't have trusted you this way last time.'

The shops dwindled, became houses. After fifteen minutes or so, they reached a sandstone wall on the right, the woodland beyond made spooky by the dark. They crossed the road and headed up a lane. He recognised the sports fields, this time to their right.

'Gosh,' he said. 'We're here already.'

They had walked a hundred yards or so when Angie stopped.

'We could stop here for a moment,' she said, nodding towards a sandstone ginnel to her left. She let go of his hand and went a little way in, the darkness all but swallowing her. He followed, making for her dark outline against the blackened bricks. She took hold of his hand once more and pulled him towards her.

'No one can see us here,' she said.

His insides flipped. He could barely make out her features, the whites of her eyes, her teeth. He wondered what she saw when she looked at him, why she would want him, she who could surely choose whomever she wanted. He heard Phyllis, a few days ago in the holiday cottage: *I wish you could see how handsome you are... Any girl would be lucky to have you.* He breathed in deeply, tried to somehow make the words part of him.

'Are you all right?' Angie asked.

'I'm all right.'

From somewhere, he couldn't tell where, cries and laughter carried on the air, the screeches of female students in a protective drunken pack. A second later, a group passed the end of the ginnel, an amorphous mass of limbs in the dark.

In breathless silence they waited, he and Angie, in their hideaway. The noise receded. The air stilled.

Women like strength, Adam had said. Christopher pushed Angie back against the wall and sealed her lips with his own, pushed his tongue into her mouth. *Not too far in*, Adam had said. *You don't want to choke 'em to death. But don't mince about on her teeth either.*

The taste of beer and cigarettes. Their bellies touched, her hands on the small of his back. Her ribs rose against his, her breasts pushed against his chest. He was already hard and willed himself to keep control. He kissed her again, and she gave a quiet hum of what he hoped was pleasure. He stroked her face and hair, her neck, the hollow at her throat. Her skin was soft, impossibly so. He pressed his mouth against the brush of her eyelashes, her cheeks, her neck. She smelled of something warm, a spice, maybe an oil.

Her skin had blended its scents together into a mix that was her, Angie, and eyes closed, he breathed her in. He kissed her mouth again, that hollow at the base of her throat.

His blood raced. He dared to let his hand slide to her breast. She caught her breath and gave a soft *oh*. Dear God. She arched her body into his. Gaining confidence, he searched out the hem of her blouse, pulled it from her jeans, slid his hand beneath. At the touch of his fingertips on the naked skin of her belly, he stopped.

'Angie.' He rested his forehead against her chest a moment.

'Hey.' She lifted his chin with her finger and kissed him gently once, twice. He felt himself swell, insist against the flat of her abdomen. He wanted to strip off all her clothes, her underwear, he wanted to…

'Is the wall all right?' he said. 'I mean, is it comfortable? Is it dry?'

'Let's go somewhere.' She led him out of their secret passageway and nodded towards some trees, bunched and silhouetted, nearer the halls. He listened for people but heard nothing.

There were shrubs too, a hedge – no more than a miniature garden, or a large flower bed. Behind the hedge, the shadows became blackness. He could see her, but only because she was so close to him. She laid down her sheepskin coat.

'It's grassy here,' she said. 'You probably can't see, but it's OK.'

He took off his rainproof jacket and laid it next to hers. The chill air bit him through his sweater, its teeth blunted by alcohol and desire strengthening by the second. No more shrieks in the air; all was silent now.

'There's no one about.' She sat down on her coat and patted the space next to her. 'Come on. Don't worry.'

He crouched then sat beside her. He could smell damp soil, flowers. 'Is this OK?'

'What do you mean?'

'I mean this. I don't want you to feel you have to.'

She gave a half-laugh, a sarcastic laugh. 'I think those days are long behind us, Christopher. Women acknowledged their right to desire some considerable time ago. This…' she slipped two fingers into his waistband, 'is a political act.'

He nodded. Dear God. 'Absolutely. Of course.'

She let her hand trail up the inside of his thigh, sending electrical currents through the rest of him. She was leading again; that would not do. Women wanted power, strength. He took hold of her shoulders and pushed her to the ground, covering her mouth with his, her body with his. He kissed her neck, unbuttoned her blouse and slid his hand inside. He wanted her naked, so badly it shocked him – the urge to rip her clothes from her and feel all her skin on all of his, the length of their bodies pressed together. He drew away and lifted up her blouse.

'No.' She pressed her arms down to her sides so that he could not pull the blouse over her head. 'If someone were to come…' But her fingers were at his waist once again, unbuttoning, unzipping. She pushed her hands down the back of his underwear, ran her fingers over his naked buttocks until she was holding them, pushing him towards her. He caught his breath, astonished. She wanted him, but clothed, perhaps as some safeguard against embarrassment should someone catch them. Her blouse fell over his hands. He reached beneath, and up. She did not object. He met the swell of her breasts, her nipples, felt the surge within him as they rose to his touch. Too much, too much. He stayed dead still and rested his forehead against the base of her neck. Breathe, Christopher. Breathe.

She pushed him back a little, drew his glasses from his face and threw them onto the grass. His world fogged, its lines faded, its colours bled. Her hands were beneath his sweater. She felt for and found the hem of his shirt and yanked it roughly from his jeans. The night fell cold on his belly and he shivered. She lay back on her coat and he eased her legs apart with his own, sank his face into her belly and traced his lips up to her small, round breasts. With every moment, he expected her to stop him, but she did not. Her bra had come loose – she must have unclasped it though he could not remember her doing it. He took her nipple in his mouth, could not believe what he was doing, what she was letting him do, and his blood bubbled through his veins like lava. He wanted all of her at once, wanted to suck her down like milk through a straw. She was pulling at her jeans now, wriggling out of them, just enough. He lifted himself up, let her pull his jeans and boxers as far as the tops of his legs. At the breath of cold air, at the touch of her fingers wrapping themselves around him, that feeling of panic came again. He groaned and closed his eyes.

'It's OK,' she said. 'No one's here.'

'I can't…'

'It's OK, Christopher. I'll hold it, that's all. I won't move my hand until you're ready. Nice and slow.'

They were half-naked, the two of them, in the dark gardens. They were hidden from view, but still… The air chilled his buttocks but her hand was warm and tight. More than anything, he felt alive. He clamped his lips shut, fearing that if he opened them he would shout so loud it would be heard all the way over in Headingley. She was stroking him towards her now, moving herself towards him. He could feel the tickle of the hair between her legs, now the warm wetness of her most private place. Oh God, oh God. He pressed himself onto her, felt her part as he pushed gently, so gently, unable to believe it was happening but knowing it was – it was. It was happening at last.

'Oh, Angie,' he said.

Her hand had fallen away. It was her body that guided him now, her insides that held him tight.

'It's OK, Christopher,' she whispered. 'I'm on the pill.' She was all around him, her skin cloud-soft against his, her arms around his back. 'Open your eyes.'

'I can't.'

'You can.'

He made himself look at her. Through the sparse light, the blur of his own short sight, the glint of her eyes, staring into his, the pale cream of her teeth. She was smiling in that mocking way she had. He wished she would not smile like that. He pushed hard into her and she threw back her head. Again he pushed, and again, enough to stop her smiling.

'Slower.' She was still looking at him – arch, knowing – her eyes boring into his. That smile – that smirk. She was laughing at him, under her breath. She thought him ridiculous, a story to tell later to her girlfriends. She, she had reduced him to this half-clothed beast, bare buttocks pumping white and naked as a gibbon. To this monster.

The inexorable rush threatened to overtake him. He searched for a focal point and found the top of her head, the pale track of her parting. He pushed hard and fast.

She cried out, as if in pain.

He glanced at her face. Her expression had changed. Her brow furrowed and something else flashed in her eyes. She looked away, towards the halls. Was someone coming? Had she heard someone? Please God, no. She cried out again. She was not smiling. She was not laughing. She looked, if anything, afraid.

'Stop,' she shouted. 'Christopher, stop.'

He pushed again, and again, his teeth gritted. Adam said women liked to resist, to play, that sometimes they told you to stop but really they wanted you to carry on.

'Christopher, you're… Stop.'

He could not. Not now. She was the one who had reduced him to this. Perhaps she thought he could not or would not go through with it well he would make her see he would show her he could he would he was close too close to stop too close too close…

With a cry that seemed not to belong to him, he felt himself empty, felt the flood of tension released in roaring, urgent silence. He fell onto her, his nose against the hollow at the base of her throat. 'Angie.'

She was thumping his shoulders with her fists. 'Get off me.' Her voice was ragged, tearful.

He rolled off her, bewildered. 'What's the matter?'

'I said stop.' She was pulling down her blouse, pulling up her jeans. She sniffed.

'Angie, what's the matter? Are you crying? I thought you wanted me to. I couldn't stop. I thought you were just saying that. I couldn't stop.'

She was zipping up her jeans. She sniffed again and gave a sob. She was crying, she really was.

'Angie,' he said. 'Don't cry. I didn't realise. Did I hurt you? I didn't hurt you, did I?'

She stood, grabbing up her coat.

'You're not *him*, are you?' She was backing away. 'You're not *him*?'

She turned and ran towards the halls. He stared after her, burning with humiliation, his jeans and underwear around his knees, his penis limp on his milk-white lap.

CHAPTER SEVENTEEN

Adam was still out when he got back. Even tonight, when Christopher had finally managed to, as Adam put it, get laid, Adam was still out of reach, going one better. Perhaps he had turned up late to the pub, picked up Alison or Sophie or both, why not, just like that. Perhaps he was with someone else, having skilful sexual intercourse with a woman who had not changed her mind halfway through, who had not left him exposed and alone in the dark. What was it that he, Christopher, had not understood? Angie had wanted him in that way, she had done everything to encourage him, but then – then she had not. Did normal men understand something he didn't? Was that what separated them from that monster on the streets, from him, Christopher? What was he then? A monster?

The following day, Adam was still asleep when Christopher left for breakfast and the library, and that evening, he did not see Adam until much later. He had expected as much, he told me, since Adam had said he was meeting Sophie in the Skyrack at eight. Christopher supposed that meant another casually successful interaction with the opposite sex, another conquest. It was a surprise his room-mate didn't have a tally carved into the wood at the foot of his bed.

When Adam came home around midnight, Christopher was in bed but still awake. He was having difficulty getting to sleep, he said, his mind too full of troublesome thoughts. Adam crept into the room. Christopher heard the creak of his bed and then first one boot drop to the floor followed by the other.

'Hello,' he said into the darkness. 'Everything all right?'

'I suppose,' said Adam. 'Got bloody stood up, didn't I?'

The great lothario had finally met his match. Despite himself, Christopher cheered inwardly. 'Oh dear,' he said.

'I wasn't even that late.'

'You mean no later than usual?' By this time, Christopher said, he had got the hang of pulling Adam's leg.

'Fifteen minutes,' he said. 'Twenty tops. I should have known. Sophie's not the type to wait.'

'She might have got there later than you. If she's wise to you, she might have known you'd be late.'

Adam pulled his shirt over his head and threw it to the end of his bed. Jumped up, dropped his trousers, which presently sailed through the air to join his shirt. He shivered, swore and got into bed. Christopher's eyelids felt heavy. He let them close.

'You could be right,' Adam said. 'I didn't think of that. Fuck. I didn't think to wait. I went into town instead. A few of the elec-eng boys were supposed to be meeting, but I couldn't find them either. Ended up drinking on my own like a Billy-no-mates. What about you, anyway? Got laid yet?'

'As a matter of fact…'

Adam sat bolt upright in his bed. 'You're kidding?'

'No, I'm not.'

'Who? When? How?'

'A gentleman never tells.'

A moment later something landed on Christopher's leg, causing him to startle. A book.

'Secretive bastard,' said Adam, and laughed.

The next evening, Adam came back to the halls in time for supper, his face stern, preoccupied. Before he even spoke, Christopher knew something was wrong.

'Christopher, man,' he said. 'Sophie's missing. I just bumped into Alison. Well I met her for lunch, actually, in the refec, and she told me Sophie never came home last night.'

Christopher had been about to go over to the canteen but instead sat on his bed. 'Oh dear,' he said, and then, 'I'm sure it's all right. The others said she's a bit of a one. Perhaps she's shacked up with someone?' He hoped that was the correct term. It sounded rather derogatory.

Adam came to sit on the side of his bed opposite Christopher. He put his thumb to his teeth and tore off a strip of nail. 'Aye, I know, but she was supposed to be meeting me and her friends knew she was meeting me and now she's gone AWOL.'

'What are you saying?'

'Well, with this lunatic on the streets, I'm worried something bad's happened.'

Christopher thought for a second. He could not deny this was a possibility. It was, quite simply, not safe out, and by all accounts Sophie was foolish, arrogant and brazen. He did not say this to Adam.

'Look, it's not even been twenty-four hours,' he said instead.

Adam had begun to scratch his head, had hooked his bottom teeth over his top lip. 'Aye, man, I know, but what if they come to me? The police? The girls have told them she was meant to be meeting me, so I'll be the first person they question, won't I? What am I going to say?'

'What do you mean, say? Just tell them the truth.'

'But that won't wash, will it? They're questioning blokes left, right and centre. I was supposed to be meeting her and now she's not turned up and I have no alibi. No alibi at all. And if something bad has happened to her… Fuck… I'm in deep shit.'

'I'll be your alibi.'

Adam stopped scratching and looked at Christopher. 'What?'

'I'll say I was with you. You're my friend. That's what friends do.'

'But you can't do that. I can't let you do that, man.'

'Why not? It's not as if anyone will have noticed me in the library, is it? I didn't check any books out, so there's no record of me even being there.'

'You'd do that?'

'Yes. Call it the big advantage of my complete lack of charisma.' It was supposed to be a joke, but Adam did not even smile. 'Look, I know you didn't do anything to Sophie,' he went on. 'You never would. Besides, she'll be fine. She'll turn up tonight, you'll see. And her friends will be jolly cross with her.' He stood. 'Let's go and get something to eat. You can tell me where we were and at what time, what we drank. I'll remember. I have a very good memory.'

Adam stood and shook his head. His face, his shoulders, the whole set of his body relaxed.

'What can I say?' he said, and threw out his arms. 'You're a true mate.'

Christopher knew what that meant and what to do. He too threw out his arms and hugged his friend.

The next day, Wednesday, Adam did not return to the halls. No one had seen him. The day after that, Christopher came back from his morning trip to the bathroom to find two policemen in his bedroom.

'Can I help you?' He pulled his dressing gown tighter around him and knotted the belt. It was odd, he said, how guilty the sight of police uniforms made you feel.

The taller of the two introduced himself and his colleague. Normally Christopher has a pretty photographic memory, but he could not remember either of their names when he came to tell me all this.

'Are you Christopher Harris?' said the taller of the two. He had a moustache not unlike David's.

'Yes.'

'And you share this room with Adam Wells?'

'Yes. Is he all right? He didn't come back last night. I was getting worried.'

The policeman nodded. 'Adam's fine, don't you worry. He's helping us with our enquiries. We need to ask you a few questions as regards your whereabouts on the evening of Monday, 3 April. Can you tell us where you were between the hours of 8 p.m. and midnight?'

'Of course. I was in the Skyrack with Adam. We wandered along there together from here after dinner and had a pint. That would have been around eight-ish, I think. I bought the drinks. I wasn't supposed to be staying because he was meeting a girl, but she didn't turn up. So we caught the bus into town.'

'What was the girl's name?'

'Sophie. Is this to do with her? Is she still missing?'

'And which bus was that?'

'The twenty-eight, I think.'

'And how do you know Sophie is missing?'

'A friend of mine told me on Tuesday she'd not come back the night before, but I assumed she'd have turned up by now.'

'And where did you go after the Skyrack, Mr Harris?'

'We went to the Union and stayed there until they closed. We were quite sloshed actually. Then we went for chips and ate them walking home. We must have got back here at about midnight, give or take. Listen – is Adam OK? He would never hurt anyone, you know.'

The policeman smiled, though not in a friendly way. 'And is there anyone who can corroborate your story?'

'I'm pretty sure the barmaid at the Skyrack would. We either go there or the Original Oak opposite, so she would know our faces. Is there anything else I can help you with? You've not found her, have you, Sophie?'

'Thank you, Mr Harris. You've been most helpful.'

When Christopher relayed this conversation to me later, I remember remarking on how easily he'd lied and how implicitly he'd trusted his friend. But, he said, he saw no reason not to lie, to trust.

'I just knew he was innocent,' he said. 'And sometimes you need lies, don't you, to protect the people you love?'

That night, Adam was still at the police station. The next day, Thursday, a grim and familiar buzz went round the Leeds campus. *He* had struck again. In the Union shop, the newspapers shouted their headlines: *Woman's Body Found in Headingley*. A student this time – a Leeds University student. It had to be Sophie. The front pages sickened Christopher to his stomach, made him feel anxious to his core. The very air was thick with talk and terror. Female students wept, huddled together, held hands. Christopher bought *The Guardian*, the *Mirror* and *The Telegraph*. Back in his room, he cut out the articles and glued them into his scrapbook with the others. The scrapbook was getting thick. He might even need another.

On Saturday morning, he was about to head out to the library when, head down, shoulders low, Adam plodded into the bedroom. How different this Adam was to the cocksure lad who had come bounding in that first day.

'I owe you my life, man.' He sat on his bed and put his head in his hands. For a moment he said nothing, and it was only when a gasp escaped him that Christopher realised he was weeping. He dropped his canvas satchel and went to sit next to his friend.

'Hey, hey, it's over now,' he said, noticing that his friend smelled strongly of body odour.

'They took my blood, for Christ's sake.' Adam's voice was hoarse, as if he had been shouting. 'They said I was *him*. Where was I this night and that night and the other? How the bloody hell am I supposed to know where I was six months ago? Not like I keep a diary, is it? They threw me in a cell. I couldn't call anyone – it was fucking terrible. I thought we were innocent until proven guilty in this country.'

'They came here.'

'I know. The barmaid backed you up apparently. Thank God we're regulars, eh?' He scratched at his scalp, violently. 'Oh God, Chris, man, it was terrible, the way they look at you, the way they talk to you, trying to tie you up in knots. She's dead, Christopher. Even when I thought it, I didn't really think it, do you know what I mean? But there's no denying it now. She's dead. I can't help thinking if I hadn't got there late… but I didn't think she'd walk off, if that's even what she did.'

'She might not have turned up at all,' Christopher said. 'She may have run into someone she knew. You can't torture yourself. All you did was arrive a little late – that's hardly a hanging offence.'

Again Adam pushed his face into his hands. 'The way the policewoman looked at me. Like I was *him*. Like I was some sick bastard who could do something like that. Poor Sophie. Poor, poor Sophie. I can't believe it. I'll never be able to thank you enough, Christopher. Never.'

CHAPTER EIGHTEEN

Dear Christopher,
   Your dad has had an accident at work. Nothing serious, he has broken his left wrist after a sink fell on him…

As Christopher pushed on the gate, his parents' front door opened and his mother appeared. He called a hello as he walked up the path and stepped inside. It was cold in the hallway. The smell of braised meat drifted out from the kitchen.

'I saw you out of the window,' Margaret said as he stepped inside. She did not kiss him or hold out her arms but stood back, rubbing her hands, in her face a worn sadness that made him too feel sad. 'Your father's upstairs.'

'How is he?'

She frowned. 'It's been a terrible business.'

Christopher took off his coat and put it on the hook. He followed his mother into the kitchen. Her back curved more than he remembered it doing, as if she were cowering. She looked smaller.

'You got here anyway,' she said.

'Yes.' He sat at the kitchen table and chafed his hands together to warm them.

His mother turned to the sink and ran the tap.

'Why don't you pop up and see your dad?' she said. 'I'll bring tea up.' She did not turn around.

The stairs creaked underfoot. As he neared the top, Christopher found himself slowing down. At the door to his parents' room, he stopped, his hand on the door handle.

'Dad?'

'In here.'

Christopher eased open the door. It brushed on the carpet, the sound like someone breathing on glass. His father was sitting in bed, fully clothed and with a white plaster cast on his left forearm. His legs were under the covers and his head was propped up by two pillows. If the hallway had been cold, the bedroom was like a tomb. His father was wearing a woollen hat, which was not pulled down and which made a strange bulbous shape of his head. He looked, Christopher thought, miserable and quite, quite mad.

'You made it back then,' he said.

'Yes.' Christopher made to sit on the bed but, seeing the outline of his father's thin legs, thought better of it and instead sat on the chair by the window.

'Your mother was disappointed you didn't come home for Easter.'

'I'm home now.'

To think, he had missed a Friday with Phyllis for this. On the bedroom floor was *The Sun* newspaper. His father must have followed Christopher's gaze because he said, 'Your mother reads me the paper.' He held up his plaster cast, as if to explain. How a broken arm affected one's eyesight, Christopher could not figure.

'How is the arm?'

'Hopeless. I'll lose weeks. You know I'd had to take on a lad.'

Christopher nodded. A reference to his own desertion. 'Yes, Mum said in her letter.'

'The idiot let go of the sink while I was on all fours welding a joint – and bang! Lucky I wasn't concussed. Lucky I wasn't killed, to be honest. Bloody idiot.'

How being killed was any kind of tragedy for someone who took so little joy in life, Christopher struggled to see. 'How come you're in bed?' he asked. 'It's just your arm, isn't it?'

'Agh.' With his good arm, his father swiped at the air, as if to swat a fly. 'Can't see any point getting up. Not like I can do much, is it?'

'You could watch television?'

'Television's rubbish. Absolute rubbish. If it's not a bunch of idiots talking about things best left private, it's some American detective twaddle.'

His mother appeared at the door with two mugs in her hands. 'Tea,' she said.

'Thank you.' Christopher stood and reached to take both mugs but his mother gave him only one. The other she took around the bed and delivered wordlessly to her husband's bedside table before creeping out of the room in silence, like a maid. Not that his father looked in any way grand. If anything, he too looked smaller, there in the double bed, wrapped in blankets, silly hat on. They had diminished, the pair of them. They were shadows even of the shadows they had been. Christopher wondered how Jack Junior and Louise found it here in the ticking silence, wondered if they longed to get out as he had done. Once university had finished, he knew he would never live here again. Twenty minutes in the place and already a heaviness had overtaken his limbs. He wanted to shout, to run down the stairs, put on a record – loud – and pogo around the living room.

For lunch, his mother made him egg mayonnaise sandwiches. He took them on a tray with a glass of milk up to his loft room, where, in the afternoon, he studied. Later, his father conceded to dinner downstairs. Jack and Louise had by then come home from their respective friends' houses and so there were five of them around the table once again. Jack Junior and Louise had changed too, even since Christmas; they were older, louder, bigger. They told him their news with an enthusiasm he had not experienced from them before, and he wondered if this was because he had not come back in so long. With distance, he had become a guest, a stranger before whom they put on a kind of performance of themselves. It wasn't unpleasant – better, in fact, than indifference.

He left the next morning, Saturday, refused his mother's offer of a lift to the coach station but accepted a carrier bag of food.

'Thanks, that's very kind of you.'

'I made fudge,' she said. She hovered over him in the dark hallway while he put on his shoes, blocking his light. When he stood straight and met her gaze, he found in it such terrible sadness that he wanted to take her into his arms and comfort her. But he did not.

'There's a half-pound of Lancashire cheese from the market,' she went on. 'It's in the brown paper, watch you don't squash it.'

'Thank you. Thank you so much.'

'Take this.' She was holding a pound note.

He waved it away. 'Don't be silly. I'm fine, honestly.'

'It was only coppers,' she said. 'From the jar on the window ledge, like. I changed them up this week once you said you were coming.'

He had to look away.

'Keep it,' he said. 'Dad said he'd not be at work for a few weeks.'

'Aye, but we've got some saved.'

'Please.' Christopher opened the front door, and with one hand holding onto the door's edge kissed his mother on the cool bone of her cheek. 'I'll see you soon.'

Margaret nodded, pushed the money into her apron pocket and closed the door behind him. At the end of the avenue, he crossed the road and turned to look back at the house. His mother was at the window, hand raised, as if she were waiting to spot him in a crowd before she could wave properly, and it seemed to him he stood on the far shore, the road he had grown up in a river, its rapid waters too wide, too turbulent to cross. He waved, turned and went on his way, but as he came to White Lund Road, he was filled with the feeling of being followed. Twice he turned back but saw no one. Then, as he waited for the coach to pull away, the feeling came again. He looked out of the window but again saw no one – at least no one he recognised. He shivered and sat back in his seat.

A month later, towards the end of his first year – June 1978 – Christopher wrote to Margaret and Jack to tell them he had a job in Leeds for the summer, which was the truth – a truth that omitted his reasons for taking it. Adam had organised a rental house in Leeds 6, the student area near the uni, for the following academic year. They would be sharing with two lads from the electronic-engineering course whom Christopher knew from three or four pub crawls up the Otley Road. It was Adam who had blagged the job: bar work for both of them in the Fenton, a pub behind the university. He had bounced back from the shock of Sophie's death, but according to Christopher had calmed down when it came to women. These days, he only had one on the go at a time.

'It'll be a good earner,' he was saying now. They were eating dinner together in the cavernous university refectory – the smell of stew, steamed pudding, thin coffee, the deafening clank of cutlery on cheap china. 'Free ale too. They're always having lock-ins there, so you'll get extra dough, and when we're not on shift we can spread our wings a bit, get over to Chapeltown and Bradford. Apparently the clubs there are better. We have to pay rent over the summer so we may as well live in it, eh?'

'Quite.' Christopher shovelled in a mouthful of partially congealed lasagne. 'Good thinking.'

'Sorted then. You can give me a cheque.'

'Right you are.'

'You ever see that Angie?' Adam traded his clean plate of what had been steak pie and chips for a bowl of apple sponge and garish yellow custard. 'I thought you and she had hit it off.'

'I walked her home a few times, nothing much to say really. All the women I meet seem to be terrified of the flaming Ripper.'

'And that's where we come in, my friend,' said Adam, smiling. Christopher wondered how he could be so flippant, especially after his time at the police station, after what had happened to Sophie. 'We can see them home safe, can't we?'

'Yes,' said Christopher. 'Safe.'

That summer, Christopher moved his meagre belongings to Chestnut Avenue in Adam's fourth-hand Mini. Christopher's room was at the top of the house – Adam had given him second choice on the rooms, and only after he had chosen did he realise he had opted for the converted loft space. There was comfort in familiarity, perhaps, even if that familiarity was becoming ever more unfamiliar. He decorated the room with posters of Marc Bolan, David Bowie and Fleetwood Mac (for Phyllis). A poster of Stevie Nicks he Blu-Tacked to the sloping eave above his bed, where she could watch over him and he could look at her. Although David could get him tapes of pretty much any album he wanted, Christopher planned to save and buy a record player. There was nothing like vinyl, *the sweet caress of the needle in the groove*, as Adam put it. And Adam had a record player – a vintage walnut Pye Black Box – so they could trade discs.

In July, on the last Friday of the twins' school term, Christopher made sure to go to Phyllis in the morning so that he could see her alone before the boys got home. He ran from the station to the bus stop, then from Heath Road by the town-hall grounds along to Langdale Road. He rapped on the door, looking up and down the street, checking for twitching curtains, like a thief under cover of broad daylight. The bubbles in the glass of the front door turned Phyllis into blobs of colour, and it was always wonderful when those colours cohered again to make her so clear, so young, this woman who always had a smile for him, who always threw out her arms and said: 'Look who it is!'

He fell towards her with gratitude and relief. There was no better place on all the earth, he thought, than here.

'Hello.'

She took his hand, as was her way, and led him into the kitchen. Once they were settled, she asked him question after question, as she always did, as if he were the most fascinating subject on the planet. How were his studies? How was Adam? Had he had any nights out? She fixed him with her brown eyes: 'And your love life?'

'Ah.' He looked down at his hands, slack and useless in his lap. Memories of Angie's naked belly flashed in his mind's eye, the look of terror she had given him in their last moments together.

'Good as that, eh?' said Phyllis.

'I've been pretty shaken up since Adam got taken in for questioning. It's not just the women who are paranoid. The men are scared someone will think it's them, and every woman you speak to, you can see in her eyes that she's wondering if you're a murderer or something. Not that I blame them.' He was exaggerating his contact with the female student community, he knew, but he could not help himself. 'But there was this girl. She seemed...' He could not continue.

'You can talk to me about anything,' Phyllis said. 'You know that.'

'I think I mistook her intentions,' he said eventually. 'She seemed to want me to kiss her, and I did. She seemed to want, you know, more, but then... she said I should have stopped.'

Phyllis took his hand, and he wondered if it were possible to become addicted to a person like you got addicted to cigarettes.

'I think perhaps it's me,' he continued. 'I don't seem to be able to get these things right.'

'Oh, love, it's not that. There's all sorts of reasons why these things don't go right. And this Ripper has got us all frightened stiff, got us all looking at the men we know, thinking, *Is it you?* Not over here so much, but up where you are, no one knows what they're up to. I heard from one of the other teachers at work that there's women accusing their own husbands. Brothers, too. The police are inundated. It's no wonder girls your age are jumpy – and it's not just working girls he's after now, is it?' She bit her lip and shook her head, seemingly lost in thought, before returning to him with another squeeze of his hand. 'And as for you, the right girl will come along – you'll see.'

She raised his hand to her lips and kissed his knuckles. 'Some people are still kids when they fall in love or when they step into the world of, you know, sex and all the rest of it. I was fifteen, and look what happened there. That's no good either, is it? Being made to give you up like that when you belonged with me. That's cruel. So it may be for different reasons but I used to think the same as you – that I'd got it all wrong, that I'd not understood something fundamental about how these things work. Other girls seemed to be getting their kicks without getting into trouble, but muggins here believed him when he said he couldn't wear a sheath. Allergic, I think he said he was. Told me not to worry, that he could control it – by which he meant pull out, I know that now, of course. And I believed him because, well, because he was older, he seemed experienced and of course he had lovely dark hair like yours and… well you can imagine.'

'Yes,' he said, in wonder. She was so frank, so honest, so modern. He could not imagine Margaret talking in this way, to anyone. Phyllis was the best kind of friend. Brave and generous enough to reveal herself with no more reason than to make him feel better.

'But then I met David,' she went on. 'I hadn't realised there were men out there who let you take things at your own pace. But by then I was in my twenties, don't forget. You're still only nineteen, aren't you?'

'Yes.'

'There, see? Plenty of time for it all to come right. So don't be worrying about all that. If this girl doesn't want to talk to you, let her get on with it. There's nothing you can do and it's her loss. There's no rush. You concentrate on getting your qualifications, and I promise the rest will fall into place, all right?'

And it was all right. He felt all right. Phyllis knew what to say. Sometimes when they parted, or even when he put the phone down, it was as if there was a physical tearing of flesh, a ripping pain such that he imagined, if he looked, he would see an open wound in his chest, blood on the ground at his feet. This was how he once described his intense love to me. I wonder now if these violent images came from this intense love alone, or from the premonition that such a love could only end in wounding, in blood. In death.

Back in Leeds, he called Jack and Margaret from the payphone in the Union. Jack never came to the phone, never had. Once she'd told him how Jack Junior and Louise were getting on, and about any changes in the road or down at the seafront, Margaret seemed to struggle for anything else to say. For his part, he told her nothing of Phyllis and his other family. He had not told her at the time, and now it was too late – the words were too difficult to find. Besides, to tell her after so much time had passed he feared would destroy her.

Christopher worked five shifts a week in the Fenton, a dingy place populated by alcoholics whose complexions ranged from red to purple, by lost young men who often left with men considerably older than them, and by lonely middle-aged women who sat all night on high stools at the bar, only to go home alone. Between times, he went to the Brotherton Library, trying to steal a march on the following year's reading list. He went out with Adam when Adam wasn't meeting a woman – once to Bradford for a curry, which they ate with their hands, once to a reggae night in Chapeltown and once to Le Phonographique, the club in the Merrion Centre. This last was a Saturday night, a night when locals emerged into the city and students, now that it was the summer holidays, were, as Adam put it, *rarer than nuns in a clap clinic*. At Le Phonographique they played disco music, songs and bands whose names he knew, of course, within a few bars of them beginning.

That night Adam had revisited his flared jeans and a new black shirt Christopher hadn't seen before, along with a silver pendant necklace. The two of them stood at the side of the dance floor, drinking cheap lager and watching the predominantly female crowd.

' "I Feel Love",' Adam shouted into his ear, bobbing about, managing to somehow smoke, talk and smile at women all at once.

'That's nice,' Christopher replied and was thrilled to see Adam laugh.

'Donna Summer,' he shouted. 'It's bloody magic, this one.'

Christopher felt the beat, which seemed to his ears frenetic, like panic rising. He thought of Angie, her skin. He thought of Phyllis and the way she held out her arms to him, the relief he felt whenever he was by her side.

'Ah, love this one,' said Adam. 'Go on then, who is it?'

'Parliament,' said Christopher.

'In one. Hold that.' He passed Christopher his drink and headed for the dance floor.

Christopher watched his friend slink through the dancers, the rhythm informing his every move. The women responded to him as if he emanated a kind of glow, like the kids on the Ready Brek commercials, and before long, he was shouting into the ear of a woman with blonde hair flicked out in rolling waves. The next song was Blondie. Christopher sang along, under his breath, picturing Debbie Harry's mouth, wondering what it would be like to have sex with her. He was normal in this, at least, he supposed.

Adam returned, a sheen of sweat on his brow. He took his pint and drank half.

'Love this stuff,' he said. It was unclear whether he meant the beer or the music. 'What's this one?'

' "Boogie Oogie Oogie",' said Christopher.

'Now that's what I call a title, man. Is that the band?'

'That's the song. A Taste of Honey, the band.'

'Page the bloody Oracle.' Adam took his cigarettes from his back pocket, offered one to Christopher, lit first his own then Christopher's, inhaled deeply, tipped back his head and blew the smoke up towards the ceiling.

'So tell me, oh lanky one,' he said, 'how come you didn't go back home for the summer?'

'You got us a job.'

'I know. But that's not the reason. And how come you're away so much at weekends? Tell me to piss off if you like, but when you come back, you're always so… I don't know, happy, as if you've been shagging for the entire weekend. Now apart from that one time, I haven't seen or heard about a girlfriend, and I think I have a clue as to why that might be.'

Christopher felt twin trickles of sweat run from his armpits down his sides. The club was hot, the air opaque. How could he explain, without having to explain everything? He would have to tell Adam he was adopted, that his adoptive parents had only told him because he'd found the note in the case, that now he'd found a family that he... he what? He preferred. That was it. That was the shameful truth of the matter. He had abandoned his old family like an unfashionable pair of jeans. Worse still, he had not told his new family that he hadn't told his old family. No – too complicated. Better to say he had a woman on the go, a married woman. It was easier.

He opened his mouth to speak, but Adam clapped him on the shoulder. 'Do you want to know why I've not gone home?'

Relief coursed through Christopher. He nodded.

'My old man,' said Adam. 'My dad.'

For the first time Christopher could remember – ever, in fact – Adam looked serious. Serious or sad or cross – something that sent his brows towards each other, that turned his smile upside down.

'Your father?'

'If I tell you this, it stops here, OK?'

Christopher nodded. 'Of course.'

'He's handy with his hands, if you catch my drift.' Adam took a drag on his cigarette, drained his pint glass. 'Violent. With my ma, but with me an' all, like. Since I was thirteen. I feel like a shit staying here, leaving her there, but it's her choice, she's made it and I have to make mine.'

In the stinging smoke, Christopher looked hard at his friend. Adam had glanced away, to the dance floor, and was lighting a cigarette from the last one. He threw the old one to the floor and squashed it with his shoe. Odd, Christopher thought, that in the thick smog of the club, this was perhaps the first time he had seen his friend clearly.

'Is he your real dad?' The question was out before he could stop it.

Adam cocked his head. 'Eh? Yes. Course he's my real dad. Believe me, I'd love nothing better than for them to tell me they found me on the street, but unfortunately, no, I am their biological progeny.'

The last words he laced with irony, bitterness – something like that. 'Come on, let's get out of here.'

They headed out onto Albion Street. Adam turned his talk to the women in the club, asking Christopher if he had seen her with the dark hair, what about that one with the silver dress, did Christopher think she was a man or a woman? Thankfully, they had left the subject of him, Christopher, behind. They turned into Boar Lane. Above them a white poster covered the wall, shouted down its message in bold black letters:

DO YOU KNOW THIS MAN?
HELP US STOP THE RIPPER FROM KILLING AGAIN
CALL LEEDS (0532) 46111

A man with dead eyes stared out from a crude photofit image. Adam nodded up at the sign. 'There's been no more since May, has there?'

'The sixteenth,' said Christopher. Vera Millward. Outside Manchester Royal Infirmary. He had cut out the newspaper article and stuck it in his scrapbook with the others.

'I know.' Adam shuddered. 'Sick bastard. They should cut his bloody balls off, man.'

Adam pushed open the door to the Griffin pub. Christopher followed him in and headed for the bar.

'It's my round,' he said. 'Same again?'

'Why aye. Good man. I'll get us a table.'

Unusually, Adam chose a table in the corner, away from the others. There were no women at all in the pub, Christopher noticed as he brought the drinks over, sat down and slid Adam's beer over to him. Taking hold of his pint, Adam made a come-here gesture with his other hand, wanting to share another confidence, no doubt.

Christopher leaned in.

'No, you prat,' Adam said. 'Fags. Your turn.'

'Oh. Sorry.'

'So that's me,' said Adam, once they'd lit up. 'Elvis, the great pretender. I know I look like I walk on water, but that's what comes from treading on eggshells your whole life.' He sucked at his cigarette, blew smoke rings, met Christopher's gaze. 'So, buggerlugs, where do you go to, my lovely? At weekends?'

'I…' Christopher began, the blaze of attention making his cheeks burn. 'It's a long story.'

Adam put both elbows on the tabletop, rested his chin on the steeple of his hands.

'Listen,' he said. 'And don't take this the wrong way. This isn't what I think necessarily, I'm just saying it's OK by me, that's all. I'm not prejudiced in any way against anyone. Black, white, yellow, straight, queer, it's all the same to me.' He paused, met Christopher's gaze. 'I'm not prejudiced, is what I'm saying.'

Christopher shook his head. 'Me neither, I don't think.'

'I mean, did you see that chap in the club? The one with the pink towelling headband on his bonce doing the big moves, the spins and all that malarkey?'

'No.'

'Doesn't matter.' Adam broke his gaze, thank goodness, and rolled his cigarette tip in the ashtray so that it made a grey cone. 'All I'm saying is, good on him. Do you know what I mean?'

'I have no idea what you're talking about.'

Adam shook his head, laid his hand on Christopher's shoulder and leaned into his ear.

'If you're gay, it's OK,' he said. 'I'm not, but if you are, what I'm saying is, that's cool, man.'

He leant back and smiled, and Christopher held his gaze for a second. Adam didn't laugh. He wasn't joking. An hour earlier, he had been one kind of person; now he was almost entirely another. How sudden the shift had been. From Adam the chancer, the dancer, the romancer, to Adam who had been beaten as a child, who when he left for university had left violence behind along with his mother, who continued to endure it. Adam who asked for confidences, who promised not to judge. With the exception of Phyllis, he was possibly the kindest person Christopher had ever known. He was still looking right at Christopher, so serious, so unlike himself, but, it was possible, utterly himself, the self he normally kept under wraps. That was what he was offering: himself – the real one.

Christopher felt a smile creep across his lips. The smile widened.

'What?' said Adam. 'I'm right, aren't I? It's OK, man, it's OK. And I won't tell either.'

From nowhere, Christopher exploded into laughter. Tears leaked from his eyes, his stomach hurt, he tried to speak but could not. Adam laughed too, but doubtfully.

'Mate,' he said. 'People are staring. Get a grip, will you?'

'I-I'm not,' Christopher stuttered, when he was able. 'I'm not gay.'

'What? What then?'

'It's my mother,' he said. 'My real mother. That's where I go at weekends.'

CHAPTER NINETEEN

Ben heads out of St Matthew's Convent grinning like a fool. Mother Superior Lawrence was a doll and he's pretty sure he caught a twinkle in those old grey eyes of hers. It is 5.30 p.m., 9.30 a.m. in California, although, he thinks, he should drop that thought and get used to what time it is here – here where he actually is.

One thing he already loves about England is how civilised everyone is. The mother superior really couldn't have been sweeter, serving him tea and biscuits in a cute little annexe full of antique furniture and pictures of JC, and talking to him for longer than he had any right to ask her to. She even let him use the phone so he could call ahead to the hotel. The wind is in his sails – turns out his mother left her address with the sisters years ago. She wants to find him; why else would she leave it? But the request for contact has to come from him. She lives near, so near, barely half an hour's drive, according to the nun. This country is so small! Tomorrow he should be well on his way to finding her. His hotel is in the same town, a place called Runcorn.

He crosses from the red-brick gothic monolith that is the convent and gets into his hire car.

Steadfastly he repeats the process of studying his map book and noting down the roads he needs. Looks like there's a river or a canal of some sort there; it might be pretty, he might even get to wander along there with her while she tells him her story and he tells her his. When he is satisfied he can find the way, he starts the car. He is getting hungry. He hopes the hotel does room service.

CHAPTER TWENTY

With the Ripper at large, it was no wonder they were all paranoid – Christopher, Adam, those girls. The whole country was in the grip of it. I remember the feeling of dread. Dread. If I could bring myself to speak, that would be the word with which I might start. Maybe the question is not *how* are you feeling but *what* are you feeling? That I could answer. I need nouns, not adjectives: guilt, shame, regret. *If you can't talk, then write.* At first I couldn't, the meds were too strong, but bit by bit I've crawled my way towards it, and now that I've started, I find I can't stop. I look forward to it – or do I? Is it simply a habit I can't break, like a biscuit with a cup of coffee?

When I think about Christopher volunteering to be Adam's alibi, I realise that was a turning point for him. Something was sealed between them in that crucial moment. Without it, would they ever have had their evening of confidences and become so very close? Needless to say, this kind of friendship was new to Christopher. He'd already told me that he'd not had a best friend at school nor a lover of any real kind – it's only now that I find myself thinking about that and wondering why I didn't think about it more at the time. And as with anything good that happened to him now, he wondered whether Phyllis lay at the root, whether having found someone like her had opened him wide enough to allow room for someone like Adam.

'I wonder if friendship or love or whatever is not a finite thing but something that under the right conditions grows and multiplies; you know, like cells in a Petri dish,' he once said to me.

I know he looked forward to Adam getting home from his evening shifts, when they would make tea and toast and smoke and talk, sometimes until the early hours of the morning. In these moments, as with Phyllis, he felt a warmth that was physical, he told me, as if his insides had been lined with fur.

Adam's father drank – too much, it transpired during one of their many long conversations. He was a miner; the work was hard and dirty, the conditions poor.

'He's got emphysema now,' said Adam, one leg over the armchair in their student kitchen-cum-living-room. 'Won't see fifty. Most of his life spent underground, and for what? Couldn't even take joy in raising his kids. Hates the fact I got to uni, hates it. Couldn't stand the sight of me then – now, well…'

'My father's a bit that way,' Christopher confessed. 'I think he'd prefer it if I knew how to unblock a drain or wire a plug.' He stared into his tea. The merest grey tinge of the meniscus broke when he put his mouth to it. 'Words were what did for my family,' he added, voicing a thought he had not known was there. 'The lack of them anyway. If they'd spoken to me sooner, I wouldn't have grown up feeling like a guest in my own house. Like an imposter.'

Adam was at that point the only person who knew about the situation regarding both of Christopher's families

'I can see how you've ended up where you are,' he said after a moment. 'But sooner or later it might be best to tell Jack and Margaret. These things have a way of coming back to bite you on the arse.'

'I will,' Christopher replied. 'One day, when I find the right moment, I'll tell them everything.'

In this way, late into the night, they unfolded their worlds like maps, the better to study their roads, rivers and contours. Like this, they hoped, they would be able to find their way through to something clearer – a destination of sorts.

*

It was in the August of that summer that Christopher went with Phyllis, David and the boys to Pembrokeshire. They had rented a bungalow in Tenby, in the grounds of a farm. Inside, the rooms smelled faintly of damp – a homely smell once the gas fire was lit, an alarming process involving a taper, the leaning back with one's arm outstretched and the waiting for a loud *woof* as the gas blew orange.

'Bloody hell,' were David's words the first evening, after he had succeeded in lighting the fire. 'Nearly took my bloody eyebrows off, that thing.'

Outside, chickens scratched at the courtyard and, in the communal garden, a rather forlorn badminton net sagged between two trees. Phyllis pronounced the place perfect, and while David went off exploring with the boys, Christopher helped her to unpack. She had brought foodstuffs in a cardboard box and in the quaint pine kitchen brought out a brick-like object wrapped in foil.

'Do you like fruit cake, Chris?' She smiled at him and wiggled her eyebrows in mischief.

'I love fruit cake.'

'What say you and I have a piece with a cuppa, while the others aren't looking?'

He smiled back, the lightness, almost fizziness he felt around her returning as it always did.

'Sounds like a good idea.' He made to sit down but stopped himself. 'Ah, I almost forgot.' From his jacket pocket he pulled the gift he had brought for her. 'I made this tape for you. It's from Adam's record collection actually. It's a selection of disco hits. I know you like disco.'

Phyllis cooed with delight and dashed to fetch the portable tape player she had brought. After a moment of static, Donna Summer's 'I Feel Love' pulsed in the cramped space. Immediately

Phyllis threw up her arms so that her bright green T-shirt rose up, exposing her white belly, her belly button. She danced like that around the kitchen.

'I love it!' she cried. 'What else is on here?'

'Everything,' he shouted over the music. To watch her dance around, grinning like a fool was to be filled with joy. She was a miracle.

'Chris, love, you're an angel.' She bent, took his face in her hands and kissed him on the cheek. He closed his eyes, but she had already let go, and when he opened them she was twirling around the kitchen again, lifting the kettle from the hob now and parading around with it like one of Pan's People. She filled the kettle with water, her bottom wiggling in her tight blue jeans. She held the kettle to the skies, spun and placed it back on the hob. With a flourish she lit the gas with a match, blew it out with a wink.

'Come on, Chris,' she cried out to him. 'Dance with me.'

'I can't.'

'Yes you can, don't be soft.'

She rounded the table and pulled him up, took his hand and put her other hand on his waist. She rocked one way, then the other, and despite himself, he followed her. He had no choice – she was leading. He thought, could not help but think, of Angie.

'All right,' he said, his voice loud under the low ceiling, and pushed Phyllis back from him. Determined to lead, to show her he could, he kept hold of her hand as he had seen Adam do with women in the clubs. She laughed and spun back, wrapping his arm around her as she went, then unwinding again, letting go of him. She continued to dance, waving her fingers at him as she backed away, laughing when she banged her backside against the dresser. The song changed – three beats in and she shouted:

' "Best of My Love"!' Her voice was still high. There was real glee in it, he thought. 'I love this one!'

He did his best to dance alongside her. He had the beat but could not make it part of him like she could.

'That's it,' she said, taking his hands in hers and moving them in time, but at the sweetness of it, at her proximity and her joy, he felt himself beginning to panic. His heart raced, his eyes prickled. He could not look at her. After a beat or two more, he broke from her and went to turn down the music – blew back his fringe, as if out of breath.

'You'll wear me out,' he said, sitting down at the table.

She stopped dancing and came to join him. She sat down and drank her tea, and for a moment he was filled with regret at having spoiled her dance. The music had fallen away to no more than tinny percussion.

'I'd like my name back,' he said.

She frowned, perplexed. 'What do you mean?'

'I've given it a lot of thought,' he said, though the idea had only come to him in that moment, through a desperate need to divert her attention. 'I want the name you gave me. That's my name. My name is Martin. I'd like to change it by deed poll or however these things are done.'

She nodded. 'All right,' she said slowly. 'If that's what you want.'

'You can still call me Christopher. Or Chris. Otherwise it's too confusing for everyone. But officially, I'd like to be Martin.'

She paused, smiled shyly. 'I may as well tell you while we're at it that David and I have talked.'

'What?' Hot dread flared up inside him – why, he had no idea.

'We want the spare room to be your room.'

He met her gaze, felt his brow knit. 'I thought…'

'I know it's already your room, but what I mean is, I want you to keep your stuff in it in a more permanent way instead of having to clear out every time. If you want to put up posters, put clothes in the drawers, what have you… I want our home to be your home.' She took his hand and held it in both of hers. 'Have a think.'

'I don't need to,' he said, feeling his face break into a smile, a great grin over which he had no control. 'I would really, really like that.'

For the rest of that week, whether it was building sandcastles with the twins at Freshwater West, picnicking at Barafundle Bay, or rockpooling at Cwm-yr-Eglwys, Christopher would catch Phyllis's eye and she would smile and he would know that she, like him, was thinking about his room in her home – his home now. His family. In these moments, he said, his happiness threatened to overwhelm him entirely until there was nothing left of him but that: happiness, pure happiness, ephemeral as tears wept into the salty pools of the sea.

Christopher became Martin but remained Christopher, if that makes sense. He studied hard, as was his way, and often took work home, where he would study in the kitchen while the twins watched television or played in their room. Phyllis pottered about. She had moved her day off to Friday so the two of them could spend the day together. Silently she slid cups of tea or coffee across the table to him, laid a hand on his shoulder as she passed or gently scratched his head. She didn't speak to him while he worked, but he could feel her near, and the thought of her helped him settle, and concentrate. Sometimes he would look up from his books and watch her work and be filled with the deepest sense of calm. When David got home, the mere sound of his key in the lock broke what was a kind of trance, as if to signal that here was a peace that could not last. David would always stop on the threshold of the kitchen, an indefinable expression crossing his face: disapproval, perhaps, though not as strong as that. Doubt?

Suspicion?

One weekend towards Christmas, Christopher arrived as usual early on Friday afternoon, expecting to spend the afternoon with Phyllis. He ran the length of Langdale Road and, breathless, rapped on the door. To his surprise, it was David who answered.

'Here he is,' he said, and though his voice was friendliness itself, Christopher sensed that something hid there, something intangible.

Christopher smiled and threw out his hands. 'I come empty-handed, but I can pop to the shop later and get some cans of lager or wine or whatever.'

'Don't be soft,' said David, reaching out to give him his customary handshake. 'I've got a surprise for you.'

Christopher stepped into the house and took off his coat and shoes. David was waiting on the bottom step.

'Follow me,' he said, going ahead up the stairs.

Christopher followed him up and along the landing to his own bedroom door.

'There you go,' said David, throwing open the door. 'Surprise.'

Christopher looked into his room, where a white desk stood against the far wall next to the window.

'Got it from a mate,' said David. 'He had it in his garage. It's been in our garage for two weeks. I've sanded it, painted it, varnished it. What do you think?'

'Golly,' said Christopher. 'It's a desk.'

'Of course it's a desk.' David laughed, more than the remark deserved. 'Can't have you cramped up on the kitchen table, can we? Need your own proper study space at your age.'

'I'm fine in the kitchen,' said Christopher, realising the mistake as the words left his mouth. He turned to look at David, tried to meet his eye. 'But yes, this is incredible. Thank you, thank you so much.'

'Call it your Christmas present.' David was still holding onto the door handle, his knuckles white. 'Should keep you out of trouble anyway.'

Christopher was not sure what trouble meant. He looked back to the desk, as if to appreciate it fully. The paintwork was meticulous – not one rogue drip, not even on the drawers. There was a dark green anglepoise lamp on the right-hand corner. Was that new? His typewriter had been put there too – also by David, Christopher supposed. The air thinned. He could feel David behind him, waiting for a reaction – another, better reaction.

'Thank you,' he said, running his hand over the desk. 'It's so smooth. You must have worked so hard on it.'

'I did.'

Christopher tried not to drift away while David rattled on about grades of sandpaper, flour paper, the superiority of satinwood varnish over gloss.

'Gosh,' he said, and, 'Really?' and .'Heavens, that's really something.'

He did not let himself say that he had no desire, no intention to work anywhere other than downstairs, in the kitchen, near Phyllis. Nor did he say what I believe he felt at that time: that he wished David would take the twins and leave him alone, alone with Phyllis, forever.

CHAPTER TWENTY-ONE

Ritual helps. We are woken at seven *on the dot* – we have breakfast. Nurse brings me my meds and makes me walk around the yard. She links my arm. She chats about nothing. She has a son still living at home. Her daughter is pregnant. I'm still on suicide watch. Yesterday Nurse asked if I felt ready to put on some nice clothes.

I brought my jeans out of the wardrobe and held them against me. They were far too big, of course. I mimed a belt and raised my eyebrows in question.

She laughed. 'Nice try, my darling. But Nursie wasn't born yesterday. Come on, let's get you outside.'

One pill, two pills, *whee*, down the throat. A tour around the yard. Coffee time. Routine, order, ritual.

Ritual helped Christopher get through that second Christmas over at Margaret and Jack's. Ritual gave him checkpoints, milestones to tick off; he only had to keep going until the next one. Midnight Mass, the exchange of gifts (he knew better than to try anything fancy this time and stayed away from politically explosive choices such as yellow cocktail mixers), Christmas dinner: *No, the turkey's lovely, not dry at all.* He spent much of the time in the loft, where, after all, he said, they had put him, hadn't they? It was no use staying downstairs. He barely spoke to his sister, and his brother, well, most of the time he just wanted to strangle him.

On Boxing Day he left, pleading a heavy workload, and travelled to Runcorn. To her – Phyllis. It occurred to him that he should invite Adam, whose home life was so unhappy, to come and stay with Phyllis and the boys, but he did not. Back then he would have said this was because he didn't want to impose. I know now it was more likely out of fear. Adam was so charming, so good with the ladies, and Christopher could not have borne anyone replacing him in Phyllis's affections.

Christopher's luck with women did not improve. As the academic year progressed, Adam still invited him out with the boys, still gave him pep talks while he, Adam, still scored *more often than Kevin Keegan on a roll*. A little before Easter, Adam announced that he had found a two-bedroom house for the third year, did Christopher want to share?

'Of course,' Christopher said.

'It's further down towards Armley but still Leeds 6,' said Adam. 'Two bedrooms. Easier to stick to just the two of us, isn't it?'

By then Christopher was supplementing his grant by working at the Hyde Park pub, up on Woodhouse Lane. Adam had talked his way into a job at the Warehouse club down on Somers Street and planned to stay in Leeds again over the summer. Christopher agreed that he would do the same, although he expected to spend a lot of time with Phyllis.

One evening at the beginning of April, a pub customer ordered a pint of Tetley's and, before Christopher could put out his hand for the money, followed it with: 'Another victim.'

'Oh yes?'

The man dropped the coins into Christopher's palm. 'Building society clerk. Not just the prozzies now apparently. Only nineteen, poor cow.'

There had been no news of the Ripper over the last few months, and the talk at the bar had been that he had committed suicide.

Clearly he had not.

The next day, Christopher bought *The Telegraph* and scoured its pages, but the kind of information he wanted was not to be found. If the girl was not a prostitute, there would have been no financial transaction, surely? Had she agreed to sex, he wondered, and then changed her mind? Was that what had happened this time? Had she initiated sex, only to tell him to stop? He cut out the article and stuck it in his scrapbook.

I could see that Christopher had become obsessed – that his preoccupation with the Ripper was more acute than it was for the rest of us. But I didn't know about the scrapbook then. If I had, I would have worried more. Much as I loved him, if I'd known, I might even have contacted the police. But thinking about it, maybe I wouldn't have, since it wasn't too much later in the year that the famous tape made it onto the news and sent everyone in a different direction entirely.

Christopher was in the library when he overheard two women whispering behind the bookshelf: *They're saying it's him. He wrote those letters, now he's sent them a tape. It's been on the news.* He packed up his books and hurried to the television lounge in the Union in time to catch the 5 p.m. bulletin. The lounge was full; he had to stand at the back, peer through the heads. The Ripper tape was the top story. The newscaster announced it gravely. The message appeared to be intended for Assistant Chief Constable George Oldfield, who was leading the investigation. The police were appealing to anyone who recognised the voice to come forward.

The newscaster paused. The silence in the room intensified, was replaced by the breathy background noise from the cassette. And then the voice: *'I'm Jack. I see you are still having no luck catching me. I have the greatest respect for you, George, but Lord! You are no nearer catching me now than four years ago when I started. I reckon your boys are letting you down, George. They can't be much good, can they?'*

The tape finished. Christopher bolted from the room, his heart pounding in his chest, his forehead slick with sweat. He headed for the Union bar, ordered a pint of Bass and drank half of it in one go. He was breathing heavily, almost panting. He downed the rest of his beer and ordered another, found his cigarettes and lit up. That voice. The Tyneside accent, the pitch, something in the way he phrased the question at the end.

Adam.

'No,' he muttered to himself. It couldn't be.

But he had been questioned by the police. And his girlfriend or whatever she was had gone missing the night he was supposed to meet her, found dead near Oxley Hall soon after. Christopher remembered him joking about how getting laid was guaranteed, since that was apparently all she wanted him for.

'I'm her bloody sex toy, man,' he had joked, and Christopher had felt the burn of humiliation. Sophie wouldn't change her mind halfway through, he had thought at the time. Sophie knew what she wanted, and Adam knew how to give her that very thing.

But of course now she was dead, along with the others. And in one of the many crude pictures that had been shown on the news and in the papers, the Ripper had been drawn with reddish hair. Adam pulled women to him without a thought. And he was often out late at night – had been since Christopher had known him. This last year, when the Ripper had gone quiet, corresponded to when he and Adam had worked together in the Fenton. Adam would not have been able to get away so easily. And now, now when only the month before last the Ripper had struck again, Adam had taken a job at a club – unsociable hours, every reason not to get home until long after Christopher was asleep in bed.

Adam didn't go home in the holidays, he had a troubled relationship with his father, had once bragged that he could go *from conversation to copulation quicker than it would take most men to eat a bag of chips*. All his shared confidences – what if they were not real? What if they were an act, designed to manufacture intimacy, trust, so better to pull the wool over Christopher's eyes? He had always wondered why Adam would choose him, Christopher, so dull and studious when he himself was so sociable, so full of chutzpah. Christ, he had even got Christopher to be his alibi! Was it possible that this whole time, Adam had been out there, in the dark, murdering women – women on the game and sometimes innocents, as they were called?

He tried to stop his thoughts but could not. It was Adam who had suggested that just the two of them share a house. Fewer housemates – fewer witnesses. Adam had chosen Christopher not despite but exactly *because* of how he was, because he knew that Christopher would never twig what was really going on: too dim, too wrapped up in history and books, often absent at weekends. And the name – Jack. Where had he got that from? Why that name in particular if not because he had heard it from Christopher?

'No,' he said again, into his beer. 'No, no, no.'

That evening, Christopher found the customary message on the table: *Gone to work. Don't wait up. See you in the morning.* Adam didn't even bother to write a note any more. He simply pulled this envelope out from the cutlery drawer where it now lived and threw it onto the table whenever he needed it. Christopher picked it up and put it back in the drawer, out of sight.

He made tea with three teaspoons of sugar and took it upstairs to bed. The sweet heat soothed him, but he was still preoccupied. Perhaps bed would be the best option – go to sleep; forget about it. Things would look different in the morning.

He got into bed but his eyes stayed open as if pinned. Above him, on the slant of the roof over his bed, Stevie Nicks looked down from on high. Ah, Stevie. He got out of bed, slid *Rumours* from its sleeve and placed it carefully on the turntable. To the opening bars of 'Second Hand News' and with the album cover in his arms, he crept back across the room and lay once more in the darkness. The second track, 'Dreams'. Stevie Nicks took him always to Phyllis, to that first meeting, to her car, to the two of them listening to that fragile, throaty voice. Stevie Nicks would lead you by the hand into the darkness – she would lay down her coat and have you lie on it with her. She would not tell you no when you were too far gone to stop. She would pull back her waistcoats and her skirts, she would unbutton her blouse made of cotton and shake her long wavy hair, and she would sing in that low voice with all its promises close in your ear, *Stay with me a while…*

He set the album sleeve down; let it slide onto the bedroom floor.

At 3 a.m., he woke. Something had disturbed him. A noise then: it sounded like a shoe dropping to the floor. Adam. Christopher lay for a moment, his insides knotted in angst, before throwing off the covers. Better to face him now, if only to reassure himself. Not as if he would sleep anyway. He crept downstairs. The smell of toast sailed up from the kitchen. Adam was whistling softly, tunelessly, all but hidden behind the kitchen wall but for the serving hatch. By the angle of his head, Christopher could tell he was spreading butter on his toast. He looked up, eyed Christopher through the frame of the hatch.

'Why aye, Christopher Robin. What's the matter – couldn't sleep?'

'No,' said Christopher, inwardly reeling at the north-eastern accent – although it was possible the pitch was not as deep as the voice on the tape. *You are no nearer catching me now…* He pulled his dressing gown tight and tied the belt.

'You look worried, man,' said Adam, appearing now at the door of the kitchen, one red-socked foot on the step that led up to the living room.

'I've been thinking. I'm not going to stay in Leeds over the summer this time,' Christopher said.

Adam frowned, bit into his toast. A blob of strawberry jam landed on his chin. He pushed it off with his middle finger and sucked it clean. 'That's a shame. How come?'

'I think I'm going to move in with Phyllis. With my family.'

'But we'll have a much better time here, you know that, don't you? God knows, you might even get laid for a legendary second time.'

Adam – always thinking of sex. He was predatory all right, but enough to follow a woman late at night? Enough to take what he wanted then kill her – or kill her if she didn't give him what he wanted?

'Late shift?' Christopher managed to ask.

'Finished at two. Had a pint after with the others.'

It was a little after three. If he'd caught a bus or walked up the back way, the timings worked.

'So. Did you hear the tape?'

Adam's eyes widened. 'The Ripper? Yeah. Fucking hell, we listened to it on the radio.' He shook his head. 'Here's us all thinking he's a Yorkshireman and he's from my neck of the woods. He sounds like my Uncle Pete. Tell you what, I'm glad that tape hadn't come out before poor Sophie was taken. What with me a bloody Geordie. Enough to send shivers down your spine, isn't it?' His eyes were still wide. He slurped his tea and took another bite of toast. 'Sorry, did you want a brew?'

Christopher sighed. His head was spinning. He pressed his hands to his knees.

'Are you all right, man? You gone dizzy or something?'

'I'm all right. Light-headed. Must've got up too quickly or something.'

'Can I get you some tea?'

Adam wasn't the Ripper. Of course he wasn't. Christopher had been ridiculous even to think it. The murders had started before any of them had come to Leeds. Adam wouldn't even have passed his driving test back then. Adam was funny and kind and loved women. He loved them. It was impossible.

The last fraught hours disintegrated in his mind. There was nothing left now but a shaky residue of shock.

'Please, yeah,' he said, drawing himself up straight again. 'Tea would be great. I might have some sugar in it actually. I seem to have gone back to having sugar in my tea today.' He reached over and took Adam's toast, bit it, gave it back. Relief cut through him. He felt easy, light, as if the world were after all a place where he could be, as if this problem that had existed in him so urgently had in vanishing washed away all others with it. If Adam was his friend, and was not the Ripper, if the Ripper could be caught and locked away, if Phyllis loved him, then everything else would fall into place. He would finish his degree, move in with Phyllis and start the rest of his life.

But on 1 September, just before Christopher began his third year, the Yorkshire Ripper struck again: Barbara Leach, not a prostitute but another student, this time from Bradford University. Christopher documented her death in the usual way, felt its sordid details run over his skin like sweat. He waited and watched for news of more attacks. At night, he looked out for anyone who fitted the description, stared at couples walking arm in arm, became alive to the rare sound of females on the street. But there were no more murders reported that academic year, which in the end went much as the second year had.

Christopher studied hard, worked his shifts, went out sometimes with Adam and the boys. He listened to Adam's tales of his romantic conquests with a mixture of amusement and confusion and spent his nights alone with his right hand and his dreams of Stevie Nicks. He did not see Angie – at the thought of her, guilt flooded into him like coffee too hot, too bitter, and so he tried not to think of her at all. Phyllis he did think of, all the time, even when he was studying. He visited her as often as he could, and when he went to her his lungs filled with air, though it felt like something more than oxygen that swelled his chest and made him run the last yards to her front door. Whatever it was, it was enough to fray the rope that for so long had tied itself too tightly around his heart. Without that rope, he could breathe.

One evening a week or two before the final exams, Adam burst through the front door, which gave directly onto the kitchen of the two-bedroom back-to-back terrace they had rented in Autumn Avenue, and said: 'Christopher. Mate. I'm in love.'

He mock-staggered across the thin scratchy carpet and collapsed onto the sofa, where Christopher had been reading *Progress and Poverty The Industrial Revolution*. Adam threw his feet over the edge of the sofa and laid his head on Christopher's lap. He blew at the pages of Christopher's book, tried to put his nose in the gap between the spine and the cover.

'Christopher,' he sang. 'Chri-i-i-istophe-e-er.'

With a shake of his head, Christopher put his book aside.

'Mate,' said Adam, the smell of ale on his breath.

'Well?'

Adam closed his eyes and knotted his hands over his chest, the pose like the stone lid of a knight's tomb.

'She is heaven, man,' he said.

'What's her name, then, this heavenly creature?'

'Stephanie.'

'Stephanie, I see.'

'I am going to marry her.'

'I say, she must be an angel,' said Christopher.

'She is.'

'So how did this meeting come about?'

But Adam was asleep. Christopher had to slide from under him, holding his head and laying it on a cushion as he stood. He made for his bedroom to fetch a blanket but had only got as far as the living-room door when his friend called to him.

'Where are you going, man? Don't you want to know the details?'

Adam had met Stephanie at the Headingley Arms and had fallen into conversation after she had dropped her earring, which had wedged itself between two floorboards.

'I dug it out with a paper clip,' he said, smiling toothlessly like an idiot. 'She said I was her knight in shining stationery.' He laughed. 'That's not her best joke. She's funny and clever and sexy as hell.'

'She sounds marvellous.'

'She is, man. Bloody marvellous with a capital M. And beautiful. I love her. I'm in love with her. I'm going to marry her. She is the one, I'm telling you. She is. The one.'

Despite Adam's relative indolence until the eleventh hour compared with Christopher's relentless diligence, both graduated with a 2:1. Christopher applied for and was accepted onto a teacher-training course in Aigburth, which he had chosen for its proximity to Runcorn – he would live with Phyllis and the family and look for work nearby once he qualified. Adam got a job as a junior electronic engineer with British Aerospace and planned to move down to the outskirts of Stevenage.

'Stephanie's agreed to come and live with me,' he said when they came to say goodbye to each other and to the tiny house they had shared. 'Give me six months to work on her. You'll be my best man when the time comes.'

'I'll hold you to it.'

Adam had already loaded his cases, his record player, his guitar and his mirror into the Mini. Wiping his hands on his jeans, he stepped up onto the pavement, where Christopher was waiting to wave him off. The moment of parting had arrived and it silenced them. They stood in the grey Leeds light and said nothing. They had felt this moment coming these last weeks, and now here it was. The memories of all they had shared flashed through Christopher's mind: Adam's silly entrance into their shared room in halls that very first day, the first time Christopher had witnessed his room-mate's virtuoso skills as he smooth-talked Alison, his pep talks – *chutzpah, mate, that's what you need* – their conversations late at night before the hissing gas fire, both tired but neither willing to go to bed. Most of all, he would miss Adam's kindness, how like a light it was. This was what it meant to be loved: to feel the light of another person shine on you, a light under which you could grow. Adam had this light. Phyllis had this light. But he could never tell Adam all that he meant to him, could never put it into words. If he did, Adam would tell him to fuck off.

Instead, he met his friend's eye and smiled. 'So this is it.'

'Come here, you lanky bugger,' said Adam.

The two men held each other, slapped each other's backs.

'You're my best friend,' Christopher said, his voice choked, his mouth close against Adam's left ear.

'And you mine, mate,' said Adam. 'And you mine.'

Once Adam had gone, Christopher found himself alone in the house. He had been alone in the house before, of course, but now without Adam, without the promise of his return, it felt emp-tier, lonelier. He went upstairs to pack the rest of his things. His clothes were already in the grotty suitcase where he had found the blanket and the note three years earlier. The thought took him back to the dark attic space behind his loft room. What had he felt? Nothing. Nothing at all. Not then. Everything he had felt about that note had come later, over years. In those first moments there had been only numbness, then in the weeks that followed action, action almost without thought.

In his chest of drawers was the Ripper scrapbook he had made. The thing bulged with articles he had cut out over the years, and yet they still hadn't caught him. The north of England was in a state of paranoia. Someone knew who it was. Or did they? He was a Geordie. Or was he? What if he had put on an accent on that tape? What if he was not from Wearside but from Barnsley or Lancaster or even Scotland? What if he was from Morecambe? Did his wife, his sister, his mother know it was him? Did the Ripper himself even know it was him? What if even he, the monster, didn't realise he had murdered those women? He might have killed them in some blind and frenzied act, only to black it out from his mind.

Was that possible – to do something so heinous you buried it deep, deep, deep until you didn't believe you'd done it at all?

Christopher flipped through his scrapbook and found the police-issue picture of the Ripper.

Do you know this man?

With the scrapbook still in his hands, he went into the bathroom and stared into the mirror. His black hair, his black beard. He removed his glasses and leant into his reflection. He looked like, could pass for that picture. Yes, he looked like *him*. Craig… or was it Darren, had said when they were in Anglesey – out of the mouths of babes… A memory: himself, washing his hands, weeping over a sink, the water trailing brown into the plughole. Brown: not red, not blood. But even so, when was this? It was something he had not remembered before – only now when he had trained his mind to it had it come up. Were there other memories, down, down with that one, memories yet to surface? Was it possible that he, Christopher, was *him*? Was he the Yorkshire Ripper?

CHAPTER TWENTY-TWO

Christopher shaved his beard off that day, I think. Certainly, by the time he was living in Runcorn more permanently, he was clean-shaven as he had been when he first met Phyllis. A clean shave was not enough to stop the monster though, I think now as I flick through Christopher's scrapbook. Here, near the back: August 1980, forty-seven-year-old Marguerite Walls, the latest victim. There are articles from *The Guardian*, *The Telegraph* and the *Daily Mail*. I picture him cutting them out, gluing them into place. I picture him and wonder what on earth he was thinking about.

I picture him. That's the problem. I can't stop the images from forming. I see the Ripper, I see him, the two of them coalescing in my mind's eye as they did in his. No matter how I try and shake off these visions, they are beyond my control.

I picture him now, returning to Morecambe for what remained of his things. In the loft room he had grown to loathe, he must have packed his clothes, which Margaret had laundered during his short stay; his tapes; his writing set; two old pairs of shoes. He remembered the letter he had written to Phyllis that first Christmas. He had put it in his old school trousers but had neglected to post it. Of his school trousers there was no sign.

Behind him came the clatter of feet on the metal steps and he turned to see Margaret, her shoulders and head at the hatch like a scrawny plaster-cast bust.

'All ready?' she said, her face set in the expression of angst he had known all his life.

'Yes. Almost done.'

She threw a Safeway carrier bag onto the floor of the room, then climbed in after it. She had not, he realised, been up here before – at least not while he was there.

'I wondered if you had room for these.' She brought the carrier bag over to the bed and sat down. The hunched set of her spine had a beaten air about it. She looked withered. From the bag she lifted a block covered in thick foil. 'It's only a fruit cake,' she said. 'Keeps you going, does fruit cake.'

'Thank you.' What was it with mothers and fruit cake?

'Aye, and there's some pickled red cabbage your father made, and some damson jam. We had a lot this year.' She looked down into her lap, as if disappointed, or sorry. For what, he did not ask.

'Thank you,' he said instead. 'I'll write once I get there.'

'So your digs, is it other student teachers, did you say?'

'It's a room in a house,' he said – a lie of omission, nothing more. 'It's near the college. I'll write my address in the book in the phone table.' A more deliberate lie; he had no intention of doing so. 'I can't find my old school trousers, by the way.'

'Our Jack's got them, love. Why, did you need them?'

'No. No, of course not.' His brother must have found the letter. Christopher wondered what the chances of him not having read it were. He would catch him before he left this place for good.

'And you start in September?' Margaret said, her implication clear.

'Yes, but I was hoping to find a job in the run-up. A bar job or something. I've paid the rent up front so it makes sense to live there.' He forced himself to stop talking – the deeper into justification he got, the more lies he would weave, and he had already woven so many.

She nodded. 'Happen you've got your car now anyroad.'

'A car, yes. Such as it is.' He bit his lip. Why he had said that was anyone's guess. With his pub savings and a little help from Phyllis, he had paid for driving lessons and bought a third-hand Escort. Starting it was a challenge, but once he got it going, it ran well enough. The words had come out wrong. They sounded like reproach, but he hadn't meant that. He just didn't want anything about his new life to appear flash – that was it. Or threatening. Or better.

'Your brother'll be pleased anyway,' she said, looking about her. 'He's got his eye on this room.'

Jack Junior, stealer of Scalextric, robber of bedrooms, of graves. 'I'm sure he'll love it. Tell him to watch the steps going down.'

'Aye.' His mother allowed herself a brief chuckle. 'I hadn't realised how tricky they were, them steps. We should have put in a proper staircase.' She frowned. 'We should have made you some blinds for the skylight.'

'It's fine, Mum, honestly. It's fine.'

'Well…' she began but said nothing more. Her eyes were wet.

He stood, and seeing him stand, his mother stood too. He could not straighten to full height so remained a little stooped under the beams, and it seemed to him that his mother stooped too, though she was smaller today than ever. She dug in the sleeve of her cardigan and pulled out the shrivelled tissue that lived there, in the darkness, like a shrew. She blew her nose, her head bowed, and he was filled with a terrible sadness.

'Mum,' he said, and tried to take her stiff and tiny frame in his arms. Her body was rigid under his hands, her arms tucked up in front of her.

'I prefer you without your beard,' she said into his chest. 'I can see your face. You will look after yourself, won't you?'

'You needn't worry about me,' he said. 'I'm all grown up now.'

'You'll be in Jack's old room when you come to visit. You won't have to go up them steps.'

Ah yes, Margaret, you were right. He would never again go up those steps. He left his family there at the door of his childhood home. If he looked back, it was only once, only enough to see the four of them lined up with stiff formality, arms by their sides, small and muted and distant as an old photograph faded in the sun.

Did he drive to Phyllis without a thought for the family he had left, this week's Top 40 in the cassette player? 'Don't Stand So Close to Me', 'Woman in Love', 'Geno'… did he sing all the way?

I don't know. There are, after all, things I don't know.

At the sight of the greenish spire of St Edward's Church, his stomach flipped. He turned left into Langdale Road and pulled up to the house. Phyllis was at the front window. She waved and jumped up and down, had run out onto the driveway in her stockinged feet before he'd got out of the car.

'You're here for good,' she cried. 'I can't believe it.' She bent her knees and her hands flew to her face.

'The first day of the rest of my life!' He threw his arms around her and kissed her on the forehead. 'I love you, Phyllis Curtiss.'

She burst into tears but she was laughing too, and she hugged him. 'And I love you, Christopher who was Martin. My lost boy. My darling, darling boy.'

And like that, his life as Martin Curtiss, known to his friends and family simply as Christopher or Chris or even sometimes Chrissy, the life he had travelled steadfastly towards since that October day in 1977 when Margaret and Jack had sat him down in the front parlour, began.

Christopher started his teacher-training course in the October of that year, 1980. In November, another Leeds student, Jacqueline Hill, was killed, her body found in the ground of Lupton Residences. Christopher cut out the relevant articles for his scrapbook and studied his old map of Leeds, curious as to where Lupton

Residences were in relation to Oxley Hall, the only female halls he had visited in his time at university.

When the Christmas break came around, Phyllis insisted he spend Christmas Eve and most of Christmas Day with his adoptive family.

'I want you here, of course I do,' she said, stroking his hair back from his face. 'But they raised you and it's not right to spend it with us. You'll hurt their feelings.' She didn't know at this point that neither Margaret, nor Jack, nor Jack Junior nor Louise had any idea of her existence.

'All right,' he said, for her, for the sake of all that he had to keep hidden. 'I'll go.'

'I've made some shortbread for you to take. And a card.'

'Lovely. Thank you.'

He went. I have no idea what happened to the shortbread and the card. They will have ended up in some rubbish bin in a service station, I should think; like so many things in his life cast aside, forgotten.

In January 1981, Christopher took up a placement at a secondary school in Widnes. In the late afternoons, while the twins were out playing football or watching television or doing their homework, he and Phyllis would work together at the kitchen table: she on her marking and preparation, he on his assignments. They had learned to keep an eye on the time, and fifteen minutes before David was due home, Christopher would take his work upstairs and finish it at the desk David had painted for him, while Phyllis would jump up and busy herself with the evening meal.

What reason did either of them give for this, even to themselves?

It was on a Sunday night in January that the announcement came. Like most momentous historical events, everyone can remember where they were when they heard. And for Christopher, that moment was at home at 6 p.m. He and Phyllis and David were sitting in the lounge with their tea on trays on their laps. It was Phyllis who had suggested they have a TV dinner, saying she wanted to catch the news. They were chatting about something or other when from the television Big Ben chimed and what followed shocked them all into silence:

'A man is charged with a Ripper murder…'

Those were the words. Not the Ripper murders, as we talk about them today, but *a* murder. I remember that press conference, the atmosphere of euphoria among the high-ranking police officers who had presided over the five-year waking nightmare. I can't remember what came out during that first broadcast and what came out later, only that feeling: he'd been caught. Finally. It was over.

A fake number plate had given him away. The police had picked him up for routine, nothing more. Saying he needed a piss, he'd tried to stash the murder weapons. He hid another one in the cistern of the toilet at Dewsbury police station. The rest had fallen into place from there.

Confession at last. To every one.

The report finished. Christopher collapsed against the back of the sofa.

'They've got him,' he said, his voice strange, strangled. 'They've caught him, the monster.' He had to put his dinner on the floor. He was panting, running his hand over his forehead. David had to go and get him a glass of water.

'Are you all right, love?' Phyllis asked, rubbing his back.

'Here.' David passed him the water and he drank it down in one go.

'I'm all right,' he said. 'Just so glad they got him. It's such a relief. It's over.'

Over the days that followed, whether it was the television news, the radio or out on the street, the talk was of nothing else. More came out. Thirteen victims: he had killed them with a ball-peen hammer and a kitchen knife – objects that hung heavy in the mind. On the surface, he was a normal man, living in a normal house with his wife, Sonia.

'It's like the last piece in a jigsaw puzzle,' Christopher said later, once Sutcliffe had confessed in full – once we knew there'd be no going back. 'I feel free. I don't know how to explain it, except for that. I feel free.'

He told me then there had been times when he thought that *he* might be the Yorkshire Ripper. He said he'd looked in the mirror and seen the image released by the police. I couldn't believe he could think such a thing, although I could see the physical similarity, especially when he had the beard – I could see how he could have compared his face to the sketches released by the police. Being such a sensitive boy, I could see how such gruesome events might get under his skin and I thought that was all it was. Now, of course, I know it was more than that.

And this is where I have to get to, what I have been aiming towards and yet avoiding all this time: April 1981. Even now I don't know if I can get there, but I will try.

It was the Easter holidays. Christopher had turned twenty-two in the March. Working backwards, it must have been the Wednesday, and I know that on that day Phyllis had gone into Liverpool with her sister to buy clothes; that David had taken the twins youth-hostelling for a few days in the Lake District. I know that the plan was for David and the twins, who by then must have been twelve years old, to return on the Saturday in time for Easter Mass on the Sunday. And I know that it was Christopher who answered the door.

I sit here now and I wonder what would have unfolded had Phyllis not gone to Liverpool but had instead stayed at home and opened the door herself. Life is series of moments, of choices, isn't it? Every moment, every choice could have gone differently, and sometimes that doesn't bear thinking about. Sometimes thinking about that one thing can drive a person mad – or even to suicide. No one knows that better than me. Regret, if that's a strong enough word, is a potent force. But listen to me, sitting here pontificating. Not like I'm any great philosopher. I'm only a person – a normal person with nothing special or interesting to say. What happened that day broke Christopher's world, broke all of our worlds, into pieces.

What else is there to say? What, really?

Perhaps I could add that it was a shame, such a shame, because by this time Christopher really had settled. Phyllis saw it: in the set of his shoulders, the line of his jaw, the way his eyes opened that little bit wider these days, seemed to have lost the anticipation of hurt she had always read there, the expression that had broken her heart a thousand times over when she had first met him and made her want to say, *Hey, it's OK, nothing bad can happen now. You are safe, my love.*

Christopher was saving for a flat. He had met a nice girl, a Spanish teacher called Amanda. They'd been out a few times. Phyllis suspected they'd slept together, since Amanda stayed in digs near the college, and besides, Christopher had taken to wearing a wide smile on his face, to whistling around the house. But he hadn't told Phyllis anything yet and hadn't asked if Amanda could stay at the house.

'No reason why she can't,' David had said when she spoke to him about it. 'They're hardly kids any more.'

'I'm not sure it's a good idea,' Phyllis had replied, with no idea how she would justify this statement. 'What about the twins?' was what came to her. 'And he's only got a single bed.'

As it turned out, Amanda staying was not something they would ever have to worry about.

It was only later that Phyllis put two and two together and came to the conclusion that somehow, in some strange way, Christopher's entry into romantic life had some connection with the arrest of the Yorkshire Ripper. The last piece of the jigsaw in place, as he put it, it was as if he could get up from the puzzle and start living in a more complete way than before. Sometimes when we think something, we have no idea how true it is, nor indeed do we realise the implication of that truth until later.

As for Christopher, the knot in his chest had vanished. He was loved. He belonged. And he felt peace.

And writing this now, no matter what happened after, I suppose I have to be grateful for that.

CHAPTER TWENTY-THREE

Wednesday, 15 April 1981

Ben wakes a little after midnight. Finding he can't get back to sleep, he writes a letter to his mother. He doesn't want to sound pushy, but he doesn't have much time. He appeals, he hopes, to her maternal instincts. He has no intention of posting the letter; it is just a back-up. If she's not in, he will post it and hope she comes to find him at the hotel.

But he's getting ahead of himself. He needs to find her first.

He turns off his light and tries to get some more sleep. When he wakes up, it is late morning. English time. He takes a shower, gets dressed and breakfasts in the hotel. Continental – fake orange juice that tastes like it's made from a powder, croissants that bend but don't flake. Yuck. He takes his time over his coffee, gets a refill. Halfway down the second cup, it occurs to him he is nervous. He is stalling.

Back in his hotel room, he brushes his teeth and checks his appearance. Wonders if when she looks at him, she will like what she sees; whether when he looks at her he will see something of himself. Slow down, Ben. You haven't found her yet.

The guy at reception gives him detailed directions, draws a map on a piece of hotel stationery. *Not too far*, he says. *About a five-, ten-minute drive.*

Ben drives back the way he came, the long, winding artery that runs through Beechwood Estate, cul-de-sacs coming off it like lungs. *Keep going, keep going*, the guy said. *At a certain point you'll see a golf club and then there'll be a wide common-type thing on the left and then a crossroads up ahead.*

Ben's beginning to think he's gone wrong when he sees the grassy area to his left. Up ahead, traffic lights, and beyond, what looks like a park. *Keep going.* He goes straight on at the crossroads, down Moughland Lane. Yes, that checks out, he has that written down. *When you get to the next junction, turn right and you're there.*

He drives on. It is all so small, so British. *Cute*, Martha would say – she would love these red bricks, these white-framed curtained windows, these neat gardens running up to the sidewalk, ending with waist-high brick walls, hedges grown for privacy. Another field opens up to his right, what looks like a sports club or something at the far end. The junction comes up faster than he was expecting. There is a memorial of some kind on the left, and as he turns right, his chest swells in anticipation. *Greenway Road.* He is here.

The road heads down the hill. He drives past the house but there is nowhere to park out front. He takes a left down a street called Balfour Road and finally finds somewhere to leave the car. By the time he has walked back to the house, his heart is beating faster. But it's OK. He has rehearsed.

A woman with thick white hair curled in the old-fashioned way answers the door. He scrutinises her while trying to look like he's doing no such thing.

'Good morning,' he says and treats her to his best smile. 'My name is Benjamin Bradbury and I'm the son of a friend of Phyllis Curtiss.'

The woman blinks and says, 'Oh yes?'

'That's right. My mom gave me this address. Forgive me, but are you her mother?' When she says nothing, he continues quickly. 'Let me explain. I live in the US, San Francisco, but my mother is from here, from Runcorn. She emigrated a long time ago but she went to school with Phyllis. I'm over here on business and Mom asked me to try and look Phyllis up. She wants to write her and find out how she is and all. Do you think you could help me?'

She still has hold of the door edge; her eyes have narrowed. Holy shit, this could be his grandmother.

'Where did you get our address, did you say?' she says.

'From my mom. I think she used to live in, let me see, is it Balfour something?'

'Balfour Road?'

'Yes. That's right. Is that near here?'

She nods, but he can see she's still unsure.

He throws up his hands. 'Listen, if it's a trouble to you, I'll be on my way. But if you can tell her that Dorothy said hello. She'll remember. I can leave her address with you if you prefer.' He smiles again, takes a step back. 'I appreciate your time.'

'Hold on,' the woman says. 'Have you got a pen?'

He heads back the way he came, the sports field now on his left. At the junction, he heads left down the long hill of Heath Road. If he goes under a bridge, he's gone too far apparently. He should look out for the town hall, just after the roundabout. *It's a white building*, she said. *With big gardens all round it and railings. After that you take the first left.*

He reaches the roundabout, sees the railings and the grounds. Everywhere is so green around here, so leafy. He reaches the left turn. Ivy Street, that's right. He turns. On his right is the big church that she said would be there: red brick, a stone JC set in the wall, flanked by a row of portholes, arched windows below. A small green spire poking skywards like a stylus from a square tower.

'Hi,' he rehearses into the rear-view mirror. 'My name's Benjamin Bradbury. I'm looking for Phyllis Griffiths.'

He takes a left, into Langdale Road.

CHAPTER TWENTY-FOUR

Nurse came late today. I have never seen her look flustered, but today she did. Her face was pink and her hair, usually combed with flat perfection into her ponytail and shining with cleanliness, had been yanked into a bumpy knot. But it wasn't that. Nor was it the tired slope of her eyes or the crackle of thread veins in her cheeks. It was the set of her mouth. She had clamped it into a smile, wide and closed like a frog's, and while every day of my stay here so far she had looked me steadfastly in the eye – and God knows this must have been a challenge – today she looked at the floor.

She handed me my dish of pills.

'And how are you this morning, my darling?' she asked me as she does every day, knowing that I will not answer.

And it struck me that this flat smile of hers was a smile of pain. And that here she was, uniform on and hair pulled back, asking me how I felt. How *I* felt. The plant that blooms no matter how many times it is cut down, and still the weed sits there trying to poison it. I wondered what in her life had cut her down. I wondered if she'd tell me as we walked around the yard, and if she was silent, whether I would find the words to ask her what was wrong.

'I'm all right,' I said. No more than a croak.

Her eyes widened; her eyebrows shot into her brow.

'Are you now?' she said. 'Well that's grand.'

I gestured for the water. She held it out to me. I took my pills and sipped.

'Nurse.' Throat still scratchy, I coughed. Gently I reached for her wrist and held it. I met her eye. 'What's your name?'

Slowly she took the paper cup from me. 'It's Betsy.'

'Betsy,' I repeated, the name giving me the woman, giving me my voice. 'You have been very kind to me. Thank you.'

But now, there's no more going round the houses. That Wednesday, it was Christopher, not Phyllis, who opened the door. It was Christopher who found himself face to face with a man on the doorstep, a man he thought he recognised from somewhere. A man with brown shoulder-length hair pushed back from his face, a lopsided smile and inquisitive dark green eyes.

'Hi there.' His accent was American, which came as a shock. 'My name's Benjamin Bradbury. Ben. Pleased to meet you.' He stuck out his hand and smiled as if a handshake was non-negotiable – as if in his world rejection was not and never had been a possibility. His green eyes creased at the edges, his pale cream teeth were even and strong. His trousers were pale cream too, as if to match, and his shoes were brown, highly polished leather. He looked American as well as sounding it, Christopher thought, leaning forward to shake the man's hand.

'Christopher,' he said. 'Can I help you?'

'I'm looking for Phyllis Curtiss... actually, what am I talking about, her name is Griffiths now, I believe, excuse me. Curtiss is her maiden name.' His voice rose at the end of each sentence, as if he were asking a series of questions. But they were not questions.

'Phyllis?'

'Phyllis Griffiths. She lives here, I believe.'

'Curtiss,' said Christopher. The word blocked his throat. He coughed – coughed again. 'I mean Griffiths. No. I mean she used to but she – she moved. Away.'

Ben opened up the piece of paper in his hands. 'That's strange. Actually, I've just come from her parents' home over on Greenway Road, and they said she lived here. Is there another Langdale Road around these parts? Maybe I'm mistaken.'

The pulse in Christopher's forehead throbbed so hard he felt sure this man, Ben, would see it: a raised purpled vein, a blood beat fit to burst. Instinctively he put up his hand to hide it. 'No. Yes. She does live here but she doesn't like visitors. That's why I answer the door, you see. She doesn't like people coming to the house. She gets… she gets nervous. She's a very nervous person. Can I ask what it's in connection with?'

Ben looked down at his shiny shoes, but from the set of his brow Christopher could see he was still smiling. 'Actually, it's kinda personal. It's real important I get to see her.' He looked up and fixed Christopher with his unflinching green gaze, his wide cream teeth.

'I would recommend you drop her a line,' were the words that left Christopher's mouth. 'If you like, you could give me a letter and I'll make sure she gets it.'

'Ah, gee.' Ben looked behind him, into the road, and back again at Christopher. 'Thing is, I have to fly back to the States in a few days and it's real urgent.'

'I'm sure if you write something now she will get it tonight,' Christopher insisted. 'In fact I'll make sure she gets it. I give you my word.'

Ben looked beyond Christopher, into the hall. 'Is there any way I could wait? It's real important I see her.'

Christopher's chest began to burn. He widened his stance so as to fill the doorway. This chap was small in build, smaller than Christopher, but he still took up plenty of space. There was something about him, polite as he was. His American-ness perhaps. The Americans were a pushy lot.

'I'm afraid not,' Christopher said. 'Nothing personal, you understand. It's just that I don't know you and one can't be too careful. Really, if you can write something down and post it through the door, that would be better.'

'No need,' Ben said, digging in the back pocket of his jeans and pulling out an envelope. 'I figured this might happen. I'd sure appreciate it if you could pass this on as soon as possible.' He handed it to Christopher. The envelope was pale blue; it looked like it was from a hotel writing set. 'Do you mind me asking, are you related to Mrs Griffiths?'

'Yes,' Christopher said, tipping his head back a little. 'I'm her son.'

Again Ben spread his big cream American teeth. 'Wow,' he said. 'That's awesome.' He stared at Christopher for longer than was comfortable before adding: 'Listen, Christopher, the note's confidential, of course. I've left the number for my hotel. I'm staying at a place called the Crest. Room 152. It's beyond the Beechwood—'

'I know it.'

'She can call me there.'

'Marvellous.' Christopher put one hand on the door now. 'I'll make sure she gets it.' He made to close the door, but Benjamin threw out his hand – another handshake. What was he, a politician? Pretending not to see, Christopher closed the door and pressed his forehead against it, exhaling heavily before running through to the living room and watching the man walk away. His gait was relaxed, almost a roll, as if he walked for the sheer pleasure of it. He got into a red Ford Fiesta parked at the end of the drive, fired the engine more than was necessary and drove away.

Once he had gone, Christopher went into the kitchen and held the envelope over the steaming kettle. His hands shook. He eased open the flap and pulled out the letter. It was handwritten, as Christopher's own letters to Phyllis had been three, maybe four years ago now.

Dear Ms Curtiss,

You don't know me and there's no delicate way to say this so I'm going to come right out with it. My name is Benjamin Bradbury but you knew me as Martin; it's the name you gave me. I am your son. Enclosed is a photocopy of a photograph of me as a baby.

Christopher dug the photo out of the envelope. It showed a nun, standing in front of a bookshelf, holding a baby in her arms.

You may remember this picture being taken. I have had this photo my whole life. It was taken in the convent over in Railton, which is where I have been today. The lady in the picture is called Sister Lawrence. She is now the mother superior, and after a lot of persuasion, she allowed me to see their records.

I have not gone through the official channels – please forgive me for that. Only I didn't have much time – I don't have much time, as I am over on vacation from the US with the sole purpose of tracking down my birth parents. The sisters at the convent were very obliging.

I grew up in Virginia and am settled in San Francisco with my fiancée, Martha. I am a graphic designer by trade and before I get married and have kids of my own, I wanted to find out where I come from and to have seen my own mother at least once and maybe even have a cup of tea with you. I am not here to make trouble. I don't need money; I don't need anything at all. I just want to say hello and ask if we can correspond a little as I go forward in my life.

I don't want to put pressure on you, but I have only a few days left of my stay here, and I would sure appreciate it if you could meet me even for a short time. It would mean a lot to me.
Your son,
Benjamin Bradbury

Christopher felt himself fold – collapse forward. There had been a mistake, that much was clear. It was he, Christopher, who had gone through the correct channels; he, therefore, who was right, who was Phyllis's son. He could not be wrong – how could he be? He had found Phyllis four years ago! He had come to her and they had both known from the very beginning that she was his mother – that it was meant to be. Didn't he close his eye in that way she did? And her nose was broad, like his, and her eyes brown, also like his, not green like the American's. Didn't they share the same sense of humour? Didn't they… Whatever, they were close, had been since that first day. He had seen nothing of Phyllis in Ben, nothing at all.

And besides, it was too late. He and Phyllis had fallen into their routines – they were practically colleagues. She had helped him so much with his teacher training, helped him plan lessons, shown him how to criticise without discouraging. She was always there when he'd had a tough day, listening to him, advising him, galvanising him to go forward. Now that he too was at work, they would come home at a similar time and sit together at the kitchen table to mark their books and plan their lessons in companionable silence. A companionable silence that had taken years!

So no. No. This man – Ben – could not simply walk into this house and claim he belonged here instead. He could not. Ben wouldn't help Phyllis prepare the dinner the way Christopher did. Ben wouldn't be able to sit at this table and eat and trade the day's tales, jokes, insults. This was not Ben's family. This was not Ben's mother. This was not Ben's life.

No. No. Christopher would go to the hotel; he would call this Ben Bradbury, this cocky interloper, down to reception and tell him to sling his hook. *Go and steal someone else's life*, he would tell him. *Go through the correct channels and don't come back here unless it's to apologise for the distress you've caused.*

The key banged into the lock. Phyllis. He knew her every sound, her sigh as she hung up her coat, the groan as she pulled off her shoes. He knew these things, and more, because he loved her more than his own life.

'Hello?' she called.

'In here.' Christopher put the letter and the envelope in his pocket.

'Hello, love.' She was at the kitchen door, clothes shop bags in both hands: Miss Selfridge, C&A, Dolcis. She bustled through, oblivious. 'I got some shoes,' she said, since that is the kind of thing people who have no idea how happy or how safe they are say to one another. 'I got three tops and a skirt too – don't tell David!'

'Good,' he croaked through the sharp sting at the back of his throat. 'That's good.'

'Tea?'

'Actually no, thanks. I've… I've got to pop upstairs a second.'

He left the kitchen before she could see his face and ran up the stairs. A second later she called up: 'Christopher?'

On the dark landing, he halted. 'Yes?'

'Are you OK, love?'

'I'm fine.' He did not move. Waited in the darkness to hear the pad of her feet retreat into the kitchen. Once he was sure she had gone, he went into his room and for the first time sat at the desk with the intention of writing something. From the pot in the corner he took out the fountain pen Margaret had given him. Margaret, whom he had abandoned. Jack too, Jack Junior, Louise, even David and the twins… all of them he had to a greater or lesser degree rejected, all for her, all for Phyllis. There was no one more important, not even himself. That was love. That was how a son loved his mother. If she weren't his mother, he would have known. He would feel it. She had to be his mother. Without her, he had nothing. He was nothing. He was no one.

He wrote: *Dear Benjamin*, and stopped. If he contested this man's claims, that would create an argument. Benjamin Bradbury would most likely return to the house and confront Phyllis. There would be a scene. He would press charges; the Americans were a litigious bunch. Liverpool Council would get involved, the whole lot. No. Far better to reject him. There was little one could argue against rejection. He bent to his task:

I am glad to have received your letter. I understand why you would want to come to the house, however I think it was perhaps better that I wasn't there. My son Christopher gave me your note this evening so I am replying as soon as I can, as Christopher mentioned you are short of time.

I appreciate your wish to see me, but what you need to realise is that I have a complete family now. I have twelve-year-old twins, and my eldest, Christopher, whom you met, also lives with us. Whilst for me it would be wonderful to meet you and to welcome you into my home, you will appreciate that for the rest of my children, this would be extremely unsettling. We are a very close family.

I wish you every success in your career and in your marriage. I am delighted things have worked out for you, and believe me, finding love is the greatest ambition there is. Please understand that I have moved on from what was a very painful time for me but that this is no reflection on you. I didn't want to give you up, but I had to. It was a long time ago and is something I wish to leave in the past. Please accept my apologies. I am sorry not to be able to give you what you came for. But at least you know where you were born and that I gave you up against my will. I wish I could rewrite the past, but I can't. I hope you understand.

Wishing you all the love and luck in the world,

Your mother, Phyllis

He sealed the letter in an envelope and wrote Ben's name on the front. He crept downstairs and lifted his coat from the hook. Silently he slid open the hall table drawer and took out his car keys.

'Chris?' Phyllis called from the kitchen. There was a smell of chocolate cake – she must be baking, he thought, for the Easter service. 'Love?'

'It's OK, Mum,' he called back to her. 'I've just got to nip out for something.'

'All right. Tea in an hour or so, once I've finished these fairy cakes, all right?'

'Yes. Yes, OK.'

'Oh, Chris?'

'Yes?'

She had come to the kitchen door and was wiping her hands on a tea towel. 'Did anyone come to the house today?'

'Anyone? Like who?'

'A chap. Only Mum said an American had called round, saying he was the son of a friend of mine from school. Said he was going to call and say hello apparently.'

Christopher felt for the latch, aware of his heart beating. 'No one came,' he said, shaking his head, turning away from her, opening the door.

'All right,' he heard her say. 'Maybe he'll come tomorrow.'

'Yes.' One foot on the step, he paused. 'Maybe tomorrow. I'll… I'll see you in a bit, then.'

'Rightio,' she said. 'See you in a bit.'

He closed the front door without a sound, as if stealth could protect him from his own roiling insides. He drove up the steep hill of Heath Road, turned left and continued past the playing fields, past the golf course and the larger detached houses, past the bus station, beneath the expressway and through Beechwood Estate. He turned right, drove a little further through yet more houses and parked, finally, at the Crest Hotel. An anonymous place, of brown brick and smoked glass, somewhere people hired for functions: weddings, christenings, funerals.

'Could you please make sure Benjamin Bradbury gets this letter as soon as possible?' he said to the girl at reception. 'It's extremely important he receives it tonight.'

'Of course, sir,' said the girl. 'I'll take it to his room now.'

CHAPTER TWENTY-FIVE

On the way back to the hotel, Ben's head is spinning like a washing machine. That guy, that tall geeky guy, is his half-brother. A half-brother around his own age. Christopher, like Christopher Robin, standing there in his cardigan and slippers like a university professor or something.

'Man,' Ben says to no one, hitting the steering wheel as he drives through the housing estate. 'Man, oh, man.'

This Christopher guy would have to be younger, wouldn't he? His mother wouldn't have given away a second child, not for any reason Ben can see, so his half-brother must be younger, maybe a year or two, lucky enough to be born when Phyllis could look after him.

The whole thing is a trip. Ben can't wait to tell Martha. And this is only the beginning. Wait till he meets Phyllis – that will blow what is left of his mind. What will she look like? She might be tall like Christopher, with black hair and tortoiseshell glasses. She might wear contact lenses. Maybe Christopher wears contacts too sometimes. Or maybe he works the whole bespectacled billionaire vibe on purpose for the girls, like Tony Curtis in *Some Like it Hot*. Christ, this is all such a rush. It's all he can do to concentrate on the road.

In his hotel room, he lies down on the bed.

A sliding sound wakes him and for a moment he has no idea where he is. The light outside is whiter, colder. He checks the time and sees that it's a little after six. He must have fallen asleep on the bed – the jet lag is killing him. Still dazed, he gets up and switches on the television. It's a local programme: *Look North*. They're the same the world over, these guys: slick hair and skin, super-straight clothes – the thought makes him smile. On the floor at the door to his room there is an envelope – the source of the noise. His lungs fill at the sight. It is from her, it must be. Who else does he know in this town?

He grabs the letter, sits on the bed, opens it. It *is* from her, Phyllis; she is glad to have received his letter. He reads on, his heart sinking lower with every word.

I wish I could rewrite the past, but I can't. I hope you understand.

'Goddam!' He screws up the letter and throws it against the wall. He checks his watch and sees that only a few minutes have passed. What time will it be in San Fran? Mid-morning. Easter holidays – there's a chance Martha will be at the apartment. He dials nine for an outside line.

The ringtone in California sounds distant, but after three or four she picks up.

'Martha?'

'Ben! How's it going?'

How he loves her. He pictures her, there in the apartment. Her smile. He tells her about the convent, about Christopher, about the letter.

'She can't dismiss me like that,' he says. 'I'm her son, for Chrissakes – what does she think I am, made of clay? It's goddam heartless. It's cruel. I didn't ask to be born. And I certainly didn't ask to be left in some goddam convent.'

'Benjamin Bradbury, calm down,' Martha says. 'Take a deep breath.'

He does as he's told.

'And another,' she says. 'It's not me you're angry at, OK?'

'I know,' he says. 'I'm sorry. But she owes me a meeting. She damn well owes me.'

'Ben. Hon. She doesn't know you is all. If she knew you, she wouldn't have written that letter. If she knew you, she'd trust your intentions. Maybe you need to write her one more time, give her more information, reassure her a little, huh?'

'You think?'

'Yeah. Besides, it's not like you to give up so soon. That's not the Ben I know.'

This time when he breathes the air reaches his lungs, swelling his chest. She's right. The thing he's learnt, the thing he knows above all else, is that with enough determination and persistence, you will get whatever it is you want. You decide what it is, you focus on it and you go get it. It is that simple.

'I love you,' he says.

'I love you right back.'

After the call, he gets up, retrieves the letter from the floor and straightens it out. Wishes he'd stayed calm – his temper catches him out sometimes; Martha hates it. Calm, Benjamin Bradbury, calm down. His full name is their code for when his anger is getting the better of him. Some things are not easy, life is not easy – doesn't mean you have to lose it, make the people around you uncomfortable. Doesn't mean you have to quit. You have to keep on, dead straight; don't let anything stand in your way. Aim – fire.

Moments later he has begun another letter, stronger this time. More persuasion is all he needs. An ultimatum. What mother can resist her own son? And if that doesn't work, he'll simply show up and not leave until she sees him.

He finishes the letter, leaves it in his room and goes down to eat in the hotel restaurant. He will post it in the morning. The timing has to be right. It's better if she has time to think it over, regret her words. Who knows, she might even show up at the hotel before the end of the evening.

'That you, Chris, love?' Phyllis called as he closed the front door behind him.

'It's me.' It *was* him, he thought. Martin Curtiss. Christopher.

She was at the sink, washing up, while on the hob a saucepan, its lid half-on, shuddered and steamed.

'Hi, you,' she said.

'Hi.' He kissed her cheek, went to inspect the contents of the other pan, where broccoli sat in cold water, ready prepared. The smell of bacon rose from under the grill. This turned out to be bacon chops – one for him, one for her.

'Dinner smells good,' he said and kissed her again. 'Thought I'd better kiss that cheek too in case it might be jealous of the other.'

She giggled. 'You are daft sometimes.'

And this was all he had ever wanted, he thought. For his mother to call to him as he came home, for her to be there doing something as ordinary and mundane as washing up while potatoes boiled in a pan. For her to say hello if he said hello, for her to giggle if he made the smallest joke. This was life. She was life. If he could have this, her, he had normality. He had everything.

He set the table then returned to her as if drawn by an invisible cord. He laid his head between her shoulder blades, wrapped his arms around her waist.

'Hi again,' he said.

She closed her wet hand over his. 'Dinner's two minutes. Open a bottle, will you?'

She brought the dinner and sat opposite him once again.

He touched his glass to hers.

She drank, as did he. He watched her over the rim of the glass. She was beautiful really. No one you would turn after on the street; her beauty came from being close to her, close enough to really see her.

'You look beautiful,' he said.

She sat back in her chair, her eyes wide. She had a mouthful of food and could not speak. Instead she waved her hand in front of her face, flustered by the compliment.

'What did I tell you?' she said once she'd swallowed. 'You are daft sometimes.'

He could not eat. The sight of her and all she meant had stopped his appetite.

'What's wrong?' she asked, and to his mortification he felt his eyes prickle.

'Nothing,' he said. 'It's delicious, but I suppose I'm not hungry.'

'What did you have for lunch?'

'That's the thing. I didn't eat lunch either.' He laid his knife and fork on his plate. Suddenly the thought of food or wine made him feel sick. 'I'm so sorry, but I feel very out of sorts. I think I'm going to have to go to bed.'

He did not sleep. How could he? How could anyone? When he did drift off, he saw Benjamin Bradbury, his assassin's grin. Benjamin Bradbury, in his pale cotton slacks, pushing his way into Christopher's home. Benjamin Bradbury, his hand flat against Christopher's chest: *I am Martin – get out of my way.* Christopher watched himself, as if from a distance, disintegrate into black dust. The dust hovered a moment before dropping to the floor...

'I am Martin.'

He was sitting up, drenched in sweat, breathing heavily. Who had said that? He looked around the room. There was no one. The voice had been his own. A moment later, Phyllis appeared at his door, her shoulders square and white beneath the thin straps of her cotton nightdress.

'Are you all right, love?' she said. 'You were shouting.'

'Sorry. Bad dream, that's all.'

'Shall I bring you some water?'

'No, it's OK. I'm OK.'

From the door, she blew him a kiss. 'Sleep well, my love.'

He lay back, but his mind would not be still. What business had this smooth American, with his easy grin and firm handshake, what business had he to turn up like that out of nowhere and ruin people's lives – ruin his, Christopher's, life? The mistake was evidently at the convent. Nuns were women of God, not professional administrators. The people at the council had systems in place, procedures, bodies set up to deal with precisely this sort of thing. Samantha Jackson was the kind of woman who knew what she was doing. She had short grey hair, no-nonsense hair, efficient hair. She wore a suit.

But if he went to the council, they would contact the convent, they would contact the Registrar, they would contact Phyllis. They would contact Benjamin Bradbury and bring him crashing into the picture. A meeting would have to take place, all parties involved. No, no. That could not be allowed to happen. He would have to take matters into his own hands. In the meantime, he would be vigilant. Whatever communication came from Ben, he must intercept it.

At dawn, sore-eyed and punch-drunk with exhaustion, he went downstairs to the kitchen. If Ben delivered that letter, he could not afford for Phyllis to pick it up.

He was still in the kitchen when at eight he heard the upstairs toilet flush, heard the water run, the squeak of Phyllis's bedroom door. He listened for her footsteps on the stairs, watched the kitchen door, waited for her to fill it. She did, her dressing gown open to reveal her thin white nightdress. She stumbled past him, ruffled his hair.

'Your tea's cold.' She yawned as she spoke. 'I'll make a pot, eh? How're you feeling?'

'Not well,' he said.

'Still? Oh dear.'

The tap ran, the kettle boiled, the toast popped out of the toaster. She slid a fresh mug of tea across the table to him. 'That's no good. I was going to go over to your grandma and grandad's today, was going to ask if you wanted to come with me.'

'You go,' he said. 'I think I might go back to bed.'

He sipped his tea, hovering on the kitchen chair nearest the door, waiting for the crash of letters on the hall mat. If Ben had written back, he had to grab the letter before she saw it but without jumping like a gun dog. He was vaguely aware of Phyllis eating her breakfast, leaving the kitchen, the rushing of the shower. The post did not come. Minutes, maybe half an hour later, Phyllis was at the kitchen door once more, her eyes emboldened with eyeshadow, her lips pinky red, her brown hair pushed into its customary ponytail.

'I'm off then, love, all right?' She hesitated, then came forward and kissed him on the head. At the touch of her lips, he closed his eyes. Her perfume was flowery, a happy spring smell. 'Keep warm. I'll see you later.'

Still with his eyes closed, he listened for the swish of her shoes on the nylon of her tights, the rush of her coat sleeves, the jingle of her keys, the bang of the front door. The hollow trot of her footsteps receding down the drive to the street, where she'd parked her Nissan. And then – not quite silence. The hum of the fridge, the click of the heating as the radiators cooled.

At half past nine, Christopher was still in the kitchen, still in his dressing gown, on the chair near the door, when from the hallway came the rustle of post and the clank of the letter box. He stood stiffly. His body had grown cold and set and he half-limped down the hall. There was nothing from Ben – only bills, circulars and the like – and the momentary relief made him sigh. He climbed the stairs and washed at the bathroom sink, put on his clothes and came back downstairs. Feigning illness had, he thought, made him feel ill. He put a teaspoon of Nescafé into a mug and flicked the kettle switch.

Another clank. He turned to see the pale blue envelope drop onto the mat, skirt along it for a moment with a soft *shush*. He hurried through the kitchen and back into the hall. Through the textured glass of the front door, the black figure of a man distorted into pools. The pools separated, dispersed, disappeared. Ben. Christopher made to open the door but thought better of it. He picked up the letter and held it in his hands. Outside, a car revved, pulled away, the rise and fall of the gears then silence. He tore open the letter.

16 April 1981
Dear Phyllis,

I appreciate your reticence about seeing me. It is one hundred per cent understandable. But trust me, I have no desire to intervene in any way with your family. I met your older son, Christopher – he seems like a nice guy and I'm sure he treats you well. I'm not asking to move in or anything, I just want to make a connection with you, you who gave birth to me all those years ago. Life is a gift; I don't take it for granted. I have that at least to thank you for.

I never really connected with my adoptive parents, you see. They are good people and they have been more than generous with me, and any problems I have had I could easily have had with my own flesh and blood. I could have been a better son to them. I was spoilt and I have treated them unfairly. I intend to put this right.

I am asking you to reconsider. I have asked at the hotel if there are any pubs near where you live and they have suggested the bar here at the hotel. It's quiet here. We could talk. Today is Thursday. You need time – I appreciate that. I will be there tomorrow evening (Friday) from 7 p.m. until they close. Think about it. I ask only that you have a drink with me. I have come all this way to see you.

I have questions, but not too many, and I believe I have a right to know the answers. I don't want to have to park outside your house and wait for you. Please don't make me do that.

The Crest Hotel. Please come. Even for an hour. It would mean a lot.

Your son,

Benjamin (Martin)

In Christopher's chest, an old fear, a knot tying itself around his heart. *I don't want to have to park outside your house...* The line rang loud in his head and pulled the rope tight.

'Bastard,' he said, to no one. 'Bastard!'

He screwed the letter into a ball and squeezed it in his hands. He threw it into the bin but minutes later took it out again. Phyllis might find it there. Not that she would look for it but she might see, she might wonder and that might make her reach, make her open it up and read. And then it would all be over. He put the crumpled paper in his coat pocket. Realising he had left the other letter in his room, he ran up the stairs, grabbed it from his desk and put it in the pocket too.

'There,' he said, though his heart battered. He went back to his room, sat at the desk and took out his writing pad. If the bastard was going to force his hand, he would bloody well force it right back.

Dear Ben,

I will meet you. I would prefer somewhere nearer to home as I can only spare an hour. I will tell my family I am going to the neighbour's or something. Meet me on Friday at the Wilsons pub in the old town. Ask at the hotel, they can give you directions. Or get a taxi. I will be there at seven. Until tomorrow evening,

Phyllis

Christopher told me he dropped the letter at the hotel and continued straight on to Railton. He said he arrived at the convent at around midday. The old red-brick building was separated from the street by a five-foot wall, also of red brick. He parked in the lane opposite and made his way back down the lane, over the road. He found the iron gates, which he had expected to be locked, but when he pushed, they opened. The convent itself was 1800s, in the Gothic style, the windows and doors thin pointed arches, buttresses and cross-shaped cut-outs in the bricks. At the dark, arched wooden door, he rang the bell. A young nun answered.

'Good morning,' he said. 'My name is Christopher Harris. Could I speak to the mother superior? It's extremely urgent.'

She nodded and let him inside, gesturing towards a stone bench and leaving him there in the foyer. He waited, trying not to stare at the replica pietà in the recessed arch in the opposite wall, the Virgin larger than life so that Christ lay small upon her lap like a child sick or dead. There was a smell of old, cold stone, of damp perhaps, but what struck him most was the silence. It occurred to him that the nun had not spoken. And yet he knew he was to wait, that she would be back. After no more than a few minutes, she returned and gestured for him to follow her down a long corridor that smelled faintly of varnish.

Maintaining her silence, she opened another wide arched wooden door to reveal an elderly nun sitting behind a mahogany desk with a green leather top. Behind her, the wall was lined with bookshelves – he was pretty sure they were the same bookshelves from the photocopied photograph Ben had sent with his letter, and he felt the rope tighten within him.

Upon seeing Christopher, the nun stood and held out her hand.

'Christopher Harris, is that right?'

He shook her hand. 'Yes, that's right. Thank you for seeing me.'

She gestured for him to sit down and sat herself, clasping her hands together on the desktop. 'You said it was urgent.'

He nodded. 'I'll come straight to the point. There's been a terrible mistake.'

It was as he'd thought. There had been another boy born March 12th, to a woman called Rebeccas Hurst. A boy named William but whom his mother had called Billy.

He came out of the convent around midday, he said. He was worried sick by now, but there was still time to do what he needed to do.

He studied the map, compared it to the address in his hand. Whitefield Road, in a place called Stockton Heath. The town lay almost equidistant, on the other side of Runcorn, from where he had come. At the realisation, he gave a sigh but continued to study the map, noting down directions for himself on the back of the piece of paper the mother superior had given him. Stockton Heath lay south of the Manchester Ship Canal – Christopher was pretty sure that was the canal that ran along the edge of the Mersey – and north of the Bridgewater Canal, the same canal that had its basin in his home town, Runcorn. It was a wonder Billy wasn't born on a barge, he thought, and for a moment he wondered if this might be the case. He imagined himself and Billy, both born on different barges, one heading up the Manchester Ship Canal and one up the Bridgewater, like Vikings en route to Avalon.

Forty-five minutes later, he turned into Whitefield Road, surprised to find it so well-to-do. He parked outside a particularly imposing Victorian house, not daring to pull into the driveway, which, he calculated, could probably have held four or five cars. As it was, there was a new BMW parked there. It looked clean enough to perform surgery on the bonnet. Breathing deeply and as regularly as he could, he made his way to the door. A cord hung next to it. He pulled on it and heard a sombre chime ring out from the depths of the house.

He waited, checked his watch. It was 1 p.m. He still hoped to be back before Phyllis.

At the sound of footsteps, he straightened his shoulders, coughed into his hand and threw back his head. The door opened. A tall, rather elegant-looking man with silver hair stood on the threshold.

'Good afternoon,' he said. He wore round tortoiseshell glasses, a pale red knitted waistcoat over a beige and brown checked shirt. On his feet were tartan slippers.

'Good afternoon,' Christopher began, all the words he had rehearsed in the car disappearing at once from his mind. 'My name is Christopher Harris. I'm looking for Rebecca Hurst.'

'Rebecca doesn't live here, I'm afraid.' The man made to close the door.

'Wait a moment.' Ben's story came back to him. 'She's a friend of my mother's, or was – a close friend. My mother received a phone call from her the other day – well, in truth, I did. I didn't realise how important she was to my mother and I'm afraid I didn't take her number. My mother was very cross and I was keen to put it right. To cut a long story short, she knew where Rebecca lived when they were teenagers and so she gave me this address.' He saw something flicker in the old man's face. He was a decent chap, kind, gentle, of that there was no doubt. 'But perhaps I'm mistaken. I'll let you go.'

'No, wait.' The man stood aside. 'She did live here. Come inside a moment. I have an address.'

As Christopher stepped into the enormous hallway, the man continued to talk. The hallway was bigger than Phyllis's living room, with a staircase that doubled back on itself, walls that continued up beyond the second flight. An antique telephone table, what he thought was called an occasional chair, and on the wall opposite, an ornate cross covered in polished coloured stones.

'She's our daughter. She did live here but she doesn't any longer. I'm afraid we've had very little contact with her for a few years now.' The man opened the drawer of the hall table and pulled out a leather-bound address book. 'Let's see. Do you have a pen and paper?'

'I'm afraid I don't. What an idiot.'

'Not at all. Let's not be hard on ourselves.' The man smiled. Really, he was so very nice. Classy, Phyllis would say. Margaret would no doubt have remarked on his lovely way of speaking, his quiet manners. 'I've a notepad here somewhere.' He dug about in the drawer, found the notepad and a Bic biro. 'There. Hardly a Sheaffer, but it will do.' He handed the pen and the paper to Christopher. 'Come through.'

Christopher followed the man, Rebecca's father, down the hall, to where there was effectively a T-junction, one way leading left, the other right. He turned right and opened a door with a frosted window in it. Christopher followed him into a spacious kitchen, which smelled of cinnamon, he thought, and sugar. He wondered if the man's wife was baking, like Phyllis, for the Easter celebrations.

'Now, if you take a seat at that table, you'll be able to write down what you need.' The man nodded towards an old oak table, large enough to seat ten or twelve without a squeeze. Beneath it was a rug worn thin, pinks and reds long faded, flowers almost indiscernible in the flattened pile.

'Thank you,' said Christopher, and sat to copy the address.

'Tea?' said the man. 'I'm Claud, by the way. Claud Hurst. Pleased to meet you…'

'Christopher.'

'Christopher, of course, you said.' Claud was staring at him. 'Have we met?'

'I don't think so.' Christopher averted his gaze. He wanted to study the man and not, all at the same time. It was like looking into the steam-clouded mirror when he was a boy.

He scribbled down the address. He recognised the name of the estate, if not the address itself, and his chest tightened at the thought of going there. Southgate was a Lego-style block of flats in the new part of the town, next to the white hulk of the Shopping City, a commercial centre full of shops, as the name suggested. The estate had a reputation for drugs, for violence. The commercial centre was where the kids he was teaching went to hang out on Saturdays. Neither place was anywhere he wanted to go.

'Thank you,' he said.

'Actually, if you wouldn't mind taking down our telephone number?'

'Not at all.'

Claud recited the number, which Christopher duly wrote alongside Rebecca's address.

'Rebecca may not be there,' said Claud. 'But it is the last address we have for her. I wonder, would you mind calling and letting me know how you find her? She's not well; she's never been well. We did our best, but…' He smiled but with an expression of sadness so deep as to be fathomless.

'Of course,' Christopher replied, thinking that sometimes a smile was the saddest expression of all.

It took him another forty minutes to find the housing estate; the road systems surrounding Runcorn were no less than a labyrinth. He parked the car on the far side of what was once a children's play area and made his way over broken glass, cigarette butts, crisp packets, takeaway wrappers. A used condom, what looked like a syringe.

Forcing himself to look up, he headed towards the brightly coloured blocks – some architect's idea of cheerful living, though he doubted the architect in question would find it cheerful to live here. The stairwell smelled of urine, as he had anticipated. More litter here – a smashed Coke bottle, its sticky brown contents dried on the concrete steps. He reached the first floor and read the numbers. Rebecca's flat was on this level, to the right. Further along the walkway, a group of teenagers dressed in tracksuits were kicking something back and forth, expletives shouted into the grey air, words that even now made Christopher wince.

Thankful he did not have to pass the youths, he rang the buzzer. After a few minutes, he rang again, only to hear someone complain from behind the door:

'Keep your wig on, will you? I'm coming.'

The door opened and a thin man with yellow skin and three teeth stood there. He was aged and ageless all at once. From him came a strong smell of cigarettes; other smells too that Christopher could not identify.

'Can I help you?' The man held onto the door. He was wearing grey jogging bottoms that were several sizes too big and a dirty green T-shirt. Despite himself, Christopher gulped, but he did not step back.

'I'm looking for Rebecca Hurst.'

'Who wants her?' He lifted his T-shirt and pulled a silver packet of cigarettes from the elasticated waistband of his trousers. He opened the packet – Lambert & Butler – and pulled a cigarette and a plastic lighter from within. 'She's out.' He put the cigarette in his mouth and lit it, sucked and blew smoke into Christopher's face.

Christopher stepped back. 'It's urgent,' he said. 'I've got news concerning her son.'

The man appeared to flinch. 'Who says?'

'My name is Christopher. It's a long story, but I have come on behalf of her son, Billy.'

'Billy?' This time the man blew his smoke to one side, but he was still squinting at Christopher as if he were a policeman, someone who could not be trusted. 'Who did you say you were?'

'Christopher. I'm a friend of Billy's.'

The man said nothing. Moments passed. Embarrassed, Christopher looked behind him, through the slice of outside world between the waist-high wall of the walkway and the floor above, to where the white hulk of the shopping centre blocked what little sky remained. Further up, he could hear the lads larking about. They sounded as if they were fighting.

'She's here,' said the man at the door.

Christopher turned back. The man nodded to him and went inside without inviting Christopher in. Christopher followed, closing the door behind him.

Inside, the flat smelled of dirt. What comprised that dirt he didn't want to think about, but he couldn't help his thoughts. The smell was body odour, cigarettes… really, he didn't know what it was: food left to go off, possibly; an unclean bathroom. When he entered the lounge, he saw and understood. Plates smeared with traces of unidentifiable food, half-full cups of tea or coffee, blue balls of mould floating at their tops, ashtrays piled high, a sofa, its fabric burned away to form black lips rudely open to reveal partially melted yellow foam. Apart from the sofa, a television and something that looked like it had once been a chest of drawers, there was no other furniture.

But worse, much worse, was the sight of the woman on the sofa: thin legs splayed, head back, mouth open, eyes closed – as if she had died where she had been thrown. On her chin, a flaky trail of dried spit.

'Bex,' said the man, stepping over the debris that covered the floor. 'Bex, there's a man here says he knows Billy.'

Christopher covered his nose with his sleeve and inhaled his own fresh laundry smell. The man turned to him. He let his arm fall away.

'Is she all right?' he asked.

'She's fine. Bit out of it, that's all.' He turned back to the woman and bent over her. He slapped her several times, softly, across the cheek. 'Bex,' he said. 'Becksy. It's about your Billy.'

'I can come back,' said Christopher helplessly. If he left now, he would never come back to this place. He glanced towards the door. If he ran, he could be out of here in seconds.

At that moment, with a groan, Rebecca woke up. She looked emaciated. There were dark scabs the size of drawing pins on her hollow cheeks. She smiled and Christopher saw she had lost several teeth. It was all he could do not to shout his disgust aloud and run from that place.

'Rebecca,' he said. 'I'm a friend of Billy's. You remember you had a son?'

The woman peered at him, through what kind of narcotic haze only she could know. 'Billy?'

'I'm a friend of his. He's looking for you. He wants to meet you. I can give you the place.'

'Billy.' This time she shouted the name. 'I knew you'd come.' She pushed herself forward, made to stand but could not.

The man – her boyfriend? – restrained her, gripped her by the forearms, though it seemed to Christopher he did so with care.

'Stay there, girl,' he said. 'Don't stand up quick or you'll go arse for tit.'

'Get off,' she said.

The man relented, stood and addressed Christopher. 'Do you want a cuppa?'

He shook his head, no. 'Thanks. I'm not staying. I have a message from Billy.'

'Billy!' the woman shouted again. The whole thing was becoming a farce. The urge to run threatened to overwhelm him.

'Yes, Billy,' he said, crouching in front of her and taking her clammy hands in his, fighting revulsion. 'Your son. You remember Billy, don't you?'

'My Billy,' she said. 'I lost you. They made me give you away.' Her voice, her accent retained some of the well-to-do household in which she had been brought up. How had she had come to this, this state, this place?

'Billy, yes, Billy,' he battled on. 'You lost him but I'm not him, I'm his friend. They made you give him up. He went to America but he's come back to find you, Rebecca.'

She narrowed her eyes at him, something in her body twitched and he knew she was listening, that it was going in.

'He was in America?'

'Yes!' He squeezed her hands. 'He's come all this way. He's going to be at the Wilsons pub at 7 p.m. tomorrow night. Is that clear? That's Friday. Friday, 17 April, do you understand?'

'I'll make sure she gets there,' said the man. With a brief nod and a frown, apparently to signal his reliability in the matter, he turned and left the room.

'I'll write it down.' Christopher let go of her hands.

'March twelfth he was born,' she said, smiling and toothless as a carnival sideshow.

Christopher's mouth filled with a sour taste. He swallowed and exhaled heavily.

'Tomorrow,' he began again. 'Look, have you got a piece of paper?'

She smiled, laughed and collapsed against the back of the sofa. Her eyes closed.

'Billy,' she said, so high and quiet. 'My Billy.'

In the kitchen, he found the man pushing at a tea bag in a dirty Kit Kat mug.

'She's out of it,' he said. 'But I'll get her there for you.'

'It's not for me – it's for her son. He's come a long way. It'll do her good to see him, it might help her.'

'You think?'

'It might.'

Christopher tried to keep his eyes on the man, tried not to see the state of the kitchen. Failed. It was like being trapped inside something decaying, a grim soup of rotten food and wasted life. There was a cooker, coated in grease, what looked like a washing machine. There was no table, no chairs, no furniture really, only the sofa and the television in the other room. One of the kitchen cupboard doors was missing. His chest tightened, the all-too-familiar rope knotting. He had to get out.

'Do you have a piece of paper and a pen?' he said again.

The man pushed past him into the living room. Christopher was unsure whether he'd heard, but he dug around in a box on the floor and after a moment produced a piece of card and a biro. 'Here,' he said.

'Thanks.'

There was nothing to lean on, nowhere to sit. Christopher pressed the card into the palm of his hand and wrote the instructions:

The Wilsons pub, old Runcorn. Friday, 7 p.m. Your son Billy will be there. He wants to see you. On Saturday he goes back to America. It is important you come, please be there. This is your only chance. Don't let him down.

He stopped, wondered whether to sign and decided not to. He handed the note to the man.

'Right. This is the situation. Billy is Rebecca's son. They took him from her—'

'I know that.'

'Right. Right, well now she has a chance to see him again. Can you try and straighten her out, at least a bit? It's very important she gets there – for her as well as Billy.'

The man nodded briskly. 'I will. She talks about him all the time. It'd break her heart to miss him.'

'So you understand how important this is? Do you know where the pub is? It's in the old town, by the canal.'

'Of course I know where it is. I'll get her there, don't worry.'

Christopher made to shake the man's hand but thought better of it. He made himself walk slowly down the dark hall and out of the flat. At the door, he stopped and dug in his pockets. There was a five-pound note and a few coins.

'Here,' he said, pushing the money into the man's hand. 'Put her in a taxi. Use this, it's all I have.' He opened the door, stepped out into the walkway. He was about to leave but stopped and turned back. The man was still at the door, as if watching to check that he was definitely going, as if this were a place anyone would want to stay.

'Listen,' Christopher said. 'This Billy. Her son. I know it won't make any difference to her, but he's not short of a bob or two, if you know what I mean. There's money, is what I'm saying.'

The man said nothing but pushed his bottom lip up against the top and shut the door.

By the time he got home, Phyllis's car was already on the drive-way. He parked on the road and sat for a moment in the silent car. He made himself breathe in and out, anxious to erase any trace of anxiety before going in to her, his family, his home. He had spent the day in the library… no, he had been for a walk on the hill. He sniffed at his clothes. Did they smell of that awful place? Was it possible the smell would stay on him forever, no matter how many times he washed himself, his clothes? Certainly the sight would remain, branded on his memory for the rest of his life. Poor Billy. To have come so far, to have spent a whole life wondering, as he, Christopher, had done, only to be faced with that, with her.

He pulled at his sweater and sniffed himself again but was not sure. Cigarette smoke – and he no longer smoked. Maybe he smelled like he'd been in a pub. He could say he'd been for a walk on the hill and called in at the Traveller's Rest for a pint on the way home. Yes, that would do. He would go in, say he needed a bath. Tonight he would be calm; he would be normal. For the next twenty-four hours he would find things to do. Keep busy, that was all he had to do. He feared he would not be able to look at her now, not until this was over. Tomorrow morning he would go with her to Good Friday Mass. Then in the evening he would meet with Billy and hopefully Rebecca would get herself together enough to come. He would reunite them and leave them to whatever conversation they needed to have. He would do this. And he would be free.

As he made his way towards the house, he saw a young lad walking towards him. Something in his gait, the way he held his head… Christopher stopped dead. His skin prickled, his breath caught in his throat.

Jack Junior. Here, where he had no business to be.

Forcing himself to his senses, Christopher continued past his own driveway.

'Jack!' he called out, and waved.

Jack's face was a scowl. He had worn it since he was a small boy – the sullen scowl of a spoilt child, and it had evidently taken up residence on his face and, like a cuckoo, booted all the other expressions out of their own nest.

'Christopher,' he said. They were close enough now to stop, to talk. They did not embrace.

'What the hell are you doing here?'

'Came to see you, didn't I?'

'What are you… I mean how did you find me?'

Jack dug into his pocket, but before he withdrew his hand, Christopher knew what would be in it. He was right. Still scowling, Jack pulled out the letter Christopher had written to Phyllis four years earlier.

'What's this?'

'Have you opened it? That's none of your business.'

'Who's Phyllis?'

So the little shit had opened it, of course he had. Shit. Christopher fought to remember what he had written. Had there been any mention of Phyllis being his mother?

'Who is she?' Jack drew the letter from the envelope.

'She's no one,' Christopher said. 'Look, is something wrong? Has something happened? Are you with Dad?'

Jack shrugged, screwed up his piggy little eyes. 'If she's no one, then why are you living with her?'

Jack. Scowling, spoilt, snot-nose Jack. He was fourteen. Christopher searched his face. Was it possible he didn't understand? What the hell had he written in that letter?

'She's… she was my girlfriend, that's all.' It was worth a punt. He looked up, as if he'd spotted something in the sky. When Jack looked too, Christopher seized the letter from his brother's hand – oldest trick in the book.

'Oi, give that back.'

He held it high, skim-read it. *I realised on the train that I had quite forgotten to wish you a Merry Christmas…* There was no overt mention of Phyllis being his mother. He handed the letter back to Jack

'Take it, since you're so interested,' he said. 'She's just a friend. We'd been corresponding. She was my pen pal. It's really none of your business.'

'So are you married to her?'

'Don't be stupid. We're friends.'

Jack's eyes widened. 'So you're living in sin? Mum'll kill you.' Poor boy. Thinking to threaten him, when instead he was throwing him a lifeline.

'Grow up, Jack. What are you going to do, tell tales? We're not kids any more. The only person you'll hurt is Mum.'

'Why don't we go to yours then?'

'Not a good idea,' said Christopher. 'You can come another time, when I've given her some warning. Look, I've got my car. I'll take you into town and we can go for a cup of tea. You can have some cake.' He was already walking back towards the car. 'Besides, there'll be too many people in the house now. The other student teachers, you know. They'll be using the kitchen, it'll be chaos.'

'Doesn't look like chaos to me,' said Jack as they passed the front gate.

'Aye, well, that's how chaos works sometimes. You can't always tell from the outside, can you?'

They got into the car and Christopher did a three-point turn and drove back the way he'd come, took a right down Ivy Street, left onto the bottom of Heath Road. Phyllis would be wondering where he was. But there was no question of taking Jack Junior into the house. He would not let his snot-nosed little brother, of all people, sabotage things now.

'There's a café by the canal,' he said. 'We can go there.'

They drove in silence. Under the expressway, and on towards the old town. The road swung left and down. To the right, they passed the Wilsons. Christopher kept his eyes on the road. The old swimming baths, then the drab parade of shops: a chemist's, the post office, a nightclub: like all nightclubs, by day nothing but dead. He turned left, parked up by the canalside.

'Why don't you ever come home?' Jack said, as if to fill the silence.

Christopher switched off the ignition and got out. 'Lock your door,' he said over the roof of the car, once Jack had dragged himself upright. 'Squeeze the handle while you shut it, then it'll stay locked.'

'I know how to shut a car door, you know.'

Christopher walked ahead. 'There's a place at the top of Ellesmere Street does a cheap cup of tea.'

'I don't want tea,' said Jack, in that sulky voice he had. 'I came to ask you why you never come home. Mum's not herself.'

'All right, let's walk. We can go along the canal.' Christopher walked up towards the water. Having no choice, Jack followed, half a step behind. They stepped onto the hump of the grass verge. 'What do you mean, not herself?'

'Dad says she's got depression. He said you dropping us like stones hasn't helped. He said you don't want to know us any more now you've got educated.'

They had reached the gravel path. Beyond, willows wept, reflected in the flat brown surface of the water. Ducks bobbed along, oblivious. An empty 7 Up bottle cruised behind them like a bald imposter hoping to pass as one of the brood. Christopher shook his head, as if he could shake his thoughts away, and looked from left to right, and left again. Further up, to the left ran the road they had driven along to get here – a bridge now, at this level, arching over the canal. He headed for it.

'I haven't dropped you,' he said to Jack, who half-ran to keep up with him. 'I haven't dropped anyone. That's simply not true.' The heat of the lie burned his insides, cut a sharp edge on his voice. 'It's got nothing to do with me or education or anything else. I've grown up, that's all. Found my place in the world. That's what happens. People get qualifications, they get jobs, they buy a house where their job is and they live there. They have kids and those kids grow up and get their training or their education or whatever it is and then they leave and have kids of their own. It's the way it is. And it'll be your turn next, Jackie boy.'

'Don't call me Jackie. That's a girl's name.'

They had reached the bridge. In its shadow, more litter huddled, concentrated here, substantial: not Coke cans and crisp packets but the dented remains of a rusted oil drum and a grimy tarpaulin. Among the dog shit and the domestic rubbish cast down by walkers, a length of rope blackened with grease, an old anchor that looked as though, if polished, it might be worth something. A mooring post lay at the water's edge where something – a barge, of course, what else? – had clearly bumped it off its foundation. Christopher turned to look at Jack. The boy's scowl had given way to confusion; fear possibly. He had never heard Christopher talk this way – with force or any kind of strength. He must think he had become someone else. And in a way, he had. He was Martin, known as Christopher, but Martin nonetheless. He was Martin because Martin was who he had chosen to be.

'Grow up,' he said to Jack, though more kindly. 'You're Margaret's son. More than I can ever be. I'm not blood. I'm not a Harris.' He was about to add, *I am a Curtiss and I have another family, my family*, but he stopped himself and said instead, 'You look after her. You're fourteen. You and Louise can take care of her. Look, does she even know you're here?'

Jack shook his head. 'I told her I had a school trip.'

'What time's she expecting you back?'

No answer. But clearly, no one knew where he was, who he was with. There were just the two of them, alone on the canalside in the falling light of a spring afternoon.

'Look,' Christopher said eventually. 'You belong there. I… I don't.'

Jack's face reddened and his eyes watered, as if Christopher had slapped him hard. 'Why are you saying that?'

'Because it's true.'

'No it's not. How can you say that? Your parents are the ones who look after you and feed you and bring you up.' He stopped, his eyes widening as they had before in the road. His mouth dropped open. 'She's your mother, isn't she? Phyllis? She's not your girlfriend at all.'

Sharp and unwelcome as a flick knife in the gut, hot rage cut through Christopher. Rage for this spoilt little shit of a boy who had taken his Scalextric, taken everything from him, even his name, without asking. They were alone. If he were to sock him in his stupid jaw, he could throw him in the canal and be rid of him forever, tie him to that broken mooring so he would sink. He could…

'It's got nothing to do with you, you little bastard,' he managed to say. 'My life is here now. It's got nothing to do with any of you. And I do visit Margaret. I'm just not some mummy's boy who's still playing with his toys…'

'Christopher—'

'… who still has his washing done for him and who still can't wipe his own arse. I'm a man, Jackie boy – do you hear me? And I'm not a Harris, I'm a Curtiss, so leave me alone, and if you tell Mum I'll bloody kill you. I'll fucking kill you, do you hear me?'

'Christopher!'

His hand was around Jack's throat. His spit on Jack's red cheek, Jack's eyes as wide as moons. Christopher shook himself, released his brother. Jack was rubbing at his neck. His eyes were full of tears, tears that leaked and fell now onto his face. On his upper lip, the mousy down of an adolescent moustache. My God, he was just a boy.

'Jack, I'm sorry.' Christopher reached out, but Jack cowered, stepped backwards. 'Be careful, you'll end up in the drink. That water's filthy.'

'What's the matter with you?' Jack's voice was ragged, his mouth the same ugly rectangle as his mother's. 'Why are you being like this?'

'Nothing, I'm sorry.' He reached for his brother again, and this time Jack let him lay a hand on his shoulder. 'I just don't want you telling Mum, that's all. It'll kill her – you must know that. I haven't told her because she wouldn't be able to cope with it. You've got to grow up and see that, Jackie. I know it's tough, but it's for the best. I can still visit, but I can't be her son, not like you. Once I buy a place, you can come and stay, OK? But not now, not yet.' He pushed Jack around to face the direction they'd come and urged him back towards the car. 'Give me a year, all right? I'll have my own place by then. You'll be knocking on sixteen, won't you? I'll take you out, how about that? Ever been on a pub crawl?'

Beside him, Jack nodded, sniffed.

'Agreed, then. Come on, I'll drive you to the station, and next time you come here, we'll get smashed. Like proper brothers.'

CHAPTER TWENTY-SIX

'You're late, mister,' Phyllis called to him from the kitchen.

He pulled off his shoes – they were muddy from the canalside – and called back to her. 'Sorry. I went for a walk. I'm… I've got to pop upstairs a moment.' He ran upstairs, tore off his shirt and washed at the bathroom sink. The immersion heater hadn't been on; the water was cold on his neck, under his arms. He shivered, dried himself with a musty towel and changed into his pyjamas and dressing gown.

In the kitchen, Phyllis was baking. As he entered, she looked at him and screwed up her nose.

'What?' He bent to kiss her.

'You're in your pyjamas,' she said. 'I was thinking we'd get a takeaway as there's only the two of us. I'm still making these bloody fairy cakes for Sunday.'

He dipped a finger into the chocolatey cake dough.

'Oi, it's still Lent.' She slapped his hand playfully, but he grinned and sucked the sweet goo from his finger.

'I don't mind going to the Chinese.' It was the last thing on earth he wanted to do. But he had to stay normal. She knew him better than anyone in this world. If he were tense, she would see it. If he lied, she would know.

'We can have cheese on toast. Won't kill us, will it?' She sighed. 'Can't wait to have chocolate again.'

'I'll buy you the biggest Easter egg I can find.' He opened the fridge door and pulled out the half-bottle of Piat d'Or for her and a can of Greenall's bitter for himself. The panic of the day was starting to ebb. He was under control. Billy would not come here, not now he had an appointment. Jack had returned to Morecambe, appeased by the promise of brotherly good times to come. Christopher would write to Margaret in the morning, arrange a visit for the end of term.

He sighed and poured Phyllis a drink. She reached for it without looking, as if the two of them were cogs in the same machine, ticking hands in the same perfect timepiece. He smiled at the idea. How relaxed it was here at the house with the boys and David away. With no kids to think about, he and Phyllis were like a young couple starting out on their life's adventure. Cheese on toast, a glass of wine; later they would curl up on the sofa together and watch *Top of the Pops* or whatever was on. This was life. If he could only keep hold of it.

The next day, Christopher busied himself as best he could: marking, lesson plans, a long run on the hill. At six, he bathed and dressed, ate with Phyllis the spaghetti Bolognese he had prepared for them both.

'I'm going out with Amanda later,' he said.

'All right, love. What time?'

'Quarter to seven. I shouldn't be back late.'

'All right. If I'm in bed, lock up, eh?'

'Of course.'

At quarter to seven, he poked his head round the living-room door. Phyllis was watching an episode of *Coronation Street* she had videoed.

'I'm off then,' he said.

'OK, love. See you later.'

He put on his coat and shoes, went to open the door. There, he hesitated a moment before going back into the lounge.

'Bye then.' He rounded the edge of the sofa and bent towards her, took her head in his hands and kissed her on the cheek. He drew back and smiled. 'I love you.'

'And I you, silly.' She looked into his eyes, her brow furrowed in question. 'Go on,' she said. 'You'll be late.'

At two minutes to seven, he parked outside the Wilsons and went in. Billy was not there, nor was Rebecca. He ordered a pint of bitter shandy, instructing the woman at the bar to make it three-quarters lemonade, and sat down. Good Friday, the pub was already busy – men, mostly. Men like his father, Jack Harris, supping ale at the end of a hard week.

Billy appeared minutes later. Christopher stood, smiled and waved. Seeing the confusion pass across Billy's face as he made his way over, he dug into his pocket and gestured towards the bar.

'What can I get you?'

'Where's Phyllis?'

'She's not here. As I said, she gets anxious. She's asked me to come and meet you. There are some things I need to tell you, but first let me get you a drink.'

Billy glanced about him before fixing Christopher with his green eyes. 'All right. Can I have a lager please? Thanks.'

Leaving Billy to take off his jacket and settle in his seat, Christopher went to the bar and held up his hand, catching the barmaid's attention almost immediately.

'Hi there,' he said, noticing this time the merest hint of a blush on the young woman's face, the way her eyes widened a little at the sight of him. 'Could you give me a pint of your strongest lager?'

The woman raised her eyebrows and cocked her head. 'That'll be the Grolsch. It's expensive though.'

'That's perfectly all right. And a shot of vodka – a double – if you will, thank you.'

He turned to check on Billy, who was talking to a bald man with a pregnant-looking beer belly. He turned back and, with a wink at the barmaid, tipped the vodka into the lager and handed over the money.

As she returned the change, she let her fingertips linger a moment on the palm of his hand. 'Know where I am if you need me.'

He smiled, almost winked. 'I do indeed. Thank you.'

He checked the door. Still no sign of Rebecca. It was possible she wouldn't come. He had been naïve to think she would. He thought of the taxi money he had given her boyfriend or whoever he was. It had probably gone on a bottle of cider or an eighth of hash by now; he had been stupid to hand it over. He made his way back to Billy, excusing himself as he pushed past the bald man, who nodded at Billy and turned to rejoin his group of friends.

'People are real friendly in England,' Billy said. He took a long gulp of his beer and set it down. 'Cheers. Thanks for the drink.'

He had not tasted the vodka – the strong lager had done its job.

'Listen,' Christopher began. 'I know it must be a shock to you that Phyllis isn't here. But the thing is, I need to come clean with you about some things and you're going to have to listen until I get to the end.'

'All right,' Billy said. 'Go ahead.'

Christopher pulled at his pint and set it down. Looked over towards the door and told himself to stop. If Rebecca came, she came. If not, he would still say what he had to say.

'So. First thing is, after you left, I opened your letter and read it before I gave it to Phyllis.'

'You had no right to do that,' Billy interrupted. 'You know that, don't you?'

Christopher raised his hand. 'Yes. And I'm sorry, but as I said, you have to listen to the end.' He met Billy's gaze and, seeing a flicker of assent, went on. 'Phyllis suffers with nerves. I was worried the letter would upset her. I was right. It did.'

'I'm sorry to hear that. But she wrote me back.'

'I know. She made me read her letter, to make sure it was all right. I was the one who delivered it for her. I knew something had gone wrong, you see. Because years ago I traced Phyllis through the official channels. I went through Liverpool Council, the court overseeing the adoption and the Registrar. You've come over with a – and I'm not criticising you at all – a whole different approach and I think, in short-cutting the process, you haven't arrived at the correct information.'

'So what? You're telling me I'm wrong?'

'Wait. Please.'

'No, you wait a second. You're telling me you're not my half-brother?'

Christopher had been about to argue back, but Billy's words stopped him dead. 'Your half-brother? Is that what you think? No. No, I'm… Look, let me explain in full and then we'll do questions, all right?'

Billy opened his mouth to speak but appeared to think better of it. He nodded for Christopher to continue and picked up his glass.

'All right,' said Christopher, his heart thumping. 'After we realised there'd been a mistake, I agreed with Phyllis that I'd investigate further and find out what had gone wrong. She was too upset to deal with it.'

'But I saw the mother superior…'

Christopher raised his hand. 'Please.'

'I'm sorry, all right, go ahead.' Billy took another long drink of his lager.

'I realise you went to the convent. But I went there also. It was a simple mistake. Two sets of documents in the same file. You asked for your details, she pulled out mine. And that's it.'

'But I have the photograph.'

'Of yourself and a nun. Sister Lawrence, who is now the mother superior. It doesn't prove anything, not a thing. I'm sure it's you, but there's nothing on that photograph to say that your mother was Phyllis. What the mother superior didn't realise when you went there is that there were two boys born the same day. I was one; you were the other. Your mother's name is Rebecca.'

'But I didn't see any documents. There was just some ledger book. I had to show her my ID.'

'Your name is Billy Hurst. Your mother's name is Rebecca. Rebecca Hurst.'

'Rebecca? What? That's not possible!'

'Wait. It's not bad news – it's different news. I know you think you've found your mother, and I'm here to tell you that you have. But it's not Phyllis, that's all. Listen, I have more to say. But first let me get you another pint.'

Billy appeared to calm down. He looked at his glass as if surprised to see he had emptied it. 'It's my turn.'

But Christopher had already stood up. 'No, I insist. My town, my treat. Besides, I think the barmaid likes me.' He winked at Billy, feeling himself blush at his own fraudulence. This wasn't him. He had borrowed Adam's personality, it seemed, to get him through. Chutzpah: so long a mystery, and now, *in extremis*, he had found it after all.

He ordered the same again for Billy, and for himself another bitter shandy – this time barely a splash of bitter in the lemonade – and returned to Billy.

'The beer's good here,' said Billy. 'Tasty, and, boy, I can already feel it.'

'I'll take you to the chippy after,' said Christopher, acknowledging Billy's attempt to break the tension – a good sign surely.

'That's the fish and chip shop, right?'

'Indeed.' Christopher raised his pint and they touched their glasses together.

'You said you have more to tell me?' Billy said.

'That's right.' Christopher checked the door. Still no one. Where was she? Bloody drug-addled waste of life, could she not turn up for her own son? What a waste of space. 'So I traced your mother, Rebecca. I knew you were short of time and I suppose I wanted to help. That's not true, actually, I did want to help you but you must understand that sorting out this matter is of utmost urgency for me too. I mean, I live with Phyllis in her home. I've been with her for four years. She and I, we have a unique bond. We are close, we are—'

'I get it,' Billy said quietly. 'I didn't want to cause trouble. But I'm going to need proof.'

'I have proof,' said Christopher. 'I have all the documentation. But I have more than that. I have your mother. I traced her. I found her parents, your grandparents. And I found her.' He stopped, drank deeply. The next bit would be more difficult. If he hadn't wanted Rebecca, there was every reason to suspect that neither would Billy.

'She should be here by now,' he said.

'Here?

'Yes. I told her you'd be here. But…'

'But what?'

'Look, she's had a difficult life. I'm sorry to say that I found her in a bad state. She was… I think she was drunk and I suspect she'd taken something.'

'What are you telling me? That my mother's a drug addict?'

'I don't know. I don't know how bad it is. But she's not well. And I realise that must be upsetting for you to hear. Believe me, I wanted to bring you better news.'

'How do I know you're not lying?' Billy leaned back in his chair. As he did so, his left eye half-closed.

Christopher stood, knocking his chair backwards.

'Oi,' said the man behind him, the bald man. 'Watch what you're doing, mate.'

'Are you all right?' Billy too had stood up. He was gesturing, as if to help Christopher sit back down.

'I… I need to use the loo,' Christopher stammered. 'Excuse me.' He lurched, pushed his way through the busy pub.

In the Gents, he threw open the cubicle door and bolted it behind him. He slammed down the loo seat and sat down, head in his hands. The stench of urine filled his nostrils. His breath came raggedly through his open mouth, his heart pounding in his chest. He closed his mouth, sickened by the smell, but sat breathing like a racehorse all the same. The metallic taste of blood, the urge to vomit – he stood and retched into the bowl, but nothing came. He spat, sat down once more and put his head in his hands.

'Oh God,' he whispered. 'Oh God, oh God.'

Ben was not Billy. Ben was Martin. He was Phyllis's son – it was clearer than the tiled floor at Christopher's feet. His eye, the way he had half-closed it on hearing something peculiar or suspicious. His eye, half-closed, revealed the rest: the brown hair that fell over his brow like hers did, his father's green eyes, Phyllis's nose and her lopsided smile. The rest came now, flushing in – Rebecca, her sunken face, her black hair, the way she had lit up for a moment before dying back on the dilapidated sofa cushions. That face, a sunken, shrunken echo of the woman in the headscarf all those years ago. *Are you Billy?*

No, I am not, he had said.

But he was. As Ben was Martin, son of Phyllis, Christopher was Billy, son of Rebecca, a mother he did not want, could not have, could not could not, could never…

'No.' The word perspired against his hands, clamped now over his face. He was weeping. He could not remember starting to cry, but his face was wet and his throat ached. 'I'm Billy.' His own voice came high in his ears like someone else's. 'I'm Billy.'

He had known. He had always known.

And if he had seen it, then so would Phyllis. She would see in Ben her son. She would see Martin. She must not see. She must not.

The squeal of the door. The splash of someone at the urinal.

He sat up, wiped his face with his hands. *Think, Christopher. This is your life in the balance. Fight for it.* Ben could still be Billy because Billy was who Christopher needed him to be. Hadn't he, Christopher, lived as Martin, Phyllis's son, exactly because that was what he had needed? Hadn't he been happy? Hadn't she? You can only live a lie if you don't know or accept the truth. He didn't accept it. No, he did not. What harm could there possibly be in sending Ben back to the US thinking he was Billy? It would not ruin his life. It would barely alter his life, over there, so far away. No. The only life that stood to be ruined was Christopher's own, and he had come too far to surrender that now. No. No and no. Ben could be Billy. Ben would be Billy.

Ben was Billy.

Once whoever it was had left the Gents, Christopher came out of the cubicle and washed his hands and face. He dried himself with the paper towel and leant in to the mirror.

'You are Martin,' he said to his reflection. 'And no one is going to take her away from you.'

Billy was at the end of his pint. As Christopher approached the table, he looked up and furrowed his brow in question.

'Where've you been, man?'

'Upset stomach,' said Christopher. 'Think I must have eaten something that's disagreed with me.'

'You don't look so great,' said Billy. 'You're sweating. Do you want to step outside?'

'Actually, yes. I think a breath of air would be good.'

Outside, the sun had gone down. The day had darkened into the first hours of night. The air had chilled. Christopher took a cold lungful.

'I'm afraid Rebecca hasn't come,' he said. 'That's disappointing. I'm sorry.'

'Sounds like she maybe didn't understand, if she was as you said.'

'Be that as it may, I left a note with instructions. There was a man with her who seemed all right. He said he'd get her here.'

Billy thrust his hands into his pockets and kicked at the pavement. 'Look, man. You seem like a real nice guy, but this Rebecca hasn't shown up and I think I'm going to need proof.'

'I have my birth certificate.'

'You do?'

'Yes. I can bring it to you tomorrow if you don't believe me. And there's something else. Come with me,' Christopher said. 'I have something to show you.'

They walked towards the town and took a left towards the canal.

'Where are we going?' Billy asked as they crossed the grass verge.

'I didn't tell you the final part,' said Christopher, thinking quickly. 'The mother superior told me how you came to be at the convent. You and your mother were brought there by the police. Your mother had given birth to you by the side of the canal, here in Runcorn, under the bridge. She must have been desperate. I'm so sorry.'

'That's terrible.' Billy had stopped and was looking out over the black water. 'She must have been scared as hell.'

'Not much to see here,' said Christopher, pushing on towards the bridge. 'There used to be barges along this far, but not so much now. They still fish here though. You see them sometimes with their big green umbrellas and their buckets of bait.' He stopped, waited for Billy to catch up. 'I'm so sorry she didn't come. I tried, I really did. I wanted to help. I can show you the bridge if you like. I can show you where you were born at least.'

'All right.'

It was after nine. The shadow of the bridge was all but black. But Christopher could make out the oil drum, the old anchor, the rope. There was an all-pervading smell of damp that he hadn't noticed before.

'Here we are.'

Billy stopped and looked about him.

'Thank God they found you both,' said Christopher before Billy could speak. 'God knows what might have happened. You might have died here. As it is, you've had a good life, haven't you? You have a good life over in America?'

Billy said nothing. After a moment, he crouched and picked up a handful of gravel chippings. He stood up and threw them into the canal. The water wrinkled then flattened.

'Do you know something?' he said – and at the catch in his voice, Christopher felt afraid. 'I'm still not sure I believe you.' He pushed his hands into his pockets, then appeared to reconsider and brought them out again and crossed them over his chest. 'It just doesn't add up. These things are always cross-referenced. What's to say it wasn't you who made the mistake?'

'That's ridiculous.'

'Is it? I don't think so.' Billy stepped closer, his eyes catching a yellow glint from the street light. 'See, I've always wanted to find my parents too. I had the same dreams you did. And the way I see it, I'm the one with the photograph. I saw the register. I have a birth certificate too, so I can't see how there can have been a mistake. And if the mother superior was the same woman who handed me over, she would have remembered who she handed me to. And she did remember. She said she gave me to Mr and Mrs Bradbury, from the US. She said that.' He stepped closer still. 'She remembered.'

'It's not true. I'm Martin. It says so on my birth certificate. The only reason I call myself Christopher is for simplicity's sake. And because my other family don't know I've found my mother, my Phyllis.' He grasped Billy's shoulders. 'Please. This is my whole life. This is who I am. Without it I have nothing, do you understand?'

'I understand, of course I understand. But unless you can prove I'm wrong, I won't stop until I get to the truth. That's my right – and I have as much right as you do. Now let go of me, Christopher. Or is it Billy?'

'Don't call me that. You're Billy. You're...' As Christopher pushed against him, he felt a numb punch that sent him reeling back, down, down onto the gravel.

CHAPTER TWENTY-SEVEN

When I started to write this, I began by giving my own account of how things had gone. But I couldn't get to Christopher that way. I couldn't find him, couldn't make sense of him. So I had to write him from his perspective, to try and explore moment by moment what he believed. What do any of us believe? How much of what we believe is in fact lies we tell ourselves, and how much is the truth? I'd had four precious years with Christopher and in that time he told me everything – not necessarily in the order I have written, but in the form of conversations, anecdotes, memories that I have pieced together. And to him, I was Phyllis, his Phyllis, but I guess you know that by now.

The scenes I struggled with most were the ones in which I myself featured. But I couldn't write them from my own perspective because that would not have helped me to understand. It's only when we remove ourselves and our own feelings that we can fully concentrate on the other person. From my point of view, there was not one hint that he was lying. Not one flicker of doubt in my mind that he was my Martin. And to understand how he convinced me of that, I had to find a way to be him, or at least process his story through him. This has been part of my therapy. If I know he loved me before he knew me, it's because he told me so. But it wasn't me he loved, was it? It was the ideal he made for himself of his real mother. And Rebecca did not fit his ideal – she broke it. I was not his ideal either, I don't think. I am not anyone's ideal. But I was all that was left.

And this is where I have to stop. If writing is therapy, then in its pages I am my own counsellor. And there are things I struggle to tell even her, my counsellor, myself. I hate myself. I hate her. I hate Phyllis. And now I must tell you the rest, the things I have not yet found the courage to say, even to her, to myself, do you see?

When Christopher came home that night, I was still awake. I was reading in bed. I've never slept well when David's away – I never used to, at any rate, when we were still together. So I was reading to get myself to sleep. I wish I had been asleep. I wish I'd never heard him come in. Maybe things would have gone differently had we faced them in the morning.

I knew from the sound of him that something was wrong. There was a heaviness to the way the door clattered against the wall, the thud of his footfall in the hall, as if he had fallen. I thought he was drunk. He'd said he was going out with Amanda; I thought maybe they'd had a few too many, ended up a little tipsy or something. Good for him, I thought. It did him good to shake loose from time to time.

'Christopher,' I called out to him. 'Chris, love? Everything all right?'

He didn't answer, and this struck me as odd. He always called back a *hello*; in fact he used to say it was one of the best things about living with us: me calling to him, him calling back, like birds. He said it was the little things that made him feel at home.

I set my book aside and listened out. I heard the water run in the downstairs loo. I heard the chain flush, then the water again. More and more. I became convinced he was drunk. His footsteps came on the stairs then, and a moment later he was at the bedroom door.

And it's funny, because I remember thinking: he's never been in this room, my bedroom. We decorated years ago, and the walls are apricot and we bought a peach-coloured bedspread to match, me and David, and when you turn on the bedside light, the whole room is bathed in this pink glow. It's heavenly; not as in the day-to-day meaning – I mean it's like what I imagine heaven's light to be: a warm light, a forgiving light. And into that light he came, and I cried out in shock because he looked for all the world like he'd been in an accident. His face was clean but his clothes were covered in mud and whatever blood he'd washed off came fresh then: bright red from his nose and eye.

'Oh, Christopher, love,' I said, kneeling up on the bed. 'Whatever's happened?'

He sank to his knees and began to cry. The sight of him crying is something I will never be able to shake from my mind. There are so many things that I'll never shake from my mind.

'Come on now, love.' I climbed out of bed and crouched beside him and held him to me. He was sobbing like a child and I thought maybe he'd been in an accident – maybe he'd been attacked.

'You're safe now,' I said. 'Come on, my love. Come and sit with me.'

Slowly I persuaded him up onto the bed. He moved as if he were in pain and sat down next to me. I pushed at his coat and he helped me pull it from him. Underneath, his shirt was clean but he smelled of sweat, as if he'd been running. I reached over and pulled a few tissues from the box on my bedside table. I dipped them in the glass of water I always take to bed with me and pressed them to his mouth.

'Here, my darling boy,' I said. 'Hold these to your lip. And your eye, love, that's it.'

He laid his hand over mine and I put my other arm around his shoulders. He was shaking, still crying. It's a terrible thing to see a man cry – any man, let alone one you love. I knew how much it cost him to let me see him like that. I knew it must have been bad, what had happened.

'Come on,' I said. 'Tell me, tell Phyllis.'

And he did. He told me everything. Between racking sobs, he told me how Ben had come to the house claiming to be my son, how he'd written to Ben pretending to be me. He told me all about Ben, how he lived in San Francisco, how he worked as a graphic designer, had a girlfriend called Martha. He told me how he'd been to the convent. The mother superior had seen him straight away, he said, and he'd told her there'd been a mistake.

'I asked her if she'd had a visitor,' he said. 'A Benjamin Bradbury.' He tried to smile at the memory but his mouth had set, would not move beyond the bare minimum required to speak. 'I told her she'd given Benjamin my details. It took all my willpower not to shout at her. I told her I didn't know how that had happened but that I'd been reunited with you, my birth mother, for some years now.

'I told her I'd been through the official channels, that I had a birth certificate at home and letters from the adoption counsellor. "The mistake can't be with me," I said. "There must have been a mistake here at the convent. I've thought about it a lot and it seems to me it would require nothing simpler than documentation put in the wrong file or a missing file or a file not sent – something administrative. Or an ankle band put on the wrong baby. Or a label on the wrong crib." '

I took more tissues, dipped them in water, pressed them to his bleeding lip. 'What did she say?' I asked him.

'I was right,' he said. 'Turned out there were two boys born that day.'

'So there was a mistake?' I said.

'She remembered you. She was Sister Lawrence.' He looked at me.

I nodded. 'I remember her. She's the one I told you about. The one I had to give you to.'

'That's exactly what I said. I told her you said she was kind. Anyway, I asked for the other mother's address. She told me she couldn't give it to me. So I stood up. I stood up because I know I'm tall and I knew that would intimidate her. My hands were clenched into fists and I pushed my fists against her green leather desktop.

' "I'm afraid you must," I said.'

He had stopped crying by now and he gave a loud sniff before carrying on.

'I knew I'd made her afraid and I felt the weight on my soul. All through my time at college I'd been haunted by that monster who made women afraid, and here I was, standing over an old woman, threatening her.'

'You did what you had to do,' I said. 'Then what happened?'

He shrugged. 'She gave me what I needed. Ben's mother was called Rebecca Hurst. Her family came from Stockton Heath. She said Rebecca used to sing to him.'

Christopher told me the sorry tale of how he'd found Rebecca, a poor, desperate woman, and how he'd given her friend the rendezvous time and place. How he'd met Ben in the pub and how when he tried to explain everything, Ben had half-closed his left eye.

'And I knew,' he said.

'Knew what?'

'Knew I couldn't lie to myself any more.'

'What about?'

He turned to me and held both my hands in his. 'Oh Phyllis.' He was crying again. 'The mistake was mine. Ben is your son. He is Martin.'

'What? What are you saying?'

'Lies. I've been lying. I knew it the moment he came to the door – I could see he was your son. Oh God.' He broke, his face in his hands.

I waited, in chaos, for him to continue.

'I couldn't let you go,' he said once he'd composed himself enough to speak. We were still holding hands. 'I can't. I love you, Phyllis.'

'And I love you. Nothing can change that, Chris.'

'But I'm not Chris,' he said, his voice ragged. 'And I'm not Martin. Don't you see? I'm not your son. I'm Billy. I'm not your son. I'm no one.'

And I knew it then too. I could not explain how or why, but when Christopher said it, it was as if I too had known. He had presented me with a truth I wanted so very badly that I did nothing to doubt or question its veracity. I didn't want another truth. I wanted my son. I saw my son. But he was not my son.

Yet he was not nothing. He was not no one.

'Did I do wrong,' he said, 'to send him away?'

'Is that what happened?'

He nodded. 'I told him he had to leave us alone. We're happy, I told him, and he had to let us live in peace. We had a fight. That's why I'm all muddy. But in the end, he accepted it. He thinks the mistake is his. He goes back to the States tomorrow. I'm sorry. I'm so sorry. I only did it because I knew if you saw him you would know and then where would I go? Who would I be? If he came and took you, I'd kill myself, I would.'

'Don't say that,' I whispered. 'Don't even let yourself think things like that. We'll work this out, the two of us, I promise.'

'I know where he's staying. You can go there now if you like.'

'No, love,' I said. 'I can't leave you here like this.'

I'll admit I felt the pull to go, to see my son just once, to tell him I had not abandoned him, that I had loved him. But I was also speaking the truth – how could I leave Christopher like that? Ben was my son. But I loved Christopher.

Christopher, whose despair was depthless. The pink light gave him a kind of halo, and his eyes were so deep and brown and he looked so sad and so innocent. He was a child, really. No more than a child. He collapsed across my lap and I stroked his tangled hair.

'I've loved you since before I met you,' he said.

'And I you.' We were both crying.

'I'm Billy,' he said softly.

'Yes, you are. But I love you whoever you are, whatever you've done. I would forgive you anything, anything at all.'

Through the crack in the curtain, the sky had begun to lighten. I checked the radio alarm and saw it was after four.

'Then I need to tell you the truth,' he said.

'What truth? You've already told me.'

'There's more.'

And then he told me the rest. What had really happened down by the canal.

CHAPTER TWENTY-EIGHT

If I close my eyes now, I can see the whole scene play out. Christopher and Ben, down by the canal. Soon there will be footsteps clack-clacking over the bridge, giggles ripe with promise. The night owls are already hooting and staggering away to their homes, to alleyways, to back terrace walls. Skirts will be concertinaed against bare white thighs, flies will be unzipped in haste. Yes, it is late. The hour for drunks and geezers has come, the hour for sex, for murder. Is that what this was? Or was it a kind of exchange for him – one life for another where two could not be? Was murder the only way he thought he could secure his place in the world?

Christopher pleads his case. Ben punches Christopher because he doesn't believe him. Maybe he realises that Christopher has brought him here under false pretences. Whatever, they fight. Who is Billy, who is Martin?

You're Billy.

No, you are.

You.

No, you.

But Christopher is Billy. He knows that now. Billy is the bigger of the two, and when Ben's punch floors him, he sits up quickly and locks his arms around Ben's knees. Ben falls backwards onto the gravel. They roll, first one on top, then the other. At a certain point, Billy grabs the oily rope from the canalside and pulls it around Ben's neck.

If I've imagined the rest, I must also imagine this. It requires little effort – these images barely leave my mind. Billy pulls hard on the rope. Ben thrashes for his life, fails, is tossed into the water.

'I killed the real Martin to become Martin,' Billy said to me as night became day. 'I baptised myself with the canal water. I named myself Martin. But I can't be Martin, can I? Not now. Not now.' He wept.

'It's OK, my darling,' I told him.

But it was not OK.

And even then, I could not have imagined what he had done next.

Christopher had run from the canal, crying and pitiful. He ran all the way back to the Wilsons, his only intention to pick up his car and drive home. And there outside the pub was Rebecca. She was hovering by the door, he said, as if she dared not go in.

'Rebecca?' It was out of his mouth before he could stop himself. He said that if he could have kept his mouth shut, he could have hidden his face, got into the car and driven away. But he did call her name and she did turn. She turned and she saw him and she recognised him.

'Billy!' A name he did not want. A mother he did not want.

'Why have you come here?' He grabbed her by the arm and shook her. Her arm was a stick – it made him sick to touch it, like touching a skeleton.

'Billy! Stop it. You're hurting me.'

He let her go.

'You're too late,' he said. 'Billy had to go.'

She laughed; her bottom teeth were pitted black. 'I might have had a drink,' she said, 'but I'd know you anywhere. Don't you remember me? I used to visit you but you never let on, did you?'

'I'm not Billy.'

Out of her bag she took her purse. Out of her purse she took a white envelope, folded in two. Out of the envelope she took a letter. 'Here,' she said. 'Tell me that's not your ma.'

He saw it before he could see it. He knew that didn't make sense but that's the way it was – he knew, as he had known things all his life. He saw the letter and knew that all the lies ended with it. In the top right-hand corner, Margaret and Jack's address in Hestham Avenue, Morecambe. Force of habit, the habit of a well-trained typist who liked to do things right.

Dear Rebecca,

Please be assured that we will look after Billy and take good care of him. We have no children of our own and this baby boy is God's greatest blessing. It must be a difficult time for you but one day we hope you will look back and know it was for the best.

We will call him Christopher, like St Christopher.
We wish you all God's love,
Jack and Margaret Harris

The writing was Margaret's, of course – her careful cursive hand. She had been moved to write to this poor woman, a woman she did not know. Surely there was no kinder act in this world? A promise between women, between strangers: to love a child in the other's stead. Margaret, whom he had judged, with no right to do such a thing. His parents, whom he had failed, for no better reason than a lack of words. But some things are not easy to say. They did not tell him the truth of his birth; he did not tell them about Phyllis. Why? Because he could not find the words. He had left them in silence, the worst possible form of cruelty. He was beyond forgiveness. He was a monster.

'Don't cry, Billy.' Rebecca took hold of the letter and pulled it from his hands. 'She was a good woman to write that. It's been a comfort to me over the years, has that.'

He heard the slur in her voice, smelled the alcohol coming out of her every pore. She took out a packet of cigarettes and lit one.

'Do you smoke, Billy?'

'No.' He hadn't smoked since university.

'Do you want a cigarette?'

'Yes.'

She passed him her own and lit another. Despite the revulsion that churned his guts, he sucked where her foul mouth had been. The tobacco made him retch. He threw the cigarette to the ground.

She blew smoke away from him. 'Do you remember me?'

He nodded. 'From the road. You wore a blue headscarf. You asked if I was Billy.'

'So you do know me! And you looked for me, didn't you? And you found me.' The glee in her gruff smoker's voice made him feel sick.

'I found you,' he said.

'I remember. And you're doing so well for yourself. Going to be a teacher, aren't you?'

'Yes.' He did not stop to wonder how she knew this, not then.

'I'm glad your life worked out for you, Billy, love.'

'I'm not—'

'My life didn't pan out so well.' Through the slurs, he was aware as he had been in her awful flat of her well-spoken diction, what remained of it, her vowels and consonants committing themselves half to her origins, half to her wretched existence now. She was not as well spoken as her father, but even so, he could hear him in her voice, and now, looking at her, could see something of him in her brow, her mouth. Something of his grandfather, the man he had met. Something of himself. Her hair, of course, was black. Dyed, he suspected, but dyed to match what it had been. She was his mother. He hated her.

'Get in the car,' he said. 'I'll take you home.'

'Buy me a drink?' She cocked her head towards the pub and smiled her awful smile. 'Little drink for your ma?'

'I'll pick some up on the way.'

'Good boy.'

They got into the car. Rebecca directed him into town, to the Threshers next to Blockbuster on Church Street.

'Get cider,' she said. 'That's what I have anyway. Get what you want for yourself.'

He left her in the car. In the off-licence, he bought a two-litre bottle of Strongbow and a half-litre of whisky. In the car, he passed her the smaller bottle.

'Here,' he said. 'This should keep you going till we get to your place.'

'You're a good boy,' she said. 'I knew you wouldn't mind helping me out once you knew the truth.'

Teeth gritted, he drove, while Rebecca talked. She had been put into the convent at eighteen. Her parents had left her there. She was three years older than Phyllis had been. He didn't care.

'I would never have given you up, Billy.'

'Stop calling me Billy.'

'I would never have given you up.' She swigged at the whisky. The smell of it filled the car. 'They made me. I didn't even know you'd gone till after. Never even got to say goodbye.' She sniffed. 'That's cruel.'

He did not look at her. 'Your father seemed like a nice chap.'

He felt her shift in the passenger seat.

'You're so good-looking,' she said. 'You look like Cary Grant or someone. Your dad was very handsome. He was cultured too.' She laughed to herself. 'His name was Richard. We were going out, you know. It wasn't a one-night stand or anything of that sort. We'd been going steady for six months. He was a funny sort. Odd, in his way, but I liked him all right. His idea of a date was to get the train to somewhere or other and go and see ruins. Ruins he loved. Couldn't get enough of them.'

They had reached the coloured blocks of Southgate flats. Christopher stopped the car.

'Let's get you home,' he said.

'Did you buy the cider?'

'Yes.'

'Good boy.'

She was swaying as she opened the door to the flat. The door banged against the inside wall. She leant against it for support.

'Do you still have the whisky?' he asked.

'Yes, Billy, love. It's in my bag.'

She went ahead, into the darkness. Billy followed but stopped to search out a light switch. He turned on the light but almost wished he hadn't. The hallway was a mess: balled-up clothes, shoes, a net bag with what looked like cans of food inside. The place stank of stale cigarette smoke, stale food, stale life.

'Come in, then, if you're coming,' she called to him from the living room.

He followed. The room was much the same as when he had first visited. An ashtray lay on the thin carpet, full of orange cigarette butts. Other butts too, browned at the edges, one with a pin sticking out of the end. He fought the urge to run.

'Where's your boyfriend?' he said.

She sat heavily on the sofa and patted the cushion next to her. 'Sit down, Billy.'

'I'll fetch you a glass.' He stepped over plates, mugs half-full, scummy. More clothes, a shoebox, one burgundy court shoe. In the kitchen, the smell of off food grew stronger. He put his hand over his mouth and nose. In the sink, a half-eaten Pot Noodle, a mug full of cigarette and reefer butts, plates thick with ketchup or something that had dried hard and brown in stripes. In the cupboard without a door he found glasses. He sniffed them, ran them under the tap and shook them dry. On closer inspection, he thought they might in a past life have been jam or mustard jars.

In the living room, Rebecca had lit a cigarette. She smiled as he came towards her, showing the black gaps at the side of her mouth. She had put on the ceiling light. It was too bright – he could see the dark scabs on her face.

'Drink?' He poured cider for her, a small one for himself.

She took the glass from him. 'You're a good boy, Billy.'

He surrendered. 'Thank you. I do my best.'

She drained her glass and held it out towards him. He refilled it. This wouldn't take long, this final thing he had to do, and then he could get on with the rest of his life.

'Do you remember me from your street?' She picked at one of the scabs on her cheek.

'Yes.' How often, he wondered, would she repeat that question if he let her?

'And you looked for me, didn't you? You looked for me?'

'Yes. I looked for you.'

'My Billy.'

She dropped forward and drove her cigarette into the hedgehog pile, sending three or four cold, spent butts over the side to the floor. When she righted herself, he saw that her eyes were shining. The sight was pitiful. She was as thin as an abandoned dog. He imagined her ribs beneath her dark clothes, contracting and expanding like the bellows on an accordion. Bile rose to his throat; the taste reached his mouth and he swallowed some cider to clear it.

He poured more cider for her. 'Did you finish the whisky?'

She winked and pulled the bottle from a fold in her clothes that may have been a pocket. She must have taken it out of her bag, he thought. She must have been drinking it while he went for the glasses. Less than a third of the bottle remained.

He teased it from her grip. 'Chaser?'

She giggled like a little girl – the effect was grotesque, and again he sipped at his cider to quell his rising bile. 'Naughty. Go on then.'

He poured a glug of whisky into her cider. While he did this, she pulled out her cigarettes and lit another, offered him the packet.

He shook his head. He felt sick.

'Cheers,' he said, handing her the gruesome cocktail. 'To family.'

'Oh, Billy.' Her voice wobbled with emotion and her eyes filled. 'To family. My boy.' She tipped the glass and guzzled its contents. It was unwatchable. He could not take his eyes from the sight.

She groaned as the alcohol hit her and collapsed against the sofa. 'I've had a lot of problems, Billy. Drugs and that. People take advantage. I've been inside, but I've never done anything bad. If they hadn't taken you, I would've been all right. But they made me work in that place and in the end I ran away. I had to.'

'I'm sorry.' He eased the glass from her hand and filled it: cider and whisky in equal measure. Surely this would knock her out like a shot horse.

'It's not your fault, love.' She took the glass from him and cradled it in both hands. 'But of course I had nowhere to go. Ended up in a hostel. I sorted myself out though, got myself the flat. It's not much, but it's somewhere to live.'

'And your boyfriend?'

She peered at him and leaned slowly to the left. For a moment she looked as if she would keep on sliding until she hit the sofa cushions, but she gave a slow blink and straightened up. 'Boyfriend?'

'There was a man here when I came to see you. I left him directions. I gave him money.'

Her mouth fell open – he averted his eyes from those black iron pits in her bottom jaw. 'You mean Bri. He's not my boyfriend, Billy, love. He's my neighbour.' She drank. It almost hurt to watch her. 'He's all right, is Bri. He's my friend.'

'He was very nice.' He filled her glass again. she had drunk about a pint, in the short time they had been there. The whisky was gone.

Without prompting, she began to weep, sucking at her cigarette and blowing out the smoke with a bitter pursing of her blackish lips. 'You'll help me, won't you?' She closed her eyes. The glass lolled but by some miracle did not spill. 'I just need a bit of cash to see me through the week.'

'You want money?' His fingers tightened around the glass.

'Don't say it like that,' she said. 'You make me sound awful. I only mean a bit, maybe something each week. I wouldn't call on Phyllis or anything. I wouldn't do that.'

'Phyllis? How do you know Phyllis?'

She gave a brief laugh, as if it were perfectly obvious. 'I've followed you all your life, Billy. I knew you were at university. I was so proud. I knew your name, the name they gave you. Christopher Harris. I followed you to the coach station once. They had no right to take you from me. If I hadn't had to give you up, my life would have been different.'

'Why haven't you contacted me before?'

She shrugged. 'You looked happy.'

'So why now?'

'You contacted me, remember?'

'Have you spoken to Phyllis? Have you been near her?'

'Not spoken, no. But I know where she lives, her and David. I sit in the town hall gardens sometimes and watch the twins play football.' She laughed. 'That Darren's a terror, cheeky little bugger. But it's not like I'd ever say anything, Billy. I know how much you like it there. Not like I'd go bowling up to the front door to introduce myself.'

She stopped and fixed him with her black eyes. And then, as if drink had taken her only in that moment, she closed her eyes and let her mouth fall open.

He caught the glass before it fell. He watched her, counted to ten.

As he crept from the room, she snored into the silence. He found her bedroom at the back of the flat. More stale smells – body odour, talcum powder, shed skin on sheets. He shivered, lifted the pillow from the bed, tried not to notice or think about the diffuse brown patch made, he supposed, over time, by the grease from her head.

She was snoring regularly now, her mouth still open. She had slid against the sofa's edge, the angle awkward. She was so thin. Patches of pink scalp showed through the oily strands of her dyed black hair, and he saw now that the roots were a greyish white. She would be what? Forty? Forty-one? He took her by the shoulders – small and square like Phyllis's, but there the similarity ended. He laid his mother, this broken bird, flat on the cushions.

'I am sorry, Mother,' he said. 'I will pray for you. And for Martin. You can find him in heaven as I have Phyllis here on earth.'

He pressed the pillow to her face.

'Oh Lord, take the soul of Rebecca Hurst. May she find peace in heaven in your care, Amen.'

She kicked, and her arms rose like the arms of a zombie in a horror film. The same choked noise as Ben had made down at the canal came from under the pillow. He could not say how long this lasted, only that when it was over his arms ached, his back, his neck. He checked the pulse at her neck. Nothing. Her face was grey even in the bright overhead light.

He poured the rest of her cider onto the sofa and wiped the glass with his handkerchief before placing it beside her slack hand. He picked up his own glass and slid it into his pocket. He took the pillow back into the bedroom and replaced it where he had found it.

At the living-room door, he stood a moment. She was stone still but he watched her for another minute, to be sure.

'Goodbye, Mother,' he said, and left that place.

*

From the moment the door banged against the wall, I had known something was wrong. And now here we were, the world turned inside out like an old coat, our life's possessions fallen out of the pockets and spread on the ground.

'What are we going to do?' he said.

'It'll be OK,' I replied. But I knew it wouldn't be. I was trying to trace a line through the mess of my own thoughts.

'You need to go back to your room,' I said.

'I can't leave you.'

'You must, love. Until we work out what to do.'

'But I can't be alone.'

'You're not alone. I'll be right here.'

I had to look away from the pleading in his eyes. Did I see a murderer? I don't know. I saw him, my Christopher, the love of my life, but everything had changed. He had killed two people, and one of them was my son. I did not know what that made him. I still don't.

'Go to bed,' I said.

He nodded finally and gathered up his dirty coat.

'Give that to me.' I took it from him. 'Leave the rest outside your room, I'll wash them for you.'

On the landing, I laid my hand on his cheek and told him to go, told him again that everything would be all right. If I close my eyes now, I can remember the way his cheek felt against my hand, the merest prickle of stubble. That moment, the memory of it, is something. But I must go on. I have come this far and now I must finish this. I *will* finish this.

So.

Once Christopher had gone into his room, I went downstairs. I was going to go back to bed but I couldn't face the sight of it, the memory of all he had told me. Instead, I made tea and sat in the kitchen. It was cold, so I put on Christopher's coat. Why, I don't know. Comfort, possibly – the smell of him. Upstairs was silent. I thought he must be asleep. I stared out of the window at the garden. I thought of the barbecues we'd had there with David and the twins that summer. I'd been happy, yes, but I'd been lying to myself. I'd been lying to myself for years. How could I have been happy when I knew something was not right? Christopher had told a lie. I had lived one. At least that's how I saw it in that moment. And now my son was dead.

I don't know how long I was there before I remembered the clothes. Christopher's sweater and trousers were on the floor outside his room. I listened for a moment at his door but heard nothing, so I gathered up his things and brought them into the kitchen, put them into the washing machine. I was about to switch the machine on when I thought perhaps I should wash his coat too. I started to empty the pockets, and it was then that I found the letters, crumpled up. I dropped the coat to the floor.

Your son, Benjamin Bradbury.

My son. My Martin. The boy who had been taken from me, who had come all the way from America to find me, and who had put his heart on this page. He wanted only to meet me and he was now lying dead at the bottom of the canal. He had died thinking I didn't want him.

I imagined him then as I have imagined him in these pages: no photos, no cine film, nothing to go on but two short letters – his life caught in no more than a glancing light. My Martin, whom I would never see, never know, never love with a love that was natural between a mother and a son. There was nothing left but mess. A man whom I had loved as a son had killed my firstborn child. He was a murderer. Whose mind, tell me, whose, could stay intact in the face of that?

I went into the hall and dialled 999.

'You need to come right away,' I said. 'It's about my son. He's murdered two people.'

I gave them the address. They must have asked more questions and I must have answered them. I put down the phone and stifled the choking sound that came out of me.

I was sitting on the hall carpet, back propped against the wall I must have slid down. I thought I heard Christopher's bedroom door open and close. Then nothing for a moment. I thought I must have imagined it. Then the grinding squeak of his window opening. I thought he must be hot, that he might come down and run a glass of water, but he didn't come and there were no more sounds from upstairs. But there was a draught, now I thought about it, and I began to shiver. I pulled on Christopher's coat once again – better to wash nothing now that the police were coming. I went into the lounge, switched on the gas fire.

I can't remember anything about the time I spent waiting; I suspect I was in a kind of trance. At about 6.15 a.m., the police came: a man and a woman, both young. I can't remember his name but I remember hers was Yvonne. I remember it because that's what the other one shouted, later.

'He's upstairs,' I said when they came in.

It's frightening, having two uniformed police coming through your front door. At least, I was frightened. The policeman headed up while the woman waited with me. She was talking to me, I think, but I can't remember what she said. I don't think I was listening. I think I was listening for what was happening upstairs.

'Christopher,' I heard the policeman say, then knocking. 'Christopher, can you open the door?' Then he shouted down the stairs. 'Yvonne! Can you get up here a sec?'

'Excuse me a minute,' she said and went out of the living room.

And then. And then. And then I was up there too, on the landing in my nightdress and Christopher's coat. Both their backs were to me and they were fighting with Christopher's bedroom door. I can remember my ankles were cold. I remember wondering where the cold draught was coming from.

'What's the matter?' I asked – and I wonder if I knew already what the matter was; when I remember it, that's the way it feels and I know I felt sick.

'The door's jammed,' the policeman said. He had his radio; he was talking into it, asking for backup.

'Christopher won't hurt you,' I said. 'If you knock, he'll probably open the door.'

'I've tried that.'

'Christopher?' I called out to him, as I always did when I heard him come home. 'Christopher? Christopher?'

But he did not call back.

CHAPTER TWENTY-NINE

Christopher had fed his skipping rope through his bedroom window. The rope his father had made for him when he was a boy. He'd tied the other end to the leg of the bed and pushed his desk up against the door. What I'd thought was the door closing was the desk, I think, banging against it. When I'd felt the cold air, that was when he'd opened the window so he could lower himself out.

He'd been dead only minutes when the police found him. That makes sense, because when I held him to me, he was still warm. I can't recall if I realised then or only later what that meant. But now, obviously, I know it means that he took his life in the moments after I'd made the call to the police, which in turn means he heard me call them. He heard me betray him. That is my weight to bear along with the rest.

They found Benjamin's body in the canal. Martin, my son, who died never knowing how much he was loved. His body hadn't gone far, tied as it was with an oily barge rope to a broken mooring post.

Now.

Here we are.

Everything I've told you so far takes us up to here, to this moment. Everything I have told you is as Christopher told me. I have tried to take Christopher's point of view because of what follows in these pages. I have done this because I was trying to understand how much he believed and how much he knew was lies. I genuinely believe that he didn't think he was lying, not in any conscious way. This was not a coldly executed deception. I believe he absorbed his lies on the deepest possible level because he needed them much, much more than truth. I believe this because I knew him, I lived with him, I loved him, and I never saw anything that made me think he was lying, even to himself.

I thought I'd understood him. But at the inquest, I realised, I'd understood nothing at all.

Oh, what a tangled web we weave.

Upon questioning, Mother Superior Lawrence revealed that Christopher had indeed been to St Matthew's Convent to search for information pertaining to his birth. But he had not been there at any time during the days leading up to Ben's death nor indeed at any point that year. When she consulted the records, she found an entry in the visitors' book for him on Friday, 28 October 1977. She remembered him. His mother had visited the convent a few months before, she said, requesting the whereabouts of her son and she had been told she would be informed should her son wish to make contact with her. Mother Superior Lawrence and Christopher had enjoyed a cup of tea together in the visitors' room, and once Christopher had shown her his ID, she had fetched the ledger for him.

'We talked about the two baby boys born that day,' she said. 'Martin Curtiss and William Hurst. I remembered his mother, Rebecca. I told him she was troubled but that she'd always sung to him, always called him Billy. And that was it. I wished him luck in his search. He set off from here so far as I'm aware intending to pursue information via the official channels, which is what he told me he was going to do.'

They had talked for about an hour, she said to the police officer taking her statement. She had told Christopher that the other baby, Martin, had gone to America because the convent had links with a church in Virginia. Martin left the convent almost two weeks after Billy. Sister Lawrence insisted that she had given no information to Christopher regarding Martin's adoptive parents. There had been no mistake there at the convent. There had been no switching of babies, no ankle band on the wrong foot, no incorrect entry of information at the Registrar's office.

It was concluded that Christopher must have read the ledger book upside down, taken a mental note of Martin's birth mother's name and address, maybe written it down later. He had a great memory. He always could sing any pop song word-perfect right the way through; always knew the title, who sang it and most of the time when it was released. He had my name and my parents' address; he was able to trace me that way. My parents have no recollection of him calling at their home. They think perhaps they might have received a telephone call around that time but they thought it was a marketing questionnaire. They couldn't be sure and their statement was not included in the final report.

I too went to the convent. My name is in the visitors' book along with Rebecca's and Ben's and Christopher's. It was Sister Lawrence who suggested I contact NORCAP, which I did, on the day of Martin's eighteenth birthday: 12 March 1977. And so, when Christopher contacted me a few months later, I had no reason to believe he wasn't my son. He wrote to me and I replied with enough information for him to reflect back to me the image I wanted so badly to see. I informed his lies. And if he found evidence of his fabricated origins in me, then I looked for evidence of the boy I had lost in him. When I half-closed my eye, he saw and adopted the idiosyncrasy as his own. When he half-closed his eye, I remember thinking it was a family tic, something only the Curtiss family did – my sister, Miriam, does it; my own mother does it too. But it was nothing of the sort. He saw it and copied it and it became his. His height – who knows? It may have been his father, Richard, an odd man who apparently shared his interest in history. And of course Rebecca's father, Claud, was tall and short-sighted, like Christopher. The black hair could have been from Mikael, I thought once, before remembering that of course it wasn't, since Mikael was not his father. It was from his mother. His poor devastated mother.

But in among all his lies, as in most elaborate deceptions, were truths. It was true that he had traced his mother, Rebecca, though not through any official channels. He had indeed found her, not on the day he said but on another day, four years earlier, using the information from the convent. He had found and spoken with his grandfather at the family home in Stockton Heath – a lovely, decent man whom I met at Rebecca's funeral. Under the most difficult of circumstances, he was dignity itself, as was his lovely long-suffering wife. It was Rebecca's father who had given Christopher Rebecca's details. Yes, this was all true, except for the fact that it happened in late 1977, not Easter 1981. By the time Ben arrived at our home, Christopher already knew his real mother's whereabouts – he may even have kept tabs on her, given her money over the years – who knows? And so, sadly, the rest of that sorry tale is a version of the truth, albeit perhaps a few different occasions woven into one. Christopher had only to go to the address he had already visited years before and persuade her to meet him in the Wilsons, and thereafter accelerate her progress on her inexorable path to destruction.

They found the note from Margaret in Rebecca's purse, the promise of one mother to another to look after the infant Billy and to call him Christopher, after St Christopher. When I think about that, I am filled with sadness. He was so particular about his name. All that love his adoptive parents had for him, love he was not able to see because it was not presented in the exact way he wanted. What is subject to hypothesis is that Christopher saw in Rebecca a mother he did not want and set about claiming one he did want. That is my hypothesis, which I have added to these pages. He was looking for me, or someone like me. He was looking for his ideal. But most of all, I think he was looking for himself. He was always looking for himself.

Back in Morecambe, there was a family in which he felt he did not belong. So he was adrift, searching for a place in this world. Aren't we all? And perhaps, knowing that the other adopted baby had gone to the US, he decided to take that baby's mother for himself. A calculated risk. He tracked her down. Her, Phyllis. Me. He found me, and upon finding me invested all his dreams. He saw a family he wanted, a home he wanted, a woman he wanted. He wanted it all so badly, he buried whatever troublesome truth stood in his way, enabling him to step into my home. And stepping into my home was all he had to do to fill a space I had already made for him. He stepped in and made my life his, in the process forsaking Margaret and Jack, who had done nothing but love him.

So what of Liverpool Council, of the friendly, businesslike Samantha Jackson and her wise, solid advice, her neat grey hair and sharp burgundy suit? Utter fabrication. Christopher never went through any official channel, never went to the Liverpool Council buildings, nor indeed to Liverpool, other than with me on shopping trips to buy clothes or with the family when we went to the Casa Italia restaurant on Matthew Street for one or other of our birthdays. He was too desperate to find what he wanted; he could not possibly have waited for official records. There was no Samantha Jackson at Liverpool Council in 1977 or indeed at any other time. I have no idea whether the offices dealing with adoption are even in Henry Street, but I had no reason to check. The day he told me he made the long, cold walk from Liverpool Lime Street to Henry Street was the day he went to the convent: Friday, 28 October 1977.

But this is the thing: when he told me how he'd found that letter from Samantha Jackson in his pigeonhole at the halls, for example, and that his heart leapt at the sight, I believed him and I still believe him. When he told me he'd known it would be there, I took him at his word as he gave me to understand it – that is, that he meant his sixth sense of things. And here again, I believe

he meant it in that way, that his need to believe his own version
of events was deep enough for him to deny the truth, which was
that he knew in the literal sense that the letter was there because
he had put it there. He had put it there because *he had written it.*
But in the moment of seeing it, in the moment of plucking it from
the pigeonhole, he had suppressed even this. His joy was real. His
sixth sense, to him, was real.

I sometimes wonder if he took the name Samantha from
Bewitched, a programme he told me he'd enjoyed when he was
younger. He loved to watch television. He had written the
letters from Samantha and stored them in the box under his
bed, along with my letters and his birth certificate. The police
found the postmark on Samantha's envelopes to be Leeds. He
had drawn official headings at the top of the pages, an almost
childish coat of arms, before typing the letters himself. As for
the court overseeing the adoption, he never contacted them. He
did not apply for Martin's birth certificate. He can't have done,
since birth certificates were a matter of public record, and had
he done so, why bother to forge one? Of course I never saw it
until the police searched his room and there it was, in amongst
the fake letters from Samantha and the real letters from me: a
sad attempt, typed up on pink A4 paper, the lines hand-drawn in
red felt-tip pen. Who were they for, these letters from Liverpool
Council, this pathetic, unconvincing fake birth certificate? Not
for me; I would never have asked him for proof. Not for anyone
but himself alone, the scaffolding for a fantasy he needed so badly
to make real – as a lonely child creates an imaginary world, or a
murderer fabricates an alibi.

And Ben, my son, whom I never got to meet or know. This
is *my* fantasy, my need to create an alternative truth for myself.
What I wrote about Ben came from the scant contents of two
letters from a young man looking for his mother. He didn't name
his parents in his letters, so at first I called them X and Y until I

found out from the inquest that they were called Dorothy and George. George was a lawyer and Dorothy a housewife, but she was not an alcoholic. I made her an alcoholic because I was jealous of her. Maybe I wanted her to have failed him as I had. In the story I created for Ben, I made him precociously successful – why not? In reality, he was working as a waiter at night, and was an intern by day. He was on his way though. He just hadn't got quite so far as I would have had myself believe. Call it my indulgence, the exaggeration of a proud mother. And Martha, his fiancée, really is a primary school teacher. She wrote to me, sent me photos of herself and Ben. She seems lovely, and I choose to believe she is. Maybe one day I'll go and meet her. In my version of events, she loved him very much and I like to think this is the truth. Of course she loved him. Who wouldn't love a son of mine?

I don't see Betsy as much now, but if she passes my door she always calls in.

'Hello there, Phyllis.'

I raise my hand, even though she is already gone. 'Hello, Betsy.'

They've taken me off suicide watch. They say I'm making progress. I have started to eat again. I answer in full sentences when they ask me a question. I can take a shower and get dressed by myself. I have written most of what I had to write. I had hoped that if I wrote it all down, it would help me understand. What do I understand?

I understand that I loved him, Christopher, not as a son but as a man. I understand that he killed his real mother because she was not the mother he wanted. I understand that he realised too late how cruelly and completely he had abandoned the mother and father who had raised him. He did at least recognise that. I understand that even after he had told me he'd killed my son, I still loved him. And I understand that whatever deception he carried out, he included himself in that same deception. None of this understanding makes any of it any easier to carry.

Why did I turn him in? Because he took lives, and that is a mortal sin. His poor mother, God rest her soul, is in a better place, but Ben, my baby Martin, died thinking that I had abandoned him. I will never come to terms with that and perhaps, ultimately, that's why I betrayed Christopher.

But now it's almost visiting time. David and the twins are coming to see me. David has been here every day.

'Phyl,' he says. He holds both my hands in both of his. 'Come back to me. We can get through this, I promise.'

David. I always thought I loved him because he was good, a good person. But now I think it is because from the moment I met him he told me that *I* was good, and of course I wanted to see myself that way too. Because the thing is, when I gave my son away, I gave away with him all perception of myself as in any way good. It was David who restored me, restored that goodness in me. I believed him once, and if he keeps telling me, one day I hope to believe him again. I will go back to him and the boys. We will in time put all this behind us.

LAST WORDS

One last point, before I lock this whole thing in a drawer and throw away the key. Under Christopher's bed, behind the box of letters, was his scrapbook. It was full of newspaper clippings, all of them about the Yorkshire Ripper, some photocopied, most actual news reports from various papers, dating from the time Christopher went to university – that is, from the time he knew himself to be adopted. The book bulged like a wallet full of banknotes.

At the back, dated Friday, 3 April 1981, a few months after they caught Peter Sutcliffe and not long before Ben appeared, was another article concerning the murder of a female Leeds University student in 1978. The article said that the police had removed her name from the list of Sutcliffe's victims. The method of killing was not his and Sutcliffe had not included her name in his confession. According to the report, sexual intercourse had taken place before her death. She had suffered some bruising but there was no forensic evidence to link the victim to Sutcliffe. The woman's name was Sophie Hampton-Scott. Her body had been found in woodland opposite Oxley Hall, behind Weetwood Lane. She had been strangled.

And I remembered that conversation in the pub, when I asked Christopher what he meant when he said he'd always known.

'Do you think that feeling came from actual concrete events,' I said, 'or was it more of a sixth sense?'

'No,' he said, shaking his head, 'but I could breathe it in the air.'

Nothing tangible, not a single event, but a multitude of little things – chance remarks, sudden silences, glances exchanged between relatives. Call it a sixth sense, call it intuition, call it the accumulation of small moments; in this life there are simply some things that even without proof we know absolutely. And so to this: what I, Phyllis Curtiss, know and what will be buried with me:

When Christopher volunteered to be Adam's alibi, he was effectively securing his own.

'I'd always known,' he used to say. How true those words were; how little I understood them.

A LETTER FROM S.E. LYNES

Dear Reader,

Thank you so much for taking the time to read *Mother*. I am thrilled that you did and hope you enjoyed it. If you'd like to be the first to hear about my new releases, you can sign up using the link below:

www.bookouture.com/se-lynes

Mother came, as many of my ideas do, from a chance remark. The book is for me about the deep need to belong and to know who we are. I have lived in many different countries, but thanks to growing up in a loving family am fortunate enough to have always known where home is. For *Mother* I have drawn from all sorts of sources, not least from my hometown, Runcorn, where I lived until I was eighteen and which formed much of who I am.

If you enjoyed *Mother*, I would be so grateful if you could spare a couple of minutes to write a review. It only needs to be a line or two, and I would really appreciate it! I am always happy to chat via my Twitter account and Facebook author page if you wish to get in touch. Any writer knows that writing can sometimes be a lonely business, so when a reader reaches out and tells me my work has stayed with them or that they loved it, I am truly delighted. I have loved making new friends online through my first novel, *Valentina*, and hope to make more with *Mother*. My next book is well underway, and I hope you will want to read that one too.

Best wishes
Susie

@selynesauthor

SE LynesAuthor

ACKNOWLEDGEMENTS

First of all, thank you to my wonderful editor at Bookouture, Jenny Geras, whose positivity, tact and expertise have been instrumental in getting this manuscript to where it is.

Huge thanks to Stephanie Zia for her generosity, love and encouragement in this new flight – Stephanie, you are an actual angel.

Thanks as always to my co-pilot in this life, Paul Lynes, who read *Mother* in its rudimentary stages and said, *Blimey, I never knew you were so devious*. Your love is the air I breathe, my darling, but one more football injury and it's over between us, all right?

Big thank yous to my MA writing group, headed up by Hope Caton and attended persistently if not consistently by my beloved writing buddies Robin Bell, Catherine Morris and Sam Hanson.

Other readers to thank are Jackie West for early reading and advice, Alison Gaskins for early reading and encouragement, Gail Shaw for a long conversation about Leeds in the late seventies (even if you did freak me out by having all your Christmas shopping done in October), Jayne Farnworth for tips on police procedure over pints and peanuts, Lynda Crellin for a long conversation about adoption practices in the late seventies, Caroline James for plot discussions over yet more pints and Richard Kipping for birth-certificate stuff and things artistic… thank you and big big love, Fleetwood Mac style.

Thank you to my kids, Ali, Maddie and Franci, for returning to me the energy that writing uses up and for sharing funnies at the end of my working day. I am so proud of all three of you, which is totally irrelevant here but these are my acknowledgements so I can write what I like.

Thanks to my creative-writing students at Richmond Adult Community College for all their love and support, for keeping me focused on this important form of self-expression and for making sure I wash my hair, put on normal clothes and get out of the house sometimes.

Thank you to all my family and friends who have supported me so massively by reading my first book, *Valentina* – thank you for your likes and shares, reviews, word-of-mouth advertising, book clubs and general flag-waving. You have helped create a readership and been a huge source of encouragement on what has been the most extraordinary journey – you know who you are.

Thank you to all the amazing bloggers, too many to mention. Little over a year ago, I had no idea what a book blogger was but now, well, all I have to say is: you rock! Huge thanks to Tracy Fenton, Helen Boyce, Teresa Nikolic and all the admin team and book nuts at TBC for helping me, and many new authors like me, reach readers, without whom I am shouting into the void, and for posting reviews of *Valentina*. I hope you enjoy this one just as much.

Thank you to Kim Nash for making joining the Bookouture authors so much fun and to Jane Selley for her amazing eagle-eyed copy-editing skills.

Big thanks to Dad, Stephen Ball, who supports me in many background ways and who, when he read my last book, provided the pithy insight: *Three months in that cottage and they've not even mowed the lawn yet.*

Lastly, massive thanks, as ever, to Mum, Catherine Ball, who reads drafts so hot off the keys they are still warm, who makes me feel normal when I think I'm mad and who is prepared to have countless conversations about my work in progress #reallyquiteboring. You are the best. This book is for you.